THE HURRICANE SISTERS

ALSO BY DOROTHEA BENTON FRANK

The Last Original Wife

Porch Lights

Folly Beach

Lowcountry Summer

Return to Sullivans Island

Bulls Island

The Christmas Pearl

The Land of Mango Sunsets

Full of Grace

Pawleys Island

Shem Creek

Isle of Palms

Plantation

Sullivans Island

THE
HURRICANE
SISTERS

Dorothea Benton Frank

WILLIAM MORROW
An Imprint of HarperCollins*Publishers*

THE HURRICANE SISTERS. Copyright © 2014 by Dorothea Benton Frank. All rights reserved. Printed in the United States of America. No part of this book may be used or reproduced in any manner whatsoever without written per-mission except in the case of brief quotations embodied in critical articles and reviews. For information address HarperCollins Publishers, 195 Broadway, New York, NY 10007.

HarperCollins books may be purchased for educational, business, or sales pro-motional use. For information please e-mail the Special Markets Department at SPsales@harpercollins.com.

FIRST EDITION

Library of Congress Cataloging-in-Publication Data has been applied for.

ISBN 978-0-06-213252-9

14 15 16 17 18   ov/rrd   10 9 8 7 6 5 4 3 2 1

For Peter

CONTENTS

THE HURRICANE SISTERS

According to Liz

My husband, Clayton, and I were at the police station getting my mother, Maisie, out of jail for brushing up against the wrong side of the law. Her actual charges were still unclear. She claims it is not against any law in the state of South Carolina to take a llama for a walk on the open road. He was, after all, on a leash. The local police beg to differ, saying this is a case of animal cruelty, endangerment, and reckless behavior. Legal or not, it wasn't normal. I was glad they brought her in to the police station until I could get there because her behavior surely demonstrates a lack of sound judgment. Or not. Maisie was crazy like a fox and we all knew it. So I sat and waited while Clayton made things right between the Town of Mount Pleasant and Maisie by writing a check.

Anyway, the jailhouse may seem like an insensitive place to begin my story, but I think it's best if you know the truth about what my family is like. Too many times we all get introduced to people who seem perfectly nice and later on you find out they're cracked. So, like people used to say, I'm cutting to the chase and telling it like it is. Every single person in this family is highly opinionated. You wouldn't *believe* how smart and clever they think they are. And even after the hurricane and all we went through with my daughter, Ashley, Maisie still can't be trusted. And maybe it's a good thing.

Clayton came back and sat down beside me on the long wooden bench.

"It's going to be about fifteen minutes until they let her out. You want coffee?"

"No, thanks. The caffeine . . . I'm already a mess. Why is it taking so long?"

"Well, apparently they're having trouble with the llama. It's skittish and spitting. I guess I'll have to go out to the farm and get Joyce, the caretaker, to calm our woolly beast down and take her back. They've got her in the dogcatcher's pen for the moment."

"I imagine that's the best plan. It's not like you can invite a llama into your SUV to take a seat."

"Your momma is really something else, Liz."

"You're telling me? She's a hundred-and-two-pound sack of pure hell. I can't wait to hear her side of the story."

"All the trouble started on her birthday," Clayton said.

"Maybe."

It certainly was the date that marked the occasion when I first realized things weren't right in my family. I looked at my husband and thought how lucky he was to be alive. And luckier for him I don't believe in packing a pistol. Clayton reached over and took my hand in his, giving it a good squeeze. I squeezed his back. After all, we were all in this soup together.

I wondered then what Maisie thought about that night. Clearly, we had not shared a point of view about very many things in a thousand years. And this llama business? Honey, it would be front-page news for the *Post and Courier* and all over Twitter. It might even make national news.

Then I understood it all. It would be perfect if it did.

CHAPTER 1

Maisie—Eighty Candles

Listen, I'm not complaining. I'm an extremely lucky woman to have lived so many years and it was very nice for my daughter and her family to arrange a dinner to celebrate my birthday with me and Skipper. Skipper is the young man who squires me all over town. He's sixty-five. I know. Bless my heart, I'm quite the scandal.

So there I was at the Charleston Grill, in my best pearls—a triple strand like Barbara Bush wore—sipping my Bombay gin dry martini with two olives, waiting for the others to arrive. I was seated right on the button of five thirty. It was late in May, and even though the streets were bulging with Spoleto Festival patrons and rush-hour commuters, I was punctual. And I live all the way out on James Island. My daughter Liz and her husband, Clayton, live right around the corner on Church Street and they're *late*. Isn't that typical? The younger folks haven't a clue about the value of time. I, on the other hand, was acutely aware of the passing of each day. Eight decades of birthdays will do that to you.

This afternoon Skipper had to go check on his llama farm way out in Awendaw and that's at least an hour from my little ranch-style house. Then he insisted on driving the whole way back across the county to pick me up. I would've been happy to drive myself to the restaurant but then everyone would've thrown a fit. They think I'm a terrible driver. I am not a terrible driver at all. It's just that on occasion I forget where I left the car. And sometimes I forget that I'm driving. That's why Liz and Clayton hired Skipper to chauffeur me and we know where that led! I'm sure having the last laugh on *that* one. And I know where the car keys are stashed should the mood strike to take the wheel again.

Yes, Skipper raises llamas. It could be worse, I imagine. He could be raising snakes. Or alligators. The first time I saw his herd I laughed my head off because they're so funny-looking, but do you know what? They are the dearest animals I have ever known! Very intelligent and affectionate. Just like, well, just like my Skipper.

I looked at my watch. Five forty-five. Obviously Skipper was still searching for a space to park. I paused a moment as I shook one olive dry and asked heaven to help him navigate the foreign throngs from other climes. Sometimes all those tourists were really just too much. But they're good for the economy and they can be interesting to talk to from time to time, if you're interested in life outside of the Lowcountry, which I am not.

Hopefully, my darling grandchildren would arrive before Liz and Clayton so we could share a civil word. And oh blessed sigh of relief, then the imbibing of a second cocktail won't be noticed by Liz who keeps a running tally. As Mother used to say, I *swanny* to St. Pete, if the pope had more than one sip of wine from the chalice during the Consecration of the Mass, Liz would have something to say about him too. Someone should count *hers,* but that's between us.

Miss Nosy Nellie Persnickety. And Mother said *swanny* because ladies of her generation did not swear.

"Why does this fetching lass seem so troubled?"

I looked up to see Skipper standing there, smiling. He was so precious with his plaid sport coat and his little Buddha belly. He had a closely trimmed white beard and blue eyes that twinkled like the waters around the Lowcountry.

"Hey there, you handsome devil. Come sit by me right this minute!"

I'd been thinking about how annoying Liz could be while I stared at a family of tourists, trying to guess if they were American or not. I decided they must be European by the way they held their silverware to cut their food: tines down, knife in the right hand. Probably French, since the father had a very Gallic profile. The mother had a Chanel bag but obviously underprioritized having squeaky-clean hair, and their two children seemed particularly sulky. I should've been a sleuth.

"With pleasure!"

He sat down next to me and kissed my hand, something he did often and something that I loved. Our waiter, Tyler, appeared at our table to take Skipper's order.

"May I bring you a cocktail, sir?"

"In the most expeditious manner you have! I'll have a Maker's Mark Manhattan with one cherry. And what about you, Maisie? Another? That's a mighty small glass they gave you, isn't it?"

"Regrettably, it was a very short pour." I smiled.

"Well, let's see what we can do about that," Tyler said as he picked up my empty glass (Exhibit A) and disappeared.

I smiled and saw my precious granddaughter, Ashley, coming

toward us, sashaying across the floor in high heels that reminded me of Betty Boop, platforms with thick heels. She was wearing a sassy black dress that seemed dangerously short. I gave her a little wave.

"Happy birthday, Maisie!" She leaned down and planted a smooch on my cheek.

Oh Lord, don't lean over too far, I thought! I reached out with my menu to cover her backside from public view. Unaware of her southern exposure, she put a small gift bag filled with colorful tissue and curled ribbons in front of me.

"Thanks, angel! Now, what's this? I told you, no presents!"

"It's just a little something I made for you," she said.

"Well then, that's different!"

I watched her take a seat, carefully pulling her skirt beneath her. I remembered how my daughter Liz wore miniskirts when she was young and they made me nervous back then too. But Liz was a professional model with a wild fashion sense, and she could always get away with murder. Although Ashley was tall, thin, and pretty enough to be a model, she was a serious artist and more modest in every sense of the word. Wasn't she? Maybe I just hated the idea of Ashley growing up. I had to remind myself that she was twenty-three, after all, and perfectly capable of deciding how to dress herself. She loved retro anything that looked like something Jackie O might have worn. There was no law against a beautiful young woman showing some leg, was there? And let's be honest, Charleston, which at one point in her history had more whorehouses than churches, was not some ultraconservative Middle Eastern country where they shroud their women from head to toe. It was high time Ashley started thinking about snagging a husband. Great legs were an asset. She gets her legs from my side of the family. Actually, in my day I could've been a kicker like one of the June Taylor Dancers. I'm not kidding. I still wear high heels. Well, not so high. But Helen Gurley Brown wore heels until she drew her last breath. And fishnet stockings. Sorry, Helen, I can't see fishnets covering my legs and the barnacles of age.

"Shall I open this now or should I wait?" I said.

"Open it now!" she said.

"Would you like something to drink, Ashley?" Skipper said as Tyler put his drink and mine on the table in front of us.

"White wine?" Ashley said.

"Chardonnay?" Tyler asked.

"Actually, if you have a New Zealand sauvignon blanc, that would be great," she said.

"Right away," Tyler said.

I looked at my granddaughter, arched an eyebrow, and thought, What's this? Since when does a girl her age know a single thing about wine? It was unbecoming for a young lady to be a smarty-pants. Especially about something like alcohol.

As though she could read my mind, she said, "We serve it at all the gallery openings because my bosses love it." She added in a whisper, "Besides, it's the only one I know." Then she smiled that smile of hers that lights up the world.

I began removing sheets of tissue from the bag and to my absolute delight, at the bottom of the bag I found a small canvas encased in bubble wrap and unwound it carefully. It was a miniature landscape of a brilliant sunset on James Island from the best vantage point at the end of my dock. Ashley had inherited my other daughter Juliet's artistic talents.

"Oh!" I said. "Ashley, sweetheart, it's absolutely beautiful! What a treasure!" And it was. I took her hand in mine and squeezed it.

"Yay! I'm so glad you like it! I took a picture of this view one afternoon with my phone and I said to myself, you know what? I'm going to paint this for Maisie!"

"How talented you are! Here's to you!" Skipper said.

"Thank you!" Then she sighed dramatically. "Maybe someday I'll live in Montmartre and paint Sacré Cœur! You know, go bohemian?"

She toasted with her water glass, smiling so wide with her dimples and all, and I thought, This child doesn't have a rotten bone in her body. She's just all goodness and light.

"Drink absinthe and smoke little fat cigarettes that smell like a sewer?" Skipper said and laughed.

"Exactly!" she said.

"Hush! I'm so proud of you," I said. "I'm going to put this on a little stand on my fireplace mantel where I can see it every day!"

"Proud of whom? For what?"

It was the grating metallic voice of my daughter Liz and her husband, Clayton. They had arrived.

"I'm proud of my lovely granddaughter and you're thirty minutes late, but who's counting?"

"Sorry, Maisie, but happy birthday," Clayton said. "I had a meeting out at Wild Dunes and traffic . . . well, you know, it's terrible. Anyway, it's my fault. Do we have a wine list?"

Clayton seated himself at the head of the table and Liz sat on his left, next to Ashley. Tyler handed the wine list to Clayton and put Ashley's glass of wine in front of her. This left two vacant chairs on the opposite side of the table for my grandson, Ivy, and his mysterious business partner, James, whom we had yet to meet. They were flying in from San Francisco just for me!

"Mother?" Liz said in a low officious voice. "Actually, the reservation was for six o'clock. We're on time."

"No, it was not," I said and wondered why Clayton took the blame if there was no guilt. But the truth about Clayton is that as aggressive as he was in his business, he was nearly completely passive with his family. He hated making waves, especially in public.

"Oh, who cares, Mom?" Ashley said. "What's the difference?"

Before I could tell Liz emphatically that she was wrong, wrong, wrong, Ivy and James arrived, straight from the skies. They were staying with me that night and heaven only knows after that. Ivy looked like a male model, all smiles and hugs with a gorgeous bouquet of flowers for me. James was quite a bit older than Ivy and appeared to be Chinese. Everyone knows Asians are smarter than Caucasians so it was a relief to know Ivy had chosen his partner with his head. Ivy and James owned a men's store in San Francisco called Ivy's. I've been told it's quite chic. And all you had to do was look at them to know it was wildly successful.

"Happy birthday, Maisie!" Ivy said and kissed my cheek.

Before we go any further, you have to know that Ivy is thus called because he is Clayton Bernard Waters IV. That's the fourth. IV. Hence, Ivy. And he started calling himself that in the third grade, immune to the taunts of the other children. We knew then that he was, well, precocious.

"Oh, aren't these beautiful? Thank you, sweetheart! And you must be James! How are you, dear?"

"Fine, Miss Maisie! Just fine! Happy birthday!"

James had lovely teeth and his eyeglass frames were very interesting. In fact I'd never seen anything like them. I didn't ask for the sake of embarrassment. What if he had some sort of vision impairment? The poor dear man.

"And how was your trip?" I asked.

"Exhausting! All that nasty recycled air!" Ivy said. "Hello, Mother. Dad."

Ivy kissed Liz with a dutiful peck and hugged his father briefly. There were pleasantries exchanged all around.

"Hey, Ashley River," Ivy said to his sister. "Y'all? Say hello to James!"

Everyone did.

"That's Miss Waters to you," Ashley said giggling and stood, hugging him with affection. Then she hugged James, too. "I know I don't know you, but down here we hug. Um, are you wearing Glass?"

I reached out to no avail to pull down the hem of her dress.

"That's fine," James said and hugged her back. "Yep. Just got 'em. They're a test pair."

"Ashley!" Liz exclaimed on seeing her daughter's bottom.

Truly, she was showing too much, well, cheek. Ashley's face flushed a bright shade of pink.

"Our friend did the colors. There's a range of them," Ivy said dramatically. "I think they make everyone look like a Glasshole."

"*You're* the Glasshole! I think they're awesome! Stupid dress," she said. She readjusted her hem and sat down again.

"Except that they are going to prove very useful for people with disabilities," James said. "If someone is deaf, they'll be able to read what someone else is saying to them in real time because it acts like a monitor and has voice recognition software."

"How long are y'all staying?" I asked, not understanding one word he said.

What was this Glass thing? A new gadget? Gadgets were taking over the world!

"Just until Sunday morning and then we fly to New York for a few days," Ivy said, taking a seat. "Does anyone think it's possible to order a drink? I'm so parched! God, I hate flying commercial!"

"Just give the keys to the doorman when you leave," Clayton said.

Apparently Ivy was staying in Liz and Clayton's pied-à-terre in Manhattan. But what did Ivy mean, that he was used to private planes now? Had he won the lottery? Was James treating him to the high life? I have heard that some of these Asian families are extremely wealthy. Ivy began to drain the water glass at his place when our waiter reappeared. What was his name? Tony? No, Tyler! Tippecanoe and Tyler Too. Yes, I know that's from way before my time but Lord, the games I had to play with my memory to make it work.

"Campari and soda with orange, please," Ivy said.

"Just Pellegrino for me, thanks," James said. "I'm going to wash my hands. Where's the men's room?" James removed his eyeglasses and handed them to Ivy. "Show Ashley how they work."

"Good thing I'm on the way out," I said, and everyone ignored me.

"You can follow me, sir," our waiter, Tyler Too, said. "And I'll get those drinks out for y'all right away. Did you choose the wine, sir?"

"No, I need a few minutes," Clayton said without looking up.

As usual, Clayton was reading the wine list too slowly. I was convinced that this annoying habit of his was what drove Liz to vodka.

James walked away with Tippecanoe.

Then the first bomb of the night was launched across the bow.

"Is he just your *business* partner, son?" Clayton said quietly, without making eye contact.

"No, he isn't. He's my life partner." Ivy put on the glasses. "Okay," he said to Ashley, "I bob my head, and see that pink light?"

"Yeah," Ashley said.

"Okay, Glass? Take a picture!"

There was a little click and somehow the eyeglasses took a picture.

"I can upload it to my iPad or e-mail it or whatever. I think it's stupid," Ivy said.

"Unless you need them," Ashley said. "I guess?"

There was an awkward but brief silence while Liz continued to process Ivy's response in regard to his relationship with James.

"Oh my God!" Liz said, gasping.

"What's wrong?" I asked.

She completely disregarded my question and began to bluster until her hair was becoming as disheveled as her face was flushed. We were a family of blushers and blusterers.

"What *is* it, Mom?" Ashley asked.

"Well, how *old* is he, for one thing?" Liz said. She was now completely red in the face and neck.

"Fortyish," Ivy said.

"Kept man," Clayton mumbled, half chuckling.

"Hardly," Ivy said. "I put in my sixty hours a week. At a minimum. Besides, half the business is mine."

"I hope you have that in writing," the ever-cautious Clayton said.

"Of course I do. Mother, what's wrong?"

"He's a . . . well, he's *Asian!*" Liz said.

I wondered what the problem was. Skipper looked at me and shrugged his shoulders.

"So what?" Ashley said. "He's gorgeous!"

"Hands off, but thank you," Ivy said and laughed. "Yes, he's from *the* Chen family of Hong Kong and he's the most wonderful, thoughtful, and generous person I have ever met. Doesn't that count?"

"You couldn't find a nice white Episcopalian man?" Liz said. "Why are you so complicated? Do you expect us to throw you a wedding now?"

"Um, nooooo," Ivy said.

"Get a grip, sister," I said to Liz, thinking, You don't have that many friends. "It's 2012."

"Um, Maisie, actually it's 2013," Ivy said in a whisper.

"It is?" I nearly fainted. "Wait! Yes, of course it is! Hold the phone! Does that make me eighty-one?"

"No, you're still eighty, Mother," Liz said, rolling her eyes.

I ignored her.

"She's right, Maisie," Skipper said. "I just did the math."

"How do you like that? I just gained a year! This is the best birthday I've ever had! Well, so far."

"So you're out there in California just having a gay time with James who wears Glass?" Liz said.

"Oh, please," Ashley said. "Here we go. Maybe we should be glad he doesn't care we're *not* Asian."

Although we had decades of confirmation, Liz had yet to reconcile with the facts, always hoping against hope that Ivy would meet a nice girl with Herculean powers of persuasion.

Ivy turned to Liz. "Mother, you *do* know that five percent of the entire population is gay and almost thirty percent of the population around San Francisco is gay? Including Asians."

"Of the entire population of the United States? That's crazy. I don't buy that for one minute," Clayton said.

It was rare for Clayton to be so insistent.

"Neither do I!" Liz said and fumbled for her purse.

"What are you doing?" Ashley said.

"I'm going to ask Siri!" Liz said.

"Who's Siri?" I said.

"Siri is this teeny tiny woman from California who lives inside

Mother's phone," Ivy said, laughing. "She's like the great and terrible Oz."

"Another know-it-all," I said. "Just what the world needs. Siri and Glass."

"Watch," Ivy said. "They're going to send me back to conversion camp."

"Horrible. Anyway, you're too old for camp," Ashley said in a somber voice.

I remembered that painful summer when Liz and Clayton sent young, flamboyant Ivy singing all the songs from *West Side Story* off to some camp that promised to send him home quiet and straight, begging to become a steady and reliable CPA or something. Years of therapy followed. That camp had become a taboo subject and we did not speak of it. So occasionally Ivy saw fit to sort of stick it to Liz and Clayton and who could blame him? Stick away, baby!

I watched while Liz and Clayton fooled around with their phones until some very weird female voice verified Ivy's claim and then they sat back absolutely deflated as though another space-age gadget had just sucked every last ounce of air out of them.

"Astonishing! Who knew?" Liz said dryly, shaking her head. "Maybe I'll have a Stoli with a twist, Clayton. By the time you finish reading that wine list, it'll be Christmas."

"Did you say, *please, dear, order a drink for me?*" Clayton said, sighing, and he slipped his phone back into the pocket of his jacket. He looked at Ivy. "I'm impressed. You could go to work for the Bureau of Vital Statistics."

"Truly," Ivy said.

"Please, Clayton, *please* order a Stoli with a twist for me?" Liz said.

Clayton raised his eyes and scanned the room looking for our waiter, gaining his attention with a nod. The vodka was ordered without one iota of concern for replenishing the drinks of the rest of the table. I have never ordered a third martini in my whole life, but someone could've asked. It was, after all, my eightieth birthday. And I wasn't driving.

James returned to the table, Clayton finally chose the wine, Liz drank her first cocktail, then another, and finally we all ordered dinner. The mood had shifted. Liz kept biting her lower lip and staring at James, then quickly averting her eyes, causing him to squirm. She knew it was the height of all bad manners to make your guests feel uncomfortable. She made me want to reach out and give the inside of her arm a good pinch. Then Ivy noticed James squirming like a little worm, figured out why, and became irritable. Clayton was chatting like a magpie with Ivy about Ashley's continued financial dependency, which irritated Ivy.

"She's still out on the island living in our beach house with her friend for the mere price of the utilities," Clayton said for everyone at our table to hear, including Ashley. "She could still live at home. Then her mother wouldn't be so lonely."

"I'm in the room, Dad," Ashley said.

"Hush, dear! The whole restaurant can hear you!" I said.

"Well, it's harder for kids today, Dad," Ivy said.

Clayton harrumphed. Ivy looked at his father with a very stern expression. I could see his annoyance boiling up to the surface.

"I guess it *is* hard if you take a job for eight dollars an hour," Clayton added.

"Ten," Ashley said and no one seemed to care.

"My housekeeper makes twenty dollars an hour scrubbing our toilets," Liz said.

Ashley was now completely mortified and struggled to maintain her conversation with Skipper about his llamas, one in particular he named Maisie as a birthday gift to me. It was just so wrong that Clayton and Liz denied their only daughter so much. They should at least give her some respect, especially in front of James, whom they didn't even know.

"Yeah, boy," Skipper said. "Maisie the llama is almost as pretty as your grandmother, as llamas go, that is. She has beautiful eyes and she can bat those lashes of hers like a movie star."

"Don't llamas spit?" Ivy said.

"Sometimes. But a llama is a great gift for the woman who has everything," Ashley said.

"She's darling," I said, trying to lighten the mood.

"I'd love to see a picture," Ivy said.

"She could be a calendar girl," I said.

Now Ivy laughed and repeated to James what I'd said and James laughed too. Lighten mood—check.

"I wonder if she's ever going to get a *real* job," Liz said.

"I *do* have a real job," Ashley said and looked to James. "Don't you love our family?"

James was now thoroughly uncomfortable. Ivy's good humor faded right in front of me. Boy, these two were awfully moody.

"Mother? What is the *matter* with y'all? You and Dad are just determined to peck everyone to death, aren't you? Like a bunch of chickens!" Ivy said. "Ashley's your *daughter*! *And* she's a fabulous painter. Why don't you and Dad climb off her back for five minutes?"

"Really?" Clayton said.

"Yes! The house was empty anyway! What's the big deal? No one ever goes there, do they?"

"Because we all worry about melanoma," Liz said. "You know that."

"You're *paranoid* about melanoma," Clayton said.

"I am not!" Liz insisted.

I began feeling anxious. "They say we're in for a busy hurricane season," I said. No one answered. "There have already been six with names. Thank goodness they blew out to sea!"

Clayton just sat back in his chair and cocked his head to one side like the chairman of the Department of Decorum and laughed.

"Well, well, well," Clayton said. "It seems at long last that my delicate son has grown a pair. This calls for champagne! Where's that fellow with the list?"

Clayton ordered a bottle of champagne and as soon as the entrees were cleared away, it was poured.

"This momentous occasion merits a toast," Clayton said.

"Are we really going to toast my family jewels?" Ivy said, snickering.

"Don't be vulgar," Liz said.

"In Ivy's defense," James said, smiling and poised, "it was Mr. Waters who introduced them into evidence."

Liz gasped. Rarely had I seen anyone speak so boldly to Liz. I sort of loved it.

"Are you a lawyer?" Ashley said.

"Yes," James said, smiling.

"Really? Where did you . . ." Clayton asked, but James answered before he could finish.

"Harvard. I don't practice too much. But I do a lot of pro bono work."

"Wow," Ashley said. "Can I try on your Glass again?"

"Sure," James said and passed the newest thing in gizmos across the table to her.

"Oh my goodness!" I said, staring at Ashley. "When you said that, you looked exactly like my Juliet!" Why had I never seen the resemblance before?

"Mother!" Liz said.

"What?" I said. "Don't you agree with me? She was just about your age when we lost her, Ashley. Just a few years older."

"Let's not get maudlin, Maisie," Clayton said. "This is supposed to be a happy occasion, isn't it?"

"I'm not maudlin one little bit!" I said. "I was just startled, that's all. I promise, y'all . . . Ashley, turn your head that way to face your daddy."

James was puzzled and said, "Excuse me, may I ask, who is Juliet?"

"My perfect sister who died of an aneurysm at twenty-seven, thirty years ago," Liz said.

"Oh. I'm terribly sorry," James said.

"It was thirty years ago," Liz said.

"Well, it's like yesterday to me," I said. "I always wonder what she would have become had she lived."

"President of the United States, Mother. Now, Clayton, you were going to make a toast? Please, dear?"

I didn't say anything to that. President, indeed. Juliet may well *have* become president. She was sure smart enough. And she could charm the birds right out of the trees. *At least she never made a living prancing up and down the runway in bathing suits,* I wanted to say. Clayton tapped the side of his glass with his fork.

"To Maisie! Happy birthday to the most amazing woman we know!"

"Hear! Hear!" everyone said.

And here came the cake with so many candles I thought if there was a sudden gust of wind we might burn down the restaurant.

"It's so pretty!" I said. "Thank you! I really shouldn't eat cake."

"YOLO, Maisie!" Ashley said. "Go for it!"

"You're not quoting that Canadian rapper to our grandmother, are you?" Ivy said and then leaned out to tell me, "YOLO means 'you only live once,' Maisie."

"I don't know about Canadian raptors, some kind of migrating bird, I imagine, but it was Mae West who coined the phrase." I gave them my very best smile.

"And, Ivy? Just to set the record straight, you're not the only man in the room who's living in sin," Skipper said.

"Not now," I said, quietly. "We can tell them later."

"Tell us what?" Liz said.

"Yes, what?" Ivy said. He seemed slightly miffed. "Not that I consider myself to be living in sin."

"Sorry, Ivy," Skipper said. "I didn't mean it like that."

"It's okay," Ivy said.

"Skipper has moved in with me," I said, "and we couldn't be happier!"

"L. O. V. E. I. T.," James said, deadpan. "Totally worth the cost of the trip."

"Maisie!" Ivy said and laughed.

"Sweet Jesus of Nazareth," Liz said and while all the color drained from her face, she drained all the champagne in her flute. She held it out for Clayton to refill, which he did.

"Now, let's have dessert, shall we?" I said, trying to gloss over the elephant in the room.

"Indeed, let's!" said Ivy, suddenly filled to the brim with mirth.

The cake was very pretty, all covered in marzipan hydrangeas of every color, just like the ones I grew. All the waiters sang and my family sang along too. Ivy and Ashley took pictures with their phones and the Glass and I smiled, thinking again I was very lucky to be surrounded by so many lovely people who cared about making me happy in that moment. We weren't perfect. I knew that. And I knew it was even more incumbent on me to see about Ashley's welfare and state of mind. All I can tell you is that every family on the planet is dysfunctional and we celebrate occasions as generously as we know how to do. We were all doing our best to appear grateful to have one another. Weren't appearances worth something?

CHAPTER 2

Ashley's Opinion

The night after Maisie's birthday party I was at the infamous family house on Sullivans Island making a bowl of pasta to share with my roommate, Mary Beth, who was also my best friend on the planet. I'm not kidding. She was practically blood. She wasn't home yet. It had been a long day at the gallery with every tourist in town wandering in, wanting cheap posters in free cardboard tubes they could take home and frame. We don't sell cheap posters in free cardboard tubes. Please! WTH? The Turner Gallery is a *serious* place on Broad Street in downtown Charleston. It's practically a museum. I mean, if an artist gets a show at our gallery, it's a very big deal. Bill and Judy Turner have dedicated their whole lives to building their business and the most important artists from the entire Southeast are in the house. My parents would have you believe I'm working at a dime store selling cheap crap from China. They make me so frustrated.

They would also have you believe that I'm living in the Taj Mahal when this creaking old house hasn't seen a plumber, an electrician, or a coat of paint in twenty years. Maybe longer. I've been carded in better-looking dive bars. But I love the beach house. I love every rusty nail in every rotten board. Like so many places in the Lowcountry, it oozes history. In the 1860s it served as a Civil War barracks. How awesome is that? I can imagine boys with whiskers and dirty hair eating from a giant pot of stew on tin plates and I can see iron bunks lining the walls upstairs and twenty or so soldiers tossing and turning at night. And I can envision them straggling back from a battlefield, all sweaty and dirty. Worst of all, when I'm miserable myself, I can feel their fear. Most of them had to be just young boys. Boys who were my age or younger. How terrible.

The land where our house stands isn't too far from where the Pest House used to be, a *truly* horrible place where some kind of officials examined slaves arriving from Barbados and West Africa to determine if they were healthy enough to put on the selling block in downtown Charleston. The old people used to say that they heard from their grandparents that if the slaves were too sick, they got thrown in the shark-infested waters. How unforgivably horrendous and uncivilized is that? Crimes against humanity! Everything about the South isn't pretty. At all.

These are two truly excellent reasons why I have always felt the island was so haunted. Sometimes, when I am alone on the porch looking out over the water of Charleston Harbor I can feel a heavy sadness in the air. And sometimes at night I think I hear the muffled voices of people quietly crying, struggling with some inexplicable grief. At first, Mary Beth thought I was really crazy but after a while she began to feel it and hear them too. I mean, just because you can't see something doesn't mean it isn't there. Right? Isn't it a little bit like believing in angels?

But when we aren't feeling the mythology of the house, mostly it is just what it is: another wooden clapboard house with warped heart pine floors, perched on towers of cement blocks, with an ancient tin roof that only leaks in the laundry room when it is a superheavy rain and screened porches all around that hold millions of secrets. Upstairs there are four bedrooms with beaded board walls and ceilings and one creaking bathroom in the hall. Downstairs there is a giant open living space with a dining table and a fireplace that hasn't worked in all my life. We have an old grand piano in the corner of the living room that was given to my father from some long-dead aunt. It is so out of tune it's ridiculous. In fact, I can't remember it *ever* being in tune. During the holidays when we were kids, Ivy would try and bang out some Christmas carols and we'd wind up laughing our brains out from the rusty noise the poor thing made.

But the house isn't without merit. The best feature of the house is the big portico on the ocean side. There is almost always a breeze and every ship that goes into or sails out of Charleston Harbor passes right by. It is where I make the world go away, just like the dumb song that Maisie says Skipper sings when it's cocktail time.

So after the mental workout from the Impossibles (a.k.a. my parents) last night, I just wanted to hang at home and get over them. Ivy and James were supposed to come by for a glass of vino after dinner but I wasn't counting on it. Ivy had so many friends downtown that I knew by the time he said hello to everyone and ate something here and there it would be too late. I'd text him and meet him tomorrow for coffee before he and James left for New York.

I heard a car door slam in the yard, the familiar clunk of Mary Beth's old reliable Camry. Her car had over a hundred and fifty thousand miles on it. My Subaru had a mere hundred and twenty-seven thousand. In one minute, she would be in the kitchen staring inside the refrigerator like it spoke English and was going to tell her what to eat that would (a) satisfy her and (b) not have any calories. Good luck with that. Ever since we'd met on the first day of classes at the College of Charleston, she'd been on a diet. Not that she needed one. Well, maybe a little bit.

"Hey! What's up?" she said, dropping her bag on the table and, like I said, opening the refrigerator. "What are you making over there, chopping away like some nut on *Top Chef*?"

"Enough pasta primavera to feed this whole island. And my day totally sucked, but thanks for asking."

"Oh? Carb alert. That's not good."

"Jammed with touristas. And, just to make sure my head explodes, we're hosting a reception for Senator Galloway next week."

"I know. We're doing the job. He's like the Prince Harry of South Carolina. Everyone says he's going to be the president someday."

"I'm going to die when I meet him."

"You and every other woman in the room."

Mary Beth worked for a very cool catering company downtown. She had a degree in elementary education but there were no teaching jobs to be had in the entire Charleston area except in schools that looked like meth labs. So, like me and everyone else we knew, except those who went to law school or medical school, she made ten dollars an hour passing hors d'oeuvres. She was also a closet chef. And Porter Galloway was the youngest person ever elected to the state senate, not that that has anything to do with anything. I just thought you should know he's practically age appropriate and that I had a mad crush on him but alas, only from afar.

"And I'm a wreck. What am I going to wear to make him fall in love with me?"

"Wear what you wore last night."

"Are you serious? That dress almost got me thrown out of the will. Here, taste this. How is it?"

She picked out a piece of pasta and popped it in her mouth, wincing.

"Too blah. Let me fix it. It needs salt and lemon zest. And garlic powder. This isn't primavera. It's pasta salad, but not primavera. Usually, primavera has roasted squash and peppers." She went back to the refrigerator and took out a lemon. "Where's the Microplane?"

"All of a sudden you're Giada de Laurentiis with a Microplane?"

We watched the Food Network like some people watched *Game of Thrones*.

"Food is my religion," she said, with such a serious face that I started laughing.

"Religion. Well, at least you believe in something," I said and giggled. "I'll find it. Want a glass of wine?"

I dug through the utensil drawer that always sticks because it's jammed with stuff from the 1960s and finally found it wedged in the side.

"Sure," she said. "How cheap is it?"

"Very. It comes with an ice pack for your eyes. Here," I said and handed her the grater. "There's too much junk in this drawer. One of these days I'm gonna start pitching stuff."

I banged it back and forth and finally forced it shut. Then I opened the refrigerator and took out the bottle of white wine with the screw cap and the flip-flops on the label. It stood up very well to ice.

"Thanks. So how was Charleston Grill? I'm starving. What's *this?* Who puts *avocado* in pasta?"

"I do. Everything is better with avocado. And bacon. My parents are completely crazy. The food, however, was beyond."

I told her what we all ordered while Mary Beth seasoned and stirred the pasta around in the big ceramic bowl that had been a part of the kitchen all my life. Funny how something that seemed so insignificant, just an old bowl with faded glazed stripes, could trigger so many memories. When I was really young, we used it for cookie dough, cake batters, boiled peanuts, potato salad, and now apparently, not for pasta *primavera,* but for pasta *salad.* But when I was little and my mother pulled out that big bowl, it meant *company* and it meant that for a few hours at least my family would do its best to look and act normal. Ah, the good old days.

"One of these days I'm going to rob a bank and go to all the great restaurants in Charleston and order whatever I want," Mary Beth said.

"I'm going to rob a bank and get the heck out of here," I said. "Or I'm going to marry Porter Galloway and live happily ever after with him in the White House. Maybe."

We clinked the sides of our glasses toasting our very uncertain futures, took a sip, and sighed.

"Either way, we have a plan." Mary Beth was always the optimist.

"Some plan," I said with a grunt.

"Want to eat outside?" she said.

"Why not? We can watch the harbor."

So we piled pasta on our plates and filled our glasses with ice and swill and made our way out to the porch juggling silverware and linens. We may have been young and broke but we had style. And standards. Frat boys ate without place mats and napkins. Not us.

The heat of the day had broken and the horizon was beginning to turn red. There was nothing more beautiful in all the world than sunset on Sullivans Island. But considering I hadn't really been anywhere outside of Charleston since I was like fifteen when I didn't care about things like sunsets, I could've been wrong. But it sure *seemed* beautiful to me. And romantic.

We set up our places and sat at the old glass-top table, taking the first bites. It was delicious.

"Wow, this is so good," I said. "Maybe you really ought to be a chef. You know? I mean, *really*!"

"Yeah, and old Larson would kick my butt! This *is* good."

Larson Smythe, her father, the Pentecostal preacher in the hills of Tennessee, didn't really believe in college educations for women. Her mother, Agnes the Weirdly Timid, played the pump organ in his church on Sundays while the congregation got moved by the spirit and spoke in tongues. Small congregation. Large snake box. Scary. He owned and ran the local hardware store in their town and Agnes, well, Agnes was a wonderful homemaker and cook but never had any prospects of a career, beyond handling the books for Smythe's Hardware. Larson would not have heard of it and Agnes wouldn't have asked. They lived quietly. (Boring.) It's not like their town was crawling with opportunity anyway.

"Probably. But your momma's a great cook. You must get it from her."

When we were in college, I used to go home with Mary Beth on long weekends so I knew this to be a fact. There was always a cake on the table, soup on the stove, and biscuits in the oven.

"Humph. I think the only thing I got from them was far, far away."

"What were you supposed to do? Work at the Dairy Queen for the rest of your life and marry some no-chin boy named Skeeter? You'd have had total brain rot if you'd gone home after college."

"Truly. At least I do some subbing once in a while. That keeps Larson's nerves in check," she said. "Makes him think the tuition was worth it. So what happened last night? Did you get career counseling again?"

"In a major way. In front of the world. While my butt was allegedly hanging out of *that dress,* according to my mother. Also in front of the world. They ragged on my job and my salary. So embarrassing. I mean, Mary Beth? How am I going to become a famous artist from here? This island has never produced a famous anything. I mean, we had Edgar Allan Poe here for like one year. Big whoop. He wasn't even born here."

"You could be the first," she said.

"Right. You know, Dad goes to New York on business every week. He used to always promise that he'd take me along so I could go to all the museums and galleries. But he never has."

"Keep asking. It's a legit request."

I was quiet for a few minutes and thought about that.

"I don't know. Maybe. I think he just likes getting away and I know he likes being by himself. Mom doesn't seem really happy. But then, I don't really know what she looks like when she is."

"It's the same with my mother. Maybe they're just out of estrogen or something."

"I'm sure my mother takes a pill for that. But seriously. Even though she's always ragging on me, I feel bad for her. She needs more fun in her life. Or something. I know she means well."

"I'd be happy if I was just married to somebody with a lot of money. I get so tired of worrying about college loans and car repairs and every other thing. I mean, I can't even afford to get my hair cut!"

I looked at her crazy red curly hair blowing in the damp breeze that was drowning the whole porch and wondered if a haircut would make a lot of difference one way or the other.

"What?" she said.

"Nothing! I'm just looking at your hair flying around and mine is too. We look like total crap! But nobody's watching us anyway so who cares?"

"Amen. I guess you can't have good hair at the beach. And what good is it to be young and gorgeous if we're broke? Nobody even knows we're here. Life is very depressing."

I scraped the plate with the side of my fork, picking up the last bits of pasta.

"Yeah. Bummer. We may as well eat ourselves into oblivion."

Just then a huge container ship on its way to somewhere on the other side of the Atlantic came into view. It inched along and because the channel was so close to our property, it seemed as if the ship was going to crash through our yard and kill us. But it wouldn't. It would veer out to sea and away from view in minutes. It always startled people when they saw this for the first time.

"You could make money with this view," she said.

"How?" I said. "Sell the house? That might be tough to do since I don't own it."

I looked at Mary Beth and she had the same look on her face as she did every time she was about to tell me something really devious.

"What are you thinking, girl? Tell me right now."

"Well, you know how we've always said this was a great place for a party?"

"Yeah. For a party that goes with my funeral. You want Liz and Clay to kill me?"

"Wait a minute. I'm not talking about a party like with our friends and kegs and drunk boys, puking and peeing and passed out in the yard!"

"What other kind is there?"

"The kind you have at the gallery! Like what if . . ."

"Stop! No way!"

"Wait. Let's do the math. What if you rented the first floor to some organization that was coming to Charleston for a conference? Or just a pop-up party? And what if they wanted to see a sunset that would blow their mind? I can get our company to cater for twenty dollars a person; we limit it to fifty people who pay fifty dollars a person. It's a two-hour deal period. You got a pencil handy?"

"I already figured it out," I said.

"We make fifteen hundred dollars in two hours!"

"And my parents will find out and I'll be homeless. So will you."

We watched the container ship adjust its course and it floated away with Mary Beth's excellent but dangerous idea.

"You're probably right," she said and sighed hard enough to blow the ship to Cape Hatteras or Greenland or someplace like that. "Paris will have to wait."

"Maisie always says I should remember that I can marry more money in five minutes than I can earn in a lifetime."

"She's right," Mary Beth said.

"Maybe, but I don't see any of the guys we know scraping their knees off proposing, do you?"

"You've still got Tommy Milano drooling over you."

"The guy who's named for a cookie. Great," I said. "Not in a bazillion years. He's asked me out how many times? Not happening."

"Yeah, no future. But he's so sweet and he's supercute."

"Maybe. Besides, I don't think it makes any sense to get married until you're ready to have children, do you?"

"It makes economic sense."

"True. Maybe. But who wants children anyway?"

"You don't? Wow. I love children! I want like five or maybe four."

"Maybe I wouldn't mind one if he looked like Porter Galloway," I said.

"Porter Galloway. Girl? He's totally gorgeous," Mary Beth said, "but messing with that man is gonna land you in a world of hurt. He's a ladies' man and you know it."

Senator Galloway did have sort of a reputation with the ladies. Allegedly, there were a lot of them in his past. To be honest, the number was practically biblical. Every time his picture was in the paper, there was a different woman on his arm.

"Maisie knows his momma, you know. He grew up on James Island. All her friends think he's like the second coming of JFK or something."

"Then you should ask her what she thinks about him. I love Maisie."

"Who doesn't love Maisie? Problem is, if I ask her, she'll tell Mom. I haven't even met him yet. I really don't want my mother all over my personal life. It's bad enough as it is."

"Okay, enough pussyfooting around. What did they say to you last night?"

I thought about it for a minute. It wasn't what they said so much as it was how they made me feel.

"They didn't say anything new. It's just that they make me feel like a loser. You know, I'm just a dreamer. That trying to be an artist is stupid and a waste of time. Maybe they're right."

"You think my parents are any better?"

"Probably not. But why are we supposed to spend our whole lives respecting them when they don't show any respect for us?"

"That's why you have to believe in yourself and never give up. Me? I just want to marry a doctor or something and have a pile of kids. But you want more, Ash. You always did. Don't let them ruin it for you."

Was money really that important to Mary Beth?

"You know, I gave Maisie that little painting for her birthday? I think she really loved it. But all Mom could do was roll her eyes because her dead sister, Juliet, was very artistic. Which was one more excuse for Maisie to bring her up."

"That's not so nice. But families are crazy."

"Truly. Just as Mom was about to sink her teeth in my neck, Ivy showed up with his partner—and I mean that in the business and the romantic way—and they suddenly had something else to focus on besides me. He's Asian. James is his name. Old Liz nearly fainted."

"Because he's Asian? You've got to be *kidding* me!"

"Nope. And he's awesome. He's from Hong Kong and he was wearing *Glass*."

"Glass? Google Glass? Wow. That is awesome. It's not even out yet! God, I'd love to go to Hong Kong."

"I'd love to go *anywhere*! Actually, Glass is sort of creepy but it's sort of cool too."

"Yeah. Makes you look like Data on *Star Trek* or something. I heard it's like fifteen hundred dollars."

"It is. I read all about it online. It's probably going to be amazing. But let's be honest. If I had fifteen hundred dollars . . ."

"I know; you'd go to Paris."

"True story," I said. "Or New York."

It was getting darker by the minute. In the distance we could see the night lights of the Ravenel Bridge come alive, and the waterfront of the city began to twinkle. Somewhere over there my mother was pouring herself her third vodka and my dad was pulling the second cork of the day. Between the Battery and the Morris Island Lighthouse, Maisie was probably curled up next to Skipper on a sofa watching reruns of *The Love Boat*. And Ivy, my sweet brother, was no doubt in his glory tonight, showing off lovely tech-savvy James and telling stories about their glamorous lives.

But me? I was on Sullivans Island, drinking really lousy wine with my roommate, mooning over a man I didn't know, who didn't even know I had a pulse, and wondering how to become a world-famous artist. Persevere, I told myself again and again, and my life would come together. I was sure of it. All I had to do was to keep trying. The more I painted, the better I got. Even *I* could see that in my work.

I thought again about what Mary Beth said about renting the house out and all that. It sure would be great to make fifteen hundred dollars in two hours. Could we get away with it? How could we plan it without them finding out? Charleston was a really small town. I hated secrets. I didn't want to lie to my parents. I only wanted to prove them wrong. Maybe I'd run it by Ivy.

I texted him at eight o'clock the next morning. He was probably still sleeping. It was five to him, body time, so no way he was up. Then again, knowing Ivy, he was probably still up from last night!

Wanna meet me at Starbucks on Calhoun Street? I hit the send button.

That particular Starbucks was probably the most convenient for him. A few minutes passed and my smartphone pinged the notice of his reply.

Sure! How's nine?

Perfect!

I hopped in my car and zoomed over the bridges to downtown, all the while thinking of how much I loved my brother. He was so smart and so sweet. And he loved me. He really, really loved me and accepted me. I wished that he didn't live so far away.

I parked on the street across from the college and for a moment I indulged in a twinge of nostalgia. A herd of freshmen were crossing the street, guys in their flip-flops and shorts wearing old T-shirts and girls with flat-ironed long straight hair, and I thought, Man, they look so young. I remembered being a freshman and couldn't remember ever looking like them. They were absolute babies.

There was a line at Starbucks so I got in it and waited, letting other people go ahead of me until Ivy showed up.

"Hey you!" I said and gave him a hug.

"Hey, Ashley River," he said.

I giggled and said, "Aren't you happy that our mother didn't name you Cooper?"

The Ashley and Cooper Rivers surrounded the peninsula of Charleston.

"Please! I have enough scars as it is! So what are you having?"

"A venti skinny latte, no sugar."

"I think I want a skinny cappuccino. Grab a table. This is mine."

"Okay, thanks."

I parked myself at an empty table, folding up a newspaper left behind by another person. I wiped the table clean of crumbs just as Ivy sat down to join me.

"So what's going on? Sorry about last night. I ran into a bunch of people I hadn't seen in years . . ."

"I figured as much. No biggie. About Friday night?"

"Isn't James fabulous?"

"Yes. Totally. He probably thinks we're completely messed up."

"No, he doesn't. All families are permanently messed up. You should hear his stories. His grandmother runs the whole family from Beijing. They call her Dragon Lily. She makes the Impossibles look normal. No lie. But you want to know what he said about you?"

"I don't know. Do I?"

"He said Mom is jealous of your relationship with Maisie. Especially when Maisie started talking about you looking like Juliet . . ."

"Oh, come on . . ."

"Listen to me, Ashley. James is an excellent judge of character. It isn't that she's jealous of you and Maisie, so much. Well, actually she sees Maisie loving you to death and it's sort of a knife in her heart. On top of that she hates getting older. She looks at you and remembers her modeling days and then she sees your youthful skin and all you've got going on and it reminds her those days are long gone for her and never coming back."

"Really? And just what should I do about that?"

"I don't think there's much you can do except be really sweet to her. It can't be easy for her to hear about Juliet her whole life and how Juliet was so amazing and got robbed of her life. It wasn't Mom's fault that her sister died."

"Yeah, you're right. I mean, she's been working to support women's rights for years. Don't you think she does that to impress Maisie?"

"Yeah, but no matter what she does, she can't live up to her sister's memory. Think about it. Liz and Clayton take us out to one of the best restaurants in Charleston and pick up the check—it had to be a thousand bucks—but what does Maisie do? Did you hear a thank-you? No. And you know I adore her. But then she exhumes her dead daughter and starts with the whole Saint Juliet business again. I was too freaked out to feel bad for Mom but when James and I talked about it later, it was pretty obvious. What was happening, I mean. Mom can't win."

"Gee God, I never thought about it like that. And every time we all get together it's pretty toxic. I just go into self-preservation mode. So what can I do? I can't avoid them."

"No, but you should start letting Mom know you're in her corner too. Know what I mean? And that doesn't have to mean you don't love Maisie."

"Well, if I can figure out how to do that without bloodshed, I'll be the next Gandhi." I stared at my brother, thinking, and said, "Do you know how much happier I'd be if you and James lived here?"

"I miss you, Ash. I remember being your age. The future is shrouded in the mists of the unknown. I used to have stomachaches all the time. What you have to do is start selling some of your paintings or else figure out another way to make money. Enough to support yourself, you know?"

"Well, actually, I did have an idea."

I told him about the scheme Mary Beth and I had cooked up and he sat back in his chair looking, well, aghast.

"You crazy little imp! Are you going to do it?"

"I would but the house looks like total hell. There's paint peeling everywhere."

"I recall," Ivy said. "Too proud to whitewash, too poor to paint. We're finally a Tennessee Williams play. It was bound to happen."

"Mary Beth and I talked about it and we think the only part of the house that really absolutely has to get a face-lift is the front porch over the water, the hallways, and the powder room. Maybe the living room. Nobody would even see any other rooms, right?"

"Okay, listen to me. If Liz and Clay hear about this, they'll disown you. You know that, right?"

"Yeah, but we can stash fifteen hundred dollars a night every night we do this. All we need is a few successful events and I can give the Sube a tune-up *and* go to Paris."

"And what would you do in Paris?"

"Are you kidding? I'd wander the halls of the Louvre and all the other museums filling sketchbooks with da Vinci and Renoir and Rubens! Not to mention Corot and Monet and Manet! And Rousseau and on and on . . . it's a long list."

"You're pretty frustrated, aren't you?"

"Yeah. I need a muse to talk to me and I think he/she/it is waiting for me in France. Maybe Italy. Maybe even New York."

"Oh, dear."

"What?"

"I'm about to become your partner in crime."

"Why? How?"

"By giving you house paint money because it's an ingenious idea. You don't have to do it forever. I mean, you choose some goal number and quit when you get there. Besides, the house isn't in a business zone. Eventually you'd get busted."

"It could be a private club, couldn't it? I mean, when we have a party at the gallery, people write checks to whatever the cause is."

"True, true. Why not? But don't ask the town fathers. They'll stop you before you can start. Just do it. I'll put some money in your bank on Monday. Text me your account number."

"Oh, Ivy. Thanks."

"Just be careful, okay? And watch the weather. It's hurricane season."

"Oh, please. It's hurricane season every year."

CHAPTER 3

Clayton—My Side

Sorry to interrupt but you need to know my story too. Here it is in a nutshell.

This is what you do when you have too much money—you blow it on stupid stuff or you hoard it. And I'm as guilty as the next guy. I had too many suits, too many shoes, too many custom shirts, watches, and ties—so much that I kept a double wardrobe, one in New York and another in Charleston. And my bank accounts were bulging. I would never admit my extreme self-indulgence to Liz or anyone else. But it was true. And I earned it, didn't I? I didn't steal it and I didn't inherit it. It was mine. I've always held a strong conviction that everyone should earn their own money. It was good for self-esteem and it strengthened character to say you built your corner of the world with your own two hands.

I'd been a Wall Street banker via Charleston my whole career, on my own terms, with a firm that made the conversion from gentlemen to animals with such ease and speed—think of Ivan Boesky back in the 1980s—it was terrifying. After the whole insider trading thing started sending some of my colleagues to state and federal facilities for character rehab, we all developed new habits for survival. We put little to nothing in writing, never spoke in an elevator or at a restaurant or while traveling commercial about any kind of hearsay, and of course we came by what we earned honestly. If you repeated this, I'd have to kill you, but the truth is that many a night passed that I thanked God my office wasn't wired.

When you're a young buck, you go into investment banking because you get off on the thrill of the deal. The money doesn't hurt either. After you've done a couple of hundred deals, the thrill is gone and you start looking for other, bigger thrills. Pretty textbook stuff—Psychology 101. My current thrill was Sophia Bacco. I never meant to have an affair with anyone. I'm not that kind of a man. An accidental screw is one thing but to really fall for someone? I guess it just happens sometimes. That's all.

I began commuting back and forth to New York almost thirty years ago when I decided I wasn't leaving Charleston. I wanted to spend my weekends smelling pluff mud and salt. I never wanted to live in Manhattan. It's too crazy for a Charleston boy. So I flew north on Sunday nights and south on Fridays except during August. For years I stayed at the New York Athletic Club during the week, which was not terribly expensive back then. After I did a few IPOs that made us all an obscene amount of money, the firm gave me a private plane to use. They knew I was ready to pack it in, but they didn't want me to retire. So they made it as easy as possible to stay. I bought a little one-bedroom in the East Fifties and just recently, I rediscovered Sophia. She was an old friend I hadn't seen in years, a model and a friend of Liz's back in the day. How's that for karma? Sophia once was a Victoria's Secret model. And to be fair to Liz, Liz was a swimwear model and even had the *Sports Illustrated* cover one year. But all that history aside, it started when *Sophia* recognized *me* in the lobby one day.

I'd never forget the first time we spoke.

"Clayton? Clayton Waters? Is that you?"

I had just hopped out of a black car and hurried into the foyer and was shaking out my umbrella. The skies were dumping snow outside and it was dark, windy, and bitter cold. It was March and everyone knows March weather in New York can be really miserable. Anyway, I looked over and there she was, wearing a red fox coat to her ankles and a big fox hat to match. She opened her coat, put her hands on her nonexistent hips, and stared at me, waiting with a smirk. She looked like a movie star and I think I stopped breathing.

"Oh, my . . . Sophia? What are *you* doing here?"

"I just moved into the penthouse. How about you?"

"I've got a pied-à-terre here on the second floor. A one-bedroom. 2F. Wow. What a wonderful coincidence!"

"Yes. It *is*. How's Liz? And the kids?"

"Oh, they're all fine. What are you up to these days?"

"Oh, let's see . . . after I stopped modeling full-time, I became the face of a line of cosmetics for Kohl's and I have a line of bed and bath linen for them too. And I do some costume jewelry for a department store chain in Argentina. It keeps me busy, hopping all over the place to cut new store ribbons and attend special events."

"I imagine it does. Are you on your way out?"

"Yeah, meeting a friend for an early supper."

"In this weather?"

"I know, but you know me. Never let a little thing like a blizzard get in between me and some fun." She laughed and leaned forward to kiss my cheek. Spontaneous laughter and cheek kissing came easily to girls like Sophia. In fact, most things in life were hers just for the asking. And why not? She smelled like something I wanted to drink. Jesus! When I felt her breath on my face, I broke a full-body cold sweat. It was ridiculous.

"Well, then . . . take care," I said and watched the movement of her fur as she passed me until she reached the door. *Meow.* "We should . . ."

"Yeah! Let's get together and catch up! 2F, right?"

"Yes," I said, committing adultery with every part of my heart and soul.

In my mind, we were naked, going crazy like I don't know what—rutting animals—with Barry White music thumping bass in the background. I was a teenaged boy again. For this reason, I didn't run upstairs, call Liz, and tell her that her old friend lived in our building. In fact, I *never* told Liz that Sophia was living in our building *and* still drop-dead gorgeous. And even though Liz was still a beautiful woman, she had lost her joie de vivre and it showed. Poor Liz.

So around nine thirty that same night, my doorbell rang. I knew it had to be Sophia. I wished then that I had shaved and showered. I got caught up in a Knicks game on cable and probably looked like hell. When I opened the door, stubbly and shoeless, there she stood with that infamous mane of thick blond hair tumbling over one shoulder. Literally, I felt weak.

She said, "I know it's a little late but I thought you might share a nightcap with me at my place. It stopped snowing and the view is incredible."

"Oh, I don't know . . . ," I said, fooling neither of us.

"Oh, come on. I've got a fire going and it's so beautiful outside . . ."

"Well, if you've got a fire and all . . . I mean, it would be a shame to waste it, right?"

I thought, Oh boy, this is dangerous.

"Get your shoes," she said, waiting in the doorway.

"Okay. Here, come inside!"

"Thanks!"

She walked in like she owned the place. I stepped back to let her pass and hurried to find my loafers.

"So I'm looking forward to meeting your husband . . ."

"Never married," she said. "Marriage just wasn't in the cards."

"Wow," I said and added, "well, marriage isn't for everyone. It's probably overrated."

I could feel her moving around behind me, knowing she was looking at everything. I pulled my shoes out from under the sofa and sat to put them on and I wondered how I could be thinking the lewd and lascivious things I was thinking when I knew she used to be my wife's great friend.

I looked up. She had a picture of Liz in her hands, staring at it hard with narrow eyebrows.

"That's Liz in Greece," I said.

"I never liked her much, to be perfectly honest," she said.

Problem solved.

"Let's go," I said, scooping up my keys.

So you know how that went. We got to the top floor and she poured a liberal amount of twenty-year-old single malt into heavy crystal tumblers. We sipped. The view was indeed breathtaking.

I remembered saying, "You can't beat the Chrysler Building at night."

She agreed. After that the details get a little fuzzy. I'm pretty sure she started it. I think she was a little looped. It doesn't matter really because neither of us tried to stop the other and now it's been going on for four months.

I needed to remind myself to tell her that Ivy and James had the keys, which by the way puts a cramp in my style. What should I have done? Tell them no, they couldn't use the apartment? Well, I didn't and it didn't work out so well.

I went back to New York a few days later, following James and Ivy's departure for San Francisco. At eight that night, Sophia knocked on my door.

"Hey, gorgeous," I said. "Come on in."

"You're not going to like this," she said, coming in, kissing my cheek, and dropping her keys on the hall table.

"What are you saying? I love everything about you! Glass of wine?"

"Bottle with a straw," she said.

"Oh dear God," I said.

From the look on her face, I knew something was deeply wrong. I pulled a '96 Latour Beaucastle from the wine rack. Serious discussion called for a serious wine. The cork was a long one that required my two-step corkscrew and some effort but a minute into it, there was a happy pop as the cork was liberated from the bottle's neck.

"I missed you," she said.

"I missed you, too," I said.

I poured a good amount of the wine into two goblets through my diffuser and handed one to her.

"Sometimes, even when I know you're not here, I'll just come down and ring your doorbell anyway."

"Really?" I thought, Wow, that's pretty sweet.

"Yeah. Really. Last week I heard music coming from your apartment so I thought you were here."

"No, that would've been my son and his, um, friend."

"I know."

She was leaning against the doorway. Her arms were crossed, and she had this sour expression, like she was pissed.

"Oh, my God. What happened?"

"Well, when the elevator door opened on your floor and I heard the music, I just assumed you were here."

"Well, sure. Who wouldn't?"

"Right. But I hurried upstairs to my place, ditched my clothes, slipped on a trench coat, and hurried back here. When they opened the door . . ."

"Oh no."

"Yes, oh no. I think I flashed them by accident."

"Oh. Shit."

"The Asian guy was wearing Glass and I think he took a picture. Or a movie."

"Shit. *Shit!*"

"I'm sorry, Clay. I really am. But you know, it really wasn't my fault."

"Liz is gonna kick my ass. What happened after that?"

"I shrieked! Then I said, *Sorry! Wrong apartment!*"

"What did they say?"

"Your son said, *maybe*. His friend said, *maybe not*."

"This is a big fat problem," I said. "I should've told you they were here. This is all my fault."

"Sort of," she mumbled.

Great, I thought. This is just great. Time to start moving assets to the Cayman Islands. All hell is about to break loose. And I'm just telling you, I am in some seriously deep shit.

CHAPTER 4

Liz—My Side

I'm really sorry about my behavior at my mother's birthday dinner two weeks ago. I know I sounded like a total witch. Sometimes, I get so frustrated and then I say the dumbest thing in the world and it makes everyone uncomfortable. I apologize. Please. Stay with me because you don't know enough about us yet to judge.

Today, as I always do on Tuesdays because I'm the dutiful daughter, I'm taking my mother out to lunch at the Mustard Seed on James Island. I've always loved that restaurant, especially their pad thai. The portions are usually generous enough to feed a family of four. When Ashley and Ivy were children I'd take them to the Mustard Seed in Mount Pleasant and we'd have a feast. It was there they learned to eat enchiladas and mussels and all sorts of daring things. Oh, they were so precious when they were young. Then the little darlings slipped right through my fingers and grew up.

Family, family. It's so frightening and, yes, almost embarrassing to muse over what my idea of family was years ago when I was dressing on my wedding day, Maisie attaching that veil to my hair. I remember it like it was yesterday. Like every other girl I knew, I thought I'd fall in love, marry, and conceive, and somehow I expected to deliver a better version of Clayton and me. Brother, was I naive!

Let me tell you, my friend, the gene pool is a mighty big place and like they say, there's literally no lifeguard. I hardly recognize myself in either one of my children except that Maisie insists my dead sister, Juliet, seems to have been reincarnated in my daughter. I know. What a creepy thought. How creepy? I've never told Maisie or anyone but when Ashley was very young she used to tell me to call her Juliet. How do you like them apples? But who knows about all that stuff?

I don't have the first clue what or who is in Ivy's DNA. It doesn't matter really. You take the children the good Lord sends you, love them with all your heart, and give them your best efforts to help them prepare themselves for life. I know Clayton and I made some mistakes with ours, Ivy in particular, but that doesn't mean we didn't or don't love them. The biggest problem I've ever had or continue to have raising our children, believe it or not, is Maisie.

Maisie was raised by parents whose circumstances had been dramatically reduced by the Great Depression. The aftershocks of that terrible catastrophe were good and bad. On the positive side, she learned to be self-sufficient, when she's so inclined. She keeps herself and her home immaculate. And she manages money well. My father used to say *she could squeeze the balls off a buffalo nickel.* There are other idiomatic expressions I much prefer, such as *she can stretch a dollar so thin you can read the newspaper through it.* Or *she's tighter than a mole's ear,* not that I've ever examined a mole's ear or ever would.

When Juliet and I were really little, our mother kept chickens for their eggs and their eventual commitment to our dinner table. My sister and I loved to play with the chicks and gave them all names. Whenever we realized that Maisie was about to send a chicken to its great reward, we'd cry and howl and beg her not to wring its neck. She'd tell us to go watch television and sure enough, we'd have fried chicken for dinner. And we ate it with a smile on our face because there was no point in being emotional. Maisie wouldn't stand for it.

Maisie would catch some creek shrimp or fiddlers, bait her own hooks, drop that hook in the water, and pull in fish by the bucketful. She would clean them outside on an old wooden table while my sister watched, completely entranced. I gagged.

For as far back as I can remember, Maisie has grown delicious vegetables and gorgeous flowers. Needless to say, she made pickles from cucumbers and string beans, and chutney from Jerusalem artichokes. I guess the only groceries she ever bought were flour, sugar, other meats, and milk. She would've kept a goat for milk but our neck of the woods on the Wappoo Creek wasn't zoned for any farm animals bigger than poultry. When Juliet and I were teenagers, we'd collapse in horror when she'd bring up the subject of getting a goat. We would've been made social outcasts forever if some cute guy came to pick us up for a date and there was a goat in the yard. Never mind goat droppings.

After Juliet died, Maisie gave up her chickens, grew fewer vegetables, and rarely fished, giving in like most of us have to filling up a cart at the Piggly Wiggly, which apparently is going to take another name. But she never gave up her flowers, saying flowers were her therapy. Somewhere along the line she learned to hybridize her hydrangeas and rhododendrons into amazing, vibrant colors and combinations only found in her yard that baffled garden club members from all over the South. It was not unusual for Maisie to find total strangers in her yard taking pictures of her flowers.

The point is she learned all this from her mother who learned it from her mother before her. Juliet could grow vegetables and make relish like Maisie. I thought it was unnecessary labor and a good way to wreck a manicure. Maybe that sounds shallow or defiant but I preferred reading or listening to music to digging in the dirt. That was one more reason Juliet was always my mother's favorite and it's also why she gave up her vegetable garden and so forth, saying she had no one to share them with, a comment that was repeated often even though she knew it made me feel sick inside. Her feelings were more important than mine.

My father, Neal (who died right after Juliet, in a hunting accident at fifty-two), was cut from the same cloth as my mother. He banked every nickel Maisie saved. My parents worked for everything they had, which was probably what attracted me to Clayton. Clayton was as completely self-made as they were. But back to my mother. With Dad *and* Juliet gone, my mother fell into an understandable but terrible depression. I was already in New York by then but I came home to visit as often as I could. We would sit across the table from each other, wallowing in silence. She thought she was the only one who had suffered a loss. She really did. Talk about denial? Over and over she'd say, *I can't believe this happened to me.*

Lately I've been wondering about the impact of all this loss on me, and one thing is certain: I've always been risk averse, almost to the point of absurdity. I knew Clayton was a safe bet when I married him. He might not have an overabundance of passion in him, but he was steady. His professional life was complicated and stressful so naturally he wanted his life with me to be reliable and calm. I could usually deliver that much without a problem. He sort of balked at my work initially, but in an odd way, it added some cachet to our family's reputation. As long as I didn't put myself in personal danger or bring too much of it home, he was fine with it. And it gave me spending money, taking some degree of pressure off him.

Way before Clayton came along, when I was a very young girl, Maisie worked as the secretary at my school, which was wonderful if I skinned my knee on the playground, but it also made it impossible to play hooky. She ran a strict house and was as hard on herself as she was on us. When Dad died, things changed dramatically. She claimed it was no longer necessary to work. She dumped her sensible shoes for kitten heels, started wearing makeup all the time, and made no secret of the fact that she was desirous of male company. The more I inched toward the altar, the more flamboyant she became. And by the time my children came into the world after Juliet was gone, she had become this other person, angry one minute and ebullient the next, as though she didn't want to be anyone's mother anymore but being a fairy godmother might suit her fine. It wasn't just a monetary issue. She spoiled my children rotten with things she never gave me—attention, approval, gifts—and darn near ruined them. She drowned them in undeserved praise while withdrawing from me at the same time.

She told Ivy and Ashley they were *special* every five minutes. Not just a little bit special, but, by golly, they were *geniuses*! They should chase their crazy dreams and don't *worry* about having a solid career to fall back on. Yes, I worked as a swimsuit model but I also had a business degree. Maisie always frowned on me as though I was some kind of slutty exhibitionist, so I took myself through night school knowing my firm thighs wouldn't last forever. But let me assure you I made ten times the money walking a runway than I ever would have earned running a small office or doing some other dreary thing. And later on when I needed it, that degree qualified me to have a meaningful position with one of Charleston's leading nonprofits that worked to stop domestic violence. Even I knew you shouldn't be strutting around in bathing suits after twenty-two. Please!

Back to my children? Yes. Maisie darn near destroyed them. Ashley actually *believes* she can support herself painting landscapes and whatever it is she's doing. Maisie always says, *Why not? Of course you can!* Outrageous! There is not one shred of evidence that this is true.

From the time Ashley was a little girl, Maisie's refrigerator was covered in Ashley's crayon scribbles. We'd be at Maisie's making cookies or something and I'd ask Ashley to recite her multiplication tables to show my mother what she'd learned. But my little girl was never a Sea World spectacle who would jump for a fish. Ashley would pout, dig in her little heels, and refuse. Maisie would say, I *know what, let's make a mural of them in Magic Markers,* and she'd produce a roll of paper and a bag of markers from thin air. It was as though she was always lying in the weeds waiting to sabotage my plans and undermine my authority. She gave my children money all the time, never came for a visit without an elaborate gift for them, and generally ignored me when I called Ashley and Ivy to dinner, to take a bath, to go to bed, on and on. Seems like I should have been able to expect backup from my own mother, doesn't it?

In fact, from the time she understood ambition, Ashley thought she was *entitled* to pursue her dreams for as long as she liked, no matter how far-fetched they were, and Maisie agreed. God gave her an exceptional talent, didn't he? Ashley is completely convinced that her talent is superextraordinary and that it would be a grievous sin not to use it. She knows that once the powers that be find out about her, the entire international art community will rear up on its hind legs and cheer her on to her certain and well-deserved immortality!

And if my son hadn't met that Chinese man . . . well, he's just lucky, let's put it that way and let's hope it lasts. I guess I should *hope* it lasts? Listen, it's just been difficult for me and hard for Clayton, too, to reconcile ourselves to the fact that there will never be a Clayton Bernard Waters V. Living with Clayton's long list of disappointments these days is just no fun. It's why I dream of running away to Bali! God knows, I wait on him hand and foot. And while we're on the subject of being driven to the edge? He's categorically mistaken to believe he can make things right between us with a little velvet box that has something sparkly inside. Just last week he did something so thoughtless I couldn't believe it. So I called him an ass under my breath and he heard me.

"Don't call me an ass," he said.

"Then don't act like one," I said.

That pretty much sums up the current state of affairs between us.

I pulled up in Maisie's driveway and got out of my car. Her yard looked gorgeous as usual, as though she was channeling Gertrude Jekyll. I had my key ready, but when I got to the kitchen door, it was unlocked. There was a pile of Skipper's laundry on the table. For some reason, it irritated me. Maisie was standing in front of the television watching *The View*.

"Don't you love the way these girls just go at it? That Barbara Walters. Boy, she still has juice!" she said and pointed to her cheek. I gave her a kiss. "Where are we going?"

"Mustard Seed," I said.

"Good. It's my favorite."

"I know."

An appreciation of *The View* that bordered on obsession was one of the few things we agreed on. She loved Barbara Walters. I thought Whoopi carried the show, but I didn't argue with Maisie. In fact, I rarely argued with her about anything because she would just ignore me and do what she wanted to do or think what she wanted to think. I would just be more frustrated. Wrestling the car keys from her was my only success. Then we hired Skipper, never expecting . . . well, Maisie is a grown woman. At first we thought he was a gold-digging gigolo, but it soon became clear that he had his own money and a llama ranch to boot. I know, llamas. Like, what's the matter with dairy cows or horses? But Maisie's happy and she rarely poses a danger to the public, only occasionally breaking our agreement and driving all over the road like she does with her nose glued to the steering wheel like Mr. Magoo. And Skipper's devotion, not his laundry, to Maisie is a relief to me. Since his arrival on the scene Maisie seems calmer and she's decidedly better behaved.

"Does he have to pile his unmentionables on the kitchen table?"

"Lord! I had no idea you were such a prude! He can pile his bloomers on my dinner plate if he wants, okay?"

I just stared at her. Her skin looked radiant. Hmmm.

"Let's go," I said. "There's going to be a waiting line if we don't move it."

"Oh, fine," she said and clicked off the television. "Cher's going to be on tomorrow."

"I thought she retired," I said.

"Guess not," she said.

"Well, she should."

"Why?" Maisie said, setting me up.

I took the carrot.

"Mother. She's sixty-seven years old. Isn't it a little undignified to be prancing around half naked at her age?"

We left the house through the kitchen door and she turned back to double-check that the door was indeed locked.

"I guess *you're* the expert on *that* sort of thing," she said. "Gosh, I'm hungry. Aren't you?"

The *expert*. On *that* sort of thing. Thank you.

"Famished," I said, and opened the passenger door for her.

Maybe I slammed the car door a little too hard, inadvertently letting her know I caught her slight. We rode to the restaurant with only the mournful sound of Joni Mitchell crooning away one of her very sad songs in the background.

At the table she scrutinized the menu and said, "So I imagine you want to split the pad thai? You always do."

"Not really. I think I'm going to have the stir-fry."

"Doesn't all that broccoli cause intestinal distress?"

Intestinal distress.

"No. What are you going to order?"

"Well, I guess I'm not having the pad thai, am I?"

"That's up to you. You don't have to eat the whole thing."

"I'll have the seared scallops." She said this with a sigh, exhaling deeply enough to dust the restaurant.

We ordered and when our iced tea arrived, it seemed the air had cleared, mainly because I just let it go. I always did. I had other things on my mind besides her snippiness.

"Did you see the Weather Channel this morning?" she said.

"No. What did I miss?"

"Well, there are a number of storms in the Caribbean. Any one of them could develop into something very nasty."

"Mother? It's hurricane season and if a hurricane's coming, I'm sure we'll have plenty of notice."

"Let's hope so. Is your bracelet new?" she asked.

"Yes. It's from Tiffany's via Clayton's guilt. I think Clayton's having an affair. Maybe." In fact, Clayton and I had not had sex in months, but I didn't tell her that.

"Why on earth would he do a stupid thing like that?" she said. "It's very pretty."

"Thanks. The reason I think he's fooling around is that the last time I was in New York our bed had not been slept in. He'd been there for three nights. And the towels were unused. And there was no half-and-half in the refrigerator. You know he can't drink his coffee without half-and-half. It was pretty obvious he hadn't needed to call the cleaning girl."

"Hmmm. He's getting sloppy," Maisie said. "Do you think he wants to get caught?"

"No man wants to get caught unless they're really Catholic or really Jewish except the politicians who think they'll never get caught. Idiots. All of them."

"Amen to that. But if you think he's dicky dunkin', you can do one of two things."

"Really? What might they be?"

"Well, you could fly up there without warning and surprise him."

"I'm not so sure I want to do that. It's not cricket, you know? What's my other option?"

"Wait a short while and see if he buys you earrings to match the bracelet. Then you'll *know* there's some funny business going on."

"They make a necklace too."

"If he shows up with earrings *and* a necklace, get a lawyer."

I knew she intended to be funny but I didn't smile. Nothing about the topic was funny to me. I just looked at her, realizing then that indeed, my marriage had a fault line right down the middle. Our food arrived.

"Let's talk about something else," I said, cutting a slice of asparagus and eating it. "This is good."

"Well, I'm happy. My scallops are wonderful. All right. Tell me about my darling granddaughter. You know, she really is an extraordinary girl."

"She's very thoughtful and sweet," I said. "But she'd starve without us."

"Liz, I don't think reminding her of that every five minutes is particularly beneficial to anyone."

"What should I do? Applaud? Mother, she earns ten dollars an hour. She's dating no one. How and when she finds time to paint is beyond me but I haven't seen anything new from her in ages. And a bachelor of fine arts? She may as well have studied indigenous cultures for all the good it's ever going to do her! I wish you'd encourage her to get her master's—at least she could teach."

"Teach? She's too introspective for that. She really should be painting all the time, you know. Working for the Turners, nice as they are . . . well, you're right. It won't put bread on the table."

"She can't even afford a *table*. Probably painting supplies either. And anyway, her work seems so amateurish to me."

"Who are we to judge? Skipper says even this new pope over in Rome says we shouldn't judge. Would you pass the salt, please?"

Skipper was a Roman Catholic. I pushed the saltshaker toward her, biting my tongue about it. If she wanted to send her blood pressure through the roof, it was her prerogative.

"Miss Maisie? We're Protestant. We don't take direction from the Vatican. You don't think I should stand in judgment of my children? Like you never judge me?"

She harrumphed and said, "You listen to your mother, Elizabeth Pringle Waters, before you get on your high horse over there. Your husband is a horse's patootie, and it doesn't matter if he's having a fling. It seems like half the men in this country can't keep their pants on. I don't know everything but I know this much. If you want to, you can put a stop to it. He loves you, and, plus, he'd die if he had to give up half his assets. And by the way, missy, I saw you having lunch the other day at Sermet's and it looked like monkey business to me."

"*What?* I was with a potential donor for the shelter, Mother. I don't like your tone."

"My big fat foot. You were drinking a glass of wine. Sitting right there at a window table for all of Charleston to see! It wasn't even one o'clock in the afternoon. Would you like a scallop?"

"No, thank you. I don't know what you're talking about."

"Take up gardening. Then at least you'll have something wholesome to brag about. You've got too much time on your hands."

"I do not!"

"And don't worry about pushing Ashley. She has a *very* special talent."

"Like Juliet had?" Oh brother, I thought. Here we go again.

"Yes, like Juliet."

"So, because Juliet died before she could fulfill her artistic ambitions, you think we should just let Ashley live her life without a solid career path and see what happens? I just find it odd, given your parents and the Depression and all that . . ."

"What? What in the world does the Depression have to do with this?"

"Self-reliance!" I knew I was speaking too loudly. "It was the most important thing you taught me! And it's odd that you don't think Ashley needs a more-well defined career path. She's got to start paying her bills at *some* point! Or do you want to keep throwing money at her?"

"Lower your voice. And stop exaggerating. I hardly do a thing for that poor child."

"Oh, right."

"She's my only granddaughter. Listen, I've never told you this before but I went to my psychic friend. She says there's a very strong possibility that Ashley *is* the reincarnation of Juliet. She says there's an unusually powerful heart connection between us."

I sat back in my chair and stared at my mother. It wasn't news. I had heard the reincarnation story at least a thousand times. Never mind what Ashley used to say when she was little, I wasn't going to encourage this nonsense. My mother was finally losing her mind. Did I need to see about her power of attorney? Pay her bills? I'd ask her doctor.

"Mother? There's also a very strong possibility that your psychic *friend* is milking your wallet."

CHAPTER 5

Ashley at Work

I was at work and organizing the catalog JPEGs for our upcoming show of artists from the coast of the Carolinas and Georgia. It was to be called *Tidal Water Gems*. I loved organizing catalogs but I couldn't decide which painting or photograph should be on the cover. The Turners had turned this job over to me a few months ago, saying I had a better eye for that sort of thing. Obviously, I wasn't so sure. I only wished my work was ready to be on a cover.

"What do you think, Mr. Turner? Should we use Jack Alterman's photographic landscape of the Ashepoo River or the Jonathan Green painting of the church ladies?"

I must have looked superserious because Mr. Turner smiled at me in that weird way grown-ups smile when they think you're precious.

"If only I was twenty years younger," Bill Turner said, "I'd steal your heart and whisk you away to the Kasbah!"

"Aw, Mr. Turner. That's so sweet!" I said. "What's the Kasbah?"

"William Turner? You stop harassing Ashley and get in here right now! You've got a pile of contracts to read and sign!"

"Yes, dear. Yes, dear," Mr. Turner said, and scurried away like a frightened mouse.

I gave him a wave with the roll of my fingers and he smiled at me again, happy he had not offended me. As if I took him seriously. Please.

Judy Turner came out of her lavish office and toward mine, which in reality was a closet I shared with the copier, the water-cooler, the cleaning equipment, the coffeemaker, the tiniest refrigerator on earth, and all the office supplies.

"Old fool," Judy said. "Don't pay him one bit of attention."

"You're the love of my life!" Mr. Turner called out and I giggled.

"That's right," Mrs. Turner called back and rolled her eyes. "And you're mine!"

"He's hilarious," I said and held up photos of the two cover options. "Cover?"

"Hmmm. Tough one. They're both so incredible. Put Jonathan Green on the front for the humanity, Jack Alterman on the back for the atmosphere. Then run the Altermans first in the catalog followed by the Greens. Sprinkle the others in between. It's equitable that way. Blame me if they squawk."

"Excellent. Another decision made. If we reprint, I can reverse it. Then everyone's happy, right?"

"Such a lovely brain! This is why we adore you!"

"Ha! Ha! Now I have to choose paper. The show's been live on our website for almost a week."

"Oh, Ashley, *dahlin,* the website gives me nightmares! Even though I've known you since you were just a little bitty thing, I never dreamed you'd grow up to be my right arm. Your momma must be so proud of you."

"Thank you," I said, unable to make eye contact. I was thinking something else entirely. The Turners wouldn't believe what it's like to try and live on ten dollars an hour. I'd bet they hadn't had ramen for dinner since Nixon left office.

The opening for *Tidal Water Gems* was only a few days away. But the event for Senator Galloway was that very night. I was so excited. I'd brought my dress to work in a plastic hanging bag from Belk. It hung suspended from the top drawer of the filing cabinet. My shoes and makeup were on the floor in a Vera Bradley tote bag I got for Christmas when I was in the eighth grade. Maybe seventh. It's hard to remember now but it was plain to see that I wasn't exactly drowning under the weight of overindulgence. And, yes, I'd brought *that* dress to wear simply because it was the best one I owned.

I wouldn't be doing anything special that night except checking in people on the guest list, directing people to the bathroom, and so on. Still, I was excited to see him in real life. Porter, that is. *Ashley Galloway!* What a beautiful name. *Ashley Galloway, First Lady of the United States of America!* Even better.

We were coming to the end of an exhibition of watercolors, which was a fortuitous thing because they were all protected behind glass. In case somebody tripped and accidentally tossed a glass of red wine in the wrong direction, only minimal damage could happen to the art, unless, of course, they broke the glass that protected the painting, which has never happened. Besides, we only rented out the gallery when there was very small risk to the installation. I was still debating my scheme to rent out my parents' house for events, and leaning toward doing it, especially when I opened the envelope containing a check for twenty-five hundred dollars from the Friends of Porter Galloway. That was what the Turners were earning for merely opening the doors and turning on the lights. Twenty-five hundred dollars was some serious bank. No doubt about it. Even though Ivy gave me enough money to give the first floor of our house a coat of paint to make it presentable, I was nervous. And even though Mary Beth had figured out how to serve decent wine and hors d'oeuvres for less than twenty dollars a person, mostly self-served, I was still nervous.

I wasn't going to do anything until I was very sure we had a foolproof plan, one where my parents would *never ever* find out. If Big Liz and Big Clay caught me in a lying scam that huge, they would throw me into the streets. I'd be living in a refrigerator box from somebody's recycling garbage, pathetically begging strangers for time on an electrical outlet to recharge my iPhone. I did not want to live in a cardboard box. No, ma'am.

The afternoon blew by. Around four, Mary Beth's catering company showed up and started setting up. It was time to take *the dress* out of the bag and attempt to put my hair up in a French twist. I thought an updo and a string of pearls might make me resemble a young blond Jackie Kennedy. With cleavage. She was my idol. I slipped into the tiny bathroom and did my best. When I came out, Bill Turner was there, using the copier.

He took one look at me, slapped his hand over his heart, and gasped.

"Great God!" he said, trying to determine the length of my legs.

"Bill? Leave that child alone!" Judy called from the gallery as though she had eyes in all the walls. Maybe she did. Or radar maybe.

I giggled and squeezed past him intending to find Mary Beth. I

had legs like a flamingo but what was I supposed to do about that?
Wear a toga?

I loved our special events. The gallery always looked so glamorous with all the flowers and the glow of all those tea candles. The
food and bar tables were draped in black to the floor with square
white cloths laid over them in diamond shapes. On the ends of the
tables were dozens of sparkling glasses in perfect lines like soldiers
at attention. All the waitstaff stood at the ready wearing black shirts
and pants with white aprons from their waists to their ankles. Very
Parisian, I thought and sighed. A sign from God that once again it was
clear I was going to have to do something drastic to get to France. Or
Italy or how about just Tribeca in New York?

I spotted Mary Beth. She was fanning stacks of cocktail napkins
with a highball glass.

"Hey, girl" I said and gave her a hug.

"Ooooh, honey! Look at you!" she said.

"Do I look okay?" I tugged at my hem a little, covering my rear a
little more but revealing more of the girls. "I mean, this dress is sort
of short, isn't it?"

"Well, it ain't PG-13."

"It's too skimpy, isn't it?"

"Hell, no. You're rocking that thing! Screw the old biddies! Wait
till *you know who* sees you."

"Let's hope. It's just not very Jackie."

"Oh, so what. And you ain't gonna believe who's on the waitstaff
tonight."

"Who?"

"Tommy Milano."

"Well, isn't that great."

"Please. He's a sweetie."

Soon people began arriving and I stood by the door, checking off names from the list provided by the Friends of *Himself*. Another girl from "the Friends of" helped the supporters attach peel-and-stick name tags to their shoulders. In no time at all there was a crowd of well-heeled people my parents' age milling about, drinking wine, looking at the watercolors, and talking louder and louder by the minute. I didn't see Tommy Milano anywhere. But to my surprise, out of the night and into the gallery stepped Maisie with some people I didn't know.

"Maisie! What a wonderful surprise!" I hugged her and delivered a peck to her cheek.

"Hello, sweetheart! Lorraine? This is my granddaughter, Ashley Waters. Someday, she's going to be a famous artist! Ashley? Say hello to Mrs. Galloway."

"It's so nice to meet you," I said, thinking, Here's my future mother-in-law. She seemed like a nice woman. I loved her earrings.

"And you too, Ashley," Mrs. Galloway said.

"Lorraine's mother, Lucille, and I went to school together," Maisie said.

"Oh!" I said, sounding like an airhead but what was I supposed to say? I mean, was Mrs. Galloway's mother still with us? Why didn't Maisie tell me she was coming with her? "Maisie? Can I get y'all a glass of wine?"

"No, thank you, dear," Mrs. Galloway said. "I'm the designated driver."

"I'll help myself," Maisie said. "It'll give me a chance to flirt with the bartender."

Oh Lord, I thought. "Okay, well then, y'all have fun! Love you, Maisie!"

"Love you too, baby!"

They drifted into the crowd and my mind began clicking away. Maisie might be able to help me with Porter. But how?

Just when my list of names was almost all accounted for, a black car pulled up to the curb. Press from the *Charleston Post and Courier,* the *City Paper,* the *Charleston Mercury,* and *Charleston Magazine* hurried to the sidewalk. Even *Garden & Gun* magazine was there. Camera flashes exploded as his driver opened the back door and Senator Porter Galloway got out and stepped to the curb. His aide got out on the street side and came around. The senator paused, smiled for the photographers, and answered a few questions. His aide began taking questions after that. My heart was racing. I couldn't swallow. Porter turned to come inside and caught my eye.

"Well, hello there," he said. "What's your name?"

"Ashley. Ashley Waters." God, he smelled so good.

"Beautiful. You have a beautiful name."

He said this so politely I thought I might faint or something.

"Thank you," I said. "I guess you don't need a name tag, huh?"

As soon as the words were out of my mouth I regretted them. How stupid and awkward could I be? Huh? Why not just say *duh?* Oh my God! I had just blown my only chance to make him notice me. Of all the things I could have said! My mouth got dry.

But he was cool.

"No, save a tree."

There was a funny little moment when he looked into my eyes and I looked right back into his, a moment of recognition that something potent was brewing. Or that something could.

"Our grandmothers went to high school together," I said. My tongue was clacking against the roof of my mouth like it had a suction cup on it.

"Really? Well, how about that? Small world. Sadly, I have to go work the room," he said, "but I'll see you later?"

"I'll be around," I said and thought, Okay, this is it, I'm definitely going to drop dead right here. But the other side of my brain was already living in the White House, pregnant with his twins and pushing our toddler on a swing while a Secret Service detail looked on with concern. I had to find Mary Beth right away.

I spotted her across the room passing a tray of mini beef Wellingtons.

"Want one?" she said. "I've had four. Delish!"

She really was packing on the pounds lately. But I wasn't saying a word about that.

"Are you kidding me? I can't eat. Did you see him talking to me?"

"Yep, so did half the room. I hate to say I told you so, but I did."

She walked away and I felt someone tap my shoulder. It was Maisie.

She whispered, "I saw that damn fool looking at you and I need to tell you something about him."

"What?" I whispered back.

"I've known him since the day he was born. He used to come around with his grandmother, God rest her soul. But he was bad, Ashley. I mean he was a bully."

"Like how?"

"Like once he was playing with some neighborhood kids in my yard? He turned the hose on all of them and made them cry. He must've been about four or five years old"

"Oh! But he was just four or five years old. Wasn't Prince William a little stinker when he was that age? He grew up to be great!"

"I'm just telling you what I know."

"Don't worry, Maisie," I said.

"Now you listen to me; I'm just saying all these politicians aren't worth a hill of beans anymore. Didn't you read the papers about that idiot, what's his name? That guy in North Carolina with the four-hundred-dollar haircut?"

"That guy? He's old. They're *all* old men, Maisie. They're from a different time. Porter is the new generation. The new generation of politicians are a lot smarter."

"Really? They're all a bunch of egomaniacs. Remember that man in New York sending his you know what all over the country by phone? How one does that, well, I'm uncertain but he did it! *He* wasn't old."

I started laughing then. It was too funny to me that my eighty-year-old grandmother was almost hip to texting but not quite.

"Um, Maisie, it was seriously gross but he's way over forty. That's old."

"Whatever. Where does that leave me? Decrepit? Just watch yourself, that's all."

"Oh, stop worrying, Maisie. Don't you think Porter exudes, you know, something special?"

"Yes. Power. And it's the most dangerous aphrodisiac on this earth. He's trouble with a capital T."

"No, he's not. He's a sweetie."

"I guess I just don't like politicians," Maisie said, shaking her head. She gave me a kiss on the cheek and handed me an envelope. "This is for you. I have to go and find Lorraine."

I opened the envelope and saw the two fifties. Now I could pay my cell-phone bill!

"Oh, Maisie! Thanks!"

"You behave yourself," she said and disappeared into the throng.

"I will, Maisie. I'm a good girl."

Mary Beth was passing another hors d'oeuvre and paused when she came near me.

"Did you see Tommy? He cleans up good."

"No. Where is he?"

"Over there with his hair slicked back, wearing black glasses."

"That's *Tommy*? Are you *serious*?"

"As serious as anything," Mary Beth said. "He's looking mighty fine, if you want my opinion."

"He's adorable. Still. Where's he going with his life?"

"Probably the Amalfi Coast for the month of August for the rest of his life?"

"Yeah, right. And sleeping in a hammock on the beach."

"Just saying. With our luck he'll wind up being a bazillionaire. Anyway, I'm having drinks with Samir."

Samir was a rich Saudi with a huge yacht in Charleston's harbor. Mary Beth talked about marrying a doctor and having a herd of children, but meanwhile she was working on sleeping with a representative of every country in the United Nations. One of these days . . . well, I hoped she'd be safe and not do anything incredibly stupid.

"Just be careful."

"Oh, come on! I'm always careful!"

"Okay. Tommy does look pretty amazing," I said and walked away from Mary Beth and in Tommy's direction.

I'd say hello to him. Big deal. It wouldn't be nice to ignore him since I worked here and all. But who was coming toward me from the other direction, waving to get my attention? Porter Galloway's aide.

"Hi!" he said and then whispered to me, "The senator wanted to know if you'd like to join him for a drink when this is over? Say about ten? He's staying at Charleston Place."

"Sure," I said. "That would be fun."

"So can I have your cell-phone number? You know, in case something comes up?"

"Sure," I said and gave it to him.

Before I could ask for Porter's number, his aide gave me his card with his own cell number.

"In case you can't make it," he said with a wide smile.

"Thanks," I said and thought, Well, it was a good thing that I didn't embarrass myself again by asking for the senator's number. Of course he wouldn't have given it to me! For all he knew I might tweet it to the entire world!

I continued across the room looking for Tommy. He was taking a tray of dirty glasses to the service area behind some pipe and drape.

"Hey!" I said. "How are you?"

"Great," he said. "Wow. You sure look, um, wow."

"Thanks! How've you been?"

"Good. Really good. You?"

"Okay, I guess. You know, working and just regular stuff."

He noticed the card I was holding.

"You going out with that jerk?" he said.

"What jerk?"

"The politician's gofer?"

I don't know why but he really irked me when he said that.

"No. For your information, I'm meeting *the senator* for a cocktail."

"Really? Well, have fun."

We were just standing there now, staring at each other. I was being reminded why I even sort of liked him in the first place (because he had this way about him that made me feel like he was in charge and I'd be better off for it, even though he had no life plan as far as I could tell) and why suddenly, Porter Galloway made me feel a little bit uncomfortable. I was meeting Porter for a drink and that was all. Big deal. Still, Tommy's disapproval made me uneasy.

When the last light was turned off, I said good night to the Turners.

"Fabulous night," Judy Turner said. "Didn't you think so?"

"It was!" I said, still floating on air, knowing where I was headed.

"I saw the senator flirting with you," Bill Turner said.

"Hush, Bill!" Judy said. "MYOB! I think Porter Galloway is absolutely adorable!"

"Me too!" I said. "Night, y'all!"

So I made my way to my car and drove over to Charleston Place, a supernice hotel in downtown Charleston. I went to the first bar, the one inside the restaurant, and there was no sign of him or of his aide. So I went to the other bar where there was a man playing piano. I sat on a sofa and ordered a glass of white wine. Was I being stood up? I opened my purse and took out the card Porter's aide gave me. George Zur was his name. Should I call him? I decided, oh, what the heck and dialed his number. He answered right away.

"Hey! It's Ashley from the gallery. Where'd y'all go?"

"Oh, hey! Right, I forgot to call. Senator Galloway wants you to come up to his room."

"Really? Well, I don't know, I mean, who's in his room?"

"Just him as far as I know. I'm hitting the sack because we have an early call in the morning. Gotta be back in Columbia by nine for a breakfast meeting."

My mind was racing about a million miles an hour. And my face was so hot I knew I was blazing red with embarrassment. There was no way I was going up to a man's hotel room, even if he *was* Porter Galloway. I wasn't like that. In fact, the idea of him expecting me to just hop on up there like a ho made me feel a little bit sick.

"What room is he in?"

"Four sixteen."

"Okay, thanks. See ya!"

I punched the end call bar on my phone and felt like crying. I drained my glass instead while I debated what to do. Should I go up there and slap him in the face when he opened the door? I texted Mary Beth.

I've got a situation. I tapped the send button.

She wrote back. *What's the situation?*

He asked me to come up to his room at Charleston Place. I pressed send.

She wrote back. *Yikes.* There was a pause and then she texted me again. *He couldn't buy you a drink in the bar first? This has an ick factor of ten on a one to ten.*

Maybe he can't afford to be seen drinking alcohol? You know how conservative all these guys have to be these days. I hit send again.

She responded with, *Look, if he can't be seen having a glass of wine with you, then you can't be seen coming and going from his room either. It just isn't right.*

She was right.

I wrote back, *Save me a glass of swill. I'll be home in twenty.*

She sent me a smiley face. *Not having drinks with Saudi Arabia. Details later.*

That was a relief!

The waiter appeared at my side. "Can I get you another?"

"No, thanks. But could you bill this to Porter Galloway in four sixteen?"

"Yes, ma'am!" he said with such assurance that it occurred to me he'd seen the Galloway act maybe more than a few times. Or maybe it was just my imagination.

"Thanks," I said and left.

I cursed Porter Galloway all the way across the Cooper River Bridge and all the way through Mount Pleasant. I double cursed him as I turned right on Middle Street on Sullivans Island. And I triple cursed him, getting out of the car and stomping up the steps to my house. Mary Beth opened the door and handed me a glass of wine over ice.

"Men stink," she said.

I took a sip and winced. That bottle had been open for a week. The ice improved it but not much.

"What kind of a girl does he think I am? I *was* going to have his babies but I didn't want to start *tonight*!"

"No kidding. Well, Momma says men only want one thing."

"She's right and Porter Galloway ain't getting this."

"Asshole."

"For real." I walked into the center hall and threw my bag on the bottom step that led to the upstairs. I was completely disgusted. "Want to sit outside for a minute?"

"Are you kidding? I want to hear every word."

We sank into the cushions on the ancient wicker sofa. We were at opposite ends and I folded my feet under me and told her the whole stupid story.

"This damn dress. I'm burning it."

"No way. It's a great dress."

"I'm so disappointed, Mary Beth! I'll never hear from him again."

"I predict otherwise."

"Yeah? Based on what?"

"His big fat ego. You said no to his nasty invitation when every other girl in the entire state of South Carolina would've run up there as fast as she could. This makes you more interesting."

"We'll see. I doubt it. What happened to Samir?"

"I stood around the marina for like half an hour. Finally, he sent a guy in his launch to pick me up. This guy hands me an envelope from Samir with five hundred dollars inside."

"Holy crap! That's a lot of money. What did you do?"

"What do you think I did? I told him to tell Samir I wasn't for sale."

"What's the matter with these men?" I said.

"Egos gone wild. Completely out of control."

"Or maybe they're just the wrong men. Wow. Five hundred bucks!"

"I thought about it for a minute but I gave it back."

"I'll bet! That's like three weeks' salary for us. But unfortunately, you're not a whore."

We giggled then in the darkness, laughing at our pathetic financial and social circumstances.

"Not yet. Anyway, Galloway might be a skunk tonight but you'll be in love with him all over again by tomorrow."

"Sad. Sad but probably true."

"I'm gonna hit the sack. My legs are killing me."

"Go ahead. I'll get the lights."

Mary Beth turned in and I went to the kitchen to start the dishwasher. Her purse was just sitting there on the counter, which was full of popcorn kernels and crumbs and needed a good wiping. I thought of my mother and felt guilty. Old Liz might've been a bitch from time to time but she never left food on her kitchen counters before she went to bed.

I got the spray cleaner from under the sink and pulled a couple of paper towels from the roll. Then I lifted Mary Beth's purse by one strap just to swipe the crumbs from underneath it. Of course, the entire contents spilled out onto the counter, including an envelope. My heart dropped. I shouldn't have looked inside but I did. Count them. Ten little oval-shaped pictures of President Grant looked back at me. This was not good. I deliberately put her purse at the foot of the stairs with the envelope positioned right inside. I would never bring it up again.

CHAPTER 6

Liz—Feeling Like Mom

The first thing Maisie did after seeing Porter Galloway looking down my daughter's dress last night was to call me at the crack of dawn. It wasn't even seven o'clock when my phone rang.

"Liz? We need to talk. I couldn't sleep all night."

"What's the matter?" I thought some tragedy had occurred. Who calls anyone at that hour without horrific news?

"Well, here it is. I was at the Turner Gallery last night with Lorraine Galloway. And her son, that scalawag senator of ours, was positively peering at Ashley's bosom. The whole room noticed it."

Really? She got me out of bed for this?

"Well, Mother? Ashley is going to be twenty-four years old in a few months. It's probably time someone had a look, don't you think?"

"I don't like it one bit." She sighed an epic sigh as only she could. "This isn't funny, Liz."

"Oh, come on now. Ashley wouldn't be interested in someone like him. He's a big flirt and everyone knows it."

"Humph. Shows you what you know about your own flesh and blood! She's positively smitten with him."

"Really? Well, that's news. Was she wearing that dress, the one she wore to your party?"

"I think so."

I made a mental note to confiscate Ashley's black dress for the sake of the family's reputation and hers.

"Well, Mother, we have to face the facts. All men like to look at pretty young women. They all let their eyes go where they shouldn't. And if they don't, they're singing big-eyed Carol Channing show tunes with Ivy, if you know what I mean."

"Well, I'm just letting you know, that's all."

"Maisie? Don't worry about Ashley."

"Maybe I'll buy her a new dress," she said.

"Please don't. Clayton would pitch a fit."

"Clayton doesn't have to know."

"It's wrong to give her money all the time, Mother. She needs to live on what she earns."

"A shrimp couldn't live on what she earns and you know it."

We hung up and thank you, now I was annoyed too. My mother had too much time on her hands. You'd have thought that Porter Galloway desecrated a holy shrine the way she carried on. Maisie can't imagine that Ashley is old enough to attract the attention of a man. In her mind, Ashley is and always will be an innocent little virgin. My mind knew better. Ashley was not a little virgin. She wasn't an easy touch but she was no stranger to the ways of the flesh. She was about eighteen when I saw it in her face. She was suddenly less moody. Maternal wisdom: when your teenaged daughter starts acting nice, she's having sex.

I never told Maisie when I found birth control pills in Ashley's bathroom, and I didn't have a fit over it with Ashley, either. I simply waited until I got used to the new reality (read: stopped weeping), composed myself, and then I had what I thought was a relaxed and civil discussion with her about being sexually active. I think I said something like it's fairly normal these days for young women to have an intimate relationship with someone when they fall in love but that it was extremely important to be safe and stay healthy.

I wasn't some prim old bat. And I didn't want to seem to be judgmental in any way. I just didn't want her to have a surprise pregnancy or catch some disgusting disease. I remember like it happened yesterday that she looked at me with that eye-rolling, head-cocked-to-one-side teenaged expression of *Duh, I think I knew this in seventh grade, Mom* and I realized we probably should've talked about sex years earlier. But with all that was going on with my son, I was too racked with fear and trepidation to even allow myself to think about *anybody's* sex life, mine included.

However, even though Ashley was now almost in her midtwenties and her private life was none of my business, I wasn't going to stand by and see my child humiliated. I mean, a relationship was one thing but a sexual encounter with a politician was entirely another. Her pretty face could wind up on the cover of the tabloids at the checkout counter in Kroger's. Politicians were what they were—an easy target for scandal. And so was everyone around them. Sometimes I thought the public's expectations of politicians were ridiculous but on the other hand, I sure was weary of being embarrassed by them.

Two hours later, the Galloway Report via Maisie was still bothering me, not the part about him having a peek but the part about her liking it. I just wanted to be sure Ashley knew who she was dealing with. Porter Galloway was not exactly a fresh-faced college boy of the ilk she used to bring home. He was a grown man on a career path that could lead him anywhere. The only real criticisms I had about her having a crush on someone like him was that he probably had a very high opinion of himself, and he was much older than she was. I knew I shouldn't be so judgmental. On the other hand, with Ashley's fascination with all things Jackie Kennedy Onassis? And she understood the role of politicians in American history from all the courses she took in college. She wasn't a stupid girl right off the farm and I halfway assured myself that there was no reason to be concerned. Except that he lived in the public eye.

I decided to approach the issue with some motherly grace. Things between Ashley and me have been sort of chilly lately and I wanted to warm them back up again. If I have learned anything about raising children, it's that keeping the conversation going is so very important. Once you stop talking to each other terrible things can happen. So I did what any sensible mother would do. I bought a box of donut holes from Dunkin' Donuts and drove out to the beach. And yes, I know she's not a child anymore. But in my heart she is still and will always be my little girl. And maybe I had been picking on her a little. Just a little. But you have to understand I can't stop myself. I just get so nervous for her.

It was still early, before nine, but I figured that Ashley would be up and about getting ready for work. It was hard to believe that she got herself up and dressed and showed up on time at her job. She was certainly growing up whether I wanted to accept it or not. I remembered the battles we used to have to get her out of bed in the morning. All that was in the past now.

She was a stunning young woman but she had been a *gorgeous* child. As I rolled from the Cooper River Bridge onto Coleman Boulevard, I could see Ashley as a young girl with those blazing blue eyes and tumbling curls so blond they bleached white in the sun like sand dollars. There were so many sweet memories—Ashley running down the Sullivans Island beach with Ivy, chasing seagulls that swooped and then scattered in every direction. And how Ashley laughed! Ivy too! The sound of them calling after each other and their peals of innocent giggles rolling across the salty air were so joyous. Whenever I remembered their music, I could almost sing along, if you can imagine such a thing. Ah me. When images of their childhoods run through my head, my chest actually swells. And to be completely honest, going over to Sullivans Island always made me sentimental. I think the island has that effect on many people because for generations it has been where families have come to relax and be together without all the stresses of life in the city. Naturally it's a depository of good memories.

Life on Sullivans Island was the polar opposite of life downtown. For example, like many other families, we set up sleeping porches. There were humble single beds with lots of pillows and old quilts that lined the walls of our side porches. The bottom half of our porch was shuttered for privacy and the louvers were opened to allow air flow. Eventually, after much pleading, Clayton had ceiling fans installed. May I just say that there were still days and nights when the heat was so unbearable, the humidity so high, and the air so still that we all felt like we could lie down and die, ceiling fans or no ceiling fans. It was like being Katharine Hepburn in *The African Queen,* minus the leeches, plus mosquitoes. Clayton didn't believe in air-conditioning the beach house, saying it destroyed the whole point of having a beach house in the first place. On those dog days and nights, the fan's paddles merely pushed around muggy hell. But for the normal hot night, sleeping on the porch was a brilliant solution to our sticky misery.

At some point in the night the tide would turn, bringing a breeze and the sounds of the waves hitting the shore and receding with a *whoosh,* which would lull us all into the deepest sleep I've ever known. Clayton was right. If the house had been air-conditioned, we would've missed all that.

We passed our days doing the same things our island neighbors did. A morning swim, a picnic lunch in the shade, a nap at home, and then back to the beach we went, moving like ducks in a line across the blazing white sand. Late in the afternoon, I would take the children home after hours and hours of building sand castles, looking for shells, and engaging in every other kind of game children played at the shore. Their skin was warm to the touch and salty to my kisses. Outdoor showers washed away the remnants of the day, and new freckles appeared like tiny trophies across the bridges of their noses and on their cheeks and arms. We'd have a supper of vine-ripened tomato sandwiches and iced tea and they were so tired from the sun that they'd be dreaming before they slept. Clayton and I would play gin rummy and enjoy an adult beverage while something like "Moonlight Sonata" or some Chopin streamed from our stereo. I'm telling you I wouldn't trade those memories for anything. And believe it or not, Clayton feels the same way—about the old days and about the island. We were so in love with each other then. And it's our mutual love for the Lowcountry that has been our glue in many of our dark moments. Well, maybe that's overstating it a bit. But loving something together seemed to help.

I was driving across the Shem Creek Bridge, looking out at the few remaining shrimp boats to my right. I slowed down to stare. The water was deep blue and so calm and still. The boats against the bright clear blue sky were as pretty a sight as I'd ever seen anywhere, begging for a photographer to document their existence. They were a dying breed, those shrimpers and their boats. Most of the restaurants used farmed shrimp these days. And farmed fish. Heaven knows what the fish farmers fed their critters but I have always thought farmed seafood couldn't be good for us.

Things change and not always for the better. Shem Creek had been a working waterway since the time of the Sewee Indians in the seventeenth century. Before the Civil War there were factories and mills on its shores. At one point ferry boats operated from there, taking people from shore to shore. But now the shrimp boats were docked there mostly to lend a decorative atmosphere.

Still, it was so lovely a sight. The water reflected the nets hanging from the trawlers' arms in the same way so many shards of dull gray Spanish moss draped the arms of live oak trees all over the Lowcountry. The old creaking boats, weather-beaten but still proud doyennes, sported names on their hulls like *Lady Eva, Miss Paula, The Winds of Fortune,* and others. There used to be many more but the town fathers, in search of increased gentrification and an ill-conceived plan to allot docking slots, had driven the fishermen elsewhere to drop anchor. Still, even with the sparse population, I could feel my heart clench from the landscape's unforgivable beauty.

It saddened me to think that by the time Ashley's children were her age there would be nothing but neon lights and valet parking on Shem Creek. Her children might never know the simple pleasure of hearing and feeling oyster shells crunch underfoot or the smells of a fresh catch or have the thrill of seeing live shrimp dance on a boat's deck as Mr. Magwood used to do for Ivy and her when they were so little.

He'd dump a bucket of live shrimp on the deck and Ashley and Ivy literally hopped, clapping their hands, eyes bulging and squealing with delight over the crazed and frenzied, desperate dance of the shrimp. Somewhere in our house downtown I had photographs of them on Mr. Magwood's boat. I made a mental note to find them and frame them for Ivy and Ashley for Christmas. I wish I'd known years ago that the time would pass so quickly. I swear, you wake up one day and suddenly your best years are behind you. I try not to think about that.

I was at the causeway before I knew it, crossing the Ben Sawyer Bridge, wondering for the millionth time just who this Ben Sawyer person was and just what he did to have a bridge named after him. Probably he was the politician who got the money to build the bridge in the first place. Who knows? A decent politician? It's possible. Anything is possible. I turned right and began the slow crawl down Middle Street toward my house at the end of the island.

The island was just waking up to greet the day. Joggers and their dogs were heading toward the beach, and young mothers and small children were enjoying breakfast on the porch of Café Medley. Someone from Dunleavy's Pub was watering the window boxes while Jamie Maher was deep in conversation with a purveyor of adult spirits standing alongside a very large truck. Dunleavy's Pub, the anchor of the business district, sponsored the Polar Plunge on New Year's Day, an event that raised tons of money for Special Olympics. It was riotous fun. Clayton and I tried to go every year just to watch all the participants in their crazy costumes run into the freezing water. Then we'd walk along Middle Street where all the restaurants had set up tables right on the street and have a plate of hoppin' John and collards for good luck. Eating collards on New Year's Day was to ensure money in the coming year. Greens bring green? Hoppin' John was a Lowcountry dish that ensured further good fortune. It was made of field peas and chopped onions cooked with smoked ham hocks. The watery juice from the pot of peas and onions, which we called pot liquor, was used to cook rice. Then, when the rice was tender, the peas and onions were combined with the rice. Was it delicious? No, it was earthy and nutty but not exactly delicious. However, it was traditional to eat it and Charlestonians were just superstitious enough to never change a tradition. This particular ritual was a good thing for a lot of reasons, not the least of which was that this particular one told you who you were. No one in their right mind would crave a bowl of hoppin' John except the sons and daughters of the Lowcountry. Maisie always said that knowing who you were and where you belonged was one component of good mental health. I believed that too.

I drove on, passing SALT at Station 22 on my left, my favorite restaurant, the hill fort, the fire department, and the tiny building that decades ago housed Miss Buddy McGinn's variety store. Every trip to the island was like looking through old scrapbooks. Finally, I came to the fork in the island at Stella Maris Church and stayed to the left, arriving at our driveway minutes later.

I pulled into the yard and turned off the engine. I knew that Mary Beth usually went to work late in the afternoon so I closed my car door gently when I got out in case she was still asleep. But there's no doubt the air-conditioning unit whirring away in her room would've drowned out the noisy clunk. I looked up and thought the house surely could benefit from a coat of paint. And it was time to clean up the boots of all the palmetto trees. We never did install central air-conditioning but we put in a few window units at the same time we renovated after Hurricane Hugo, the infamous storm that packed a mighty wallop to the Lowcountry in 1989. Our old house withstood the storm but we lost all our windows and rugs and other furnishings from wind and water. We kept the piano for some reason I can't recall. Probably sentiment.

But folks have short memories, and they continue to come in droves to live on the islands, despite the erosion and storms. The new residents weren't like us. They were from Lord knows where, hither and yon, showing up here with bulging wallets and driving the cost of real estate through the roof. Those people wanted central air, ice makers, and media rooms. We natives were reluctant to give in to things like going wireless and irrigation systems on timers, but eventually we probably would too. And if we didn't, our children, who had already bought into the many vagaries of consumerism, surely would.

I walked across the yard, stopping to pick up palmetto fronds that had fallen from the trees. The yard and the entrance to our property were a mess. It annoyed me that the front steps were littered with beach sand and debris. They could have used a good sweeping. I thought, Good Lord, these girls live here for practically nothing. The least they could do is sweep the darn steps. The door was locked so I used my key and let myself in. I could hear Ashley rattling around in the kitchen.

"G'morning, sweetheart!" I called out.

"Mom? God, you scared me to death! I didn't know you were coming!"

Was she telling me to call before I came to my own house?

"I brought donuts for you and Mary Beth. I was just thinking about you and decided to take a ride over and see you," I said, going into the kitchen. I gave her a hug and a kiss on the head. She was wearing a pair of plaid cotton pajama bottoms and an old T-shirt looking more like a teenager than an adult. "You know, sometimes I just want to see my daughter!"

"Oh, well, that's nice. Thanks! Me too! You want coffee?"

"Sure, but I'll help myself."

I reached in the cabinet for a mug and placed it on the counter, the counter covered in crumbs. Well, not completely covered. As though she intuited my annoyance, Ashley quickly dampened a paper towel and wiped them away.

"I made toast earlier," she said, balling the paper towel up and tossing it in the overflowing garbage can. "I actually cleaned this all up last night."

"Oh, honey! I don't mind!" I poured myself coffee and opened the refrigerator looking for some milk. The refrigerator was stuffed with take-out containers and jars that were older than some of my shoes. "So what time do you have to be at work today?"

"Noon," she said, eyeing me carefully. "I just woke up early."

"Well, either that means you're stressed over something, which is ridiculous," I said, smiling, "or you went to bed early, and I can't imagine why someone your age would."

"Right," she said and popped a donut in her mouth. "I'm usually up all night partying."

I looked at her sarcastic face and thought, Oh boy, this isn't going to be much fun. I came here bearing sugar and she shows no signs of sweetening up anytime soon. So either I could continue to be nice or I could take her on. Two could play at this game.

"Well, you may not be out having fun but you're sure not sweeping the steps or cleaning out the refrigerator either, are you?"

"Mom? It rained like hell this week."

"Please don't curse. It's common."

"Whatever. You know that rain always messes up the yard. And I'm sorry the refrigerator isn't squeaky clean. I was going to throw out a lot of stuff this morning. I got up early to do laundry and clean house. It's not like I have a housekeeper, you know. And I work forty hours a week. Sheesh!"

She stomped out of the kitchen. I could hear her feet and in a few minutes she returned with a stuffed hamper of dirty laundry.

"Excuse me," she said, squeezing past me to the laundry room. There was a little bit of twenty-three-year-old balsamic vinegar dripping from her voice.

"Want some help?" I asked.

"Nope."

"Okay." What could I say next? "So, babe? I need to talk to you about something."

There was silence, except for the water filling the machine, and then she said, "I knew there was another reason you showed up."

I heard the lid of the washing machine slam, and I could feel her annoyance radiate from the other room. Well, too bad, I thought.

I sat on a barstool at the counter.

"Come sit with me for a minute," I said.

She sat down, pushed her hair back from her face, blew some air, and rolled her eyes.

"Okay, what's going on, Mom?"

"Look, Ashley, you're practically a grown woman and I know you don't think you need any advice on anything . . ."

"No, that's not it. It's that I just wish people in this family told the truth more often. If you wanted to come over here to talk to me, why didn't you just say so?"

"Maybe I was hoping the subject would come up naturally in the course of conversation."

"Porter Galloway?"

"Yes," I said.

"Maisie called you?"

"Yes, but please don't tell her I told you."

"Sure. Another secret. Look, Mom. Porter Galloway is a douche."

"Really?" Douche? What did that mean beyond the normally accepted definition of a feminine hygiene product? Or in French, a shower?

"Yeah. He asked me to come meet him for a drink last night. So I went to the bar at Charleston Place Hotel expecting to find him there. Turns out he wanted me to come to his room. I was like, yeah, right. In your dreams, Senator. So I left, but I charged my glass of wine to his room."

I knew she was telling me the truth.

"Good for you! How insulting."

"I thought so too. He can kiss it."

"Well, yes." I searched her face. Her disappointment and annoyance were all over her. I didn't blame her. "Men can be so stupid."

"Yep. Mom? Don't worry about me. *I'm* not stupid and I'm a good girl."

I reached out and ran my hand down the side of her face.

"I know that, baby. Anyway, I thought I might take you shopping. You know, somewhere out there is a little black dress that's slightly less lethal. I'd be happy to help you find it. We can make it an early birthday present?"

"Maybe sometime this week," she said. "Thanks. So Maisie thinks my dress is dangerous?"

"Don't you?"

"Maybe." The tiniest of all smiles in Christendom crept across her face. "Anyway, say what you want about Porter, but he's going places. I wouldn't mind being the governor's wife."

"Governor! Darling, I think he's got a long row to hoe before he gets that job. Although there is talk. And would you really want to be a politician's wife? Politics are such a sordid business."

"So is everything. He's got to marry somebody, doesn't he? Then I could paint all the time."

"Baby? I think that price tag for your artistic freedom might be way too high. Besides, according to the papers, he's showing no signs of settling down just yet."

"I know. Maisie told me. Well, it doesn't matter because he probably already forgot my name."

"I'll bet he hasn't. I'll bet you a new dress *and* shoes. Call me when he calls you."

"You seem pretty sure about this. How do you know?"

"Because all men want what they can't have. Every last one of them."

"Well, I'm not holding my breath."

"Listen to your mother. I know more about men than I care to divulge." I laughed when I said that.

"You sound just like Maisie," Ashley said and laughed with me.

"Lord, save us all. Listen to me, sweetheart, I just hope that when you do marry, that you are dead in love and that your lucky guy feels the same way about you."

"I agree."

"Love is the most important thing there is, Ashley. Love, family . . . these are the things that matter; the things to cherish."

"Who could argue with that?"

If nothing else transpired, at least I had made her laugh with me and peace was restored.

Shortly after that I left her and drove back downtown. She promised to sweep the steps and take out the garbage. And she promised to be more diligent about the house in general. It couldn't be easy to be her age in today's world. I thought about it as I passed over the causeway and through Mount Pleasant. Ivy was the one who rightly pointed it out. It couldn't be easy at all.

CHAPTER 7

Ashley—Party On!

Another advantage of staying in the family beach house, besides the killer view, was that we had a tiny ancient cottage in the yard. My family used it for sort of a metaphorical purgatory—a way station between a yard sale (heaven) and the dump (hell). It was filled with abandoned junk, stuff you no longer wanted to use but you couldn't bring yourself to throw away—old box springs, rusty bicycles, broken chairs that never got fixed, et cetera. I had no memory of it being anything other than what it was. At one point I had thought about fixing it up and renting it, but it was *such* a wreck and I had, as we all know, limited resources. Besides all that, I didn't have the first clue about being a landlady.

Mom and Dad mumbled around and finally said they didn't mind if I used the cottage as a studio so I configured it to suit myself. This meant the death of a million trees as cases of paper towels were squandered, many bottles of vinegar and cleaners were spritzed to their last breath, and the backbreaking work was done to haul ancient possessions and garbage to the curb. The neighbors must have thought we were total hoarders. Nasty!

Originally, the cottage was a kitchen house back in the days of the Civil War, or the Recent Disturbance, as Maisie liked to call it when she was feeling her years. It was pretty common for kitchens to be separated from the main house because they were always catching on fire from flying embers, badly maintained chimneys, and so forth. I could only imagine someone rushing from the cottage to the house in pouring rain or gusting winds, hanging on to a platter of pork chops for dear life! How stupid. I minored in American history and it never failed to blow my mind how awful it was to be a woman a hundred years ago, much less in colonial times.

Anyway, even after I cleaned up the cottage, it was still a serious dump. The walls were old Sheetrock and particleboard, cracked from abuse, and the ceiling was open with exposed rafters. The roof was missing so many shingles that it leaked like holy hell. But a little indoor precipitation didn't bother me. I just placed garbage cans and pots under the drizzles and went on with my business. Who cared? I had my own studio! It was the rat droppings that were more bothersome.

Actually, it was a *good* thing that the cottage was a pit because when you paint, you don't want to have to worry about the floors. The floor of the room where my easel was set up was covered in the cheapest linoleum mankind ever produced fifty years ago, and now it was splattered with every color found in nature or not—my homage to Jackson Pollock.

But hey! It actually looked like an artist's studio! The living room held a huge piece of half-inch plywood laid over two old sawhorses where I stretched my canvases over frames and prepped them with two or three coats of gesso, depending on the quality of the muslin or the texture of the material I was using. It was just way cheaper to make my own than to buy them already finished. And this way I could put together canvases of unconventional sizes and textures too. I mean, I could paint on denim or burlap. How to stretch a canvas was probably one of the most practical things I learned in college besides how to stretch a dollar.

Anyway, in the back of the cottage there was an old tin sink where I could clean brushes and a creepy bathroom if I was desperado. In the other little room, where they probably kept pantry items and so forth back in the day, I stored my paintings in open vertical bins made of two-by-fours just in case David Zwirner's or Larry Gagosian's car broke down in front of our house and they needed shelter. In case you've never heard of them, they own some of the most amazing galleries in Chelsea, if not on the whole planet. They'd say, *So, young lady, what do you do here on Sullivans Island to pass the time?* And I'd say, *Well, I like to paint.* And then they'd say something like *What a coincidence! We're art dealers. In New York!* I'd whip out all my canvases and give them a cultural experience they'd never forget. They'd beg to represent me and fly me and all my paintings off to New York. There I'd have a one-woman show that would astound the press and everybody in the art world and I'd be an overnight sensation.

Maybe not.

Ah, let the girl have her dreams. I know, I know. Pretty over the top. Oh well.

Most of my current paintings were landscapes. I envisioned them in bold colors and sometimes painted them on other materials like seersucker or denim for texture and dimension. But I loved figura-

tive painting too. For the pure fun of it, I'd been working on a portrait of Maisie as Mona Lisa, complete with that all-knowing smile.
I loved taking people I knew and dropping them into a context that
said who they were. And instead of having the pastoral background
that da Vinci used in his painting, I painted a landscape with a llama.
It was *so* Maisie. She'd get a hoot out of it if she ever saw it. Unfortunately, since the day the Impossibles confiscated her car keys, she
rarely came out to the beach anymore. Maybe one day I'd surprise
her with it. Meanwhile, it hung on my bedroom wall.

And I had a painting I did of Ivy as a little tiny boy, sitting all
alone on the steps of a giant brick building, sort of like him in a big
cold world. I used to worry about how he kept so much to himself.
Our parents were really terrible to him when he came out. In fact,
he didn't even have the chance to come out as gay before they packed
him off to that horrible camp. The camp made him believe he was
a sinner bound straight for the fires of hell if he didn't go straight.
How was he supposed to do that? When he came home, he wouldn't
talk to anyone for months. All he did was stay in his room and cry.
But eventually he got angry enough to rebel and he went back to
normal—his normal. And my parents allegedly apologized to him
but holy crap, there was a lot of damage already done. Their disappointment in Ivy was so obvious. I just kept telling him that they
were dead wrong, that it was like hating your child for having kinky
hair or one blue eye or some other thing that the child was born
with. And while we're being honest, who wanted to be like Clayton
and Liz anyway? Amen to that.

Oh, Ivy! My sweet brother! One of the first paintings I ever did
was a small acrylic of us playing on the beach when we were children. I copied the composition from an old photograph and gave it to

him to hang in his first apartment to remind him how much I loved him. And then we broke down and cried. I hated it when he moved out of the house and left me with *them*. I knew the minute he left they'd begin a new campaign to mold me into some new improved version of themselves, which of course they did. After a while they gave up, probably because, as Dad said, I was just a girl and I'd wind up married and having babies and maybe painting when my own children went off to college. Their current hope was that if I couldn't get a better job, then I'd make a brilliant marriage. Up until the other night, I thought marrying Porter Galloway would've been brilliant. Maybe I was just too sensitive but I was still so disappointed and plenty insulted. Big-time.

In fact, if I was going to paint stupid Porter Galloway today I'd put him up on a barstool and give him a wolf's tail and fangs. You know, like that wildly famous Coolidge painting of the dogs playing poker? The other figures around him would be straight-up wolves and I'd be at the end of the bar, emanating purity with a big halo. I wonder how he'd like to see *that* hanging in a museum or a gallery? Or maybe I'd make him something even more menacing. I'd have to think about it. God, I was still so mad at him I could have slapped him right across the face. Although I'd been tempted to tell Ivy about the Galloway Insult the next day when I called him in San Francisco, I instead put it out of my mind and asked him about his and James's stay in New York. When I asked, "How was it? Did y'all have fun?" there was an odd pause. I said, "What? What happened?"

"What? Oh? New York. Well, it was the same as always— crowded, dirty, scary cab rides, great food . . . you know, the usual. I got fabulous shoes at Barneys for half price and James got a three-hundred-dollar massage!"

He wasn't telling me everything.

"Ivy? How long have I known you?"

"All your life."

"What are you not telling me?"

"What do you mean? I'm not hiding anything!"

"Yes, you are. There's something else, isn't there? Does Dad have like a collection of sex toys or something like that in his apartment?"

"No! Jeez, Ash. Sex toys. No. Yeah, Big Clayton? No. No way. The only things he's squirreling away are chronologically organized receipts for every nickel he spends."

"No surprise there," I said.

"I think I'm getting a cold, that's all. I'm a little out of it."

"Okay," I said and let him off the hook. "I'll dig it out of you later. So listen, thanks again for the money, Ivy. I'll pay you back, I swear."

"Whatever. Don't spend it on clothes!"

"I would never!"

"I know. I'm just messing with you. Consider it a house gift for the old homestead."

"The old homestead needs so much, it's ridiculous. It's sort of falling down in places. I mean, maybe it's my imagination, but I think there's more slope to the floors than ever."

"Maybe it's sinking."

"Prolly. Anyway, Mary Beth and I are going to Home Depot tonight and we planned to start painting the house this weekend. Any thoughts on how to make this party the coolest thing ever?"

"So you're really doing it, huh?"

"Ivy, if I don't do something drastic I'll be stuck in this life forever."

"Okay, look, here's my advice. Try to do everything first-class, you know what I mean?"

"You mean, I shouldn't serve Singapore Slings out of a garbage can using a soup can as a ladle?" I started laughing just thinking about the look on his face.

"Mon Dieu! Quelle horreur!" he said, laughing. "Listen to your big bubba. Go to whatever restaurant supply place there is in Charleston and buy one hundred all-purpose wineglasses. No plastic! Be sure they fit in the dishwasher. Don't spend more than a dollar apiece, okay?"

"Wait a minute. I need to write this down." I grabbed a pencil and started making notes on the back of a junk mail envelope from AARP. The AARP mailings always pissed off my parents. "Okay. Continue."

"Buy one thousand white paper cocktail napkins. Then go to Home Depot or someplace like that and buy ferns. Big, bushy sword ferns. Six of them. Buy white tea candles and little clear votive cups, like two dozen at least, to put up the front steps, all around the portico, in the bathroom, on the tables."

"I'll get four dozen."

"They're cheap enough. And ask Mary Beth . . ."

"Mary Beth," I said in disgust and thought about telling him about her whoring around. Then I decided to save it.

"What about her?"

"Nothing." I knew he knew I was holding back. That's how it was with us.

"Oh, okay. Anyway, ask her where to get the best price on four bar-height twenty-four-inch round tables for the porch. And you'll need two rectangular tables—one for a bar and another for stationary food."

"Wait a minute! Aren't Mom and Dad going to see all this stuff?"

"Hello? Hide it in the cottage. Is there still a refrigerator out there?"

Mom kept an extra refrigerator around for winter holidays and summer beer. She hadn't touched it in a decade.

"Yeah, but it's encrusted with who knows what."

"Girlie? Get a sponge and put it to work! You can stash stuff in it. And tablecloths. You'll need linens."

"Right! What about booze?"

"I'll text you a list of what to get."

"Okay. Whew! You make it sound so easy!"

"I've been around the block, Miss Rivers. I've thrown a few soirees in my day!"

"Dang! I guess so!"

So for the next ten days, Mary Beth and I did our best to transform the entrance to our house, the halls people would pass through, the powder room, and the big portico facing the ocean. I had decided by then that if she wanted to take money from a man it was her business, because it was. I had all sorts of thoughts about that, like how it's prostitution, but I really didn't want to talk about it. Besides, I needed her help to throw this party. It darn near killed us, but on top of painting like mad, we pushed the two-ton piano out into the hall by the door to the portico and polished it until we could see our faces in it. But something had definitely changed between us. She knew that I knew she had done something really awful. We pretended that she had not.

"I'm never moving this again. I don't care what my mother says."

"You can say that again! But to be practical, we can put a fruit and cheese display on it," Mary Beth said. "We can use that big cutting board? I'll give it a good waxing."

"Great idea."

Next we pulled the old brass telescope out from the hall closet and buffed it up the best we could. It also seemed to weigh two tons.

"This thing is a real relic," Mary Beth said.

"Yeah, I think my grandfather bought it in London or it came from London. I don't know. It's got an old story though."

Then we fell in love with it, using it to watch people on the passing ships in the evening light and the stars later on at night.

"I didn't know how awesome a telescope could be," Mary Beth said. "I mean, I knew, but I never had one around."

"Growing up, I always thought it was lame. But I liked it when Maisie would show me Mars."

"Do you still know where it is?"

"Yeah, it's up there," I said and pointed to the ceiling.

"Yeah. Very funny. FYI. That piano is a twanging machine," Mary Beth said. "Should we get it tuned?"

"Nah," I said. "Who would play it anyway?"

"Um, did you know Tommy Milano was like a child prodigy or something?"

"Are you kidding me?"

"Nope."

"Think he wants to come and play?"

"Maybe if it was tuned he would. And for you he'd play for nothing."

"Piano music could be very chic, right? How much does it cost to tune a piano?"

"No clue, but we could ask him. Why don't you call him?"

"Oh Lord, do we really want a third person in on this?"

"We can give him a tip jar," Mary Beth said, with an expression that said she thought she'd just come up with a piece of genius.

I just looked at her wondering if my parents were going to kill me by beating me to death or by slitting my throat.

We were in deep.

We painted, we shopped, we obtained—and Tommy Milano said yes.

"Are you kidding?" he said. "I can tune it myself."

"Really?"

"Yeah, really."

"Wow." What couldn't he do?

Sure enough, as we were putting the last coat of paint on the door frames, Tommy was bringing the old piano back into pitch.

"Amazing," I said, when he sat down and hammered out a little Beethoven.

"Thanks," he said, smiling and switched to Paul Simon classics. "So what ever happened with you and that asshole?"

"Do you mean Senator Galloway?"

"That's the one."

"He's unworthy." I said this so seriously, as though I'd made an important life decision.

"You're telling me?" Tommy said and grinned.

As much as I hated to admit it, Tommy was pretty sweet when he wanted to be. And I did not speak of Porter Galloway again.

"By the way, y'all can't use this as a buffet table. I have to open her up. Otherwise, we aren't going to get the maximum sound out of this baby."

"Fine! Do what you have to do. Something tells me you know what's best."

I was so nervous my stomach was in knots and I wasn't sleeping. I mean, what if my mother just showed up with more donuts? She would totally lose her mind and kill me dead.

When the mutually agreed-upon date arrived, we sent a tweet to the list of people we had from Mary Beth's company and Tommy's contacts too. I had a few people I'd known since we were kids but I didn't really expect them to show. In any case, we all tweeted the following: *Mango Sunset Party tonight at 7:30! Ash and Mary Beth's on Sullivans Island. First fifty with fifty. Cash. Vintage cocktails and hors d'oeuvres with piano music and a view!*

We had decided not to use Mary Beth's caterer, thinking we'd make a little more money if we did the work ourselves. One of the older women she worked with said she'd help us for a nominal fee. It seemed like we had a plan. I was a wreck.

Mary Beth orchestrated the menu and I helped her fix all the food—millions of tiny meatballs in some Hawaiian pineapple–tomato sauce, pigs in blankets from Costco, giant wedges of cheese, also from Costco, and tons of crackers and strawberries. Basically we were serving what Lucy and Ethel cooked up for Fred and Ricky. And we made pitchers of mai tais to garnish with pineapple wedges and cherries on a toothpick. We got white wine too. And liquor. Everything on Ivy's list was found and bought. One of Tommy's friends, Ed something, was there to tend bar, which was all set up and looking very professional. The votive candles cast just the right amount of warm light as day faded before our eyes. Everything seemed to conspire in harmony, creating the perfect atmosphere. Even the ferns were lightly swaying in the breeze. We were as ready for a party as we could be. Maybe we wouldn't get caught.

At six thirty the first car arrived. Four people got out. They looked normal enough to me. Young professionals. Mary Beth and I were watching through the windows. That was when I noticed her new watch, probably bought with the money from Samir.

"Nice watch," I said.

"Thanks," she said and blushed deeply, running her hand around it, almost hiding it. "My mom sent it to me."

"Really?" She was lying like a cheap rug. No way she bought a Michael Kors watch in the backwoods of Tennessee. "Do you believe we're really doing this?" I said to change the subject.

"Yes. It's okay. I know them," Mary Beth said. "Should I go to the door?"

"No, you get the food going. I'll take care of the money."

She shot me a look but didn't say anything. She knew right then I didn't trust her because she had lied to me. She didn't try to defend herself.

Without missing more than a half beat she said, "Right!" She started toward the kitchen and called out, "Tommy? Start playing!"

"What should I play?" he yelled back.

"What? Now we have to tell him what to play?" I yelled to both of them.

"I got this! I got this!" he yelled, laughing.

The next thing we knew, old Billy Joel songs filled the air, two more cars pulled into the yard, then three more, and soon my pockets were absolutely bulging with money. Every so often, I'd slip into my bedroom and throw handfuls of cash into a shoebox. Eventually cars stopped arriving and I felt like it was finally okay to mingle a little. The sun had fallen into the horizon and the edge of the earth was painted red as deep as a string of rubies. It was a gorgeous sunset. Just gorgeous.

People seemed to be having a wonderful time. I picked up empty glasses and balled up paper napkins. Almost every guest seemed to be around thirty, and Mary Beth and Tommy seemed to know lots of them. Must be nice to have fifty dollars to spend, I thought.

Tommy's tip jar, which was actually a vase, was jammed with one-dollar bills and even a few fives! He seemed pleased. Mary Beth was flitting all over the place with trays, smiling and seemingly having a blast. Our guests were watching container ships go by and taking selfies like mad. It was a very dramatic night.

I hardly knew anyone. Tommy and Mary Beth must have been passing the word in the last few weeks. I counted heads and we had a few more than fifty. And most people were well behaved, marveling at the sunset. I thought, Whew! What a relief! Well, there was that one unfortunate couple who locked themselves in the powder room.

I noticed that three women were lined up in the hall, waiting.

"How long has somebody been in there?" I asked.

"Like twenty minutes?"

"There's another bathroom down that hall," I said, pointing. "Not as nice but it works."

"Thanks," they said and wandered off.

I knocked on the door.

"Y'all all right in there?"

There was the distinct sound of muffled voices, giggles, clothes being zipped, and the toilet flushing and the water running all at once.

"Yeah," a male voice called back. "I'll be out in a minute."

I waited and I waited and I waited. Then I knocked on the door again.

"Do you need a doctor?" I called through the door.

The door slowly opened and a guy with tousled hair and a very snide expression just looked at me and passed by. Behind him, a pretty younger woman appeared, looking discombobulated as all hell. I grabbed her arm.

"Oh!" she squealed.

"What's your name?" I said.

"Amy."

"Amy what?"

"Smith. Let go of my arm!"

"And who's the guy you're with?"

"Joe Blow."

Joe Blow indeed. She didn't even know his name. Or maybe he was a coke dealer.

"Yeah, well, don't you think it's pretty tacky to screw in somebody's house who you don't even know?"

She just stared at me as though she had every right to have sex in the middle of Highway 61 if the opportunity presented itself. How dare she?

"Get out, okay?" I said. I was blistering mad then.

"Really? Then I want my money back," she said.

"Sue me," I said. "It's going to cost me a hundred dollars to fumigate!"

"You're a bitch," she said.

"That's okay. You're . . . you're a *skank slut*! Now go get your skank friend and get out of my house!"

She gasped and stomped off. My heart was pounding so hard I thought my eardrums might explode.

"Hey, Ash?"

It was Tommy. He had stopped playing and was standing at my side.

"What?" I said, still thinking I might faint.

"Nicely done," he said and patted me on the back.

"Thanks," I said and went out to the portico to make sure I could still breathe. I inhaled and thought, Well, that was nice of Tommy to step up to my side, wasn't it?

I spotted Joe Blow at the bar and took a bold stride right up to his side.

"Joe Blow?"

"Pritchard," he said. "What's your problem?"

"This is my house and you're too much of a badass for me. I want you to get Amy and leave. Okay?"

He looked at me in disbelief. Then he pretended to be cringing in fear. What was the matter with people?

"Ooooooh! Amy? Is that her name?"

The music had stopped again. Tommy was watching and Ed the bartender was on point too. Joe realized that Tommy and his buddy Ed could totally kick his butt so he headed back inside. I watched as he grabbed Amy and made way to the door. She gave the one-finger salute as they left and I breathed a major sigh of relief.

"Another asshole," Tommy said.

"Boy, you can say that again," I said. "I think I'm gonna have a glass of wine now."

I went back to the portico. Some people had walked out to the beach to get an even closer look at a passing cruise ship against the fading light. I thought then that I would never get used to how spectacular the sky was at sunset. Just because the sun was below the horizon didn't mean it was dark. The remaining clouds in the sky changed colors every few minutes, from jagged streaks of deep-hued rose quartz to wisps of amethysts and under lights of transparent shimmering gold. All these colors were laid on top of one another, changing in their depth and shape every few minutes. No two sunsets were ever the same but they were almost always mesmerizing. I helped myself to a glass of wine and spotted Mary Beth passing hors d'oeuvres through the thinning crowd.

"What happened in there?" she said.

"Two jerks screwing in the powder room," I said.

"Well, at least someone's having sex," she said and giggled.

I rolled my eyes, passing up another opportunity to nail her.

"Puh-leese! There's a time and place issue here?" I smiled then. Poor Mary Beth. "Some people are so stupid!"

I felt a tap on my shoulder.

"Hey! Aren't you Ashley?"

I turned around to see a really nice-looking woman dressed very professionally, like a doctor or something. You know, she was wearing clothes that inspire trust. And not too much makeup, except for concealer that was failing to mask some dark places around her eyes. But she looked good. I mean, there's that fine line between looking like that bleached-blond red-lipped stripper/ho in the shoe ad on television and the kind of girl who's contemplating a cloistered convent. What I'm saying is she was hitting all the right notes.

"Yes, I'm Ashley."

"This is your house, is that right?"

"Well, it's my family's home."

"What a view!" she said, adding, "Oh! Where are my manners? I'm Cindy Elder! Cindy Lue Elder. But my friends call me Cindy. Ever since I got out of law school, I dropped the Lue."

"I know what you mean. I used to be called Ashley Ann but now I'm just Ashley or Ash. So how'd you hear about tonight?"

"I work on Senator Galloway's staff and one of his aides picked it up on Twitter. I was at the Turner Gallery for his fund-raiser but you probably don't remember me."

"Oh! No, I'm sorry, I don't."

"It's okay, I mean, uh, there was an ocean of humanity there. But what a coincidence!"

"Yeah, small world."

She stared at me for a moment. It flashed across my mind that she might have had a personal interest in Porter and it was quickly apparent that she did because she seemed so nervous. And in that same moment of knowing that I knew, she recognized me as competition. She was at least thirty. Ticktock.

"Politics are impossible," she said with a sigh of resignation.

"Come on, Cindy," I said, "let's get you a big old mai tai and a pile of meatballs."

"I like you, Ashley. And I'm not even sure why."

Later on when everyone had gone home we counted up the money. We gave a hundred dollars to Ed the bartender for two hours of work and seventy-five to the lady who cleaned up the kitchen. Tommy's tip jar was his take and it had almost two hundred dollars.

"I think my waiter days just ended. Well, if I can get gigs like this anyway. Are y'all gonna do this again?"

I slid another hundred dollars across the table to him.

"Um, yeah," I said. "You didn't make enough for all you did. You didn't know bouncer was in your job description."

Mary Beth didn't say a word and I had thought she might object.

"Wow, thanks!" Tommy said.

After expenses, we netted almost sixteen hundred dollars. And, best of all, we didn't get caught.

I called Ivy first thing Saturday morning.

"How did it go? Are you calling me from the hoosegow?"

"No! You big crazy! Ivy? It was a screaming success! And we made some serious bucks."

"Fabulous! But speaking of the bank, you'd better open a new account."

"Why?"

"Don't the parental ones have access to yours?"

"Right! Jeez! But don't worry, I have it hidden. You know what, Ivy?"

"What?"

"I'd make a terrible secret agent. I hate lying."

"Me too. I think we're not wired for social espionage."

CHAPTER 8

Liz—Working It

It was Sunday afternoon. I had a case of the blues and I hated myself for giving in to them. It felt like weakness to succumb. Maybe it was my imagination, but it seemed like Clayton couldn't wait to finish repacking his briefcase for New York and get out of here. Sadly, I knew it was not my imagination. His body language told me everything. He was consumed with a heightened level of enthusiasm I rarely saw at home. God, his excitement completely depressed the hell out of me. I felt like a bloodless hologram, fading into the woodwork, the paneling imprinted on my skin. But because there's a side of me that's like a puppy, I decided to be nice anyway.

"Would you like me to take you to the airport?"

He was organizing a stack of manila folders and looked up at me as though he hadn't seen me in ten years.

"What? The airport?"

"Yes. The airport."

"Oh, right, right. Uh, no, actually Walter is picking me up in a few minutes." Walter Whaley, who owned Chauffeurs Unlimited, was Clayton's favorite driver. He managed a weak smile. "What does your week look like? Busy?"

All it took was the slightest inquiry and I felt my blood begin to flow again. Just throw the old girl a bone.

"Well, I'm giving a dinner tomorrow night to try and find some new funding. I've been trying to get these two couples to the table for nearly a year. Now I have them both in one night. Pretty stressful. It's not easy raising money these days."

"Was it ever?"

He pulled the tab through the handle of his briefcase and it clicked into place in its lock. I had given Clayton that briefcase for Father's Day a few years ago. It was Italian and had cost a small fortune. Clayton loved beautiful leather goods and I had wanted to make him happy. There was a time when his happiness was all that mattered. I wondered then for a moment or two which came first? Him not caring or me being sad?

I watched as he looked at himself in the mirror over the hall table. He was preening. For whom? Something was deeply wrong between us. He was so distracted and indifferent toward me and had been for some time. I mean, his indifference was one thing, but posing like a peacock was another.

"No, I guess not. But donor dinners are a good way to begin, especially if they're smaller events."

"Really? Why's that?"

"Well, because people can talk about themselves a bit."

He didn't say anything. I just watched him neaten his collar around the lapel of his jacket.

I continued. "Listening to them helps me to figure out how important they want to be to the organization. I mean, they know why they're invited. They're not stupid. So I'm cooking for these folks. They finally said yes. Finally!"

I may as well have been reciting the Gettysburg Address in Portuguese.

"Well, that should be nice. I'm sure it will go well. I hope you've got some help coming. Save all your receipts."

"I know," I said. "I do. Actually, Ashley's roommate, Mary Beth, is coming to help. And Peggy will be here."

"Well, good. No point in wearing yourself out. Anyway, you can't be much of a hostess if you're in the kitchen all night. Is that a new dress you're wearing?"

"No. It's from a few years ago."

"Well, why don't you take yourself shopping? Buy some pretty new things for yourself? My treat."

The doorbell rang. Walter had arrived.

"You'll be home . . . when?" I said.

He picked up his bag and started toward the door.

"Thursday night late, if I can. But probably Friday. We're taking a small Australian pharma public so I have to see how it goes. I'll call you."

"Sure. I need to plan my time, you know?"

"Don't work so hard," Clayton said and smiled.

"I'm just trying to make my life mean something, Clayton."

He took a deep breath, stopped, and turned to say something to me and then hesitated.

"What?" I said.

"I just hate it when you talk like that. I mean, why couldn't you go to work for something less controversial like, I don't know, a library?"

We looked at each other then, right in the eyes. For the first time in ages. It was the old argument again. He hated my work. Men define themselves through *their* work. In Clayton's Ozzie Nelson mind, women were supposed to have complementary careers if they had one at all. My career was a very messy business. Too many unpleasantries. Of course, in this day and age, not working was as ridiculous as it was impossible, especially when you're married to a world-class tightwad. I've heard there are places in India where fat wives are a trophy, testimony to the man's earning power, and the wife doesn't work outside of the home. She has servants and she eats great mountains of noodles and other goodies like steamed buns stuffed with candied guava or papaya. Or maybe that was in Africa. No matter. I didn't live in such a culture, and my husband's ideas about women's roles were as weird as Skipper's llamas.

And besides that smorgasbord of neurotic delights, I'd have preferred to work as a ditchdigger than ask Old Moneybags for a new pair of shoes. He had some outrageous control issues, and for a long time now experts in my field have acknowledged that the need to have control over another human being was an example of abuse. In Clayton's case I felt like it was just ego based. But maybe my work hit a little too close to home for him. Hmmm. It didn't pay to overanalyze it. It was best to encourage Sunday to become Monday and just keep moving forward. Maybe I should go shopping and spend every dime of his that I could.

"Go on to New York," I said. "Travel safely and call me, okay?"

"I'll call when I can," he said and I closed the door behind him.

No good-bye kiss. Not that I wanted one.

I'll call when I can was Clayton-ese that meant he'd be calling when he felt like it, not because he missed me or even out of some sense of duty. He always left me feeling sad for the old us. But that *old us* had been gone for so long I couldn't even imagine what that looked like. I decided to call Maisie.

"Well, he's off to Yankee territory again," I said, sounding like the dog died.

"Why should *that* put you in the dumps? He's been commuting for as long as I can remember."

"I don't know. I guess sometimes I just miss being madly in love, that's all."

"Oh, snap out of it! You've got a dinner party to plan!"

"True. You coming?"

"Can't. You know I hate those things. Anyway, I just joined a new Bunko group and our first meeting is tomorrow night."

"Bunko? Mother! Aren't you a little . . ."

I heard her gasp before I could even finish.

"Old? I'll have you know that most people say I can pass for seventy any day of the week! And I was invited to join by a very nice divorcée Skipper and I met at the garden center."

"Better watch out. She might have her eye on Skipper."

"Sweet Mother! I hadn't thought about that."

"I'm beginning to think everyone has a secret agenda," I said, apropos of nothing except Clayton's attitude. I had a mental flash of him bolting toward the bright lights of Manhattan, flailing his arms, running up the FDR like a madman. He must be having an affair. But guess what? I didn't really want to know.

"I'll get my hair done," she said, "if I can find a salon that's open on Monday."

"That's the spirit! Maybe I will too!" I said and we hung up.

Get my hair blown out? Maybe I'd have a manicure too. That was what I needed—some pampering. *Affordable Pampering*. It sounded like an Obama program.

My foul temper had practically dissolved so I decided to work on my table for the dinner party. I looked around my dining room and suddenly it seemed cluttered, like a grandma's house. Where did all this old lady stuff come from? I must have had a dozen candlesticks on the sideboards and dining table. Too many tureens, too many tchotchkes. I had collected all these things and was saving them for my children who didn't want them. Well, someday Ashley might like some of my things but Ivy? Probably not. He had more sophisticated taste.

So while I waited for Monday, I took the small table apart and added a leaf so I could seat my guests. My dining room was very small, as was the scale of my house. Most houses on Church Street were two hundred years old and built for smaller people with smaller possessions. I loved it because it was like living in a dollhouse and also because every room downstairs opened onto a terrace or a porch. And yes, I had one of those well-known Charleston hidden gardens with miniature specimen plants, an ancient handmade brick walkway, and a fountain in the center. The walls of my garden were trellised with Confederate jasmine and fig ivy. In the east corner stood an old live oak tree that produced enough Spanish moss to thrill the camellia and azalea bushes nestled below with some partial shade, protecting them from the lethal sun. But it was deep summer and very little remained in bloom then. Somehow the lack of color gave all the varieties of ferns a chance to take center stage because that was when my garden became more about different textures and variations of green. The only flowers were the water lilies in the fountain and the ones in my hanging baskets. On an ironic note, Maisie did not consider me to be a gardener. Isn't that nice?

I was debating inviting another trustee and her husband. I knew it was probably dangerous to have Mitzi Summerset because she loved the sound of her own voice way too much. I could see her batting her eyes like a schoolgirl and going on and on about herself while my other guests went catatonic waiting for her to relinquish the mike.

Common sense prevailed and I didn't invite her. But I did have my hair blown out and Monday night finally arrived. Mary Beth was in the kitchen with Peggy plating salads and arranging cheeses on a huge platter with fruit and crackers.

"I'm so glad you could come, Mary Beth," I said.

"So am I," Peggy said with a laugh. "There'll be a hundred glasses to hand wash!"

"A hundred?" I said and narrowed my eyes at her. Lordy, Lord. Peggy did love to exaggerate.

"Okay. Fifty," Peggy said.

"No, problem, Mrs. Waters, happy to help!"

"Great! Peggy? Show Mary Beth where the extra wine is and the bottled water. Let's fill those water goblets at ten to six, okay?"

"Done!" Peggy said.

"I don't know how we use all those glasses but we do. Sorry."

"Honey? Use them all! Dirty glasses are my job security!" She laughed again.

With only seven of us for dinner Peggy probably didn't really need Mary Beth's help. But Peggy was getting older and she liked to go home early. Two extra hands would cut her work in half and I knew Mary Beth needed the money. It was a tiny win-win in my domestic life.

The delicious smells of roasting meat were wafting all over the house like mythical sirens calling out to sailors to throw themselves on the rocks. Maybe my prospective donors would be so intoxicated by my roast beef and mashed potatoes that they'd write big fat checks for us, and good women and children would be able to sleep safely. I almost had to laugh because a simultaneous thought crossed my mind that dreamers give birth to dreamers. Ashley came by her dreamer personality honestly. Ah, me. Another maternal insight— you always dislike about your children that which you dislike about yourself because you understand the danger of that trait. But who knew? Maybe the community relations person from All Air, Inc., *would* like to fund a new shelter. Maybe the retired real estate developer would *like* to endow our counseling services. Until somebody emphatically turned me down, the answer was still yes.

The doorbell rang promptly at six and our executive director, Tom Warner, breezed in, gave my cheek a polite kiss, and stood back.

"It smells like heaven in here! Roast beef?"

"Of course!" I said. "Where's Vicki?"

"Allergies driving her crazy. Sneezing and hacking. God! Smell that? These fellows don't have a chance. Am I the first?"

"Yes. Come on in. Let's open a bottle of wine."

"Excellent idea," he said. "Is Clayton here?"

"In New York."

We walked through the living room to the dining room where the wine was chilling. "Too bad. I haven't seen him in ages. Your house looks beautiful, as it always does."

"Oh, thanks, Tom. Peggy and I packed away a ton of stuff this morning and lo and behold, suddenly there was room to set up a bar!"

"It's important to have our priorities straight," he said and smiled. "Now tell me again; who's coming? I mean, I know who's coming. I just want to hear their names out loud. Every other nonprofit in Charleston is dying of jealousy tonight."

I giggled and Tom opened the bottle. I removed Vicki's place setting from the table.

"David Malcolm from All Air and his wife, Annie, and Steve Karol, the real estate mogul of all times, and his wife, Michelle. Steve and Michelle are living on Spring Island right now but thinking about moving here. And for a sledgehammer finale, Karen Jones is coming in at eight for dessert and coffee."

Karen Jones (formerly known as Anne Marie Wilson) was a physician's assistant whose husband, Leonard, was once a well-respected orthodontist in Myrtle Beach. Karen came to us three years ago, black and blue from head to toe with her two small equally battered children and with just the clothes on their backs. For every good reason, she was fearful for all their lives. But when she took him to court, she blew the lid off his deviant and, yes, criminal behavior and that was the beginning of the fat lady's song for him. His practice dwindled until he moved to Salem, Oregon, but not before he threatened revenge. Leonard Wilson was as angry a man as you could ever imagine and as mean a son of a gun as you could find on this earth. An order of protection signed by any authority you could name was still a joke to him. He'd kill somebody eventually—I had no doubt of that—but for the moment he was in Oregon and Karen was living in Charleston with her children and new identities for all. She was the head of our Survivors Council and could tell the story of domestic violence with such passion that it gave me chills no matter how many times I heard it.

Mary Beth came into the room carrying a tumbler of something and said, "Here you go, Mizz Waters, I believe you favor vodka?"

I looked at her and thought, This child doesn't know a thing about the real me.

"Mary Beth? Throw that thing right down the drain. Only Pellegrino! This is a very serious work night."

"For real!" she said. "Pellegrino it is!"

"Thanks. Listen, these two couples who are coming here for dinner could change my world. I'm looking for money to build a new shelter that is so desperately needed. I need you and Peggy to keep your ears open and remember everything you hear, okay?"

"Yes, ma'am! I mean, Ashley told me you were involved with a crisis center, but I had no idea . . ."

"She probably thinks I answer the crisis hotline for Butterball turkeys," I said and watched Mary Beth's face fall. "I'm sorry, that wasn't nice. But I have to tell you, Mary Beth, for what it's worth, no one in my family has ever taken an interest in my work."

"I'm gonna wash my hands," Tom said.

"Down the hall on the right. You know where it is."

He nodded and walked away, sensing he shouldn't hear whatever confidence Mary Beth wanted to share with me.

"Maybe they just don't understand what abuse really is," she said.

"But you do?" I said. What was this child saying?

"I'm just saying that all kinds of things go on and some people are too afraid to say anything."

I looked at her face and searched her eyes for meaning and to my great sorrow, there was nothing there I hadn't seen in the faces of so many damaged women we counseled and tried to help at My Sister's House.

"If you ever want to talk——" I began, but she interrupted me.

"I'd better help Peggy get that roast out of the oven instead of standing here running my mouth. And I'll get you that Pellegrino. Lime?"

"That would be great. Thanks."

On another night I would've encouraged her to sit down and talk about herself but my doorbell was ringing again. Maybe I'd call her and take her out to lunch. Yes, I would do that.

When Annie and David Malcolm arrived, I took an immediate shine to Annie. Minutes later we were gathered in my little courtyard, and they were all sipping a glass of wine. Mary Beth was passing steamed shrimp with a cocktail sauce.

"Stay right here, young lady," David Malcolm said to Mary Beth. He popped one into his mouth, then another and another. "God, I love these things."

Yes! I thought. I was so relieved that I wasn't dealing with a Mr. Fancy Pants. This would make the pitch go much easier.

I took a moment to check the temperature of our party's waters. The chatter was going nicely. Fortunately, the mosquitoes weren't biting or the no-see-ums, because my landscaper had sprayed for us earlier in the afternoon. Maybe it was the fact that I used a landscaper that made Maisie think that I wasn't a real gardener. Well, I could think about that another time. There was an intermittent breeze, laced with some sweet, Lowcountry perfume and another day began to fade away. Please, Lord, make them sympathetic to the cause. Amen.

"So how long did y'all live in Seattle?" I asked Annie.

"Twenty years. We raised our children there and we had wonderful friends. Seattle is a very special place."

"Rains a bit?"

She laughed and said, "It's really not all that much rain. It's more like gray skies and the drizzles for months on end and then we have gorgeous summers."

"Yeah, that's actually what I've heard. So are you enjoying Charleston? Did you find a house?"

"We did! We bought a nice place on Daniel Island. You'll have to come see it! It's a great location for David's commute. And I am absolutely loving Charleston. Every chance I get, I go to a plantation or a house museum. There's so much history here!"

"Well, it's not ancient Rome or Athens but for American history? You could spend a lifetime learning all there is to know. Anyway, I'm so glad we could finally get together."

"So are we," Annie said, and somehow I knew she meant it.

I looked up to see Mary Beth showing Steve and Michelle Karol out to where we were. There were hellos all around. Mary Beth left to get them some refreshments and more Pellegrino for me. For the moment, Tom seemed to have them all enthralled. He was his most charming in any kind of social situation. I was a bundle of nerves.

When Mary Beth came back, she whispered to me, "Are you all right, Mizz Waters?"

"Of course! Why?"

"You just seem so serious. I just thought, you know, maybe something was wrong."

I looked at her.

"Mary Beth? Let me tell you what's going on around here. In 2010, there were almost fifty thousand victims of domestic abuse in South Carolina. Tell me what could be more serious?"

"Plague?" she said and made an odd face.

"This *is* a plague, sweetie," I said. "It's a bona fide plague. Is the roast out of the oven?"

"Yes, we should be able to sit in about ten minutes," she said and hurried back into the house.

"Sorry, honey," I muttered to myself as soon as she was out of earshot.

I hated myself when I fact-bombed people but I was so nervous, trying to hold my anxiety in check. I also realized then that Mary Beth was probably a long way away from coming to terms with the secret she was holding. But why in the world this subject wasn't on the tip of every woman's tongue, not just here but all over the country, I simply didn't understand. Annie and Michelle caught my attention.

Michelle said, "Tom just told us you're beginning a capital campaign for a new safe house. Is that true? How do you go about doing something like that?"

"Girls like us put the squeeze on our husbands and the money somehow materializes!" Annie said, laughing. "Am I right?"

"I think we're going to be best friends," I said. "I wish it was always that easy."

"I was on the board of a battered women's shelter in Seattle," Annie said. "I've got the drill."

"Oh my dear long-lost friend! Would you like to be on ours?" I said.

"Wait a minute!" Michelle said. "What about me?"

I hugged them both, all of us knowing that after the nominating committee heard about and interviewed them for two seconds, they would certainly be given the most serious consideration for board positions. We were always in need of good trustees, especially ones of means and experience.

The French doors to my dining room opened wide and Mary Beth sang out, "Dinner is ready anytime y'all are."

Well, Mary Beth was as cute as a bug in her white shirt and black skirt, but she shouldn't have been clanging the proverbial triangle like we were back on the Ponderosa climbing off a dusty mule train. This was Church Street in Charleston! I'd have a word with her later.

I turned to Tom and whispered, "Well, shall we knock the mud from our boots and go get us some grub?"

"Oh, don't be so prissy, Emily Post," Tom said and smiled again and held the door for our guests to go in ahead of us.

"You're right. I'm just nervous."

This was why he was the executive director and I wasn't. He was unbothered by almost anything except our mission, which bothered both of us deeply and in the most profound way.

We were seated at the table, wine was poured, and a toast was offered by Tom.

"Thank you all for being here with us tonight and a special thank-you to Liz, our development director, for this lovely dinner in her beautiful home! Cheers!"

"Cheers!" we all said and began to eat our salads.

"It's my pleasure!" I said and then, "Michelle asked me earlier about how exactly do we go about a capital campaign and I didn't have the time to answer her. The truth is there are as many ways to launch a campaign as you might imagine."

"But basically the mission is to raise money, I imagine. Right?" David Malcolm said.

"Yes," I said, "but it's just as important to raise awareness. And my gorgeous state of South Carolina bears the shame of being the state where more women are killed by men than any other state in America. It's based on a per capita number but still it's just horrible."

"Good grief!" Michelle said. "Number *one?*"

"Yes. We are always in the top ten," I said.

"It has to stop," Tom said. "It's hard to understand how Charleston can be the number one tourist destination in the country and the state still has this unspeakable problem."

"I did a huge Google on y'all last week but I can't remember everything I read. How many people died from domestic violence in South Carolina last year? Like thirty?" Steve asked. "And it's not just women, is it?"

"Right at forty," Tom said. "And you're right. Men are victims as well, and children, but the national average shows that eighty-five percent are women. And then there are all the unreported cases."

"As a rule women are peace-loving creatures, but when it comes to this kind of crime, you have to take mental illness into account as well," I said.

"Dear Lord!" Annie said. "How terrible! Why do you think South Carolina . . . or just how did this happen? Number one is really bad."

"Well," Tom said, "there's not just one answer. It's racism, sexism, homophobia, unemployment . . . the fact that the world is still so patriarchal . . . it's a combination of circumstance, drug and alcohol abuse, economics, environmental conditioning . . ."

"Environmental conditioning! Good grief. Tom! Could you be any more antiseptic?" I had to laugh even though it wasn't funny at all. "Look, what Tom means by environmental conditioning is, and this is another terrible truth, a boy who is a witness to domestic violence is ten times more likely to become an abuser as an adult."

"It's true," Annie said. "That statistic is true everywhere."

"Um, maybe this is a dumb question, but why don't people who are being abused just leave?" Michelle asked. "I mean, I'd just get in my car!"

"It's not a dumb question at all," Tom said. "In fact, it's the first one most people ask. What we ought to be asking is, Why are all these men behaving this way? And the answer is complicated. Domestic abuse crosses every socioeconomic line. Some of the nicest people you've ever known terrorize their families."

"Tom's right. Of course, you have to know how abusers operate," I said. "They're superpossessive; they monitor their spouse's every move. And somehow, over time they manage to put up a wall to isolate her from the rest of her family. Friends too."

"Meanwhile," Tom said, "the guy you think is Cary Grant on the golf course is, at home, yelling his head off at her, berating her until she believes that she's worthless. The next thing you know, he pushes her, then there's a slap with the next argument, and next is a punch with a closed fist. The woman can't understand why this is happening. The harder she tries, the shorter his fuse becomes. But he cools off, apologizes profusely, begs her to stay, and swears it will never happen again."

"Until it does," I said. "It's this slow process of drawing in the victim until she's trapped and ashamed because he's manipulated her into believing she's the cause of his anger. So she becomes meek and withdrawn and can't find the courage to leave."

"It's true," Annie said. "We saw it all the time in Seattle. It's classic. Then he says he will kill her if she leaves. Nice, right?"

"Yes. And sometimes women die," I said and then added, "and sometimes their children are killed too. Look, imagine this. Your husband loses his job, can't find another one, and the bills start to pile up. He's drinking more than he ever did, and suddenly he has a trigger temper. What do you do? The dog barks or the baby cries or he hates having to be home by seven for dinner so he loses it. You get very quiet and let him rant and rave, hoping it will blow over. Does this sound plausible?"

"Sure, unfortunately . . . ," Michelle said and the others nodded their heads.

"So tension builds and stress builds and then really awful things begin to happen. The king is no longer in charge of the castle. He is completely demoralized."

"Well, this is terrible!" Michelle said. "We have to do something about this!"

"We're trying to," Tom said.

"Well, building just another safe house can't begin to solve a problem like this," Steve said.

The table got very quiet then. Steve Karol was absolutely right. It was going to take an awful lot more than one new safe house to change the entire culture of abuse. Had dinner gone wrong?

"Let me say something here," Steve said. "First of all, I'm a peace-loving man. I love my new home on Spring Island for that very reason. It's peaceful. I can ride my horses, catch a nice fat fish, watch birds, and think my thoughts."

"Me too. But sometimes it's a little too peaceful, which is why we're thinking we need a little getaway spot in Charleston," Michelle said.

"That's right, sweetheart," he said. "I mean, I have to give this a lot of thought but I'm thinking you need a much larger campaign. If you really want to change things dramatically, that is."

"We want dramatic change more than anything in this entire world," I said and realized I was becoming more emotional than I would have wanted them to see.

"Tell us what you're thinking," Tom said.

"Well, you need housing. That's not a big problem, right, Malcolm?"

David Malcolm, who had been pretty quiet, perked up.

"The cost of a house? You're right, Steve. Not a big deal. But I'm thinking that house has to change all the time. I mean, what happens when the angry spouse finds the hiding spouse?"

"Mayhem," I said. "You're right. Keeping the location of the safe house a secret is a very serious concern for everyone."

"Okay, so what if a recently retired real estate developer joined forces and resources with a major manufacturer of airplanes that they've been building housing for like mad . . . what if they built and donated a house to you and as soon as it was say, a year old, you gave it back and we gave you another one in a completely different location." Steve Karol was grinning from ear to ear.

"And what if the manufacturer donated counseling for these battered women and their families and also underwrote a PSA campaign to educate the public? You know, give the victims the courage they need to leave?" David Malcolm said. "And wouldn't it be great if that airplane manufacturer provided you with some lobbying services that already cost them a fortune anyway?"

I was almost blown off my chair. Did these people fall from heaven?

"I don't know what to say," I said.

"Something tells me, Liz," Tom said, smiling so wide I could see his bridge, "that Mr. Karol and Mr. Malcolm have already met."

Steve Karol and David Malcolm reached across the table and shook hands with each other.

"Nice to see you again, Steve," David said.

"Same here, David," Steve said. "Every time I turn around there are the Malcolms! And just so you know, Tom and Liz, we'd never come to a dinner like this unless the answer was already yes."

"Amen! Listen, All Air is all about the skies being the limit. We've just taken up residence in your beautiful state. We'd like to be good neighbors. A leadership presence in a campaign like yours will give all our employees a tremendous sense of pride," David said and sat back in his chair. "We should start with a board challenge, don't you think, Steve?"

"Great idea! What do you say to a ceiling?"

"How's fifty thousand?"

Basically, this would be a challenge to our board to raise fifty thousand dollars and they, the Karols and All Air, would match it.

"Perfect. Michelle and I need a cause. This is probably the most important problem we've ever worked on. We're going to make South Carolina number fifty and we won't rest until it is. Of course, we have a lot of work ahead of us but that will be good for us."

"We can't live in this gorgeous place and stand by doing nothing," Michelle said and smiled like an angel.

I couldn't help it. I started to cry.

The kitchen door opened. "Are y'all ready for some gorgeous roast beef?" Mary Beth said. "Oh, and Mizz Waters? Karen Jones called and is stuck in traffic on the bridge. I guess there's a wreck or something."

Tom said, "Mary Beth, please call her back and tell her she doesn't need to come. Mission's accomplished. Y'all will meet her soon enough. Remarkable woman."

"Sure thing," she said.

I looked at the table. We'd barely touched our salads.

"Wait! Don't go. Who cares about radicchio and endive anyway?" I said and began to blubber like a baby. Between my gulping I managed to say, "Please clear the table, Mary Beth. Ask Peggy to open the champagne and for goodness' sake . . ."

"Bring Mrs. Waters a healthy shot of vodka on the rocks and a box of tissues on the side," Tom said.

"Two limes," I sputtered.

Annie put her arm around my shoulder and gave me a squeeze and Michelle reached across the table and patted the back of my clammy hand. I was so happy and I was just a mess.

CHAPTER 9

Ashley—In Red

I was blow-drying my hair. Mary Beth was standing next to me talking my ear off about my mother and some big deal about My Sister's House. Sadly, and maybe selfishly, I didn't want to hear anything about it at that moment. I was so excited I could feel my heart fluttering in my chest. I was having dinner with Porter. Everyone was right. He called. Yes, ma'am, he sure did! And he sent flowers— beautiful red roses! He was so, so darling.

"You should've seen her in action, Ash. Your mother is like amazing!"

"Yep. She sure can be. Did you see the dress she bought for me? Totally Jackie O circa 1965. It's in that dress bag on the back of the door. And she bought me killer pumps from Bob Ellis. I guess she figured the world had seen enough of my bootylishiousness!"

"You're terrible," she said, laughing. She unzipped the bag and took out the dress. "Holy crap! This is Jackie, all right! It's screaming for a circle pin. Don't you think?"

"Right? I think it takes guts to wear a red dress though, don't you?"

"Well, I look like a freak in red with my red hair and freckles but on you? I'll bet it's gorgeous! Put it on! Galloway's gonna faint. Where's the dog, read SOB, taking you?"

"In a minute and Mary Beth? He's not an SOB. Really, he's not. He's just crazy busy, that's all. And can't you imagine he's got so much stress all the time. I don't know how he handles it. He was very sweet when he called. And, news flash, we're going to Hall's Chophouse downtown. He said he was dying for a good steak and I said I think Hall's is supposed to be amazing. I'm just glad it's not located in a hotel."

"Boy, no kidding." She shook out the dress and hung it back on the hook. "You are going to look so pretty in this."

"Thanks. We'll see. Hey! Did I tell you I saw Tommy downtown this afternoon? He was at Starbucks on King Street. He actually bought me an iced coffee."

"He's such a cutie," she said.

"He wants to know when we're having another sunset party."

"What did you tell him?"

"I told him we'd think about it. What do you think? Should we do it again?"

"Heck, yes! Don't you think the last one was awesome?"

"Yeah, but to do it again . . . I don't know. I think it should have a new theme or something."

"Like what?"

"I don't know. Let's think about it. Meanwhile, Senator Fabulous is going to be here in like ten minutes."

"Okay. I'm going to go wallow in my loneliness with some micro fat-free popcorn and last season of *Downton Abbey*. Take a picture of the food for me."

"Right. No date?"

"No date. No work tonight. It's a sad story."

"Oh, please." I threw the dress over my head and Mary Beth zipped me up while I stepped into my new shoes. Then I put on some red lips and fake pearl earrings that looked as good as real ones. I stepped back to look in the mirror. "What do you think?"

"I think . . . I think you look like a movie star!"

"Too flashy?"

"No! You look terrific! Now spritz something in all the target points and be ready when the doorbell rings."

"Right." I pushed my lipstick, my cell phone, and my house keys into my little black bag and sprayed some perfume all over my hair and my wrists.

A few minutes later we heard a car pull up in the yard. Mary Beth went to the living room to peek out the window. It was him.

"It's him! He looks pretty cute, I guess," Mary Beth said.

"You really don't like him, do you?"

"Ash? It's not that I don't like him. Any girl who's with him can't be just herself. She's going to have to be what he wants her to be. Because if his girlfriend/woman/wife can't help him get what he wants, he's gonna dump her. That's just politics, you know, like Hill and Bill? So I'm just saying . . ."

"Be careful, right?" I knew she was right. "I will be. Anyway, I like teamwork. I'll just let him talk about himself. Guys like to do that."

"Good idea."

"Hey, Mary Beth? When'd you get so smart about men?"

"You don't want to know," she said and I thought she looked a little unhappy.

"We'll talk later on. Okay?"

"Sure."

We both looked out the window then. He was standing in the yard talking on his cell phone.

"What the heck is he doing?" I said. "Isn't he going to come to the door?"

"Maybe he expects you to go running to him," Mary Beth said.

"Like Maisie would say, hell will freeze first," I said and I meant it. "Our table's for seven o'clock."

It was just after six thirty and the restaurant was a solid twenty minutes away without traffic. So we watched him and we watched him. He was just chattering away like he wasn't in my yard and I wasn't waiting and we didn't have a reservation. Time kept passing and he kept talking.

"Don't you think he knows what time it is? Maybe he thinks they'll just take him anyway."

"I don't know what he thinks but it seems a little weird to just be standing there talking forever, doesn't it?" I had an idea. "I'll be right back."

"Where're you going?"

"Watch me."

I opened the front door and stood there. Finally, he looked up at me and waved. Then he made a motion with his left hand for me to come to him. I slammed the door and stayed inside.

"What in the world are you doing?" Mary Beth said in disbelief.

"Just wait a minute," I said.

A minute later the doorbell rang. I paused, took a deep breath, and then I opened it.

"Hey, Ashley! Gosh! You look beautiful tonight. Why didn't you come to the car? We're going to be late."

"Not my problem. You were on the phone."

"Yeah, I was! I was talking to the head of the Senate Finance Committee about a very important vote that's coming up and . . ."

"Porter? I don't care if you were talking to Barack Obama. If you want to take me out, well then, you're going to have to come to the door like a gentleman."

He stopped, stepped back, and looked at me. The strangest expression came over his face and then he smiled.

"I knew I liked you," he said. "An old-fashioned southern girl with manners and everything. You are too cute!"

"I won't be too late!" I called back to Mary Beth. I caught her eye, well, *both of them* and they were rolling around the ceiling.

He opened my car door and waited until I was all settled before he closed it. I thought, See? He *is* a gentleman. As soon as he backed out of the driveway he took out his phone again.

"I have to finish this phone call. You don't mind, do you?"

"No, no, of course not."

"Okay, and just so you know, anything you hear cannot be repeated. It's state business and lots of times things are said that might sound rough or peculiar to the uninitiated."

"No, I get it. Go right ahead and make your call."

So for the entire ride to Charleston I was held captive and unable to speak because Porter and Mark were discussing the state budget, who was going to get funded and who was getting frozen out because they didn't support something. It was just about the most boring conversation I had ever heard in my entire life. That would be a capital B.

"Sorry that went on for so long," he said as we pulled into a parking spot right in front of the restaurant just as another car pulled away from the curb.

"Gee, you'd think they saved this spot for you," I said. "Talk about parking karma."

"I know. Hey, I'm a lucky guy! Look at who I'm with tonight!" I started to get out of the car and he said, "Don't you touch that door handle! I'll be right there!"

"Yes, sir!" I said and giggled.

So he opened my door and extended his hand to me. I took it and stood on the curb. He locked the car with his key, it chirped like a bird, and then he held the door of the restaurant open for me too. I thought, It's pretty nice to be treated this way. Boys my age expected you to do everything for yourself and then maybe split the bill at the end of the night unless it was your birthday. And then you were supposed to jump in bed with them when you got home like sex had no meaning whatsoever. I mean, you shouldn't assume that having sex meant you were in love or something. You could hold out for two or three dates, but if you had no intention of sleeping with a guy, you shouldn't date him more than a couple of times. This was exactly why I didn't date that often. The difference between Porter and the guys I dated appeared to be vast, at least so far. Porter wasn't a boy; he was a man. And he was a senator, for heaven's sake. All these crazy thoughts were swirling around in my head as we climbed the steps to the second-floor dining room. Of course, the maître d' recognized Porter and offered him his choice of tables downstairs but Porter mentioned something about wanting some privacy. So upstairs was the best choice. And we were led to a table at the back of the room that was about as discreet as you could ask for in that restaurant.

"Would you like a glass of wine or champagne?" Porter asked, motioning for the maître d' to stay for a moment.

"Sure! Maybe a New Zealand sauvignon blanc?"

"Very good," he said, "and for you, Senator?"

"I'll have what the lady is having," he said.

"I'll get those drinks brought over to you right away!" he said and left.

Porter turned back to me and his face was just incredulous. "Excuse me? Are you like a sommelier or something?"

"No," I said and smiled. "I just happen to like the taste of that particular grape."

"Oh?"

"Yeah. I think chardonnays are too oaky and heavy and German wines are too sweet. But if my roommate and I are sharing a bottle of something, it's usually on sale at Bi-Lo for like ten dollars or less. And it *might* be a chardonnay."

There was no reason to tell him that sometimes we bought wine in a box from Costco. By the ton. This fact would not have showcased me in my most sophisticated light.

"You mean yes, not yeah."

"Yeah, I guess so. Ha-ha! Just kidding, Porter."

"Got it. It's just that *yeah* sounds so, I don't know, undignified. Public eye and all that. I have to watch everything."

I'd never say *yeah* again or *yep* and I imagined that saying *yup* carried the same penalty.

"We were talking about cheap wine?"

"Right! Well, I remember those days. Roommates and all that. It wasn't that long ago, actually."

"Oh, please, you're not that old."

"No, I'm actually the youngest guy in the state senate."

"I know that," I said.

"You do? What else do you know, Ashley Waters, with the biggest blue eyes I've ever seen?"

I giggled. I wanted to tell him right then that he smelled so good and that I loved his eyes too but I didn't. I opened my menu and began to consider my options. I was going to have the petite filet mignon and a baked potato and maybe the Caesar salad. Did I want creamed spinach too? No! I'd smile at him and have spinach in between my teeth hanging like Spanish moss on a live oak tree. Spinach was out of the question.

"I know that I'm really starving and that's about all I know. Are you going to have an appetizer?"

"Absolutely!" The waiter put our goblets of wine on the table in front of us and left. "Well, may I propose a toast?"

"Sure."

"Here's to the most beautiful girl in the restaurant!"

"Me?"

"Yes, you. And, Ashley, I owe you an apology."

"For what?"

"Well, for expecting you to come up to my room the night I met you. I promise it was harmless enough. I mean, they give me a suite with a completely separate living room and all that. My aide clearly neglected to tell you that. But I should've realized how it sounded to you and I didn't even think about it. In any case, I apologize for my manners."

"No problem. And the flowers you sent were gorgeous. Thank you."

"You're welcome."

"Look, I guess you may as well know this about me now, Porter."

"What's that?"

He looked at me in a way that made me feel like a tiny bug about to be eaten by a big hairy spider but first the spider wanted to interview his food. And maybe toy with it too.

"Well, for one thing, I don't think I'm like the other girls you date."

"And how's that?"

I took a sip of wine followed by a deep breath.

"I don't just go out all the time. Like just to party and all. I don't do any drugs. I go to church. Well, most Sundays." This was not true. "I don't sleep around. And I'm pretty serious about my career. And I actually love my family, crazy as they may be." Did I sound like a fool to say these things?

He reached across the table and took my hand in his.

"Somehow I already knew all that about you, Ashley. Maybe that's why I haven't been able to get you out of my mind."

"Really?"

"Yes, really. I've been thinking about you constantly, and I think I've just about come to the conclusion that I've been waiting all my life for someone like you to appear. I walked in that gallery and there you were, just standing there glowing with goodness."

What?

"Are you serious?"

"Dead serious. Don't you believe in love at first sight?"

"Well, I believe in *love* but I'm a little less sure about first sight."

I felt my face burning with surprise. Did he really think he was in love with me?

"Are you going to tell me you don't feel the electricity between us?"

What was he saying? Did I feel it? Excuse me for pointing this out, but what I felt was like an ongoing explosion of nuclear energy. *Yes,* I felt it. Suddenly, our smirking waiter was standing next to Porter's shoulder, ready to take our order. My jaw was still dropped.

"Um, I think . . ." I nodded in the waiter's direction.

"Oh!" Porter said. "I didn't see you there. Uh, I think I need a few minutes."

"We have a few specials tonight. I'd like to tell them to you now, sir."

The captain or the waiter or whatever he called himself went into a food litany that included preparation. I didn't hear a word he said. All I could think about was Porter and how gorgeous he was and I was visualizing walking down the aisle in a gorgeous bridal gown with miles and miles of tulle and him standing at the end of the aisle, waiting for me . . . a cathedral . . .

"Ashley? Are you okay?"

"What? Oh yes! I'm fine."

"Do you know what you'd like to have for dinner? Would you like to share the porterhouse?"

"They named a steak after you? Gosh, that is *so* nice!"

"No, sweetie, it's a big steak for two people."

"Oh, well, sure that sounds great," I said and felt like an idiot.

"How do you like your meat prepared?" the waiter said.

"However the chef likes to serve it," he said.

"Very good," he said and made a note. "And would you care for appetizers?"

Porter ordered something for both of us and I couldn't even tell you what it was. I ate whatever was placed in front of me. It was only the most delicious food in the world, that's all. What really mattered was that Porter felt the same way about me as I did about him and I have to say, I was unprepared for this. Completely unprepared. I know we had dinner because plates kept coming and going. The last one had an unmistakable residue of chocolate.

"Would you like to have coffee, Ashley?"

"If you're having coffee, I will."

We had coffee, Porter paid the bill, and we left. We drove across the Cooper River and into Mount Pleasant, heading toward Sullivans Island.

"What a wonderful dinner," I said. "Thank you!"

"You're welcome," he said. "You know what I hate?"

"No! Tell me!" Had I done something wrong?

"I hate that this night is coming to an end."

"Oh! Well, me too! I thought . . . well, never mind. I wish it could go on too."

"Unfortunately, I have to drive back to Columbia tonight. I have committee meetings starting at ten in the morning."

"Gosh, that's awful."

"Yes. It's a little rough. I should've booked a hotel room. I just didn't think it through."

"Well, Porter, I'd offer you the sofa, but my roommate would have a heart attack."

"Oh. No, no!" He started to laugh. "I'll bet she would! She's that redhead, right?"

"Yes, Mary Beth Smythe. From Teeny Town, Tennessee. We went to the College of Charleston together. She's my dearest friend. Like a sister."

"Nice. Wait! You never told me about your career and all. All we did was talk about me all night. So tell me about what you do, what's your plan?"

"Well, I'm a painter and I'd *like* to make my living as a painter. But it's awfully hard to do that when you live here and besides, I need a larger body of work. Then maybe I can get a show somewhere." I didn't tell him that not so long ago I'd thought of painting him as a wolf. Why spoil the moment?

"So here I thought you were happily working in fine arts management when you're an artist yourself! I should've known! Can you show me something you've painted?"

We pulled into my yard, and he stopped the car next to the cottage. Mary Beth's car was there next to mine.

"Sure! That's my studio."

I pointed to my pitiful hovel and tried to remember if I'd left it unlocked. I thought I had.

"Wow! She has her own studio! Impressive."

"Well, painting's messy and smelly so it's a good idea to have a place outside of the house."

He just sat there in the driver's seat and stared at me.

"What?" I said.

"Nothing," he said. "Don't move and I'll be right there."

He hurried around to my side of the car and opened my door.

"Mademoiselle?" he said and offered his hand to help me out.

He was a little bit short and I was a little too tall so in heels, I was actually a shade taller than him. I wondered if that bothered him at all. I was about to find out. As soon as I stood up he hurried to the steps of the cottage and stood on the first one. Yep, he had to be taller. Oh, so what, I told myself.

"You have to let me pass so I can turn on the lights."

"Come here," he said.

"What?" I said and stood in front of him.

He took my face into his hands and said, "Ashley Waters? I am going to kiss you right here in the moonlight."

And he did, and oh my goodness, this was sure not his first kiss. No, ma'am. I'm not quite sure how to describe the effect of it without sounding completely inexperienced but it sort of left me breathless. And weak. And I felt an unfamiliar but thunderous flutter deep inside of me, somewhere below my stomach and above, well, you know where I mean. I hope.

"You are so beautiful. You have no idea how beautiful I think you are."

Now I was officially having a near-death experience.

"Porter?"

"Yes?"

"I don't think I've ever been kissed like that before. Can we do that again?"

He kissed me again and I promise you I thought I was going to faint dead on the ground.

"I'd better leave soon."

"Yes. I can show you my etchings any time."

So we just stood there for I don't know how long, an eternity, just staring at each other. Maybe it was a minute or more. My mind began to race. When would I see him again? Would I see him at all? What was the appropriate amount of time to wait before I, well, you know, did the obvious deed? Were the rules different with senators? This required thought.

"Ashley? What are you doing this weekend? Do you want to come to Columbia? There's a dinner I have to go to for the SCDOT."

"Where would I stay?"

"With me? In my apartment?"

"No way."

"Really?"

"Really. I'm not like that, Porter. Sometimes I wish I was but I'm not. Find a nice lady to chaperone me and I'll come. Otherwise, I'll see you the next time you're in Charleston."

"You're killing me," he said.

"Are you going to walk me to my door or what?"

So Senator Porter Galloway walked me to my door and we said good night. I watched him walk down the steps and to his car. He turned and waved and I blew him a kiss. If I had not thought that running down the steps to him would land me in bed in ten minutes, I would've run down those steps like a track star with my hair on fire. My instincts told me to let him go.

I went inside and Mary Beth called out, "How was dinner?"

"Mary Beth? I'm in love and I'm going to marry him."

"Does he know this?"

"I have not told him yet."

"Yeah, first date and all that. Prolly better to wait a bit. We don't want to scare the boy."

I slept the sleep of the dead, right through my alarm until almost ten o'clock. It was my cell phone that woke me up. And to my surprise it was Cindy Lue Elder calling me, the woman who showed up at our party, the one who worked for Porter.

"What time is it?" I said instead of even saying hello.

"Ten. Oh! I'm sorry! I woke you up, didn't I?"

"Who's this?"

"Oh, Lord. Ashley? It's me, Cindy Elder from Senator Galloway's office. Do you remember me?"

I untangled myself from my sheets and sat up on the side of my bed.

"Of course. Listen, I can't talk now. I'm supposed to be at work and for some dumb reason I slept through my alarm. Can I call you later?"

"Sure. I just wanted to take you out for lunch. How's tomorrow at one?"

"Um, that sounds fine. Want to meet at my gallery?"

"Sure. We can decide where to go then."

We hung up and I broke the world record for getting dressed and out of the house, calling the Turners on the way. Mr. Turner answered the phone. He was totally cool.

"Don't worry! Take your time! Be careful driving. We'll see you soon."

What a sweetie he was. I began to relax. Why did Cindy Elder want to have lunch? What in the world was on her mind? Well, it obviously has to do with Porter, I thought. She must have heard about us. Maybe she was a jealous nut who was going to throw acid in my face or something terrible! No. I was being overly suspicious. No way would she do something awful like that. She was way too sane. Well, I told myself, I'd just have to wait and see.

The next day came and Cindy walked into the Turner Gallery on the stroke of one.

"Hey! How are you?" I said.

"How am I?" She took off her huge sunglasses and revealed red and swollen eyes. "What do you think? Nice, right?"

She'd obviously been crying for a long time.

"Oh, God! How terrible! What happened?"

"Let's go eat and I'll tell you all about it."

"There's a little sandwich place right down the street."

It was crowded and we got the last empty table for two. I sort of hoped she'd keep her glasses on while we had lunch because who could eat and look at that?

I ordered a salad with grilled chicken and she ordered egg salad on white bread with potato chips and we both asked for sweetened iced tea, which is sort of the state drink if you don't count PBR. And I was sitting quietly just waiting for her to tell me something about which I had a growing suspicion I *really* didn't want to hear. Our tea came and I practically drained the glass in one gulp. She was quiet too, probably not knowing where or how to begin, and the longer she waited to talk to me, the more certain I was that whatever it was she wanted to say was going to be horrible.

"Okay," she finally said, "I'm going to tell you this and you can believe it or not. I know that you're seeing Porter and I just want to warn you. He's not so nice."

"What do you mean?"

Our waitress put our food in front of us and refilled our tea glasses.

"Y'all need anything else?" she said.

"No thanks," I said.

"I'm fine," Cindy said.

"Okay then," the waitress said and walked away.

"We've been seeing each other off and on for about a year. I wanted a commitment from him and he didn't want to give me one and so we began to fight. We'd break up and then I'd beg to see him again, because I was in love with him, you know? So we'd go along for a while and then we'd start fighting again. He just yelled at me, telling me I was lucky that he'd go out with me at all. Well, we finally broke up after he saw you at the gallery fund-raiser. But even then, at least I still had a job."

"Gosh. I'm sorry."

"I know. Listen, I'd disagree with him about a policy position or something in a meeting and then later on that night he'd go nuts, screaming at me, telling me I was out of line."

"What are you saying, Cindy? That's terrible."

"Yeah, terrible is right. Soon after the fund-raiser I went over to his house in Columbia to try and make some sense of what was left of our relationship and he *fired* me. I've never been fired from *anything!* I graduated at the top of my class and I worked so many hours for him it was ridiculous. All I had to do was disagree with him over a few tiny things in a meeting and it cost me my job?"

"I am so sorry."

"Yes, he fired me and I'm going home to Cleveland. You don't want to get involved with him, Ashley. He may seem like a nice guy but he's not. And he's not looking to settle down and get married."

"It's different between us, Cindy. He's the one pursuing me."

"You mean that love-at-first-sight line?"

I didn't answer her. I couldn't believe he'd used the same line with her. My heart sank.

"You don't have to tell me another thing," she said. "Here's my card. Even though I'm unemployed at the moment, that is my cell-phone number right there. Call me if you ever want to talk, okay? I don't even know why I'm telling you all this except I liked you and you didn't seem like somebody who wouldn't get her heart broken. God knows, he broke mine."

"Thanks," I said. My appetite was gone. "I can't eat."

"Me either," she said.

Something about her story didn't hang together quite right. Either Cindy Elder was one of those superpossessive, supersensitive women who couldn't take no for an answer or Porter simply dumped her for me. Nobody likes to be the dumpee. It's humiliating. Poor Cindy.

CHAPTER 10

Clayton—On the Ledge

I was lying in her bed and thinking about the fact that I was in deep shit. I mean shit right up to my nostrils. If I blinked or moved in the slightest way, I would drown in shit. And while I'm throwing the word *shit* around like a Frisbee, I'm also thinking about how amazing Sophia is in bed and how delicious her skin is to me. It's like tasting Tuscan olives and smelling the subtle fragrance of some kind of flowers at the same time. My God.

From my vantage point, propped up on pillows covered in linens from some outrageously priced store on Madison Avenue, I was watching her take a shower through the clear glass walls in her bathroom, trying to memorize her beautiful, beautiful body. Sure, she'd had a little work done, but it was money well spent if you asked me. I had tried to talk Liz into at least getting a little liposuction on her chin but she wouldn't hear of it. It's not supposed to hurt too much and God knows we had the money. But oddly, now that I'd loosened the purse strings and told her she could spend what she wants to spend, she doesn't want my money anymore. True, I don't want her spending money on things she doesn't really need. But a little nip and tuck is good for everyone after fifty.

But back to my original statement of my whereabouts? I was in deep shit because in my gut I knew Sophia was not as in love with me as I was with her. Maybe I should ask my doctor for some Viagra or something to make things more exciting from my end. Everyone seems to use it these days. In fact, I'd bet it's the number one prescribed recreational medication in America. And while we're on the topic, how about I heard that the insurance companies only pay for four capsules a month? Now they're going to decide how often we can screw? Are they kidding? This is much worse than National Security Agency surveillance! Just my opinion. I'd rather give up my dental plan.

My cell phone rang. I reached over to see the caller ID. It was Liz. *Shit!* I hopped out of bed and let the call go to voice mail, but I knew I had to call her back right away. That was our agreement. She called; I answered. Otherwise, there would be suspicion that could lead to some very ugly stuff. So I yanked my shirt off the chair to cover myself and I hurried to the terrace. Then I was afraid Sophia would get out of the shower and start calling me or something. I knew she was in a hurry to get to a meeting. I pulled the sliding glass door behind me to close it and put on my shirt, just in case a neighbor had a telescope focused on Sophia's terrace. I called Liz back.

"Hi, Liz!" I said, sounding upbeat because it was sort of titillating to be almost naked on your lover's terrace while talking to your wife. "What's going on?"

"Well, I wanted to tell you about my donor dinner. Clayton, it was just a dream . . ."

Liz went on and on and I listened, not realizing that Sophia had locked the terrace door and left the apartment. I started to panic. I checked the door. I was locked out of her apartment, on her terrace, wearing only a shirt.

"Clayton? Are you all right?"

"Yes, yes! I'm fine, dear, just on my way to get coffee—I was feeling like a cappuccino, you know, something different."

"Oh, well, good. Sometimes it's good to change things up."

"Yes, I agree." I thought, Oh boy, this is going to be embarrassing. "Well, I'm really glad to hear that your dinner went so well."

"Clayton, I've been raising money for twenty years and this is like Christmas finally came. I mean, I was so surprised that I cried."

"You cried? Actual tears? Right in front of them?"

"Yes. I mean, I know it sounds weak but you know what? They understood the cause! David Malcolm's wife, Annie, was even on a board of a battered women's shelter in Seattle! I can't wait for you to meet them. They really want to make a difference in this whole domestic violence issue. They want to be national role models for education and change. I swear I was checking their backs for wings! Remember that movie with John Travolta? His wings hanging out of his topcoat? What was it? *Michael*? Yes, that's it. Oh my, Clayton? I'm telling you . . ."

I was really happy that Liz's dinner was so successful, but my best friend was swinging in the breeze and I needed to get to my office! Why did Sophia lock me out? Didn't she see the rest of my clothes draped across the chair? What was she telling me? Did she lock me out on purpose? Did she think this was funny? I pulled on the terrace door about fifty times.

This was not funny.

I was finally able to get Liz to stop talking and we hung up. I had to think for a moment. I could not call Liz back. Or 911. There was no way to get out of this situation without a major awkward moment. I had to call the building super. It was much better than trying to scale the side of the building to see if maybe the bedroom window was unlocked. I could just slip inside a window and none of us would be worse for it. But if I did scale the side of the building—the ledge was wide enough—and I couldn't get in or back to the terrace? Everyone below would see and they'd call the fire department and I'd be on the six o'clock news all around the world. I called the super.

"Manuel? This is Clayton Waters calling. I've got a bit of a situation and I need your help. Right away?"

That was when I heard the sirens. I looked over the side of the balcony to see them pulling up in front of my building.

"Manuel? There's a hundred dollars in it for you if you get me out of this in like two minutes."

"Mr. Waters? The police are here and I have to go to see why first. Then I come to you."

"Manuel? The police are here because I am locked out on Ms. Bacco's terrace. Without my trousers. Please tell the police they can go home. It's a big mistake. Just a big silly mistake."

There was a momentary silence as the lightbulb clicked on in the brain of my superintendent's head.

"Ah!" he said. "Just give me a few minutes."

I leaned over the balcony and watched Manuel talking to the police. He pointed up to the roof and they looked up. I waved at them and they waved back. One officer even took a picture with his phone. Eventually they got back into their cruisers and pulled away from the curb. An eternity later Manuel was on the other side of Sophia's sliding glass doors pulling them open.

"There you go, Mr. Waters. Now about that hundred dollars? Let's forget about that. I mean . . ."

He wasn't kidding me for one second. He wanted his money.

"Just give me a minute, Manuel. It's not like I had my wallet with me out there." I went to my trousers and took out my wallet, handing him two fifties. "I know I can depend on your discretion."

"I don't see anything," he said and struggled to suppress a smile as wide as the Mississippi River.

Why was Sophia treating me this way? This had to be intentional.

CHAPTER 11

Ashley—Late for a Date

Porter and I have had three dates, not including the stupid night he wanted me to come to his room. First was steak night at Hall's, second was dinner at Langdon's in Mount Pleasant, and the third was also in Mount Pleasant at Basil's. I guessed that he wanted to go places where he thought he wouldn't be recognized right away. This was pretty dumb because in our neck of the woods it was like going out for dinner with Stephen Colbert or Joe Riley, both of them huge homegrown talents whose faces were plastered everywhere. Was he for real? Little old ladies could recognize Porter by the back of his head. They'd come up to him all the time and ask for a kiss or a photograph with their cell phone. Yes, even grannies in orthopedic shoes knew how to use cell phones that took pictures. They probably put them on their Facebook page for all I knew. Anyway, I didn't mind dinners in what he considered to be *off the beaten path* restaurants because we didn't need big attention as a couple. Not quite yet anyway. Somehow we had escaped the notice of the newspapers and I was actually glad about that. It took some pressure off both of us. And we talked on the phone like every other day. That was enough for right now.

And somehow, so far I had managed to avoid sleeping with him. There was a lot of heavy-duty kissing and fooling around and points where I was sure I was going to lose my mind, but so far, nada on the big one. We'd almost get there and then something would make me stop. Of course, the more you tell a man he can't have something, the more he wants it. And I wanted him too, in the most urgent way, but something was holding me back.

I had not gone to Columbia for that dinner he asked me to go to because it made me feel uncomfortable. And staying in a hotel wouldn't have been the answer either. I didn't think it was right for him to pay for a room because the whole world would know it in about five minutes. Columbia may have been the capital of South Carolina but it was still a small town where everyone knew everyone's business. Anyway, I didn't feel right about the whole thing. I kept thinking about what Maisie would say if she knew I went on an overnight with him and the decision was made. Weirdly? Porter understood. He probably went home and thought about it too, deciding it was more trouble than it was worth because taking me to some official event was making a public statement that we were a couple. We weren't quite ready for that.

So time was running out on not having sex but I was holding out for as long as I could. He was not exactly angry about it not happening but I thought his patience was wearing thin. He was probably used to girls throwing themselves at him. I guess that at the end of the day I just didn't want to hop in the sack with him before I felt like there was some real substance to our relationship and that we weren't playing a stupid game of cat and mouse. And maybe this is super old-fashioned, but I didn't want it to be *sex*. I wanted it to be *romantic*. Besides, if I was going to marry him, he wouldn't want a total slut to be the mother of his children, now would he?

I had not forgotten about what Cindy Elder said. I never heard from her again, which suited me just fine. The poor thing. Porter a screamer? Not to me. She must've really done something terrible that mashed all his buttons at once, I thought. Suddenly I remembered what Maisie said to me at the gallery the night I met Porter. It was one of the few times I could remember that she was wrong. He may have been a bratty kid but he wouldn't have gone this far in his career if he wasn't a great guy. Between the Internet, the media, and the government, there was no such thing as personal privacy anymore. Even I knew that. Every time you picked up a *People* magazine there was an article about some famous actor or actress and what some obnoxious reporter found in their garbage cans and used to ruin their reputation, like kiddie porn or something just as disgusting. I mean, I can't think of anything more disgusting but there probably *is* something out there. No, Cindy Elder was just a really sweet girl but a poor thing who didn't know how to handle a powerful man like Porter.

In any case, it was the evening of our second sunset party. Guests were to arrive at seven and be gone by nine. Sunset was to happen around twenty minutes after eight. Funny how they could predict that, wasn't it? Tommy, Mary Beth, and I were at the house prepping everything with Mary Beth's catering friend, Ursula, and Tommy's bartender friend, Ed. I had told a white lie to the Turners, that I had a dentist appointment, and asked could I please leave early. Of course they said yes. It was a ton of work to set up an event for fifty people, as I now knew. But at least we already had glasses, ferns, candles, and a piano that was tuned.

Yesterday, on our Twitter blast we'd said it was a black and white party, meaning guests should be wearing black, white, or a combination of black and white. I liked the idea of theme parties because it would keep it interesting. Tommy said it was only one step above a toga party and Mary Beth agreed with him.

"Oh, come on, y'all," I said. "Do you really think we wouldn't let someone in if they were wearing pink or green?"

Tommy said, "I'd be more worried about who won't show up because they wore the wrong color to work today. You could lose a lot of people."

"Oh, no!" I said. "I didn't think about that!"

"Besides," Mary Beth said, "black and white clothes don't have much to do with my sort of Mexican themed food."

"True," I said. "Maybe we should have margaritas?"

"Tequila is nasty," Mary Beth said. "It really is."

"Yeah, I guess. And margaritas are a sticky mess to clean up," I said.

"So that's settled," Tommy said, like he thought he was entitled to an opinion.

So we sent out a second tweet that forgave all other colors and patterns and mentioned optional south of the border. We'd just have to see what happened.

"We sure do have a lot of chicken salad," Mary Beth said as she began placing tiny sandwiches on a large tray with sprigs of curly parsley all around the edges.

"And a lot of sangria," Ed said. "Y'all might've gone overboard on this one."

"Honey," Mary Beth said, "that wine's so cheap we won't lose too much. Costco was having a major sale on Chilean malbecs." She picked up a handful of minced parsley and sprinkled it all over the tray. "We call this confetti in the food world."

"Confetti," Tommy said deadpan and shook his head.

We had planned for four hors d'oeuvres—chicken salad on white bread, no crusts, thank you very much; pigs in blankets with mustard for dipping because everyone loved them; cheese and fruit of course; and a Mexican shrimp salad in phyllo cups because shrimp was also on sale at Magwood's. We had big bowls of corn chips and small bowls of salsa on two of the tall tables. It seemed like a feast to me. I sure hoped that our *guests* would think they were getting their money's worth.

At six thirty, I double-checked the powder room, hung the ferns, and began lighting tea candles. Ed and Tommy had the bar under control and Mary Beth had the food ready to go. Cars began to arrive and I answered the door, directed people to the portico, collecting their money. One cute guy came in wearing a giant sombrero with his pale blue seersucker suit and his red bow tie. He looked like a Broad Street lawyer gone loco. His date was wearing a Mexican wedding dress with a sprig of red oleander stuck behind her ear.

"Love the hat!" I said.

"Gracias!" He bowed and smiled.

"Olé!" His date threw her arm over her head and snapped her fingers.

"De nada!" I said and thought, Wow, there went all the Spanish I remembered. "Make sure someone takes y'all's picture!"

Tommy was playing some Billy Joel and I was humming along, feeling pretty good about the world. When people stopped arriving, I stashed the cash in my shoebox and went outside. I gave the crowd a solid once-over and decided they were a good group and that there was no harm in what we were doing. The crazy sombrero was traveling from person to person, flapping in the breeze. People were laughing and snapping pics with their phones and peering through the telescope at the ships leaving and entering the harbor. I thought I recognized a few people from our first event and took that as a good sign. As they had the last time, people were out in the yard by the gate to the beach taking more selfies with Fort Sumter in the background. The sun was low, on a slow descent, turning the horizon every color you had ever seen in an evening sky—rich purple, delicious mango, and deep rose, all of it streaked and swirled with a strange gold light. It was just beautiful.

Finally, it began to get dark and I slipped inside the house to check the bathroom, because, ahem, recently the bathroom had been a cause for concern. Thank goodness, it was unoccupied and reasonably clean. I took the wastebasket to empty and on the way to the kitchen I looked out the window. To my surprise Porter's car was pulling into the yard.

I'd be lying if I said my heart didn't skip a beat. I wasn't expecting him! I knew he had to be in Charleston today for some meeting about dredging the Cooper River and some business with the cruise ships and what a nuisance they were with their sooty smoke and how it got all over the houses downtown or something like that. Anyway, Porter was coming up the steps and I was holding a wastebasket so I stuck it on the floor behind the curtains and went to the door.

"Hey!" I said. "How nice to see you!"

"You too! What are all these cars doing here? You having a party without me?"

"Never! Come on in!"

He gave me a kiss on the cheek and walked past me into the house. Then he stood in the center hall, facing the portico and all the people outside. He put his hands on his hips and then in his pockets and then he looked at the floor.

I hadn't thought a thing about what he might think of this excellent adventure until he showed up. He was obviously dumbfounded.

He turned to face me.

"Ashley? If this isn't a party, would you mind telling me just what the hell is going on here? You've got a yard full of German cars and a pile of people here who are probably close to ten years older than you."

He was upset and he didn't like what was happening.

"Well, of course, there's an explanation."

He started back toward the front door.

"Tell you what. It's probably better if I'm not seen being here right now. So I'm going to go down the island to that restaurant—what's it called?"

"Poe's? Dunleavy's? High Thyme or SALT?"

"SALT. That's the one. So when all these people leave, come there to meet me. I'll wait. When do you expect this whatever it is to be over?"

"They'll be gone by nine."

"One would hope. So you'll be there at nine."

"Sure," I said. I kept trying to smile as though nothing was wrong, but I knew in my heart that he was really pissed. "Maybe nine fifteen."

Porter couldn't get out of my house fast enough or get to his car and back it out of my yard fast enough either. Nice, I thought. I knew exactly why he was angry. He was angry because this, that is to say my scheme, might not play well in the media. Did he think CNN was following him around all the time? I mean, he wasn't like Justin Timberlake or something. Was he always this judgmental? Well, my good mood was gone.

I went around the house, picking up dirty glasses and wadded-up napkins. Tommy stopped me. I noticed that his tip jar was jammed with money. Good for him.

"Somebody made out like a bandit tonight," I said.

"I guess. What's wrong with your pretty face?" he said. "Wasn't that Galloway?"

"Yes, it was him but don't tell anybody," I said.

"Oh? Why not?"

"Well, he stopped by to surprise me and when he saw all these people, he completely freaked."

"He's a total asshole," Tommy said.

"Well, think about it from his side. He's in a weird position, you know. And what we're doing isn't exactly legal."

"Oh, for God's sake, Ashley. You're not dealing drugs. You're not running a whorehouse. Nobody's gambling or getting hurt. Right?"

I looked at Tommy and thought, Right! If Porter gave me a hard time, that's exactly what I'd tell him.

"Thanks, Tommy! You're absolutely right!"

"I'm just telling you, this guy's a self-righteous asshole who thinks he's God or something."

"He can be a little arrogant. I'll give you that. But he's really a pretty nice guy. And I guess politicians can't be too careful these days. Remember Sanford?"

"Uh-huh. Okay. Whatever you say."

I looked at Tommy and thought, You know, he's really pretty

sweet to even notice that I didn't seem happy. But honestly, just between us? I think he's jealous.

When everyone left, we cleaned up the house and divided the money. This time we made a little more.

Mary Beth counted up her share. "I think this went great!"

"Here, Tommy." I slid a pile of twenties across the table. "And give this to Ed."

"Thanks! Maybe I'll have a glass of sangria now," Tommy said. "Is there any left?"

"Not much but go on and help yourself," Mary Beth said. "These folks drank like fish! How about you, Ash? Want a glass of El Cheapo sangria?"

"No, thanks. I've got to go meet Porter."

"Oh? I didn't know you had a date with him."

"Well, I didn't. He came by earlier and almost had a breakdown when he saw what we were doing. I think he's upset with me."

"Why don't you get going?" Tommy said. "I can help Mary Beth clean up."

Mary Beth said, "Yeah, well, you've got a pile of money in the bank that you didn't have a month ago. Hey! Why don't you ask him how you'd go about getting a license for a private club so you could serve alcohol? Don't the firemen on this island run the island club? "

"Yes! They sure do! Thanks, Tommy. What are you up to tonight?"

"Like what if you wanted to rent the house for a wedding or something?" Mary Beth said.

We all paused for a moment to consider that.

"Nah," Mary Beth said, "too complicated. Anyhow, Samir's boat is in the harbor and he's invited me to come over to meet some of his friends and sail around."

My face must have looked odd. The minute she told me what she was doing I started getting anxious for her.

"Just be careful, okay?" I said.

"Ashley? I'm a big girl. I know how to take care of myself."

"Okay. I know. It's just that . . ."

"Please, don't worry. If it gets funky, I'll leave."

"Okay. I won't be late."

"Me either."

I looked in her eyes and I wanted to tell her what I knew but I couldn't. It wasn't my business and I wasn't her mother.

"Thanks, y'all!" I said and hurried to the powder room. I ran a brush through my hair and put on some lipstick. Well, I didn't look like Miss America but I looked just fine considering I'd had a very long day—one that wasn't over.

All the way down the island, Mary Beth's plans for the night haunted me. I thought, Sure, if things get too nasty, you can always jump overboard and ride a dolphin back to shore. Better yet, a shark. Good luck, Mary Beth. You're playing with fire.

I pulled into the parking lot of SALT at Station 22 and gave my keys to the parking attendant.

"Will you be dining at SALT tonight?" he said.

"Yes," I said.

SALT had its own parking lot. Apparently they had a bit of trouble with people parking in their spaces and then going somewhere else to eat. I mean, who would do that? There was a big sign that said PARKING FOR PATRONS OF SALT ONLY. You'd have to be as blind as a bat and raised by wolves to park in their lot if you weren't going there. Worse, I could eat there every night of the week and the parking guy would ask me the same question, like he'd never seen me before in his whole life. Okay, I was nervous. I'll admit that. I knew Porter was going to give me total hell and even though I thought I was ready for it, I wasn't looking forward to it.

I looked up and down Middle Street for oncoming cars and when traffic allowed I scooted across, marveling at how many cars there were these days. It never used to be so crowded but lately it seemed like the island might sink from the weight of them. SALT at Station 22 had just been renovated. The building was a classic island cottage complete with porches that gave it a breezy atmosphere that belied its serious kitchen. I thought the new changes to the interior were so pretty, especially the long bar. Mary Beth and I would stop here for a drink once in a while or brunch on Sundays when we had some extra money. Anyway, we came here often enough to know most of the staff.

I climbed the steps to the porch and spotted Porter sitting at a table with Richard Stoney, one of the owners. It was nine fifteen on the nose.

Richard stood up to greet me.

"Miss Waters, I believe?"

"Hey, Richard. How are you?"

"Old but I'm still game." He laughed and kissed my cheek.

He was a big flirt but he didn't really mean anything by it. Well, maybe he did but he was old enough to be my father. Honestly? I think his flirting was just habit. He just liked women and southern guys who were raised right always tried to say something nice.

Porter remained seated, and I could tell immediately from his expression that he wasn't happy. Well, he'd had a little time to marinate in his irritation.

"What's wrong?" I said to him.

"I'll let y'all have your dinner," Richard said. "Sauvignon blanc?"

"Yep. I mean, yes. Thanks!" I said to Richard and sat down across from Porter.

"I'll send that over right away," Richard said and left.

"You're late," Porter said.

"No, I'm not. It's nine fifteen."

"I said nine, Ashley. I hate being kept waiting."

"Porter, *you* said nine. *I* said nine fifteen. It's only fifteen minutes. What's the big deal?"

"Okay, okay," he said and looked across the room to see if he knew anyone. "Let's not quibble over details."

"Okay. You're right. It's not important." My favorite waitress, Trudy, put my glass of wine in front of me and I said, "Thanks!"

"You're welcome! I'll get menus for y'all," she said and walked away.

"She's a sweetheart," I said.

"However," he said in a hushed voice, "we do have to address what was going on at your house."

"I guess so. Okay. What about it?"

The night air was gorgeous on the porch. It seemed a shame to ruin the night over something that had already happened. It wouldn't change anything.

"You don't seem to understand how you've jeopardized my reputation and career. Do you know how it would look in *The State* newspaper? 'Senator Porter Galloway's Girlfriend Caught in Raid!'"

Did he think of me as his girlfriend? Wow! This was pretty fabulous news!

"I'm sorry," I said. I *was* really sorry. I didn't want to jeopardize anything.

"Why in the world would you do something so stupid?"

"Why? I mean, how about none of us make any money? Everyone has a university degree and we all make something like ten dollars an hour because there are no jobs. Porter, I'm an artist and I've never been to Rome or Paris. I want to go so bad I can taste it in my mouth. It's the same with Mary Beth. We have dreams. You know what I'm talking about?"

"Yes, of course I do; but do you think it's right for you to dream at my expense? You're so young! Do you have any idea how hard I've worked and the sacrifices I've made to get this far?"

"Probably a lot?" I thought, He's probably had to shake a million hands and kiss a million butts.

"Yes, ma'am. A lot. Look, Ashley, I really, really like you. I've told you I even think I'm falling in love with you, but there's not a politician left in this whole country who can weather a big scandal, especially a young guy like me."

"I'm sure you're right," I said and thought, Yes, they do. They get reelected all the time. But there was no point in arguing with someone when they were furious. They won't hear you. Maisie taught me that. "I'm sorry, Porter. I really am."

"Just don't let it happen again, okay?"

"Yes."

"Good. Now let's eat something. I'm starving. I can't decide between the scallops and the shrimp. Why don't you get one and I'll get the other? Then we can share."

The verbal spanking was apparently over. His mind had moved on to dinner. Porter liked to order for both of us. I thought it was sweet, even though I wasn't a big fan of scallops.

"Sure. We'd better get our order in. It's getting late."

We ordered and Trudy brought our food out pretty quickly. While we ate, we talked about what it was like to live a politician's life. Maybe he thought he was giving me an orientation.

"Well, your personal life has to be above reproach, for one thing. I'm sure you've heard enough stories about politicians and their zippers to hold you for a while."

"I'll say. But gosh, Porter, no one's perfect." The list of philandering politicians was a long one, to be sure.

"That's right. There's temptation everywhere you look. So it's very stressful. You have to be so careful who you associate with, who *they* associate with, and who *those* people know. It's endless. And being a politician's wife isn't any easier, you know."

"Porter Galloway! Are you asking me to marry you?" I laughed.

He smiled and his dimples showed. God! He was so cute!

"Oh sure, three dates and he proposes. Maybe on our next date, but I just think you should know what you're getting into with me."

"Was Jackie Kennedy afraid of the White House? No, I don't think so."

"Right. Jackie Kennedy?"

"She's my idol."

"Oh, well, look, I'm sure my life looks all glamorous and whatever but let me tell you, it's not. There is tremendous scrutiny and terrible stress. Were you ever a Girl Scout?"

"Yes. Why in the world would . . ."

"People will want to know. And were you a good student?"

"Oh, boy. Yes. I graduated in the top ten percent of my class at the college. Porter, are you playing with me?"

He paused for a moment and took my hand in his.

"No. Ashley? If we go the distance? I'll take you to Paris and Rome. I swear."

"Really?"

"Yes, really. Your innocence is such a beautiful thing to see. I'd love to see your face when you see the great museums. And I understand how impatient you must feel. I really, really do. Ten dollars an hour is tough to live on. But please don't let what happened tonight repeat itself. It just can't happen again."

"Okay," I said, as I thought, Mary Beth is going to kill me because she was already planning another one. Needless to say, I decided not to ask him about getting a license.

When the food arrived, I sort of devoured my half of my entree, which wasn't a big portion. I had not eaten all day and I was feeling a little light-headed. Trudy brought me another glass of wine and I reminded myself to sip it. Porter ate all his scallops and then reached across and took my plate.

"Sorry about the scallops. I forgot to share. It was delicious. We can order you something else if you want. I just want to taste your shrimp."

"No, thanks. I've had plenty."

He pointed to the french fries on my plate that was now his plate.

"Here, have some fries. They're good!"

"No, that's okay," I said and ate them anyway.

"Did y'all save some room for dessert?" Trudy said as she picked up our plates and handed us menus. "We've got homemade donuts with cinnamon vanilla ice cream. And, of course, all the other things on the menu."

"Donuts?" I said, my eyes growing wide.

Porter laughed and said, "Please bring the lady donuts and ice cream. I'll just have coffee."

Later, at home, he walked me to the door. Mary Beth's car wasn't there, which was good and bad. Good because we'd have a little privacy and bad because where was Mary Beth?

"Want to go look at the water?" I said. "Maybe walk on the beach?"

"You know I do! Look at the stars?"

This was code for, *Do you want to go make out like crazy?*

"Would you like something to drink? There might be some wine. Mary Beth caught a sale on some kind of red from Chile, I think."

"I will if you will," he said.

"Maybe a small glass," I said, thinking he wants to get me all liquored up and take advantage of me.

Nonetheless, I hurried to the kitchen and as I thought there might be, several opened bottles of wine were there on the counter, leftover from the party. I filled two goblets halfway and went out to the portico to join him.

"Look at that moon," he said and took a glass from me. "Thanks."

"Amazing," I said. "You know, there *is* something very powerful about the moon. Come on. Let's walk."

We went down the stairs toward the gate that opened to the beach. We kicked off our shoes and left them there. He rolled up the cuffs of his pants.

"Watch your step. People used to think that full moons could turn you into a lunatic but I don't believe that."

He held my elbow until we reached level sand.

"Me either. If you've got the crazies, the moon's not going to make it better or worse. But I love moonlight. When I dream, this is what the lighting is like. Just like this. Light enough to see but dark enough to make you uncertain about the reality around you."

"Really? You remember things like that?"

"Yeah. I mean, yes, I do. It's the details that matter, isn't it?"

"Yes. Sometimes, the details make all the difference."

We walked a short distance down the beach and stood by the edge of the water as the waves washed over our bare feet. He had his arm around my shoulder. This is what it felt like to be falling in love and I knew it then. I was absolutely certain of it.

"Let's go back," he said.

"It's getting late," I said.

When we reached the gate I put my heels back on and he slipped on his loafers. We went up on the portico to finish our wine. He looked at me and I knew the moment had arrived. The balance of the evening would be played by the damsel trying to hang on to her virtue while hoping her roommate would arrive in time to squash the ambitions of her lover. No such luck. He seemed to be completely overcome with the urge to hold me against the railings of the portico while the waves splashed madly against the jetties like in an X-rated version of *Wuthering Heights* or something. It would be seriously nasty to describe what the senator was attempting to do, but it entailed exposing parts of us to the elements and to, I think the most gentle description might be, *go for it*. He didn't seem to care that we were standing. Luckily, I was just tall enough to escape the impact of his intentions.

"Take off your heels," he whispered.

I panicked. "No!" I said.

He stopped, made some personal adjustments in the area in which I had forbidden my eyes to travel, and then to my surprise he pushed me hard by my shoulders, nearly knocking me over.

"You have to stop doing this to me, Ashley." He was pissed.

"What are you talking about?" I said.

"Telling me no."

I was quiet for a moment and then I said, "You shoved me, Porter."

"I did. I'm sorry. But you can't keep on teasing me like this."

"I'm not teasing. I'm just not ready."

"Well, get ready. Or maybe you think this is fun; is that it?"

"Maybe we should say good night," I said. I could feel tears welling up in my eyes.

"Maybe we should say good-bye," he said.

"If that's what you want," I said. *Oh no!*

"I'll call you," he said. He started to leave.

"Porter! Wait!"

He stopped and turned to me.

"What?" he said.

"Look, I just didn't want it to be like this. I wanted it to be romantic, not standing up, outside here on the portico like we were. And I wanted to have, I don't know, I wanted some assurance from you, I guess."

"Assurance of what?" he said.

"I don't know . . . maybe that this wasn't just nothing to you or something like that."

"I don't have the patience for this, Ashley." He was still angry.

"Sorry," I said. With that, traitorous tears began sliding down my face, and my nose began to run.

"Look, either we want the same thing or we don't."

"I want what you want," I said. "I do."

I was practically whispering. I was not listening to my inner voice that was telling me to say good night and send him home. He had shoved me! But at that moment, I was so conflicted and miserable. I didn't want to lose him. I wanted to *marry* him! But then he came back to me, put his arms around me, and held me against him.

"You're so young, Ashley. But you're so damn smart that I keep forgetting just *how* young. I'm sorry too."

"Okay," I said.

"Okay, what?" he said.

"Next time," I said. "We can, you know . . ."

We both knew what I meant.

CHAPTER 12

Liz—Bad News

I could not *believe* my ears! It was Maisie on the telephone, calling me at seven thirty in the morning again. But this time it was for a very different reason.

"Liz, Skipper's had a stroke. Please. Meet me at MUSC."

Maisie was calling me from the hospital. Her voice was low pitched and had almost no inflection. That's how I knew she was frantic with worry.

"Dear God. Don't worry, Mom, I'll be there as fast as I can."

I had just called her Mom, something I had not done in recent memory.

I was stepping out of my shower when the phone rang. My hair was soaking wet. As quickly as I could, I towel dried it and pulled it back in a rubber band. All I could think was, Oh Lord, please let Skipper be all right. I can't handle Maisie by myself! Please help me dress and get out of here as fast as humanly possible. Please keep Maisie calm. Please don't let there be traffic.

Right before eight, I jumped in my car and backed out of our driveway, nearly taking out a couple of tourists and my neighbor who was walking her dog.

"Sorry! Medical emergency!" I hollered out the window.

My neighbor called back, "Let me know if I can do anything!"

I gave her a thumbs-up and turned left onto Church Street. I didn't even know her name much less her phone number. All the way to the Medical University hospital my mind raced. Skipper was supposed to be taking care of Maisie. Was Maisie now going to take care of Skipper? What if he was paralyzed? She couldn't lift him in and out of bed or a wheelchair! She can't be a caretaker! She was too old! Did we now have to hire a driver for the driver?

I called Clayton. No answer. I left a detailed message.

"Clayton? Call me. It's urgent. It's Skipper. He's had a stroke. Dear God, I wish you were home," I said, knowing I sounded uncertain and probably a bit panicked.

He would call back. It was the one thing he was pretty good about. I called my office and Tom answered.

"Wow, you're in early," I said.

"I've got a pile of stuff to get together that I promised David and Steve. What's up?"

"Well, I got bad news just now. My mother's partner has had a stroke and I have to go to MUSC to meet her right now. She's beside herself."

"She's probably scared to death," he said. "Of course you have to go! Call me later on, okay?"

We talked a few more minutes about the very exciting gift from the Karols and from All Air. It was the best news we'd had in a long time.

I called Clayton a second time. Voice mail again! I'd left a message to say it was a matter of life and death. Just how bad did it have to be for him to return my call or to take it in the first place?

I pulled into the front drive of MUSC and left the car with the valet, hurrying into the lobby. I stopped at the information desk. There was an EMS worker there prattling on with the receptionist like it was a chat room instead of an emergency room.

"Excuse me," I said. "I'm here to see Skipper Dempsey, my mother's, uh, driver. He just arrived a little while ago with my mother, Maisie Pringle? He had a stroke."

"That's your mother's *driver*?" the EMS worker said with a big stupid grin that infuriated me immediately.

"Is he okay?" I asked. "Where are they?"

I could see that the receptionist was struggling to maintain a straight face. The EMS worker just looked at the floor and shook his head. I wanted to slap both of them right across their smug little faces. What had Maisie done now?

"He's already in NSICU. Eighth floor. Just ask at the desk."

"Thanks," I said. My face was in flames.

On the elevator ride upstairs, I braced myself. Never mind the antics of my mother, I knew the situation could be dire. Skipper could be near death. He could be so damaged that he might be unable to speak or see or any number of things. I said another prayer for him. I also knew that if Maisie lost Skipper, it would kill her. For as much as I disapproved of Maisie cavorting around with a man fifteen years younger than her, he made her happy, and I was probably getting old.

I asked the nurse at the desk and I was directed to his room. When I got there, I opened the door slowly. Poor Skipper was asleep and hooked up to so many machines and monitors it would make your head spin. And he looked so small in the bed, like he had shriveled up to nothing since the last time I saw him. Maisie, who was seated by his bed, looked up at me. Her hair was disheveled. She wore no makeup. Her eyes were puffy and red. In her hands were wet tissues, wadded into golf-ball-size lumps. She'd been weeping. And she seemed like she had aged twenty years overnight. That was when it dawned on me that Maisie really loved Skipper and she was indeed deeply frightened.

"Hey," I said quietly and gave her a kiss on the cheek. "How's he doing?"

She blew her nose and cleared her throat, putting on the brave face she had earned over the years.

"Well, he's getting this special aspirin treatment—tPA, I think it's called—and it's supposed to help him recover all his faculties. We'll see. And they gave him an ultrasound that showed some more blockages. He's going to have to have carotid artery surgery when he gets stronger."

"Good grief," I said. "What happened? Did he just collapse?"

"I'll say he did! I called 911 as fast as I could. Then I threw all his meds in a Ziploc—I saw a tip about doing that on Dr. Oz's show. Next I threw on some clothes and before I could tie up my sneakers the EMS people were knocking on the door."

"What do you mean? You weren't dressed?"

"What do you think caused the stroke?"

"Oh, my God. Maisie Pringle." Sometimes my mother could be shameless.

"Oh, for heaven's sake, Liz. I'm not dead yet," she said and stood.

As she stood it was clear to me that in her haste she had neglected to don her foundation garments. Another horrific detail. It was no wonder that the EMS worker was snickering. Most likely, he had probably regaled the receptionist with all the details of how he found my mother's lover in the sack. I guessed HIPAA laws didn't apply in this situation. But then, an incident like this would produce more gallows humor over gossip for people like them. The important thing was that Skipper's life had been saved.

"Obviously. Would you like me to go to your house and bring you a nice outfit and your makeup?"

"Oh, Liz! Would you really? That would be so nice if you would. I must look a fright! If he wakes up and sees me like this, he'll have another stroke." Maisie's wit was on the road to recovery.

"I doubt it." I smiled and turned to leave. "Is there anyone we should call?"

"No, I don't think so. He has a sister in Florida but they're estranged. I mean, if something terrible happens, I'd try to find her."

"Of course. Okay then."

"Wait! Do you need a key?"

"No, I have a key to your house right here." I held up my key ring and rattled it. "I'll be back as soon as I can. Did you eat?"

"Are you kidding? I haven't even had my morning coffee."

"Okay, I'll make you a sandwich and I'll pick up coffee."

"I think there's egg salad on the second shelf in a little blue-and-white bowl."

"Got it."

"Liz?"

"What?"

"Thank you. Thanks for everything."

I smiled at her. This was my eighty-year-old mother before me, a woman filled with conflicts and wacky ideas about so many people and things, but she loved Skipper. He was perhaps the first man she had cared about since my father died.

I left the room and felt the *whoosh* of the door behind me. Walking down the hall to the elevator, I told myself then that I needed to look way beyond the unconventional nature of their relationship and focus on the genuine affection they felt for each other. It was hard enough to find somebody to love without worrying about obvious differences. Then my bothersome conscience, that irksome nuisance of a chatterbox in my brain, reminded me that I should apply that nugget of insight to Ivy and James as well.

As I passed through the lobby I noticed the receptionist was a different person. I was glad for that. I'd endured enough embarrassment for one day, but wasn't this a great example of precisely why we shouldn't judge each other? How could one person see inside another person's heart?

As soon as I got to Maisie's house I called Ashley to tell her what had happened. She got very upset.

"Oh, *no*! Is he going to die?"

"I don't think so. And listen, sweetheart, he's in a special ICU for stroke victims and head injuries. He couldn't be in a better place. They have him plugged into so many monitors that they probably know when he hiccups."

"Oh, I just *hate* this! What can I do?"

"Not much. Say a prayer for him and maybe tonight or tomorrow you might want to pay him a short visit. Don't bring flowers. Not allowed."

"Okay. Gosh, Mom. This is terrible."

"Yes, it's not wonderful but I'm just glad Maisie was there. She called 911 and went to the hospital in the ambulance with him."

"How's *she* doing? Is she like completely freaking out?"

"Actually, no. Maisie's a rock, you know."

"She's so great. Tell her I'll see her after work, okay?"

We hung up and I called Ivy, not that he could do anything from the whole way out in San Francisco.

"Ivy?"

"Mom? Is everything okay?"

"Well, not exactly. Skipper has had a stroke. He's in the ICU at MUSC."

"A stroke? How bad?"

"Well, right now they don't seem to think it was too bad. They've got him on a special aspirin drip and I think he's expected to recover pretty well, but he's got to have another surgery."

I told him everything I knew and naturally, he was concerned.

"How's Maisie holding together?"

"Just like you'd hope. Stoic. I'm actually at her house now to get her some things. Then I have to go to the office. We're launching a huge challenge grant with our board. I guess I'll be running Maisie back and forth to the hospital. Of course, your father's in New York. I've called him twice but does he call me back? No. Sorry, that's my problem, not yours."

"Sounds like a lot. Do you want me to come to Charleston for a few days? I can take care of Maisie. I mean, I'd be glad to help out, you know, take the load off you a little?"

"Oh, Ivy, that's so sweet of you, but don't. Listen, for all I know, Skipper will be home in a few days."

"Well, if Dad was there he could help." He paused for a moment. "Mom? Don't you ever wonder why he spends so much time in New York?"

"Yes. Yes, I do. Why? Do you think something is going on?"

"I don't know but I thought the idea when y'all bought that apartment years ago was that you'd spend more time there too."

"Well, I did while Ashley was in college and had her own apartment. But in the beginning of the summer this year two people at work up and left. Another one retired. I just picked up where they left off because there was no money to hire someone to replace them. So now I've got a *real* job on my hands, one that seems like it will never be finished. And to tell you the truth, son, right now it's easier for me with your father gone all week. I don't have to cook and all that."

"Still, I wouldn't leave him alone for too long or too often, Mom. He is a man, you know."

"Hmmm. What are you telling me? Do you think your daddy is on the prowl?"

"I think if I were in your position I'd let him know I was watching."

"But you don't know anything?" He knew something.

"No. You know I'd tell you if I did."

No, he wouldn't.

"All right then. I have to go make Maisie a sandwich and take her some clothes. I just thought you'd want to know about Skipper."

"I do and listen, if you need me, all you have to do is call."

As we hung up I had the thought that as awful as it was that Skipper was so ill there was nothing like an actual near-death experience to pull the family together. Everyone except Clayton. Just what was he doing?

I went in Maisie's closet and pulled out a pair of pants I'd seen her wear recently and the blouse she'd worn with it. When I opened her lingerie drawer, I gasped in shock. It took some digging but I finally found a pair of panties and a bra that didn't look like they belonged to a pole dancer. Didn't she know I would see all this sleazy stuff? Wait! Of course she did and she didn't care! I was holding a red garter belt in one hand and a bra that had actual feathers on it in another and I collapsed on the foot of her bed, laughing hysterically.

"Maisie? Girl? You are too funny!" I said this to the empty room and added, "I think I might need some of what you're smoking!"

My cell phone rang in the other room. Hoping it might be Clayton, I hurried to reach it before it went to voice mail. It was him.

"Hey! What's going on?" he said as nonchalantly as ever.

"Don't you listen to your voice mail?"

"Liz? I've been in back-to-back meetings since eight this morning. Let's not play games here. I saw you called so I'm calling you back."

Did he have to be so brusque? I told him the whole story and he didn't really seem moved by it.

"Well, there's nothing you can do about it, is there?" he said.

"No, but now I get to be Maisie's driver and I've got a full-time job."

"Tell her to take taxis, for God's sake. That's what they're for."

"Oh, for heaven's sake, Clayton, this isn't Manhattan."

"Well, then suit yourself. Anyway, keep me in the loop and give him my best, okay? And Maisie."

"So I guess this conversation is over then?"

"Look, Liz, I've got a conference call in ten minutes. I'll call you later, all right?"

"Sure," I said and pressed the end call button.

Something was definitely going on in New York City with Clayton and when I found out what it was, I knew I wasn't going to like it. God, he was so rude. But I didn't need to think about him then. I needed to tend to my mother. I folded her clothes, took some cosmetics from her bathroom, made the sandwich she wanted, and put it all in a paper bag from the grocery store with a couple of pieces of fruit and some paper napkins. Driving back to the hospital, I stopped at a drive-through Dunkin' Donuts and got two cups of coffee and a dozen donuts for the nurses. Whenever I went to see anyone in the hospital I always took donuts or cookies for the nurse's station. I felt like they were so overworked and underappreciated. And many times they were more knowledgeable than the doctors and therefore more important to the patients than anyone knew. Doctors came and went, but nurses were there, on hand, around the clock. They had their proverbial fingers on the literal pulse of the patients.

I went straight to the eighth floor, thinking I might come back downstairs and get Maisie something to read from the gift shop. I stopped at the desk. There was a nurse there named Dee Dee.

"I brought y'all some donuts," I said to her.

"You did?" She looked at me like I might be lying and said, "Well, that was awfully nice of you! Claudia? Come over here!"

Claudia, who was reading a chart with a grimace, put the chart down and wandered over smiling.

"You got a Boston cream in there?" she said.

"I think so," I said. "Well, y'all enjoy them, okay? I'll just be in Skipper Dempsey's room."

"Okay. We sure will," Dee Dee said, opening the box. "Thanks!"

"Here goes my diet, y'all!" Claudia said. "Hello, hips? Look what I've got for you."

I walked away quietly until I reached Skipper's room. Maisie was right where I had left her, staring at Skipper with a terrible expression of morbidness and trepidation.

"How's he doing?"

"No change," she said.

"Well, here's coffee and your sandwich, and other things are in this bag."

"Thanks," she said and reached out for the coffee.

I put the bag on the floor next to her and took the plastic top off my cup.

"No problem." I took a deep drink. "I love Dunkin' Donuts coffee."

"I like Folger's. They have the best ads."

"Ashley likes Starbucks and I don't have a clue what Ivy likes. Probably something exotic like a West African blend of beans I've never even heard of in my life."

"From a country you've never heard of either," she said. "I guess everyone in this family has to have their own taste buds."

"Sometimes I think my children don't like something only because I do," I said and I thought about how absolutely true that was. It also included Maisie. "Even Clayton."

"Does he know about Skipper?"

"Oh, yes. He sends his best to you and Skipper. And so do Ashley and Ivy. Ashley will probably come by tonight."

"Well, I'm going to stay. I want to be here when the doctors come so I can hear what they've got to say."

"Okay. Do you want me to stay too?"

"No, you go on to your job. If anything changes, I'll call you right away."

"Okay. I can pick you up and take you home after work. If you'd like, we can have dinner too."

"Liz! Please! How could I possibly eat a meal with Skipper lying up here in this infernal place in a room that looks like Dr. Frankenstein's laboratory with all these machines?"

I got up to leave. She was going into martyr mode. I was in no mood to spar with her over anything.

"Right. Well, call me if anything changes, okay? Or if you need anything."

"Oh, Liz, I'm sorry. I'm just all out of sorts."

"Well, you've had an awful shock. Not as bad as Skipper's but bad enough. I'll talk to you later."

I left and thought, One of these days I was going to tell her I was tired of her not being so nice to me. In fact, I was going to tell Clayton too. And maybe Ivy and Ashley. Why not?

When I got to my office, Tom wasn't there. I asked Teesha, our receptionist, where he was.

"Gone out to All Air," she said. "He said he'd be back by three."

"Okay. Good. I'll be in my office."

I decided to call Annie Malcolm to see if she was free for lunch. I was in need of some cheering up; seeing her would definitely do the trick.

"I'd *love* to have lunch with you," she said. "Do you want to meet somewhere?"

"I was thinking about a crazy little place I haven't been to in ages. Ever hear of Martha Lou's Kitchen?"

"No, I don't believe I have," she said. "Where is it?"

I gave her the address and we agreed to meet there within the hour. Martha Lou's was one of those places you'd only know about if you were from Charleston or if a local took you there. The location was in, how do we say this diplomatically, a *reemerging* neighborhood, the building was as pink as a bottle of Pepto-Bismol featuring a sort of fabulous fish mural on the exterior wall, and the interior decor was a little to the left of chic. That said, you'd never put a better piece of fried chicken in your mouth. Martha Lou's was one of the few places left in the culinary world that didn't use flambé or coulis on the menu. It was authentic, down-home, southern fare with no highfalutin nonsense. A holy place, where a meal was a transformative experience. Everyone *in the know* ate at Martha Lou's, including a visiting food critic from the *New York Times*. He loved it, and we all know how persnickety critics can be.

I arrived before Annie and had to wait a few minutes until a table was free. While I waited I read the specials—okra soup, chicken-fried steak, fried medallions of sweet potatoes in maple syrup, black-eyed peas with rice, lima beans, and fried okra. Of course, there was fried chicken, fried fish, pork chops, and sides of red rice, collards, macaroni and cheese, coleslaw, and a choice of hush puppies, biscuits, or corn bread. Couldn't I just have some of each? I was finally seated, sipping on a tall glass of sweet tea with lemon, and Annie walked into the restaurant. I was already thinking about dessert.

Debra, Martha Lou's sweet daughter, brought Annie to my table and handed us menus. I thought then that some of the five-star restaurants in New York could learn a thing or two about hospitality from her. Annie gave me a hug and then slid into the booth opposite me.

"Where am I?" she said, laughing. "This place reminds me of Pam's Kitchen in Seattle. Only locals know about it but the food is off-the-wall good?"

"Yep. You'll see. Debra's mother, Martha Lou, is in the kitchen cooking up a storm every day except Sunday."

"Well, let's do this thing. I'm starving," Annie said.

"Would you like sweet tea?" Debra asked.

"I'd love it," Annie said.

Minutes later we were buttering hot biscuits and waiting for our entrees to arrive.

Annie said, "So David is having lunch with Tom and Steve today."

"Yeah, I know. I thought it would be fun if we got together too. Tom said Michelle wasn't in town or I would've called her too."

"Yes, she's in Boston. She's a doll, isn't she? We see them all the time. So tell me about *yourself*."

"Ask away," I said, wondering when the last time was that anyone wanted to know about me.

"Well, do you have children?"

"I do indeed. My daughter, Ashley, is in her early twenties. Wait, I can show you a picture." I pulled out my phone and scrolled through my photographs until I found one that was very flattering. "Here she is."

"Oh my, Liz! She's a screaming beauty! I can't believe she's still single!"

"They don't get married so young these days, you know? They wait until they can afford to be married and, besides, she's an artist. She paints and she also works in the Turner Gallery on Broad Street. And I think she's dating one of our state senators. Children get to a certain age and then they clam up about what's going on in their social lives."

"Boy, that sure takes the romance out of things, doesn't it?"

"Yes. I think so. But as you know, things have changed since you and I were out there. Women are so much more independent. Ashley has always said she doesn't want to have children until she's thirty," I said.

"Women are having children later and later these days."

"Well, in a way it makes sense, but if you wait too long there are risks."

"Yeah, that you'll be too tired to raise them! So you only have one daughter?"

"No, no. I have a son who we call Ivy—long story. He's older and lives in San Francisco. He and his partner own a men's retail store. He's very hip, I guess is the word."

"I have a gay daughter. I know what you mean."

Hip was the new gay?

"Oh!" I said. "Well, I love my son just as much as I love my daughter. His lifestyle just took some getting used to for us, I guess. I mean, for my husband and me. He's our only son and I think my husband wanted an heir to his dynasty, you know? But what are you going to do; it just is what it is, right?"

"Liz, I'm sure he's a wonderful man with a beautiful heart."

"He is." I showed her a picture of him. "He's really wonderful."

"Very handsome! What more can we ask of our children? My daughter is a Rockefeller Scholar and the chief of neuro-oncology at Columbia Presbyterian in New York. She saves lives every single day. She's my hero!"

"Wonderful! Look, I don't want to sound like I'm whining. Just today Ivy offered to fly home to help me. What a day this has been. I didn't even tell you this but my mother's boyfriend had a stroke this morning and someone has to drive her back and forth to the hospital. Ivy would fly across the whole country just to help drive his grandmother where she needs to go. Ashley would help too, but Ivy's time is more flexible. But really? I think he just wants to be the savior. That's how good he is."

"Good grief! A stroke? Was it serious?"

"Well, in the scheme of things I think no. But they're all serious. And he's young enough to recover if he's lucky."

"How old? Gosh! I'm so nosy!"

"No, it's okay. He's sixty-five. We hired him to be my mother's driver because she loses the car and can't see where she's going but one thing led to another and now they're living together. And did I mention? He owns a llama farm."

"Llamas? And your mother's how old?"

"Just turned eighty. We call her Maisie. She drinks martinis and Skipper drinks Manhattans and she's never been happier. Him either."

I thought she was going to spit her tea across the table. We were both grinning from ear to ear. It really did sound so odd to tell it.

Annie slapped the table. "Oh, my Lord! I love them! Don't you love their spunk? Maisie, huh? Even her name is great!"

"Yeah, well, sometimes her spunk and preciousness can drive you right out of your skull but basically? She's a rare bird and I'm glad she's mine."

"Hang on to her. My mother died twenty years ago. I'd give every piece of jewelry I own to see her again for just one hour."

"Oh, Lord, Annie. I'm sorry. She must've been awfully young."

"She was. Dad was away on business and she was home alone. She choked to death on a glucosamine chondroitin supplement. How stupid is that?"

"Sweet mother! How terrible!"

Debra put our food in front of us. We looked down at our plates and then across the table at each other.

"This is a mortal sin of the first order and I'm going to eat every last crumb," she said.

"Save room for the bread pudding," I said. "It is so good."

We took bites of the fried chicken and moaned. It was that delicious. Then we started to giggle. Annie was the girlfriend I needed. We were going to be the best of friends.

"Well, if I can stop stuffing my face for long enough," she said, "we need to talk about My Sister's House."

I sat back, wiped my mouth with my napkin, and thought about it calmly.

"What is there to say? You know? I just want domestic violence to stop. Right now. I want adults to get it together and act like civilized people. I want men to know it's a felony to terrorize and do physical harm to their wives and children, and that pounding someone with your fists is not how you show someone you love them. I just want it to stop." I thought about all the women who are turned away from shelters because there are no beds, and I thought about the women who were so terrified of their husbands that they feared for their lives and the lives of their children. And I always thought about the women who were too afraid to call the authorities. "It just seems like this problem is almost impossible to solve."

She nodded her head.

"I'm gonna help you, Liz. We're gonna make some noise."

I believed her.

CHAPTER 13

Ashley—Too Much

"The red-eye is killing me. Do you have any Visine?"

I turned around to see my brother standing right there in the Turner Gallery with his hands on his sassy hips. I was so surprised I gasped and then I squealed with delight to see him. He squealed too.

"Ivy!" We threw our arms around each other and hugged tight. "What are you doing here? You look fabulous!"

He was wearing supertight longish pants, a schoolboy blazer with a skinny necktie, and roundish tortoiseshell glasses. He looked adorable.

"I came to help Maisie and to see for myself how Skipper is doing. Can you go out for lunch?"

"Let me just ask!" I started to go find one of the Turners and stopped. "This is the best surprise I've had in years!"

"She said as though she was a world-weary thousand years old . . . ," he said.

Okay, he rolled his eyes but let me tell you, he was plenty glad to know how happy I was to see him. Who wouldn't want someone to be totally excited to see them walk in a room?

Judy was squirreled away in her office, paying bills online. She looked up at me with a tired scowl.

"Sorry to interrupt, Ms. Turner. I can't believe this but my *brother* just showed up!"

"From California?" She took off her reading glasses and smiled such a pretty smile. "How nice!"

"Yes! He wants to take me to lunch. Is that okay?"

"Of course it is. Go! Have fun!"

"Thanks! I'll be back in an hour."

"Honey? Take the day. It's not like you see him that often," she said. "Life's short."

"Really? Thank you! I'll see y'all tomorrow."

"Fine, fine. It's a gorgeous day. By the way, how's your grandmother's friend doing?"

"Skipper? I saw him last night. He's talking and walking—not exactly like before but they say he's making huge progress."

"Well, that's fine. Now shoo! Don't keep your brother waiting!"

"Okay! Thanks!"

Ivy and I walked down Broad Street in the sizzling heat, talking about Skipper and his recovery.

"When I first heard the news, I figured he was a goner," I said. "But apparently this aspirin drip they gave him worked a total miracle."

"They have made all sorts of incredible strides in medicine. Especially the human genome thing."

"And what is that in English, please?"

"Well, as I understand it, they do a map of your whole DNA or something and then they can tell you what you are likely to catch— you know, like cancer or heart disease. Then they can design meds to suit the individual. It's pretty expensive to do all this but if you had a lot of Alzheimer's or something really horrible ran in your family, it might be worth it, you know?"

"I'm twenty-three. I've never done anything to defile my temple except to drink some very cheap white wine. I can't fathom mapping my anything."

"Right. Me either. It was just something I read in the science section of the *San Francisco Chronicle* on the way here. I'm hoping that by the time I get something, they'll know how to cure it."

"Me too."

We were headed to the Blind Tiger to have lunch and we were shown to a table in the courtyard.

"I love this place," he said. "I haven't been here in years. Did you know it used to be a speakeasy?"

"No kidding?"

"Yup. True story. Do they still have fried pickles?"

"Yes," I said. "Right there in the appetizer section. I'll share if you want."

"Perfect."

Despite the heat, it was very comfortable in the shade of the garden. Maybe I was just used to it.

"Are you gonna stay with me this time?"

"No, precious. I'm staying at Maisie's for obvious reasons. But I will see you every minute I can. I just figured our mother needed some pressure taken off. And besides, I need to talk to you about something."

"Rats. Okay. S'up?"

"Well, let's order and then I'll give you the skinny."

So we ordered fried pickles and corn fritters, chicken salad and crab cakes, and, of course, two huge glasses of sweet tea. Ivy hemmed and hawed around, not stuttering exactly but obviously not getting to the point of what he wanted to tell me.

"Is everything okay? I mean, with you and James?"

"Oh, heavens yes! We're like two old men, set in our ways, saving up our strength for better things than work, although sometimes it seems like all we *do* is work."

"Then what are you not telling me that you wanted to tell me?"

"Oh, my dear. I don't know where to begin."

"Okay, process of elimination . . . if this isn't about you or James, is it about Mom or Dad?"

"Yes. It's about Dad."

"Is he sick?"

"No. Well, no more so than most men. In the head, I mean."

I thought for a moment. It was about Ivy's last trip to New York with James. He found something out.

"You never actually came down with that cold, did you?"

"Cold? What cold?"

"Ivy? You're the worst liar on the planet!"

"I never was much good at it. That is true."

"Remember when you went to New York and then we talked later and I asked you what you were hiding from me and you said . . ."

"I think I'm getting a cold?"

"Yes. So Dad's up to no good in New York?"

"I'll say."

"Oh, no." I felt my heart sink and slouched in my seat. I hated to know this. "Poor Mom. Does she know?"

"I don't think so. But I think she's suspicious."

"Because you made her suspicious?"

"Maybe."

"Oh, Ivy. Now what? Give me the details!"

"It all happened so fast. James and I were in the apartment getting ready to go out to meet some friends for cocktails and the doorbell rang. We opened the door and there stood this gorgeous *amazon* of a woman with hair for days, wearing a trench coat, but under it? Honey? She was just as jaybird naked as the day she was born into this world."

"Oh, no! Did you like faint?"

"Almost. But you know my James. He whispered, *Glass? Take a movie.* So Glass starts filming and boom, we've got a short film we could submit at Sundance. This woman says, *Oh sorry, wrong apartment,* which was pretty fast thinking on her part. I said, *Maybe.* James said quietly, *Maybe not.* Anyway, we have the file. And she was not selling Girl Scout cookies, okay?"

"Holy crap. I'm sure she wasn't. What did you do with the film?" I said.

"Well, I have it on my phone. I was debating showing it to Mom and then I thought about showing it to Dad. Then Skipper had his stroke, which gave me an excuse to come home and I thought, you know what? I'm not telling Mom about this. I'm just going to encourage her, in the strongest possible terms, to pay Dad an unannounced visit. I'd like you to back me up on that."

"No problem. Ivy? Don't let Mom see the film. It would just hurt her."

"I agree. But I feel like e-mailing it to Dad, you know, anonymously. What's the *matter* with him?"

"I don't know. It's pretty terrible to run around, and especially for him to do this to Mom. I really don't like this. I mean, she annoys me to death sometimes, but she's faithful to Dad, even if they do bicker. Are you absolutely positive this woman was there to see Dad?"

"Yes. Look, I know Mom annoys you. She annoys me too. So does Dad. They can be pretty thoughtless and rude. That's why we call them the Impossibles!"

"And they are. It's the bickering I hate the most. But on a brighter note? Guess what? I'm in love!"

"What? You are? With who? Gosh, I love these stupid little things."

At that point we were making fast work of the fried pickles and the fritters.

"Porter Galloway. He's a state senator and cute as a bug."

"What? Wait. I think I know that guy. I think. Or maybe not. How old is he?"

"He's thirty-one so he's not so old as all that."

"I think I remember him . . . he was a little badass, if memory serves."

"Well, he's not a badass anymore. We're having dinner tonight."

"Yeah but, thirty-one? That's an eight-year difference!"

"And how old is James? Hmm?"

The waiter took away our appetizer plates, on which there was not one single crumb left, and put my chicken salad and Ivy's crab cakes in front of us.

"Thanks," he said to the waiter. "Okay, okay. I see your point. How long have you been seeing him?"

"Off and on for a while. He picks me up, we go out to dinner, he brings me home, and that's about it."

"That's *it*? Is he gay?"

"Ivy Waters! You can't ask me . . . of course not!"

"Ashley River? Listen to your big bubba. If he's not trying to throw you down, there's something tragically askew in his southern clime."

"Well, let's just say we're traveling on the road, but we're not there yet."

"Fine. Holy Mother McCree, the idea of my baby sister having a love affair is just too weird. Change of subject. How was your last soiree?"

"It was great. I mean, this idea is like the smartest thing ever! No one gets hurt, everyone has a good time, and we make money!"

"How many people showed up?"

"Like fifty. Totally manageable. This chicken salad is delicious."

"The crab cakes are awesome too. So how many more times are you planning to do this? I worry about you."

"Well, I was ready to keep doing it until I had like ten thousand in the bank, but Porter thinks we should stop now."

"Well, he probably doesn't want to see you get into trouble."

"Yes, and it wouldn't be good for him either. In fact, he sort of threw a fit about it."

"Well, he's not wrong, Ash. You are serving alcohol without a license."

"Oh, please. It's not like we were selling drugs or running a whorehouse or something terrible like that."

"I know, I know. Well, it looks like this Porter fellow grew up and turned out all right. At least he's well behaved."

"Oh gosh, yes! Ivy, I know what, why don't you join us for dinner tonight? Then you can see for yourself!"

And maybe I would be able to avoid the bedroom for at least one more date if my big brother was there.

"No, you go have your date. I'm a little anxious to go see what's going on with Maisie and Skipper. Let's pass on dessert and get over to the hospital."

"Okay. Wait, I know! Come meet us for a drink at Cypress! Six thirty? Just one little dwinkie? Please?"

Ivy looked at me, shook his head, and smiled.

"Does anybody ever tell you no and stick to it?" He pushed his plate a few inches away. "If I eat another bite, I'm going to explode. Let's get the check."

We paid the bill and decided to drive my car over to MUSC.

"I'll take you back to your car later," I said, clicking the locks open on my SUV, wondering why I locked it.

We climbed in and it was as hot as the nails in the planks on the bottom floor of Dante's hell.

"Lord! Crank the AC, will you? I do not miss this heat and humidity!"

"I'm sure you don't. It's a beast."

I blasted the air-conditioning as high as I could, not that it made a difference until we were well down the street.

"How many miles do you have on this thing?"

"Half a billion," I said. "But it's a Subaru, therefore I can leave it to my children."

"What kind of a car does the senator drive?"

"Porter? Oh, gosh, it's like an unmarked police car. You know, a gray four-door sedan with no sex appeal whatsoever. What are you driving these days?"

"My same little two-seater Beemer with a stick that's ten years old. But hey, I get my thrills in the hills of San Francisco by reenacting the chase scene from *Bullitt*. Right?"

"I guess. Porter's not a car person. It's something we have in common."

"You're not a car person because you can't afford to be one. But once you become a famous artist, you won't have to drive—you'll be *driven*! Maybe in a big ol' Rolls, powder blue to match your eyes!"

"Wouldn't that be amazing? What a nice dream."

We pulled into the parking lot, got out of the car, and walked across the street.

"You know where you're going, right?" he said.

"I got this one," I said and went straight to the elevators.

As we rode up Ivy said, "Do I need to brace myself for some ghastly scene?"

I giggled. "No, only an old dude in a hospital gown and a bunch of monitors."

We pushed the door open and there was Maisie sitting in the same chair she was in last night. Skipper, who was also sitting up in bed, perked up to see us.

"Well!" Skipper said, and I could see it was a struggle for him to get that one word out of his mouth.

Maisie jumped to her feet, surprised and thrilled to see Ivy.

"Ivy! I *knew* you'd come! I told Liz you would! She's such a party pooper. Oh! I'm so happy you're here!"

She smothered him with kisses and hugs and Ivy was ridiculously happy.

"Thanks, Maisie. You know I couldn't stay away. How are you feeling, Skipper?"

"Pretty good," Skipper said and nodded.

It seemed then like he was speaking naturally and not forcing himself to find his words and I thought that was an awfully big improvement over yesterday. The first day he could barely nod yes or no but my imagination could be exaggerating. All I knew was this— strokes were cruel and mean. It was like Skipper had been made a prisoner and had to fight his way out of his brain to freedom. I was so happy to see him getting better every day.

"I'll just wait outside," I said. "Visitors are limited to two people for ten minutes every hour during whatever the visiting hours are. I might be wrong. Anyway, I'll be outside."

I wasn't sure if Ivy even heard me, but it didn't matter; I was certain Maisie knew the rules and they'd find me. I found a vacant chair in the waiting area and plopped down to check my e-mails. Porter and I were now in the habit of sending each other smiley faces when we were missing each other. It was innocent enough—so innocent, in fact, that if the whole world found out they'd probably sigh, go *AW!*, and think it was sweet. I had two smileys from him so far that day. I mean, maybe there was something in Porter's personality that was a little off but he was being so great to me. I sent him back a smiley with a small x. I couldn't wait to see him that night. He'd been so busy in Columbia all week and my whole world was a little crazy too, with Skipper's stroke and all. We'd have lots to talk about, that was for sure. And I couldn't wait for him to meet Ivy.

It wasn't long before Ivy came out of Skipper's room.

"So here's the plan, Ashley River," Ivy said. "Skipper wants us to go out to his llama farm and check on his animals with the caretaker, not that we know what to check. Then I need you to bring me back here to get my car, and I'll pick up Maisie. Next, I'm going to take her to the grocery store, get us some supper, and bring her back here. Then I'm going to come meet you and *The Senator* for one drink. And last for the night, I'm coming back here to get Maisie and take her home. I called Mom. She knows I'm here."

"What did she say?"

"She said, 'Great!' and that was about all. Apparently, she's all involved in some new project. She hardly had time to talk to me."

Maisie walked out from Skipper's room to say good-bye to us.

"Yeah, she's trying to build a new safe house," I said.

"Too bad the city needs one," Ivy said.

"I'll say," Maisie said. "Men who hurt women and children should be strung up by their you know whats. The ones who shoot them should be shot too."

"Maisie!" I said.

Sometimes my grandmother said the most outrageous things!

"Sorry," Ivy said, "I'm with Maisie on this one."

"You're such a sweet dear," Maisie said to him.

"See you in an hour or two," Ivy said.

"I can take Maisie back and forth tomorrow night," I said to Ivy as we headed up Highway 17 North. "Then you can go see your friends."

"That's great," he said. "Thanks."

"No problem. What's wrong?"

We were quiet for a minute and then Ivy said, "You know, here's the thing that upsets me. One day Skipper was living his life, mixing it up with Maisie, and the next minute he's in an ICU struggling to say his own name. Awful."

"I know. What causes strokes?" I said.

"How the heck would I know?" he said. "Brain tumors? Aneurysms? Head injuries? High blood pressure?"

"Maybe too much salt? Who knows? All I know is I don't want to have one."

"Boy, that's for sure. Take the next right."

"Thanks for the navi. I've only been here like a thousand times! Did Maisie call Joyce to say we were coming?"

"Yes. I think so. Well, she said she would. Jeez, Ash, Skipper is a mess, huh?"

"You should've seen him two days ago. You can't believe how much better he's doing."

I bumped along the dirt road to the cattle gate and Ivy got out of the car to open it. Then I drove through and he closed it behind us.

"Llamas," he said, slamming his door shut.

"I know, but they're hilarious," I said.

We continued on, passing llamas grazing in the fields, until we reached the barn that also had an office, which was where we figured we'd find Joyce Cerato, Skipper's manager. Her car was parked right where it should've been. I thought my car was old but she drove a restored 1947 Ford Sportsman Woodie convertible. It was absolutely gorgeous with highly polished wood on the sides and the trunk, and the color was something called pheasant red. Luggage leather interiors. Someday my Subaru would be a classic. I was counting on it.

I remember she said, "It was the best thing that came out of my first marriage."

And I said something like, "Oh Joyce! You're so awesome! You never got married again?"

And she said, "The right car just never came along." And we laughed like crazy.

Anyway, I liked her a lot. She must've heard us coming because the door of the office opened and she came out to greet us. Ivy was already out of the Subaru inspecting her car.

"Hey! How y'all doing?"

Now, even though she was a little older than us, I had to say Joyce was a beautiful woman. She had naturally curly black hair and the prettiest hazel eyes. She was tall enough to look Skipper's llamas right in the eye and so Zen that when she went into the fields they all gathered around, nuzzling her, as though her pockets were stuffed with treats for them.

"Hey, Joyce!" I said. "You remember my brother, Ivy, don't you?"

"I sure do. How are you?"

"Great, thanks. What a car! I love it!"

"Thanks! You here for a while?" she said.

"Well, actually, I came here because of Skipper."

"That was awfully nice! How's he doing? I'm going to pay him a visit later on after I give the kids their supper and put them away for the night."

She hooked her thumb in the direction of the llamas. They were the kids? Goats, maybe, but llamas? Ivy and I smiled at each other, then at her.

"He's doing really well," I said. "Considering what he's been through."

"He just asked us to take a drive out here and see if you needed anything."

"He did? Now, isn't he the sweetest man alive? He's in a hospital and worrying about me and the farm. That's Skipper, all right. No, I don't need a thing. Maybe two weeks in the south of France but that's all I can think of right now! Or a big bag of fifties? Ha-ha!"

She laughed and we laughed with her. She and Skipper had very similar personalities. They laughed easily and were supermellow.

"Have you ever seen a llama up close?" Joyce said.

"No," Ivy said. "I live in a city. We have little dogs and the occasional cat but no llamas, at least none that I know of."

"Well, they're really sweet. Did you know they hum all the time? Come with me," she said. "I'll introduce you to the one named for your grandmother. She's in that pasture with all the girls."

"You separate the males and females?" I asked.

"Are you kidding? If I didn't, they'd never stop breeding! They're like the sexiest animals in the world! It's Saturday night all the time!"

"Wow," Ivy said. "I did not know that."

"Yeah, nymphos! Ha-ha!"

We followed Joyce over to the fence and she called out.

"Maisie? Maisie? Come on over here, girl!"

One of the llamas lifted her head and looked in our direction, chewing a mouthful of something I imagined was grass.

"She's curious, I guess. I mean, is she curious?" I said.

Maisie the llama began coming toward us.

"Yes, she is. Llamas are very curious and they're good listeners. That's a good girl," Joyce said. "Come on, come say hello!"

"She's a beauty," I said.

"Look at those eyes!" Ivy said and held out the palm of his hand the way you would for a dog to sniff. "Come here, Bette Davis eyes!"

Well, Ivy must have frightened Maisie because she walked right up to the fence, took one look at Ivy's hand, lifted her head, and gave a projectile spit of grass—and who knows what else was in that nasty wad—that landed a direct hit in the center of his face. It reeked.

"Oh, shit!" he screamed.

"Maisie!" Joyce yelled. "Bad girl! Bad girl!"

"I guess she doesn't like Bette Davis," I said.

We rushed Ivy back to the barn and quickly cleaned him up. He was complaining in a nonstop diatribe that had Joyce and me dying laughing. What else was there to tell about our visit to the llama farm? That about covers it. I drove him back downtown to his car.

"See you later!" I said and blew him a kiss.

"Llamas," he said, still completely disgusted. "Foul creatures."

I didn't blame him.

It was around four o'clock when I finally got home to take a shower and get dressed for the evening. Mary Beth was almost out the door; she was working that night. Some Broad Street lawyer was throwing his wife a fiftieth birthday party at Boone Hall Plantation for two hundred people. They had a twelve-piece Motown band coming to play and valet parking and everything you could think of that would make a party spectacular.

"Even fireworks!" she gushed. "Can you imagine somebody loving you so much that he had fireworks for your birthday?"

"No! That's like really amazing. Take pictures!" I said to her as she was leaving. "There might be some good ideas for my wedding!"

"Wedding?" she said. "What wedding?"

"You'll see!"

Porter arrived on time. We were having an early dinner because this was supposed to be the night that we, well, went to the next level in our relationship. At least that's what I was thinking. I was a little nervous for a lot of reasons. But when I saw him I knew he would be completely impossible to resist.

"Gosh! You look so pretty!" he said when I opened the door. "And you smell like spring in the Garden of Eden! Come here, girl!"

It was another weak-in-the-knees kiss and I thought, Oh, Lord!

"Do we really have to go to dinner?" I said, thinking all I wanted to do was, well . . . be a very bad girl. "We could just walk the beach and order pizza?"

"The night's young," he said. "First, I want you fed and then we'll see to your other needs. Besides, it's not even dark."

"Oh? Does it have to be dark? I didn't know that."

"You are too adorable," he said.

"Well, then let's get going because I actually have a surprise for you." I locked the front door of the house and practically skipped down the steps, trying to keep up with him.

"Oh, what's that?"

"Well, my grandmother's boyfriend, Skipper, had a stroke two days ago . . ."

"Your grandmother Maisie who went to school with my grandmother? That's too bad."

"Yes, the same one. Anyway, he's in the hospital and . . ."

"Is he going to make it? I mean, he's got to be pretty elderly."

"Well, not exactly. He's actually younger than she is."

Porter opened my car door and I slipped in. Then he closed it and came around to the driver's side and got in.

"Okay," he said. "How much younger?"

"Fifteen years. He owns a llama farm out in Awendaw."

"A llama farm in Awendaw?" He cleared his throat. "Why?"

"Why Awendaw or why llamas?"

"Llamas. Why in the world would someone want to raise llamas?"

"Well, they're very sweet. Practically domesticated. And their wool has a lot of value. It's much more fun to raise llamas than say, alpacas because *they,* alpacas that is, are not nearly as friendly. Alpacas are more like sheep. Have you never seen a llama? Up close, I mean. They hum to their babies. Isn't that awesome?"

"Do you know how often you say the word *awesome*?" He was

smiling when he said it but I knew it was another lesson in how to be a politician's partner.

"Probably too much. I'll try to be aware of that. Anyway, have you ever seen a llama?"

"No. Can't say I have, except on *Animal Planet*."

"I love that show. So, would you like to?"

"Maybe someday," he said. Porter was smiling. I thought he liked the idea. "So is that your surprise? You're going to take me out in the country to a llama farm?"

"No. Well, I can, any time you want. But my big surprise is that because Skipper had his stroke, my brother, Ivy, flew in from San Francisco to see what he could do to help . . ."

"What kind of a name is Ivy for a man?"

"Well, it's a nickname because he's Clayton Bernard Waters IV, so the IV is like ivy. Anyway, we've all called him that since he was really little."

"I see." He was quiet for a moment. I could almost hear the wheels turning in his head. "And so?"

"So he's going to meet us at Cypress for one drink and then he's got other things to do. I just wanted him to meet you."

"Okay. If it's only for a drink. I really want this night to be ours, you know?"

He seemed slightly miffed but maybe I was imagining things.

"Of course, I know. I feel the same way. But Ivy's hardly ever here and he's just so great. So I thought it was a good idea."

"Then let's park the car and go find your brother who's named for a houseplant." He snickered and I thought it was funny. At least he had a sense of humor.

We pulled into the parking lot and paid the attendant.

"Hello, Mr. Senator? He's also named for a category of very select schools. And for Old Moneybags, our father."

Porter turned off the engine and looked at me. His smile was a little too wide then.

"So I imagine then that your father is a gentleman of means? Not that I googled him or anything."

"Massive. Not Rockefeller or Bill Gates fortunes but enough to live a pretty large life. I guess. But he's pretty frugal so what can I say?"

"And your mother works, doesn't she?"

"Yes. She works for a nonprofit that helps battered women and children."

"That's a nasty can of worms, isn't it?"

"I don't know about that. I mean, I'm sort of proud of what she does."

"Yes, I'm sure in many ways you would be. But I just think it's strange for your father, if he's so successful, to let her be exposed to that kind of thing."

What did he mean? People who were rednecks on drugs? Or that it was too unpleasant a business for a lady of refinement?

"I don't think he thinks of it that way."

"Okay. Well, I'm just glad to know he can pay for the wedding," he said and reached over to tickle me on the inside of my knee, a move that totally creeped me out. He got out of the car and came around to open my door.

However, he had said that magical word—*wedding!* That wasn't my imagination, was it?

We went into Cypress and took the elevator upstairs to the bar. There was Ivy waiting at a small table. He stood up and extended his hand to Porter.

I could tell that Porter hated Ivy on sight. It might have been because of the way he dressed. Ivy was a cutting-edge fashionista. Porter was not. We all ordered a glass of wine. They made pleasant enough conversation about San Francisco and Ivy's business and James and the state of politics in the South and across the nation. We talked about Maisie and how she was living with Skipper and the unfortunate accident with the llama spit. It should've been a home run but the night was lost. What had happened? Why was Porter so uneasy? Ivy, for some reason beyond me, seemed to get an unspoken signal from Porter that he should leave and so he stood to go. His wineglass was still half full.

"Well, this has been very nice, but I have to get back to the hospital to see about Maisie," he said and gave me a kiss on my cheek. "We'll talk in the morning?"

"Of course!" I said. "Love you!"

"Love you too, Ashley River," he said and pressed the elevator button.

I thought, What happened here?

Porter paid the tab and a few minutes later, we went downstairs to dinner. He ordered a bottle of red wine because he said we were sharing chateaubriand and Caesar salad, which in my mind was the perfect dinner. But what was supposed to be an amazing night seemed like it had already gone to hell in a handbasket, as Maisie liked to say.

"Okay," I said. "Are you going to tell me what's wrong?"

"Nothing's wrong, Ashley. What could be wrong?"

"Well, your jaw is twitching, for one thing. It does that when you're nervous."

"Look, I'm a high-profile guy, representing the people of our state. Your family is just a lot more colorful than the folks I'm used to, that's all. Give me a little time to process the llama farm and Maisie and battered women and Ivy, okay?"

"What is there to process?"

"You're kidding, right?"

"No."

He finished the wine in his glass and refilled his and mine before the waiter could get to him.

"Sorry, sir," the waiter said.

"No problem," he said and then turned back to me. "Okay, here's a really superexaggerated example of how I see it. Do you remember the television show called *The Munsters*?"

"I think so, why?"

"Well, everyone is either Frankenstein or a vampire or a were-wolf except for the niece, Marilyn. She's blond and beautiful, just like you. And she doesn't realize she's surrounded by a family that's very odd. That's all."

"And I'm Marilyn?"

"But in a much more subtle way. How's your salad?"

I had not realized that the salad was in front of me. I took a bite and smiled at him. I drained my wineglass and he refilled it. Did he think I came from a family of freaks? Was he trying to tell me that my family flunked the interview? Oh my God! He was going to dump me. He was going to try and sleep with me because I had said we'd go to bed together on this, our next date. Then he was going to dump me! I was supposed to be his wife and eventually the first lady of the United States of America! Now it wasn't going to happen? What were my options? I had to think fast!

While I sliced and ate my roast beef, and he talked about himself and his important political future at the national level while I nodded in agreement, I had this thought. It had probably been a long time since he had sex with someone my age. I was sure I had more stamina than that last one, what was her name? I couldn't remember. Cindy something? And my generation of girls was a lot wilder than his. We'd do anything. The wine was definitely going to my head but I was still feeling pretty damn bold. Whoops! I used a curse word.

I hardly remember the drive back to the island but I remember thinking I was going to have to seduce him because he was acting pretty chilly. I'd get him out on the portico. That portico was my secret weapon. Yeah, baby! I mean, *yes,* baby!

We pulled into my yard and he stopped the car.

"Want to take a look at the moon with me?" I said and thought I sounded like a sultry temptress.

"Ashley? I don't want you to ever think that I would take advantage of a tipsy girl. Do you know what I mean?"

"Porter? I'll let you know when I think you're taking advantage of me and besides, I'm not tipsy."

I could barely make out the details of his face.

"Right. Come on, I'll walk you to your door."

So he helped me out of the car and he walked me up the front steps. I fiddled with the key and finally got the door open.

"Thanks for a nice evening," he said.

"Don't you want to come see the ocean with me?"

"Okay. For one minute. Then you need to go sleep it off, honey chile."

I thought I was being clever to pull him down the hallway to my bedroom instead of out to the portico.

"Stop! Ashley, stop!"

He got pissed and pulled away, which under normal circumstances wouldn't have amounted to anything. But because I was wearing some really high heels I lost my balance and fell, hitting my head on the edge of the door on the way down to the floor. I could feel something warm running down my forehead and I knew I was bleeding.

"If you weren't so aggressive, this wouldn't have happened," he said. "Besides, I make the call on who I sleep with and when it happens. I'm sorry."

I remember him handing me a face cloth and I remember the sound of the front door closing. And I remember that I started to cry.

CHAPTER 14

Liz—Headed North

The hospital moved Skipper to a regular room yesterday, which was much less stressful for him. And it was nicer for us because we could come and go as we pleased. It was late in the afternoon, and I had just arrived at MUSC after a long day at work. A very nice young woman, a speech pathologist, was taking Skipper somewhere for a session. I just caught him for one second on the way out the door, but that brief moment was long enough for him to dazzle me with a clear and coherent greeting with only the smallest hesitation.

"Well, hello, Liz! Are those nice flowers for me?" he said.

I nearly clutched my bosom and gasped like Melanie from Twelve Oaks. But of course I didn't. Still, his words were a wonderful surprise.

"Yes, they are! How are you feeling today, Skipper?"

"Right as rain," he said and smiled.

"Let's go, Mr. Dempsey," the pathologist said.

"Later!" he said and shot me a peace sign.

He left, walking with just the support of her arm. I was left to talk about Skipper's recovery with Maisie and Ivy, who had probably been there all afternoon.

"Hello, hello!" I gave them both a peck on the cheek. "This room is so much more cheerful," I said, putting the vase of flowers I had brought on his chest of drawers. "At least now he doesn't have to feel like his life is hanging by a thread."

"Hard to be cheery in an ICU anyway," Ivy said. "How was your day?"

"Just fine. My Sister's House got a gift from All Air today for two hundred and fifty thousand dollars. Not a bad day's work. Thanks for asking. How are you, Maisie?"

"Fine, thank you. Here's the *really* good news. I think his doctors are going to release him tomorrow," Maisie said. "Then he's going to have to endure a lot of physical therapy until he's strong enough to have the carotid artery surgery. What an ordeal he's facing!"

Did Maisie say congratulations? No.

"Like he hasn't been through enough?" Ivy said. "And so have you! That's why I'm here, Maisie. I can drive him wherever he needs to go. And you too. Ivy's Limo, at your service! And I can stay for as long as you can stand me."

"*Stand* you? I *adore* you!" Maisie said.

"That's awfully nice of you, Ivy. You're so dear!" I said.

"You're just finding that out?" Maisie said. "Humph! I've known that for years!"

"Now, now, girls, don't fight over me," Ivy said and laughed. "So, Mom? I met Ashley and Porter Galloway last night for a drink."

Maisie could be so persnickety.

"Oh? I didn't realize she was seeing him for sure."

"Oh, yeah," Ivy said. "I think she's pretty sweet on him."

"Oh, dear. What did you think of him?" I asked. I could tell from his face that it didn't go well.

"He wouldn't be my first pick for a brother-in-law," Ivy said. "That's for *sure*."

"He's nothing but a scallywag," Maisie said.

"And it was pretty clear that I made him uncomfortable," Ivy said.

"Why?" Maisie said.

"Please, Maisie," I said. "We don't have to spell it out, do we, Ivy?"

"No. First, I wasn't wearing a seersucker suit and, second, I'm probably the first gay man he's ever engaged in conversation. He was a nervous wreck, like it's contagious or something."

"Son? Don't worry about him. He'll be out of her life before you know it."

"One can only hope," Maisie said. "I don't like him for our Ashley."

"Me either," Ivy said. "Too conservative for my taste."

"Hmm. I'm sure he'd be crushed if he knew," I said.

"Probably not," Ivy said. "Have you heard from Dad?"

"Not really. We've only had the briefest conversation earlier this week about Skipper. You know, when the stroke happened."

Ivy and Maisie looked at each other with the strangest expression and I knew I was about to be on the receiving end of news I didn't want to hear.

"Don't y'all have a habit of calling each other at least once a day or something?" Maisie said.

What business was that of hers?

"James and I totally have a bed check every night."

This conversation had been rehearsed without me. Obviously.

"Why would we?" I said.

"Because if he's not obliged to check in with his wife, it makes it easy to forget he's *got* a wife."

"Mom, all I'm saying is there might be too much slack in his leash," Ivy said.

"I really don't want to discuss my marriage with my mother and my son," I said. "It's completely inappropriate."

"Well, you can't live your whole life in a state of denial," Maisie said. "It just isn't a mentally healthy thing to do."

"*Denial?*" I said to her. "You're going to lecture *me* about denial? You're kidding, right?" I could feel my temperature rising.

Maisie didn't take the bait. She said, "I'm sure I don't know what you mean by that. I'm just suggesting that you might like to take a few days and go see what's going on in New York. That's all."

"I couldn't possibly go now. We're just in the middle of a new campaign at work and Tom needs me. Besides, Clayton will be home tomorrow."

"Well, then, next week or the next," Ivy said. "I agree with Maisie and I just think you should slip into Manhattan unannounced and drop in on Dad's life to see what he's up to these days."

"Unless *work* matters more than your marriage," Maisie said.

"Yes," Ivy said. "That's completely your call."

I couldn't expect Ivy to understand how critical my work was but it would've been nice if Maisie acknowledged I made a real contribution toward making the world a better place for a helluva lot of terrified people with nowhere to turn.

"I'll think about it," I said. "Well, I've got to get moving." *Because this conversation had gone on long enough.* I stood up and went to the door and stopped, turning to face them. "Listen, I know y'all mean well. This is just so personal . . ."

"It's okay, Mom."

"It's because we care about you, Liz. Just think about it, all right?"

Why did I feel like every time my mother said something like that that she was being disingenuous? She just sucked the soul out of me. And why did it *not* bother me that Ivy was a partner to this sudden gush of marital advice?

"Sure. I will."

When I stopped at Ted's Butcher Block and picked up steaks to cook on the grill for Clayton's supper, it occurred to me that we probably ate more red meat than we should. But Clayton loved his steak and truthfully, I did too. And, when he came in from running around Manhattan all week, the last thing he wanted to do was go out to a restaurant. He was exhausted. Truth? So was I. So on Fridays we usually stayed at home and I'd prepare something simple. We went out on Saturdays. And he usually left for New York on Sunday evening. Sometimes if we had something we *had* to do that night, he'd leave at the crack of dawn on Monday. But it was odd that he was coming home consistently on Fridays and had been for months. In the dead of summer he always came home on Thursdays. At least he used to. That gave me a serious moment of pause.

After the butcher's, I zoomed over to Whole Foods in Mount Pleasant for everything else I needed. Somewhere between the parking lot of MUSC and the parking lot of the grocery store, I began to hatch a plan. I was going to organize a dinner for him that would be so gorgeous it would astound him. And while he was busy drinking too much wine and overeating, I would look for any kind of nuance that might betray his secret, if he was keeping one that is.

On further reflection, I seriously doubted that Clayton was having an affair. His hair was thinning on his flaky scalp, he had a paunch and bad posture that came from too many client lunches and too much time at a desk, and his teeth were yellowed. Bleaching teeth would never occur to someone like Clayton. He would say it wasn't manly. He squinted, he wore his reading glasses on top of his head, and he rarely wore anything other than a dark suit, a white shirt, and some kind of silk tie. He always had coffee breath and I had to remind him to clip his fingernails and his nose hairs. So let's be honest about his pretty profile. Who would want him besides me? I mean, listen, I knew Clayton could be an obnoxious ass but he was *my* ass. I reassured myself again that Clayton wasn't fooling around. It just wasn't his style. When he would tell me about one of his friends stepping out on his wife, he'd say, *Can you believe him?* Then he'd call the guy a sleazy bastard. He knew a lot of sleazy bastards. Was it possible that my Clayton had become one too? No way.

At Whole Foods, after I picked up three bunches of flowers and everything I needed for a great salad, I worked my way through the cheese section, choosing two small pieces. They had so many choices it was always a bit of a conundrum to decide, but finally I chose a soft wedge with blue veins that was encrusted with crushed walnuts and a small block of an aged Gruyère that I'd serve with a special fig jam from some exotic place like Madagascar or Pasadena. They grew figs everywhere these days. Then I debated the merits of smoked Pacific wild salmon versus gravlax marinated in ginger and green tea and decided on the gravlax. More interesting and refreshing. By the time I got to the checkout counter with a fresh roasted chicken for my own dinner that night, I had convinced myself that Clayton would do no such thing. An affair was a tawdry business and beneath his dignity.

Later on at home though, while I dined alone with my prewashed lettuce, sliced chicken, and a healthy shot of vodka over tons of ice to console my restless mind, I was deep in thought. I was unnerved by Maisie's and Ivy's opinions, and I began to doubt my convictions. I told myself that I should listen to them. No matter how they acted, especially when they didn't have their behavior in check, I knew they cared about me. And we were a family. A small but interesting collection of somewhat peculiar characters, but a family all the same.

They would not make me suspicious unless they had a good reason. And most of all, why would Ivy take the incredible step of telling his own mother that she had better go see what his father was up to if he didn't already know something? Something that he had already told Maisie. That would explain why they confronted me together. I poured a small shot of vodka over a ton of fresh ice. The fact that he went to Maisie first and not me was very annoying and troubling. Why had he done that? Well, the obvious answer was that he thought he should. This running to Maisie business was long overdue for an intervention. It had to stop.

Was there anything about Clayton that really set him apart from other men? Was he a candidate for sainthood? Hardly. If his friends could fall victim to their fading prowess at a certain time in their lives, couldn't he? And when was the last time we had a night of big-time ooh la la? Ages. Oh, Lord, I thought, not Clayton too.

Anything was possible, so the next day I did what any normal red-blooded woman would do. First, I called Tom and told him I needed the day off from work for personal reasons.

"No problem," he said. "Vicki and I are entertaining the Malcolms tonight and I thought we might try to find another date with the Karols over the next two weeks."

"I'll make the call first thing Monday," I said. "Thanks, Tom. Give my best to Annie and David. And Vicki, of course."

Next, I begged my hairdresser to squeeze me in so I had my hair done and my nails too. Later in the afternoon, I showered, shaved my legs, creamed my skin, and sprayed perfume up one side and down the other. Then I put on a pretty summer dress and sandals. I turned on some music we both loved and arranged the flowers in a low bowl for the dining room table. I put one flower in a bud vase in his bathroom along with a fresh bar of his favorite soap. As a final touch, I turned down the bed and put on low lights. All this should give him the message that, yes, his wife had expectations.

The phone rang. It was Maisie.

"So we brought Skipper home. I thought you'd like to know." She was irked. Well, two could play that game.

"Okay, good. Can I do anything?" I had forgotten to call them and it was nearly five o'clock. So kill me.

"No, thank you. *Ivy and I* have it all under control and *Ashley* is bringing dinner."

"Well, that's lovely. Tell me, how is Skipper doing?"

She began to calm down. Skipper's well-being was all that mattered to her then (besides the number of her minions) and the relief in her voice was nearly palpable.

"Talking like mad with some hesitation here and there and walking just fine."

"That is such wonderful news."

"I haven't prayed so hard since, well, when Juliet . . ."

"Me too, Maisie. It just wasn't Skipper's time, I guess."

"Liz, it certainly wasn't Juliet's time either. You *know* that."

I didn't say anything for a moment or two and then I cleared my throat and spoke.

"Okay. Well, if I can do anything, you'll call me, won't you?"

"Yes, I will. Clayton's coming in tonight?"

"Yes, and I've not forgotten what you said. I want to see how the weekend goes."

"Fair enough. All right then . . ."

We hung up. *Fair enough?* What an odd comment. Did she really believe because she was suspicious of Clayton that I *had* to be suspicious of him too? Poor meddling Maisie. But this was more about Juliet than some diabolical need to control me. Juliet's death was a terrible dark cloud that colored her every day, and her rage over losing her was always right there. She'd spent all her life since Juliet's death looking for signposts that bore witness to her loss, and she pointed them out at every opportunity. And she laid the guilt on me with a thick impasto. Why did I survive and not Juliet? I tried to take it in stride. Some days were easier than others.

Clayton arrived around seven thirty. I heard the front door close in his signature style—the creak of it opening wide and three beats later, a gentle closure.

"I'm home!" he called out.

I put my best smile on my face and went out to the foyer to greet him. I was going to get to the bottom of this nonsense.

"Hi, sweetheart!" I said, as though we were newlyweds. "How was your trip?"

"Uh, you look nice," he said and glanced toward the dining room. "We having company tonight?"

"No, just us. Would you like a glass of wine? I just opened a French pinot."

He looked at me so strangely.

"Um, sure. Let me just put my things down and wash my hands," he said.

"Great! I'll meet you in the kitchen."

On the kitchen counter, I had already arranged a platter of the gravlax with toast points and wedges of lemon, and the cheeses were on a wooden cutting board with slices of apple and some crackers. The open bottle of wine stood there too, next to two goblets. I could smell the potatoes as they baked in the oven. The colorful salad glistened with olive oil and lemon juice and the steaks were seasoned, ready to sear to a juicy medium rare on my grill pan. I poured a glass of wine for him and vodka over ice for myself. I squeezed two wedges of lime into my glass with a spritz of tonic water.

"No point in wasting too much tonic," I said to the room.

Clayton ambled into the kitchen with the day's newspaper tucked under his arm and surveyed the counter. He picked up his glass and tossed the newspaper into the recycling bin.

"Well, this is very nice. What's the occasion? I didn't forget a birthday or an anniversary, did I?"

"Noooo! I just thought we should have a romantic dinner and see where the night leads us. What do you think about that?"

"I think . . . I think, um . . ." He paused for a very long moment. "Why not? Cheers!"

Then I saw something in his eyes, something he was trying to mask. Some sorrow, some disappointment. The soft skin around his eyes crinkled more deeply than usual as he forced a smile. Maybe he was just very tired. I could feel him giving me credit for trying to make the evening intimate and special, and I knew also that he would prove to be a reluctant partner.

"Cheers! Welcome home." I raised my glass in a toast and he immediately did the same.

"Thanks. How's Skipper?"

"It's unbelievable how well he's doing and guess what? Ivy flew in to help! Isn't that wonderful?"

"Really? Yes! That's great. Well, maybe we should try to have a family dinner tomorrow night. What do you think?"

I wanted to say, *Why, because the last one went so well?* But I didn't. I just said that I would call Ashley and Ivy and ask them what they wanted to do.

The conversation proceeded very nicely. We were very civilized with each other and very polite, but there was no tangible spark of anything sensual. So I didn't object when he left the dinner table to open another bottle of wine. What was the point? We weren't driving anywhere anyway. And the night had all but dissolved into a puddle of disinterest. At least on his part.

Let me tell you something you probably already know. It's that second cork that should remain in the neck of the bottle. You can liberate one, but two bottles of wine for two people is one bottle too many. There was a reason the French bottled wine the way they did. Two and a half glasses was plenty of wine for two people to consume with dinner. But that's not how it went with us. I had a cocktail or two. He had a glass of wine and then maybe another. By the time we got to the table, he had drunk most of the bottle and there was not much left for me. I didn't want vodka with steak. So, pretending to be the gentleman, when in actuality he was feeding his habit of numbing himself with alcohol, he opened another bottle. Needless to say, the plans I had for the bedroom were a dismal failure.

Saturday morning I got up more determined than ever to discover what was going on with Clayton and to pull my family back together. So I called Ivy and Ashley and asked them to come to dinner at seven that night. They didn't exactly jump at the invitation but they knew they couldn't refuse, especially when I asked them to help me with their father.

"And, Ivy? Would you do a small favor for me?"

"Sure. What?"

"Would you say something nice in front of your father about the food tonight? Or about how I look?"

"Sure! Why's that?"

"Because before I fly to New York and expose his secret life, I want him to know I'm still alive and viable. And I want him to see what he's at risk to lose."

"So you do think he's up to something?"

"Yes. For no particular reason but I do."

"No problem. Did you invite Maisie?"

"No. Frankly, I was just thinking it would be nice to have my children around the table without the running critique of my mother. But let's keep that ugly detail between us, all right?"

"Sure," he said. "I understand. She would probably say no anyway. She's mooning over Skipper and fussing around trying to anticipate his needs like a love bug. She's not ready to leave him home alone."

"Okay, good, then seven?"

"I'll be there."

I called Ashley.

"Ashley? Do you have plans tonight?"

"Nope. What's going on?"

"Well, I'd like you to come to dinner with Ivy and your father and me."

"Sure. Where're y'all going?"

"Actually, I'm cooking at your childhood home on Church Street. Remember that place?"

She didn't even groan but I knew I had to stop being so sarcastic with my children. It wasn't nice.

"You're cooking? Wow! Mom, you haven't cooked for us since like, Easter!"

I was quiet for a moment. On my father's grave, she was right.

"Oh! My! Word! You're right! Well, I'm inspired to bring my family together and I'm going to do it, starting tonight!"

"What are you making?"

I hadn't gotten that far in the thought process.

"I have no earthly idea *what* to cook!" I laughed at myself then.

"Make baked ziti! Please? Remember how much we loved baked ziti when Ivy and I were little?"

"Okay, I will! With garlic bread and salad and peaches and ice cream!"

"Mom, that sounds amazing. I'll be there as soon as I get out of work."

"Just one thing I need you to do for me, okay?"

"Sure, what?"

I told her I wanted the night to be fun for all of us. I wanted laughter and teasing—but only if the teasing was kindly delivered—and I wanted stories of their best memories to be told across the table.

"Why in the world?"

"Let's just say Mom's feeling nostalgic, okay? How's that?"

"It's okay with me. Did you ask Maisie to come?"

"No, she's got her hands full with Skipper. I'll give Ivy something to take home for her."

That sounded reasonable to her. There was no need to tell her that Maisie was on my naughty list at the moment. As soon as Maisie realized that she was, she'd do something nice or she'd say something nice to be in my good graces again. Maisie was the queen of passive-aggressive behavior.

It was one more trip to the grocery store and the butcher and I surprised myself by remembering how to cook baked ziti. It smelled like my children's childhood. The bread was in the small oven and I had prepared a big board of antipasto with olives and cheeses and dried meats with another loaf of bread for dipping in two different flavored olive oils. Clayton opened a bottle of a pretty good Barolo and he even made a vodka martini for me. Ivy and Ashley had yet to arrive.

"Dirty, right?" he said as though he couldn't remember.

"Yes, I like it dirty," I said and wiggled my eyebrows at him.

"What's come over you, Liz?"

He didn't even grin. True, he was a cool character but in the old days he would've grabbed me and made a big silly smacking noise on my neck or something like that.

Maybe he had convinced himself that I didn't want him anymore and therefore he could justify an affair? Was that how the business of infidelity worked?

"What's come over me? Clayton? Are we ever going to have sex again?"

"Of course we are. Don't be ridiculous."

"Well, then, one of us has to make a move, right? Send a signal?"

"And you're thinking tonight might be good?"

"Why not?"

"Well, let's see what we can do about that." He finally smiled at me. At least he smiled at me.

The front door opened and closed and my heart lightened to hear the voices of our adult children fill the air. When they reached the kitchen, they gave me a kiss, acknowledged their father with hugs, and poured themselves glasses of wine.

"Wow! Mom! This looks delicious! I don't know where to start!" Ivy said and picked up a little chunk of aged Parmesan marinating in olive oil and cracked pepper. He popped it in his mouth. "Like butta!" Then he went to work on the prosciutto, winding a slice around a little ball of mozzarella. "Here, Pop!"

Clayton put it in his mouth and said, "This is good. Quite good. Actually."

"Quit hogging the whole board!" Ashley said, reaching over Ivy for a piece.

"Oh, please," he said. "Wait! Mom? Do I smell *baked ziti?*"

Ivy came around the island and took an oven mitt from the counter, opening the larger oven, peering inside.

"Yes. I made it for y'all but especially for you."

Ivy's sass dissolved right in front of me.

"It was always my favorite."

"I know that."

"I love you, Mom. You know that too, don't you?"

"Ivy? I love you with all my heart. I do. And you too, Ashley. And you too, Clayton."

"What's happened, Liz?" Clayton said.

Everyone stopped talking.

"I'm not sure," I said. "I guess I just want us to all be how we used to be. With each other, I mean. Somewhere along the line there was a shift and I want to make things right."

"I don't know about a shift, but I think this is going to be a wonderful night!" Ashley said, pushing her hair back from her face.

That's when I saw the scab on her forehead that went into her hairline.

"What happened to you?" I asked.

"Oh, you know those black high heels I love so much?"

"Yes," I said.

"Well, they're dangerous little monsters. I was out with Porter and I slipped and fell. Unfortunately, there was a corner of a wall right there waiting for me and I slammed into it before I landed on the ground."

I didn't like the story. It didn't ring right. Ashley had never fallen like that. She was a gazelle.

"Why didn't he catch you?"

"Because he was like ten feet away. It all happened pretty fast."

I went over and gave it a closer look. It wasn't so terrible after all.

"Stupid shoes," I said. "Let's get you a safer pair on Monday."

Clayton popped up with uncharacteristic generosity saying, "Buy two pairs and give me the bill."

"Thanks, Dad!" Ashley said. "I should hit the wall more often!"

Well, then the lighthearted mood was restored and we went on to have dinner. As I had asked them to, Ashley and Ivy told stories and because they were talking nonstop, Clayton was eating and drinking nonstop. He opened a third bottle and he was the only one still drinking wine. By the time I put the peaches and ice cream on the table, Clayton was fast asleep on the sofa.

"What happened?" I said to Ivy and Ashley.

"I don't know," Ivy said. "He just got up and went over there. Next thing I saw was him kicking off his loafers. But he was smiling."

"Well, at least he knows better than to put his shoes on my sofa," I said. "I'd kill him."

"He's probably just really pooped," Ashley said.

"You think?" Ivy said.

"Honey? Your daddy's hammered," I said. "This is not good."

Ivy and Ashley helped me clean the kitchen and I gave them each a large plastic container of ziti to take home. It had been a truly wonderful night, except for Clayton slipping into the deep end of the vineyard. When the kids left, we all hugged and kissed but Clayton disappeared to the bedroom to snore like every hog in hell and without a word to anyone. It was all right. I was going to New York.

I almost didn't make my flight on Tuesday because there was another tropical storm becoming a hurricane and heading our way. For the record, I flew commercial. If it became a hurricane, they were going to call it Lorenzo. We were already up to the *L*s. That's how many storms we'd had over the season. Fortunately, it turned out to sea.

Anyway, I was going to put an end to all the suspicion about Clayton and then we'd see what we would see. Either he was having an affair or he wasn't. It was pretty simple. I would just tell him I came to take in an exhibit at the Frick I'd heard all about. Everyone who read the arts section of the newspapers knew that Vermeer's *Girl with a Pearl Earring* was there for a short period of time. And I packed a pretty nightgown hoping to pick up where our good intentions left off. We landed at La Guardia and I hopped in a taxi, telling the driver to take me straight to our apartment building.

Our doorman, Eduardo, was very surprised to see me.

"Mrs. Waters! What a nice surprise! I haven't seen you in a long time."

"Thanks, Eduardo," I said, when he took my tote bag. "It's nice to see you too. How's the family?"

"You know my daughter got into Princeton? We're very proud of her."

"Wonderful! She must be very smart like her father!"

"Like her mother, Mrs. Waters. Like her mother."

He held the elevator door for me and I stepped inside.

"Do you know if Mr. Waters is at home?" I asked.

Even though Eduardo was dark skinned, he blushed deeply.

"No, ma'am. I don't know." He was staring at the floor.

"Okay, thanks."

He wasn't getting involved.

The elevator landed at the second floor and I got out. I fished around in my purse for my keys and found them. When I opened the door of our co-op, my heart sank. It was lifeless. Going from room to room only confirmed my worst suspicions. Clayton wasn't sleeping here. His clothes were in the closet and there was some recent mail tossed on the kitchen counter, but there wasn't a drop of anything in the refrigerator and not a piece of bread in the drawer. The bed was freshly made, the bathroom dry as a bone. But there was vodka in the freezer and bottled water in the refrigerator. I'd call out for Chinese or Thai food and I'd live until the morning.

The only other sign of life was some dirty clothes that were thrown on the bottom of his closet, shirts and socks and underwear, leading me to decide that he slept elsewhere and came home to change before going to the office.

I'd be in the lobby at seven in the morning to greet him.

Don't ask how I got through the night without calling his cell and screaming my head off but I did. And at seven A.M. I repacked my things, put my bag in the bedroom closet, and went downstairs. I sat on the lobby couch reading the *New York Times*, waiting like a black widow spider. At seven fifteen my patience was rewarded. The elevator door opened and out came my old friend, actually archnemesis, Sophia Bacco, followed by Clayton. They were engaged in a vigorous argument and didn't notice me at first. I stood up. Eduardo wisely headed for the sidewalk.

"Sophia? Is that you with my husband so early in the morning?"

"Liz! What are you doing here?"

"Hello, Clayton," I said.

"Yes! And for God's sake, will you please take him home? He's hounding after me like a schoolboy!"

"You always were a whore," I said, evenly.

"And you could never keep a man," she said.

I lowered my voice to a whisper. "Fuck you, Sophia, and get out of my sight before I scratch your nasty Botox and Restylane face off and feed it to the dogs!"

Everyone was frozen in place. This was not the kind of building where you used an obscenity in the lobby.

"Not *my* face, you won't." She all but ran from the lobby to the street.

"I never liked her. So, Clayton? What do you have to say for yourself?"

He began to weep.

"She dumped me," he said, covering his eyes with his hand, "for an Argentinean polo player. Some asshole named Armando. He doesn't even weigh one hundred and twenty pounds! He's only five four! I loved her, Liz. I did."

He *loved* her?

"Clayton?" I said as quietly as I could, given the gravity of the moment. "Your sorry ass had better hire a lawyer. I'm going back to Charleston."

CHAPTER 15

Clayton—I Blew It, Didn't I?

What have I done? I can't eat. I can't sleep. And I can't stop crying. I've never done anything so stupid and reckless in my entire life. Sophia is nothing but a self-centered, and I hate the word but she is one, bitch. I mean, she *really* is! There's a reason why people use those words and they fit her to a tee. Why couldn't I see it from day one? I don't know. But when I was locked out on the terrace I got an inkling of what was to come. I should have stopped the affair right then but I couldn't. I'm so sorry I didn't.

I *fell* for her like a starstruck kid. I was so foolish! No, I *am* a fool! Liz must have known something really bad was going on to show up at the apartment without telling me she was coming. And now I had blown it with her too.

There was only one way she could have found out. Ivy. Ivy was at the bottom of this! He must have told Liz about Sophia! Or maybe he showed her the picture James took! Oh my God! Whatever. He had definitely done something big enough to prompt an unannounced trip to New York. That film was evidence they could use against me in court! What was I going to do? I might just fly out to California and wring his skinny neck. That's what.

I mean last weekend? There was Liz trying to make everything right by having the kids over and making an incredible meal. It was like old times. Family dinner. She had flowers on the table and everything. And what did I do? I drank myself into a stupor and then gave her nothing but a *thanks for a great night*. She didn't even complain. At least she had some grace. If I'd had any at all, I wouldn't have gotten bombed and I would've taken her to the bedroom and done what a good husband does. And Sunday night I just left as though everything was fine between us when we both knew it wasn't.

I'd been avoiding her for months and she knew it. And she also knew, because women are so damn smart, that if we resumed our intimate life, and that if there *was* something going on with me and another woman, it would be more difficult emotionally and psychologically to continue the affair. But what did I do? I avoided my wife. I had been actively choosing another woman over my wife for months. I just couldn't help it. I was just like a drug addict, hopelessly addicted to Sophia.

There *was* a time, right in the beginning of our affair, when I really believed that I was in love with Sophia. Maybe at one point I even tried to see myself married to her. But the truth? Recently it had become clear that she'd lost interest and that she was trying to figure out how to end it. Even though she said it was an accident, I should've taken the hint when she locked me out on the terrace. In an ideal situation in Sophia's mind, I'm sure she hoped I'd just go back to Liz and no one would get hurt. But I couldn't give her up! I just couldn't. You see here was the thing. Sophia was forbidden fruit. She was the only thing I ever wanted that I couldn't have. And I thought I was dead in love with her. Now I wished I was dead.

My life was in ruins and I had no one to blame but myself.

Things started to unravel with Sophia about the time James and his Glass took the pictures or the movie or whatever he did. I could trace it back to then. I came back to the city and Sophia told me what happened. That was definitely the moment Sophia began to lose interest. I could see it in her face. She was in it for the game, but she didn't want to wind up in the tabloids. It wasn't like she was carrying the weight of celebrity like Martha Stewart or Cindy Crawford but her clients wouldn't like to hear that she was the home wrecker that she was.

I called Liz at least a hundred times since Wednesday and she wouldn't talk to me, she wouldn't pick up the phone, and she wouldn't return my messages. I was at my wit's end and didn't know how to fix the mess I'd made. There was only one thing I could think of and that was to go home and tell Liz I was sorry. God! I was so filled with regret and shame. How could I stoop to such a sordid business as I had?

And here's the killer: Did my poor sweet Liz deserve this? She was a good woman. I really didn't deserve *her*. I could see that now. I had humiliated her and myself. Why on God's earth did I tell her that Sophia had broken my heart? How colossally stupid was that? Was that some Freudian behavior that I thought in the moment that Liz was my mother and I was running and crying to her to help me? In my entire adult life, it was the only time I'd ever lost control of myself. There I was wailing like a baby in the lobby.

I called the office and told my secretary I was taking a few days off. I could hear the surprise in her voice because I never took time off.

"I'll be available on my cell if anyone needs me."

"Very good, Mr. Waters."

Luckily, it was the middle of August and the markets were dead quiet. Most of the partners were out in the Hamptons or cruising around the Mediterranean on their yachts. I decided to go get some fresh air, such as it is in the dog days of summer in the city. I took my sunglasses and my keys.

This was a time when I wished I had a dog. People in Manhattan walked their dogs at all hours of the day and night. It gave them purpose. No one ever said, *Oh, what's that fellow doing out at this hour?* They said, *Oh, he's walking his dog, a dog has to be walked, there's nothing unusual about a man walking his dog.* But there was something highly suspicious about a man my age, dressed for the office, wandering aimlessly up Madison Avenue in the middle of the morning. So in order not to look like a mental patient, I put on my sunglasses, squared my jaw, and took manly strides that made me appear to be on the way somewhere. No one even tried to make eye contact, but this was a typical thing in the big city. Eight million people walking the streets ignoring one another. Why? Because that's just how it is.

If people talk to you, they're going to mug you or they're crazy persons off their meds or they're from out of town and have lost their way. Given the odds, two out of three, that an encounter with a stranger would not have a good outcome, it was best not to make eye contact, but to exhibit purpose in your stride and preselect a destination.

This was particularly pitiful for me because for years and years I had walked these streets knowing exactly where I was headed.

Now I had no direction and my life was destroyed. I walked and I cried and every so often I stopped at a storefront and wiped my eyes. After twenty or thirty blocks of this manic behavior I turned around, crossed over to Fifth Avenue, and walked back toward my apartment.

Somehow, I overshot my block and I looked up to see St. Patrick's Cathedral was right in front of me. I was not a regular churchgoer and when I was, I'd go to Grace Episcopal in Charleston on Easter and Christmas or for a funeral or wedding. I don't know why. I just never got much out of it, I guess. I didn't object to organized religion, I just wasn't a subscriber. But I thought, and freely admitted to my slothful sinner's soul, that there was an enormous charm about the grandeur of St. Patrick's and maybe, just maybe, there inside I could have a word or two with the Almighty. I mean, once you get past the Cathedral of St. John the Divine, St. Patrick's had to be the Lord's next stop. I went inside and took a seat in a pew toward the middle of the church.

I sat and tried to pray but I'm afraid I wasn't very good at that either. All I heard in my head was—*Go home! Ask for forgiveness!* Was this Divine advice? It didn't matter. I got up and left, making a donation to the poor box on the way out of the doors and back to the lonely streets brimming with so many people that it was almost frightening.

I knew this much about relationships. In business it was always best to nip problems in the bud. I also knew that if Liz divorced me, not only would I be miserable for the rest of my days but I wouldn't be nearly as liquid. I had to at least attempt to put things right, and the longer I debated the sense of doing that, the wider the abyss between us would grow. I didn't want to go home and see the disappointment in Liz's face and I didn't want to be berated forever and have this brought up all the time. Like, what if she marked it with an anniversary of sorts? *Well, it's two years ago today I caught you in the lobby with Sophia!* Or, *Remember the time you cried because you were in love with Sophia?* No, I didn't want to hear it. I really didn't.

But I also realized, as I stood there watching taxis switch lanes and people nearly get killed crossing Fifth Avenue, that I had better just go on and get it over with.

Okay. Decision made.

Good or bad, I was back going to Charleston, beautiful Charleston where things moved at a more graceful pace and people were kinder. I was going to try to make peace with Liz. She had given me and our children her whole adult life. She was a wonderful woman, really she was. She would stay with me through old age and having grandchildren, prostate issues and cataracts, and whatever else life decided to sling our way. She understood what it was to devote yourself to a cause. I only knew how to devote myself to a fat bank account and the world of food and wine. Pretty shallow.

And Sophia? Sophia was a bottom-of-the-pile, amoral, soul-crushing demon.

Liz was thoughtful and sensitive and she had loved me steadfastly forever. And I was thinking of throwing that away? I was whining to her that I loved Sophia? Dear God!

"Dry your eyes, asshole," I said to my bathroom mirror when I got home. "Call NetJets right now and get the hell out of here."

Then in a moment of genius I called Bottega Veneta and ordered Liz the duffel bag she'd always admired. It would thrill her. If I was going to win her forgiveness I was going to need more genius than I had ever had.

"Think, man! Think!"

Maybe I'd take her to Bali. She used to say she'd like to go there. But maybe I'd put the apartment on the market right away. I didn't want to keep running into Sophia in the lobby. In fact, I never wanted to see her again. She was the devil incarnate.

So I called NetJets and I took myself out to Teterboro in a taxi. They had a Citation IV available and the IV reminded me of Ivy all the way to Charleston. I thought about him and Liz and Ashley and wondered what kind of a head of the family I was. Not so good. I was supposed to lead my family and I had not done that at all. I sort of gave Ivy and Ashley the sink-or-swim kind of parenting and just left Liz to her own devices. This was my greatest sin and I knew it. I had no idea what I was going to say to Liz. No idea at all. *I'm sorry* didn't seem sufficient to mend this wound.

I sent a text to Walter to meet me at Landmark, the private airport I usually used. Walter was a great guy. He'd been married for a thousand years. Maybe he could give me some advice. Surely he'd had at least one big argument with his wife.

I felt so lonely then. All the way to Charleston I thought about my life and this horror show with Sophia and how I'd cried like a damn fool to Liz. I needed some advice but there were so few people whom I could turn to, talk to; I had so few friends. All I had left was one brother in Oregon whom I hadn't heard from in ten years. Should I have called him then and cried like a girl? No. Real men were stoic.

In New York, all I'd ever done was work and entertain clients. And when I was in Charleston, I was always with Liz and the children and Maisie. Maisie demanded and got an extraordinary amount of attention and now there was the situation with Skipper. Sometimes I felt like there was no room in their lives for me and it *had* to have been too much for Liz. And through it all, the years of commuting and family responsibilities, somehow, I'd forgotten to make a life outside of work for myself. I was almost sixty years old. Maybe it was time for me to sort out and reestablish all the relationships within my family. If Liz would forgive me, that is.

Then maybe I'd do something for fun, like take up tennis or golf. Why not? Fun had never been very high up on my list of priorities. In retrospect that seemed like a pretty Spartan way to live. Who said I had to be a Spartan? Why had I denied myself friends and fun? It wasn't that I ever intended to but the commute had sure cut me off from a regular social life and turned me into a working machine. It surely wasn't how I grew up. All the guys I went to school with belonged to a country club, had second homes and boats, and took vacations with their whole family. Between the demands of my career and the crazy commute, we rarely got away. Maybe that was one reason Sophia seemed so enticing—I had been starved of personal stimulation. I know that sounds like I am making excuses for what I did but it is also true.

We touched down and rolled to a stop. It was time to face the proverbial music. I climbed down the steps to the tarmac, and the heat and humidity slapped me in the face full force. There was little to compare to the heat and humidity in the Lowcountry of South Carolina except maybe the hinges on the back door of hell. That's what folks in these parts always said and it was fact. I should get familiar with hell because if I couldn't gain Liz's forgiveness, that's where I was going.

Walter was waiting for me in the parking lot.

"Mr. Whaley!" I said.

"Mr. Waters," he said, shaking my hand and then opening the rear passenger door.

It slammed shut and I took a deep breath. It was nice and cool inside his car, which for the record was pristine. There was a chilled bottle of water in the armrest cup holder that I opened and began to drink. He started to drive.

"So how's everything, Walter?"

"Good. You?"

"Well, Walter, to be honest, I've had a bit of a run-in with my wife. A little trouble in paradise. You've been married a long time, haven't you?"

"Seems like all my life. Joyce and I got married and then we grew up together. She's the best thing that ever happened to me."

"Tell me, what's the secret to a long marriage like yours?"

Walter burst out laughing.

"Mr. Waters? People ask me that all the time. The truth is it's all because of Joyce. She makes sure we operate as a team. The other thing is that I don't criticize and I thank her every day for sticking with me."

I never did any of this. I never said I was grateful to Liz for being my wife, I hardly ever told her I loved her and we weren't even close to a team. That was my fault because I liked flying solo. That was going to change too.

"I wish I'd asked you this about six months ago. I could've saved myself a lot of heartache."

"Well, I'm sure you'll work it out. The sun doesn't shine every day but it will shine again."

"Thanks, Walter. I sure hope you're right."

Soon we were winding our way through the historic district of downtown Charleston and over to Church Street, where we lived. I was a nervous wreck. I had called Charleston Flowers and had them send over every flower they had in their coolers. That would be a start. Hopefully, it would set a tone.

In my head, I started rehearsing what I was going to say.

We pulled up in front of the house and I got out. I felt like a very old man. An old man who was very, very tired and drowning in remorse. The truth was that if I lost Liz, I'd have no one. No one. I waved good-bye to Walter, and thinking he was very wise, I watched him pull away from the curb.

I pulled out my key to unlock the door and realized that the locks had been changed. What? Why would she do such a thing? What was I going to do?

I called Maisie. Maybe she knew something about this.

"Maisie? It's Clayton."

"I'm glad you called, Clayton."

"Well, first of all, how's Skipper?"

"Skipper? Why, he's jam up and jelly tight! What's new with you?"

"What's new is that I'm locked out of my house. Do you know any reason why Liz would change the locks?"

"I told her not to do it. I told her to just sit down with you and sort things out. But she's really angry, Clayton."

So Maisie knew everything. Great.

"Well, we can't sort things out if she won't answer the phone or return my calls."

"I told her that too."

"So what am I supposed to do? Spend the rest of my life standing here on Church Street, waiting for a miracle?"

"Do you want me to talk to her?"

The last thing I wanted in the entire world was to have Maisie position herself in the middle of my marital problems and exacerbate them.

"I don't know. This is really between Liz and me."

"No. What's between you and Liz is a locked door and a lot of hurt feelings. Why don't you come over here and I'll make you some supper. Ivy went back to San Francisco and left me with enough food to feed the army and the navy."

Maybe she was right. Maybe I needed someone to intercede on my behalf. What other options did I have?

"Well, let me see if I can get my car out of the garage. And if I can, I will."

"Good. Pick up a handle of gin for me on the way, okay? Bombay. I'm all out and it's getting dark soon. Skipper says he can drive, but I don't think he's quite ready for that. His balance is still a little out of whack."

"Sure."

"Thanks. Don't worry. I'll talk some sense into her."

I thought then, Just what the hell is the matter with this family? My eighty-year-old mother-in-law just promised to talk some sense into my wife for the price of a bottle of gin?

CHAPTER 16

Maisie—Final Soapbox

I put the chicken Parmesan in the oven to warm it up with the potato tots and opened a bag of salad, dumping it in a bowl. Then I set the table for three of us and when there was nothing more I had to do, I called Liz. I was in no rush to have this discussion with her.

"Guess who's coming to dinner?" I said to her.

I really hated being put in the middle of Liz and Clayton's trouble but someone had to stir the pot and get things moving. Standoffs never solved a thing.

"Who? Clayton?"

Who else? The president of the United States?

"Of course Clayton! He's in town and on his way to my house because . . ."

"He couldn't get in my house," she said.

"Oh? Now it's *your* house? Since when did it become just *yours?*"

"Since Wednesday morning."

"Okay. So you want a divorce? Is that it? All those years together, he makes one stupid mistake and now it's 'good night, Alice'?"

"Maisie? What else am I supposed to do? He went out, had an affair, and fell in love with another woman. Am I just supposed to forget what I saw, what he did, and what he said?"

"If you want to stay married, you have to *forgive* what you saw and heard. Never mind what he did. You don't have to forget."

"Forgive? Forgive, hell! You have to be kidding me!"

It appeared that Liz was not yet prepared for reconciliation.

"No, I am not kidding you. Liz, you have a decision to make. This is actually quite simple. Either you want to stay married to Clayton or not. That's it. It's as black and white a case as there could be. But at the very least you have to talk to him and hear what he has to say. You owe him a conversation and you owe it to yourself."

I heard Liz choke up and start to cry. It was only then that I realized how much pain she was in. She began to wail. Then I *really* didn't know what to say.

"Where are you?"

I hoped she wasn't carrying on like this at her office and making a spectacle of herself.

"I'm at home."

That was a relief. I tried to make her laugh, which was the worst thing I could've done.

"Listen, if you want him back you could really have some fun with this. You could make him grovel. You know, a trip to Paris? A cruise around the world? A door-knocker diamond?"

Then she exploded at me.

"Stop! You think that my family falling apart might be *fun* to put back together? *You don't understand! You never have! God!* Isn't there *one* person in this world who can see inside of my heart?"

"Liz! Pull yourself together! Half the men in America screw around on their wives. At least that's what Jon Stewart says."

I heard her sniff and then blow her nose, which is terribly rude to do when you're on the phone with someone. But in this situation I overlooked it.

"Jon Stewart is not a reliable news source. And I don't care about half the men in America. Is Ivy there?"

"No. He ran back to San Francisco this afternoon. James was arrested for wearing his Glass while driving or some fool thing. Before he left he told me to call taxis to take Skipper back and forth to see his therapists and send him the bill. Can you imagine? I'll do no such thing. Anyway . . ." Frankly, I was so unnerved by her crying that I was out of things to say. She was too. She was just sitting like a lump on the other end of the phone. "Look, Liz, I just want you to get what you want. And I want what's best for you. But I think you have to talk to him."

"I'll think about it," she said.

"Okay. I just heard a car door slam. It's probably Clayton. I hope he bought vermouth too."

"What? You asked Clayton to go to the liquor store for you?"

"Why not? It was on the way."

"I'll talk to you later, Mother."

She hung up. How about that? She called me Mother? And she was provoked over a bottle of vermouth? Well, she was always a little high-strung. I hurried to the front door no one ever used to let him in. Not that I was so anxious to have a cocktail but it was a quarter to five. Who knew how many happy hours I had left in this life?

"Hello, Clayton!" I smiled at the poor son of a gun. He'd had a rough week and it showed. He had literal bags under his eyes, a terrible five o'clock shadow, and he seemed drawn, as though he'd lost weight. Why was it that men could merely *think* about losing weight and then they lost it?

"Maisie," he said in acknowledgment and dutifully kissed my cheek.

"Come in, come in!"

"Thanks," he said.

It might have been the first time Clayton had been in my house without Liz in decades. He stood there in the middle of my living room like he didn't know what to do. Sit? Stand? Lie down on the sofa and tell me all his troubles?

"By any chance, did you get vermouth too?" I asked, taking the bag from him. It had more than one bottle in it. "Thanks!"

"No. You didn't say anything about vermouth."

"Well, I'm sure there's enough for tonight. Can I get you something?"

"I actually bought a bottle of wine. Do you have a corkscrew?"

"Of course! Come on in the kitchen with me."

He followed me to the kitchen. I dug around in my utensil drawer and found it.

"Great," he said and I handed it to him. "Nice apron."

I was wearing a retro apron Ashley bought for me at Anthropologie. It had black kittens all over it with a red ruffled edge and a big sash I tied into a bow in the back. It really was a hoot. And of course, I had on my single-strand pearls because the occasion called for something sedate. Somebody in this drama had to be glamorous and I decided long ago that it was going to be me.

"Thanks!" I said. "It was a birthday gift years ago from my precious granddaughter."

"Nice. Ashley can be a very thoughtful young lady. So how's

Skipper? Is he awake? I'd like to say hello. Can I fix your martini?"

"I believe that's still my job!" Skipper said.

We turned and there was my sweet Skipper in the doorway wearing khakis and a knit shirt and his loafers with no socks. He was adorable.

"Skipper!" Clayton said and smiled. "How great to see you! I thought you were a goner!" Clayton hurried over and shook Skipper's hand and slapped his shoulder. "You look fine! Really! Just fine!"

"Thanks," Skipper said and smiled. "I feel fine and I'm glad to still be here! You get your wine opened up and I'll take care of Maisie's daily double. Ha-ha-ha!"

Skipper hadn't changed in any profound way since the stroke, but he laughed even more easily than he had before and he seemed happier all around. I guess he was just plumb happy to be aboveground.

Clayton pulled the cork of his bottle and poured a generous amount of wine into the goblet I handed him.

"Cheers!" he said and took a big gulp.

"I guess you earned this one," Skipper said. "Maisie tells me you're in a bit of a kerfuffle, that is, you and Liz, I mean."

"Yeah, you could say that," Clayton said. "You sure could."

I took the olives from the refrigerator and put them on the counter next to Skipper with the toothpicks and quickly got the vermouth and bourbon from the liquor cabinet in the living room. I didn't want to miss a word.

"Well, let me fix this drink for my queen and a tiny drop for myself and I'll tell you a story about getting my hand caught in the cookie jar. If I can survive a stroke and all the exercises I have to do with my occupational therapist, who might be trying to kill me, a cookie jar episode ain't bubkes!"

This was the most animated I'd seen Skipper since he came home from the hospital. Maybe it was just that men needed the company of other men. Not that Ivy wasn't a man, but he was still very, very young. I decided to let them just talk and then I'd tell Clayton about my conversation with Liz. I filled the shaker with ice cubes.

"I'd love to hear," Clayton said. "I sure could use some advice."

"Oh, I've got plenty of that," he said.

Skipper shook my gin and vermouth in the shaker and even managed to put two olives on a toothpick. His fine motor skills were greatly improved. To tell you the truth, the olives were in a dish and they were large ones, purposely chosen to make it easier for him to handle. And this is how it was going to be until he regained all his faculties. He maintained his dignity because I was doing small things to pave the way for him. Just tiny mercies. He still needed a little more time. But he filled the martini glass I had placed there next to a tumbler for him and handed it to me without a problem. That small gesture that we would've taken for granted just two weeks ago seemed like a miracle now, and that his health was so improved made me so happy.

"Here you are, sweetheart," he said.

"Thanks, angel," I said, adding, "cheers!"

I had also filled a small bucket with ice so he could make his own drink exactly how he liked it. Basically he drank bourbon on the rocks. Sometimes he threw in a cherry or some sweet vermouth. But since coming home he seemed to prefer it straight because he said the sting of the liquor in his throat reminded him that he was still alive.

Clayton was sitting at the kitchen table and Skipper joined him. I opened the oven door and poked the potatoes with a fork. Not crispy enough yet.

"Dinner still needs a little time," I said. "Would y'all like some cheese and crackers?"

"No, no," Clayton said. "My appetite hasn't been the best for the past few days."

"Understood. You look like the devil," Skipper said and raised his glass. "Cheers!"

"So talk to me, Skipper. Tell me what you were going to tell me."

Skipper took a drink of his bourbon and put his glass down on the table.

"Ah! That is so good. Okay, well, it was a very long time ago. In fact, it was the summer after I graduated from high school. I got involved with a very sweet girl, sweet but a little wacky. Nancy was her name. She got pregnant so I married her. We weren't passionately in love but I wanted to do the right thing by her. I didn't even know what love was then. Anyway, I couldn't find work that would support us and it was the height of the war so I joined the army and wound up in Vietnam. While I was there in the countryside around Hanoi I met another girl, a beautiful Asian girl, and I fell in love. I mean, I fell in love, Clayton—hook, line, and sinker."

"Skipper! You've never told me this story!" I said.

"There was never a reason to until now, and I'm only telling this because I think it might help Clayton."

"Go on," Clayton said.

"It was just . . . well, I'd never met anybody like her before. Her name was Lien. I was completely knocked off my feet. She treated me like a god. And Nancy, my kooky wife back home, didn't. Nancy didn't write very often and all the other guys were getting mail from home almost every day. It was hard for me. And I was scared all the time. For all I knew Nancy had already run off with another guy. I was gone for a long time. Then Nancy sent me a letter saying that she lost the baby. I didn't know if that meant our marriage was over or what. I was very young and stupid. But I wrote her and told her how sorry I was and that I hoped she was okay."

Skipper paused then, looking serious, as though he was reliving those days.

"What happened?" I said.

"Well, we, Lien and I, started sort of halfway living together and she conceived a child. Somebody in my unit must have told their wife in a letter because Nancy found out. I got a terrible letter from her saying she was going to divorce me. I was very upset. But then one day when I was out on patrol, Lien's village was attacked and she was killed. She was six months pregnant. Her whole village was massacred."

"How terrible!" I said. "How terrible!"

"Good Lord, Skipper!" Clayton said.

"Yeah, it was horrible. I came home, got divorced, found out crazy Nancy had had an abortion and was running around like I don't know what. I was so blown away by it that I never got into another serious relationship until I met Maisie. I was too terrified. It just wasn't worth the pain."

"Gracious, Skipper, I'm so sorry," I said.

"I think I would've been terrified of another relationship too," Clayton said.

"The lesson in all this," Skipper said, "is that the heart wants what it wants. But when you can't have that person—in my case it was a fatal loss—you have to ask yourself some fundamental questions about yourself and the mess you've made."

"Such as?" Clayton said.

"Such as how did you get in the mess in the first place and now that your mess is out in the open, do you want to clean it up or walk away?"

"Oh, Skipper! I'm just so sorry!" I felt like crying for him.

"I don't know the answer to the first part, and I'm not so sure the second part is up to me," Clayton said. "Did you talk to Liz?"

"Yes," I said. "I did."

To be sure, the irony of all this horrible discussion wasn't lost on me. I knew perfectly well that Clayton had fallen in love with that whore Sophia in a way he had never loved my daughter and here I was attempting to encourage him to make up with Liz. And I was about to serve him dinner. I should have socked him in the nose.

"Well?"

"Clayton. She's very upset. In fact, she wept this afternoon. I haven't heard my daughter weep since her sister died."

"I don't think I've ever seen her weep," Clayton said.

"I think you have to be nicer, Clayton," I said. "Not that you're not nice, but you're not engaged. It's always like you have one foot out the door."

"Yes, I can see how it would seem that way," he said.

"If you want her back, go to her," Skipper said. "Beg her forgiveness."

"Beg?" Clayton said.

"Yes, beg," I said. "Her heart is broken."

"And it's all my fault," he said.

"Time for dinner," I said and got up shaking my head.

"I understand that," Skipper said, "but if you don't go to her and beg her forgiveness, you could wind up empty-handed and empty-hearted."

CHAPTER 17

Ashley—Bad Night

It was Thursday night after work and Mary Beth and I were catching up with each other at the beach house on Sullivans Island. She had a catering job later that night after a concert and she was getting dressed to go to work. We were in her bedroom and I was sprawled on her bed watching her fix her hair and put on her makeup.

"I told Porter I didn't want to see him anymore but the truth is I'm dying inside. I miss him so bad."

"No, you're not dying. You know, I love you like a sister but I don't like him one little bit."

She was putting her hair up with combs and clamps. Little tendrils kept escaping but she looked good, like *The Birth of Venus,* the superyoung and supercute redheaded version.

"You have to stop saying that all the time. Besides, he said he was sorry about leaving the way he did. He said I was being hysterical and I guess I sort of was."

"I worked with Tommy last night and when I told him you broke up with Galloway, you should've seen his face."

"Cookie Boy? Please!"

"If you want my opinion, I think you'd be better off with Tommy or someone like him than Porter Galloway. Galloway's too weird or something."

"No, he's not. You don't know him. Anyway, he wanted to have dinner tonight and I told him no."

"Good."

"Well, I said no because I'm not so sure I still love him after the way he acted last week."

"No shit! I walked in and found you lying in a pool of your own blood, passed out on the floor. You could've been dead for all I knew! And he left you like that? It's like Ted Kennedy and that poor girl he left in the river!"

"She died and I didn't and Porter apologized like crazy. He was so upset. You should've heard him, Mary Beth. He said, 'If I only had a chance to do it all over again, I would. Please forgive me, Ashley, you know I love you!' "

"He's saying that because he wants to get in your bloomers."

"That's what I'm afraid of. I don't know if I'm ready for that yet. I'm just not so sure I can trust him, but I miss him, you know? But I just keep thinking that if I could see him one more time I might get him out of my system."

"Well, I sure wish you would. Get him out of your system, that is."

"I think I have to see him one more time to be sure."

"You just said that. Just watch yourself, Ashley, okay?"

"Should I call him back and say yes?"

"No. I wouldn't."

The front door chime sounded, the one hooked up to the alarm system, and I got up to see who was walking in the house without ringing the doorbell. It was almost seven thirty.

"Anybody home?"

"Dad?" I said. I hopped off the bed and raced to the front door. "Hey! What are you doing here?" I gave him a hug. "What's going on?"

"Well, it seems that your mother and I have had a disagreement. Can I spend the night? Just one night. I'm sure we'll have it all sorted out by tomorrow."

"Dad? It's your house! Of course you can!"

"Thanks, Ashley."

"Did you eat supper?"

"Yes. I ate with Skipper and Maisie."

"Okay. Hey, Mary Beth! My dad's here! Put on your clothes!"

"Very funny!" she called out to us. "Hey, Mr. Waters!"

"Hey, Mary Beth!" he called back.

I knew immediately that Mom's trip to New York had been a total disaster, especially because Dad was standing in the hall. But I wasn't going to say one word to him about it. No, ma'am. My lips were sealed. I also felt that having Dad in the house was good because I could have dinner with Porter and he wouldn't try anything stupid with my father around. Perfect!

"Do you mind if I go out? I sort of had a date."

"No, no! Of course!"

I went to my room and called Porter.

"Hi, Ashley."

"Porter? Hey, did you make plans for dinner yet?"

"No. I was just going to get something at the hotel."

"Oh. Okay."

"Why? Did you change your mind? Did you decide to give me a break?"

"No." I was ignoring that. "I just didn't like the way things ended the last time we talked. So do you want to get something to eat?"

"Okay. Actually, I've been riding around the island trying to figure out what to do with you. Anyway, I'm close by. Whose car is that that just pulled into your yard five minutes ago?"

"What? That's my dad's car. Come in and say *hey!* I just need a few minutes to get myself together."

"Okay."

I quickly freshened up my makeup and pulled a brush through my hair. My clothes were fine. I was just wearing a sundress and sandals because it was so hot. We'd probably go somewhere close by that was casual. Most restaurants in Charleston were very casual, and even more so this time of year.

I heard the doorbell and went to answer it after I took one last look in the mirror. My stupid head hadn't completely healed. I still had a big scab that I covered with makeup. I wagged my finger at my face and started laughing. I was so happy that I was seeing Porter. There had to be a way for us to figure out how to get along. I just needed to be more careful and realize who he was. He had stress I couldn't even imagine trying to handle, so it really was no wonder he got mad so easily. I hurried to the door.

"Hey," I said and sort of melted when I saw him standing there. He had on an aqua linen shirt and white linen pants. For once he wasn't wearing a suit. "You look so nice." He looked younger than usual but if I told him that he'd flip out.

"Thanks," he said and smiled. "So do you."

"Want to come in and meet my father?"

"Of course I do," he said.

I took his hand and he followed me inside. This time he didn't jerk away. And I loved holding his hand.

Dad was on the portico, reading and watching a huge container ship sliding into the harbor. He looked at us and stood up.

"Dad? This is Porter Galloway."

Porter stuck out his hand and made eye contact with Dad, giving his hand a solid shake. It was something I'd bet Porter did a hundred times a week.

"How are you, sir?" Porter said.

"Fine, Porter. You?"

"Just fine, sir."

Dad gave Porter the biggest hairy eyeball from head to toe I'd ever seen him deliver. It didn't faze Porter in the least.

"So where are you young people off to this evening?" he said.

"Just going to grab a bite. Probably somewhere on the island," Porter said.

"High Thyme has crab cakes tonight," I said.

"That sounds good to me," Porter said.

I guess my scab must've been showing on my head because Dad said, "Glad to see you're wearing flat sandals, Ashley. You don't need another head injury."

"Oh, that was my fault, sir. I should've caught her when she fell over the coffee table."

"Oh?" Dad said. "I thought you said you tripped on your high heels?"

"Over a coffee table," I said.

"I see," Dad said, and he knitted his eyebrows, smelling a lie. "Well, try to get her home at a reasonable hour, Porter."

"I will. It was nice to meet you."

I could tell Dad was suspicious and Porter must've sensed it too because as soon as we got in the car and backed out of the yard, I got another little blast of Porter's temper.

"You know, you just made me look like a liar to your father when we were explaining how you hurt your head."

"Look, Porter, my parents asked me what happened and I told them I had a fall because of my high heels. Whoever said anything about a coffee table? You just totally made that up. I don't even think there is a coffee table in the house. Anywhere."

"That doesn't matter. Here's what you don't understand, Ashley. This is about my reputation. My credibility is everything. This might sound nuts to you, but if the smallest thing makes someone think I'm lying, then they begin to wonder about everything else that comes out of my mouth."

"But it *was* a lie, Porter. There was no coffee table."

"Okay, here it is, Ashley." We had just pulled into a parking space right in front of High Thyme. "If I say there's a coffee table, there's a coffee table. You must *never* say *anything* ever to contradict me. Not the smallest thing. In private? When it's just us? That's different. Got it?"

"Got it."

I got it but I didn't like it. It would sure make our relationship feel strange. I wondered if Jackie Kennedy ever disagreed with JFK. Probably not. She was the ideal political spouse and I guess that was the point he was trying to make.

I understood what he meant. I read the news. Politics weren't totally my thing, but I knew enough about these mayors and governors saying and doing stupid stuff and getting caught. They looked like idiots all the time. And then people laugh at them for saying one little careless thing. I mean, you can't even whisper on television because people can lip-read and catch you saying something really awful like when somebody dropped the F-bomb during President Obama's inauguration. That was terrible.

"I understand what you mean, Porter." I said this after I drained half a glass of sauvignon blanc. "If the world is going to hold you to a higher standard than the normal person, then you have to live up to that standard. That's got to be hard for you."

"You have no idea." He said this with such a somber tone. Then he smiled. "How's your dinner?"

"Wonderful," I said and smiled back.

"I'm really sorry about the last time we were together," he said. "I know I've said it over and over but I really am. Anyway, I think you need to watch how much wine you drink for a couple of reasons. One, people are counting your glasses . . ."

"Oh, come on, Porter." That was totally crazy.

"Believe me, they are. They count mine? They count yours. Have one glass and sip it."

"Gosh, I guess you're right." Maybe he *was* right.

"And, two, you never would've had the accident if you weren't a little loaded."

"That's true too. I was just looking for courage that night. I didn't expect a couple of glasses of wine to go to my head like that."

He leaned back in his chair and stared at me sort of sweetly.

"Don't worry. I forgive you."

I hadn't really looked at things from Porter's point of view and he was right. Cracking my head open was my own fault. He didn't pour the wine down my throat. I did.

"Thank goodness!" I said.

"And just what did you need courage for?"

"You know. We were supposed to . . ." Did I have to say it out loud?

"Ah! Well, don't worry. I'll let you know about that when the time is right. Now are you going to eat that other crab cake?"

"No, actually, I wasn't going to. Would you like to have it?"

"Yes, because if you're going to have fish breath, I might as well have fish breath too."

"You're right! It's delish!" I handed him my plate and took his empty one.

He looked at me with that look guys get when they're thinking about you naked and right then, I knew tonight was the night. Oh no! Suddenly, I wasn't ready. I knew he could sense my nervousness.

"Okay, just this once, why don't we get you a second glass of wine?" he said, confirming my clairvoyance.

He signaled the server who brought the new big glass of wine almost instantly. I didn't chug it but I didn't sip it either. Porter thought he was going to take me home and *you know*. Had he forgotten my dad was there? Ha-ha-ha!

Or had he seen my dad's car drive by the restaurant? Because when we got back to the house, Dad and his car were gone. Yikes.

We went inside. There was a note on the kitchen counter. Porter stood behind me and we read it together.

Dear Ashley,

Went home to Mom. Thanks for everything. Behave yourself, young lady!

Love,
Dad

"What does that mean? *Behave yourself*?"

"It means you have to be a good little girl and do what I tell you to do," he said.

"No, it doesn't," I said and walked over to the refrigerator, opening it, pretending to be looking for something. I closed it and opened the freezer.

My dad may as well have been standing in the room with me because if I had ever been excited about being seduced by Porter, that excitement had fizzled out. But not for him. He started making moves.

"Come here to me," he said and turned off the lights.

"What's with you and the dark? Do you want ice cream?" I said, trying to ignore the fact that he was about to pounce on me like a leopard. Maybe a little Ben and Jerry's Chunky Monkey would cool him down a bit.

He was utterly uninterested in ice cream.

"No," he said, and moved in, closing the freezer door and grabbing my arm.

Okay, now this sounds a little sicko but he twisted it behind my back and held it there while he kissed me. And as knee buckling as his kisses were, he was hurting my arm. I knew there were some people who thought a little discomfort was sexy but I didn't.

"Porter?" There was no answer. His mouth was working its way down the side of my neck and giving me chills like crazy. "Porter!"

"What?" he said, in a weird sort of drowsy voice.

"You're hurting my arm! Please stop!"

"Okay. Let's go. Where's your bedroom?"

"Porter! Wait!"

He was already pulling me down the hall looking behind doors for my room.

"Come on!"

"No! This is my parents' room!"

"Oh," he said and yanked me back into the hall. "Fine."

"That's my room," I said and pointed to the door across the hall.

I wasn't trying to encourage him, but the last place I wanted to fool around was in my parents' bed. That's just me. But at that point Porter would've thrown me down on the bare floor.

"Let's go," he said and pushed the door open with the heel of his hand. "Get undressed."

"Come on, Porter," I said, "can't we go slower?"

"And do what? Make out like a couple of teenagers on the sofa?" He unbuckled his belt.

"No, I just . . ."

"What are you saying, Ashley? Do you love me or not?" He took off his trousers and folded them across a chair.

"I think I do, Porter. It's just that this all seems a little rushed and I don't know . . ."

"You *think* you love me? You *think*? Ashley, are you trying to make a fool out of me?"

Holy crap! Senator Porter Galloway was standing in my bedroom in his boxers! And next he was unbuttoning his shirt . . .

"God, no! You know how I feel about you! I love you, Porter!"

"You're afraid, aren't you?"

I nodded my head.

"Baby, there's nothing to be afraid of! I wouldn't hurt you for anything in the world. You know that, don't you?"

He stepped over to me and put his arms around me and kissed me again. Then I felt him unzipping my dress. Is this how I wanted it to be? No. But I was afraid that if I didn't let him have what he wanted I would lose him. My dress hit the floor.

"I know that," I said, but I was very uncertain. "But I just want to wait a little . . ."

"You belong to me, Ashley, and what I say goes."

"No! I said, no, Porter!"

I happened to glance at the clock. It was just a little after nine. He pushed me down on the bed. I didn't even get to kick off my sandals. His mouth was on mine and no matter how much I tried to object, it wouldn't have made any difference.

"No, Porter! Stop!"

"Shut up!"

Then it seemed that it was happening, but I didn't feel anything. Nothing! He kept whispering my name and telling me he loved me. I didn't even know I was crying until it was all over. I looked at my clock again. It was only ten minutes after nine. Good grief. It was the worst sexual experience of my life. Then I cried for real. Didn't I tell him to stop? Why didn't he stop? How was I supposed to spend the rest of my life with this passing for sex? We were completely incompatible. It wasn't going to work, and knowing it just broke my heart into a million pieces. Plus, I hadn't wanted to do it and he knew it.

"Oh, great," he said. "I guess it's time for me to leave."

"I wasn't ready," I said, not knowing what else to say. "I just wanted to wait, Porter."

"Well, it's a little late to clarify your position, isn't it?"

"I guess so."

"And I wasn't enough for you, was I?"

"Oh, no, Porter . . . it's just that . . . I don't know. I don't."

But he *knew* and he was so angry with me that he was almost hyperventilating. He practically jumped into his pants and he threw his shirt on without even buttoning it. He stepped into his loafers and then he slapped one hand across my face. Then he was gone. Just like that. He was gone.

Mary Beth got home sometime after two in the morning and I

was on the portico, sobbing my eyes out. I'd left the door open so she'd know where to find me.

"What the hell happened?" she said. "Are you all right?"

"No! Oh, Mary Beth. It's over!"

"You and Porter?"

"Yes."

"What happened?"

"Oh, God, he *hates* me now! We . . . you know . . ."

"Had sex?"

"Yes. And it was *terrible!*"

"The sex or that you did it in the first place?"

"Both! Oh, God! I could just die!"

"Stop! Listen to me, Ash. Are you telling me he forced you to have sex with him?"

"Yes. I mean, he knew I didn't want to do it and then he just sort of did it to me anyway."

"Ashley? That's called rape. Call it *date rape* if you want to soften up the term but it's still rape. Did you object?"

"Of course I did, but it didn't make any difference. He didn't care."

"The bastard! Let's go to the emergency room. Come on. Let's get your purse."

"No! Mary Beth, listen to me. I'm *not* going to be the one to ruin his career. I'm not! I'm just saying that we were so incompatible and that's what breaks my heart. It was impossible."

"Oh, Ash." Mary Beth came and sat next to me on the glider. She threw her arm around my shoulder and gave me a good squeeze. "There's nothing worse than lousy sex. I'm sorry. Was it really that hopeless?"

"I'm pretty sure. Oh, hell. Yes. It was that hopeless. Less than ten minutes of sheer nothingness. When he realized I wasn't thrilled, he slapped me and then he stomped out. I've been crying ever since."

"What? He hit you?"

"Yes."

"That shit. Don't cry, Ashley. He isn't worth it."

"He said terrible things to me."

"He'll calm down. He'll call and say he's sorry. He will."

"It doesn't matter, Mary Beth. I'm just so sad because I thought we were so good together. I was going to be his Jackie O."

"Would it make you feel better if I told you a secret?"

"I don't know. Depends on the secret."

"Okay. You know Samir and his five-hundred-dollars thing?"

"Sort of." Was she going to confess at last?

"Well, he can only get it up if he tells himself he's with a prostitute."

"And so he pays you to have sex with him?"

"Yeah, the same five hundred dollars every single time. He gives it to me, I take it back to him, he gives to me again, I take it back again . . . I mean, men and their you know whats are a very complicated business. At least we don't have to worry about *that*!"

I actually laughed! One, I was seriously relieved to know my best friend wasn't a total whore and, two, her story was as bad as mine!

"So your momma really did send you that watch?"

"Yes. She bought it on the Internet. Why, what did you think?"

"I thought I was going crazy! Oh, my God," I said. "Men!"

"Men is right."

CHAPTER 18

Liz—Another Chance

It was early in the morning, and the weather was overcast and humid. I was making pancakes. He was sleeping in the guest room. Clayton, I mean. I called him after Charleston Flowers delivered last evening. The parade of people bringing in flowers was a little bit insane. Every surface in the living room, dining room, kitchen, my bedroom, the guest room, the kids' old rooms—everything was covered in vases of heart-stopping gorgeous flowers. It was as though someone terribly important had dropped dead and my house was a funeral parlor or as though *someone* was drowning in regret. I'm going with regret, although I almost dropped dead myself when I saw all the flowers. Like the women I championed, flowers had something hardscrabble in them, rugged enough to climb through tons of stone and earth to emerge as a beautiful thing. Beautiful, but fragile still. I decided that I would take most of them to the safe house and share them with all the women and children. But for that lovely moment I was going to enjoy them and photograph them so I would remember that this was the greatest gesture of apology that ever came from Clayton.

So I called him last night after the flowers arrived and he begged me to let him come home. What was I going to say? *No?* I couldn't do that. Maisie was right. He deserved at least a conversation, a chance to explain himself. I'd done a lot of thinking since New York. A lot. The truth was that Clayton was as vulnerable to temptation as the next man except that he got caught. And now he was desperately sorry. I believed him. And, as much as I hated to admit it, the extraordinary abundance of blooms softened my heart.

When Clayton arrived at around eight, I asked him if he was hungry. I opened the front door for him but I averted my eyes from his. I just couldn't look in his eyes because I knew I'd burst into tears. He followed me to the kitchen, and I was trying to act as though everything was calm because I really didn't want to fight. What was the point of a screaming match? And to be honest, I was more sad than angry and that was what I wanted him to know.

Anyway, I had made some pasta from what I had in the house and what I didn't eat was still in a pot on the stove. It would taste even better tomorrow.

So I said, "You hungry?"

He said, "No."

This surprised me because I couldn't recall him ever turning down food of almost any sort and certainly not pasta. And maybe, just maybe, he could see the irony in expecting me to serve him a meal juxtaposed by the fact that it was unacceptable for him to just help himself. I took this as evidence that he was deeply and genuinely upset.

"Someone send flowers?" he asked.

I had to smile then because we were truly surrounded by a virtual botanical garden bonanza.

"Yes. Someone sent flowers."

He smiled and picked up a bottle of wine from the rack in the kitchen and considered it. To my surprise he put it back and said, "Let's talk first and then maybe we can share a bottle later?"

"We'll see," I said. "That depends."

"I know. Do you want to sit in the kitchen? Or the living room or where?"

"The kitchen is fine," I said.

After all, the kitchen was where most of our family's drama had always played itself out. And the important conversations, whether they were about science projects, math problems, college applications, hurt feelings, or family illnesses, all happened in the kitchen. Usually you'd find us around the ancient walnut trestle table I bought out in Summerville from an antique dealer right after we moved into this house. I wished then that I had a dollar for every meal I had cooked and served on this table. Or for every problem solved, hand held, and heart mended.

"Okay," he said and took a bottle of mineral water from the refrigerator, moved several arrangements to the floor, and sat down. Apparently, taking water was not overstepping whatever boundaries he had imposed on himself. It was interesting that instead of sitting at the head of the table where he'd sat since the children were little, he took a chair on the far side. Maybe that was some unconscious signal that he was uncertain about his position in the family. I sat opposite him where I always sat. And waited. He just stared at me through masses of pink roses and Stargazer lilies.

Finally, he took a deep breath, ran his hand through his hair, and spoke.

"I made a terrible, terrible mistake, Liz."

"I'd say so," I said.

"You couldn't know how profoundly sorry I am. I never meant to hurt you or anyone."

"Do you want to tell me why this happened? I didn't know you were so unhappy with our marriage. I really didn't. I mean, I know it's not fabulously exciting every day of the week, but it's dependable and solid. And we've had lots of wonderful things happen to us, haven't we? Happy years?"

"I wasn't unhappy with our marriage. I really wasn't. I guess the only explanation is that I was weak. And I don't know why I was so weak with Sophia . . ."

"*Wait! Stop!* Stop right there. I never want to hear that nasty filthy name in my house again. Ever."

"Okay. I'll never say it again, but my point was that I don't know what made me so weak because I've said no thanks to lots of women over the years."

"You have?" What kind of a thing was that to say? "Where are we headed here, Clayton?"

"Oh, come on. Like you haven't said no to other men?"

"Actually, only once." Okay, maybe there was one other guy but that was so long ago.

"Who was it?"

"You don't know him," I said.

"Okay," he said and looked at me as if the guy's name would appear across my forehead as though it was hidden under my makeup. "Okay. But remember the rush of excitement you felt when he first came on to you and you realized he *wanted* you? That he was practically possessed with you?"

"Yes," I said, remembering how I blushed then and how exciting it was that someone else found me attractive and even desirable enough to suggest something so dangerous and illicit. It had been almost staggering to consider but in the end nothing happened. It wasn't that I didn't want to sleep with him. And it wasn't because I stood on some high moral ground. Nothing happened simply because I was a coward. But that decision had almost nothing to do with Clayton. In fact, for the duration of the flirtation, Clayton rarely came to mind. What Clayton was trying to tell me was that his affair with her, the Wanton Whore of the Upper East Side, had nothing to do with me or our marriage. I understood that this was possibly true.

"I was seduced," he said. "Like Adam and Eve and I took the apple."

"I'm sure she seduced the hell out of you," I said. "She has a long history of leading men down the path to her well-worn mattress. She's horrible. She's a man-eater."

"Yes, she is. I'm so sorry, Liz. I don't know what in the hell I was thinking."

"I'm so disappointed, Clayton."

"I am too. I've never been the kind of man who did those things and I don't want to be that kind of man now. It's despicable and tawdry behavior. I'm just so glad it's over."

"You cried, Clayton. You cried to me. You cried like a *baby* and told me that *you loved her.*"

"There was a moment that I thought I did love her. Then I came to my senses. And I have the deepest shame and the most horrible regret that I said those things to you. I must've been out of my mind."

"It's possible. You wouldn't be the first man who ever took a leave from his senses over a pair of outrageous implants. But that's not the problem. *Do* you love her?"

"Absolutely not."

"Are you really and truly certain of that?"

"Yes. Listen, Liz. I've done more soul-searching in the last two days than I think I've ever done in my entire life and I've made some important decisions."

"I'm listening . . ."

"First of all and most important, I realized how much I really do love you. You've been a wonderful wife and mother all these years. You deserve better than what I've given you up until now and I am determined to make this up to you."

"We'll see."

"And I'm retiring. I don't really need to work anymore. We have plenty of money. I'm putting the co-op on the market and selling it. I want to be here all the time."

"To do what?"

"Well, a friend of mine who has been married for a long time told me the secret to a happy marriage is to operate like a team. I've been flying solo for too long. So I want us to take up golf."

"*Golf? Golf?* Are you *serious?*" I burst out laughing. He didn't even crack a smile. "Holy mother! You *are* serious! Clayton? You think a sport like golf can repair a broken marriage? That is the most ludicrous thing you have *ever* said for as long as I have known you! *Golf?*"

"Okay, tennis then. Or kayaking. Or hiking. Something. The point is we need to find something to do that brings us together that we can do all the time that we like."

"What's the matter with grilling or gardening or traveling?"

"Nothing! Those are all great ideas too! Let's go to Bali!"

"Really?"

"Yes! The point is we should enjoy what we have earned. You know, it's time to spend some of the fruits."

"Or we can leave it all to the children."

"Dumb idea."

"Well, at least we agree on something. Look, Clayton, here's what it comes down to. Either we're staying married or we're not. But one thing's for sure, if we remain married, we're not going back to how things were."

"I completely agree."

"You'll have to accept the fact that you're not the center of the universe."

"What do you mean by that?"

"Just that. You are no longer going to stroll out of here when you feel like it and stroll back in expecting my world to stop and for me to wait on you hand and foot. We're at a different stage in our lives now. The children are gone. And now I want you to pay some attention to me, be nice to me, and be my friend. Start acting like you love me. Even if you don't love me, maybe you can convince yourself you do if you act like it long enough."

"No, Liz. I do love you. More than anyone in my entire life."

"And you are never going to utter one syllable that devalues my work. Is that understood? What I do literally saves lives and you know it. You and Maisie act like I'm working with gunslinging, drug-addicted lowlifes who live like animals when nothing could be further from the truth. Just look at all the abuse among the clergy! And the police officer in Beaufort who was beating his wife for years until she finally shot him? It's the people who are supposed to protect

us that abuse us! There's so much anger and rage out there . . . it has
to stop."

"You're right. I know that's true, and I promise to learn more
about your work and your mission. I swear I will."

And then what? I thought.

"This work is my legacy, Clayton. What's yours going to be?"

He stopped and stared at me again. He surely didn't want the
world to say that he was nothing more than a philandering money-
making machine with the soul of a miser.

"I don't know. I guess it would be good if our family knew that I
changed. That I became a changed man. A much better man. Maybe
I'll join forces with you? I do love you, Liz. When I realized I might
lose you, I thought I would *die* because I don't want to live without
you. It made me see how much you mean to me and how much our
family means to me. And I want to be your best friend, the best one
you've ever had. Please, I'm begging you, Liz."

"You're begging for what?" I said.

"I'm so, so sorry and I'm begging your forgiveness. I swear on
everything that's holy that I will be a better husband and that nothing
this stupid will ever happen again!"

There was a long silence then as he waited for me to respond.

"Okay, Clayton. You've got the new ground rules committed to
memory?"

"Yes," he said.

"Then we're going to put this ugly business behind us and never
speak of it again. Is that clear?"

"Clear as a bell. So I'm forgiven then?"

"I'm going to work on forgiving you, Clayton. You can sleep in the
guest room and maybe you can seduce me into full forgiveness over time."

"Can we kiss?"

"Oh . . . okay."

He stood and came around to my side of the table and pulled me to my feet. Then he kissed me like he used to and I felt a wave of something wonderful radiate through me like I just stepped into the warmth of the sun for the first time in years. He put his hand on the back of my head and ran it down my hair.

"I love you," he said. "Thank you, Liz."

"For what?" I said. I looked at all the little wrinkles around his eyes, the deep creases in his forehead that appeared when he worried, and I knew I loved him too. I did.

"For another chance," he said. "Um, is that spaghetti over there on the stove?"

"Yes. Would you like for me to heat it up for you?"

"Please. I'm starving. Would you like a glass of wine?"

"Oh, why not?"

Ingrained behaviors are hard to change. I was like the proverbial horse to the barn as I served him a plate of pasta and he poured wine for us. We truly were creatures of our habits. I watched with some measure of satisfaction as he twirled and devoured every last strand and with a heretofore unwitnessed gusto, declaring it was the best thing he had ever tasted in his whole life. At least that's what he said. It didn't matter if it wasn't so. I'd had enough truth for one night.

Nonetheless, we stayed up late, talking and talking. And we wept together as we made a vow to take his affair off the list of topics for discussion. Tears were so rare between us that we were reduced to a kind of vulnerability I hadn't known since my sister's death when I learned that anything can happen. He told me I was beautiful and smart, no, brilliant and such a wonderful woman, so selfless and generous and he praised how dedicated I was to my family and how none of them, the wretches they were, deserved me. The whole time he was running his mouth, telling me what a magnificent creature I was, I kept thinking, This is some bodacious bullshit coming out of his mouth. But I sort of loved it. I did. Bullshit, used smartly and with discretion, could be a very pleasant change of pace.

So that's how I wound up here at the stove making pancakes this morning. It was almost eight and I planned to leave for work by nine, to avoid traffic. I put some bacon in the microwave to cook and melted some butter into the syrup over very low heat. I was no Barefoot Contessa but I could put the hurt on breakfast food. All I needed was a box of Bisquick. I set the table, and a few minutes later there was Clayton in the doorway, in his bathrobe and flip-flops.

"G'morning!" he said. "Do I smell bacon?"

"Yes, sir! Coffee?" I poured him a mug because I knew the answer and handed it to him.

"Thanks," he said. "You know what?"

"What?"

I poured some batter into the pan and took two plates from the plate rack and set them on the counter by the stove.

"You should try the guest room mattress. It's fabulous."

I looked at him and he raised his eyebrows in amusement.

"Maybe I will," I said and smiled.

"I meant what I said about taking a vacation, just you and me. Someplace really exotic where we've never been before. Like what about Bali? You always wanted to go there, didn't you?"

"Yes. I'd love to go. Who wouldn't want to see Bali?"

He already sounded more like the Clayton I'd fallen in love with so many years ago. Most important, he was thinking of a future with me, a future of mutual discoveries, a starting-over adventure.

"Well, then, let's do it!"

"You arrange it and I'll pack. Meanwhile, I'm going to be late for work."

We had a quick breakfast.

"Liz, I've been thinking."

"Seems like we've been working overtime in that department." I smiled at him. A smile didn't cost anything. "What are you thinking about now?"

"Well, I've got to retire from work. And I want to put the apartment on the market. So I was thinking of leaving for New York on Monday and I'd come back as soon as I can, if this is okay with you?"

"I think that sounds great, Clayton. I think that sounds like a good plan."

"I can just call a mover, right?"

"Absolutely. They'll pack up everything for you."

"What are we gonna do with all that stuff?"

"We can put it in the beach house. It needs refreshing."

"Perfect," he said and added, "God, I love pancakes. And I love you too."

"Who doesn't love pancakes? And I sort of still love you maybe." I laughed. "Would you like more?"

"No, no." He patted his tummy. "I'm completely satisfied."

"Well, good," I said, and I got up to put the dishes in the dishwasher.

"I'll do the dishes," he said. "New rule. You cook? I clean."

"I like that," I said. "See you tonight."

I got in my car and while I was buckling my seat belt I was thinking that Maisie was right about two things. One, a reconciliation might be fun after all and, most important, I wasn't going to let the one really stupid thing that happened in all these years tear my marriage and my family apart. But hell would freeze before I'd admit that to her.

I had no intention of discussing my marriage with anyone but Clayton, except to say here that I'm really glad I went to New York and that privately I was grateful Maisie and Ivy gave me the impetus to make the trip. I feel like facing the problem and dealing with it as I did was the only course I could have taken. Was I certain that forgiving Clayton and letting him come home would work? No, I was not. Not at all. But listen, Clayton didn't have a history of catting around and I had known Sophia for what she was a long time ago. She was not a nice girl. Men were playthings to her. I'd seen her melt them and pour them in the sink like cold coffee, watching them circle the drain without a care for the havoc she left in her wake. She was heartless and jaded. Clayton didn't know women like her. I did. There was a reason why they called the catwalk a catwalk—there were some dangerous felines up there slinking around. Mostly there were nice girls in the modeling world, but every now and then you'd run into one who was so narcissistic it would blow your mind. Sophia was a sparkling example. I hoped she'd have fun with her five-foot-four-inch-tall polo player. Poor Clayton. But at the same time I was saying *poor Clayton,* I was hoping he never completely healed from the stinging humiliation of his encounter with her.

My cell phone rang. As expected, it was Maisie.

"All right," she said, "tell your mother. Is everything hunky-dory between you and Clayton?"

"We are going to be fine, thank you." That was all I said.

"Well, for the record, it was Skipper who told him he should beg your forgiveness."

"How's Skipper feeling this fine sunny day?" I said, wondering if she had told the story of Clayton and Sophia to the mailman and the UPS deliverywoman and the woman who did her hair too.

"Skipper's fine. He's like Lazarus!"

"Well, I'm so glad to hear it. What a relief."

"So I guess you're not going to give me any details?"

"As I said before when I was cornered by you and Ivy? I think it's inappropriate to discuss the details of my marriage with anyone. I don't mean to seem rude, but Clayton and I have to work out our issues ourselves. It can't be a topic for conjecture or judgment with anyone else or how can we maintain our dignity?"

"You're right," she said.

For a moment I thought I should pull over to the side of the road so I could faint. I could count the number of times I'd been right in Maisie's eyes on one hand.

"Okay, then. I'm driving so I should probably hang up. Maybe we'll see y'all this weekend? And if you need a thing, like a ride to the doctor's office, call Clayton. He's going to be home until Monday. Then he's going back to New York to take care of a few things."

"Really! You trust him?"

"Maisie! Let's not go there, okay? And he's planning a vacation for us. He needs to relax a little."

"Yes, that's probably the best thing for y'all. Where are you planning on going?"

"We were thinking about something exotic like Bali."

"I wish I could go on a vacation like that."

"Well, I'll be your guinea pig and I'll tell you all about it when I get back. Okay! Love you! Gotta go now!"

If she thought I was taking her and Skipper to Bali or wherever Clayton decided we should go to rediscover our romance, she was really cracked.

The phone rang again. The number was unfamiliar but I took the call anyway.

"Mrs. Waters? It's Mary Beth. Ashley's roommate?"

"Hi, honey! Is everything all right?"

"Oh, sure. I guess. I just wanted to talk to you about something and I was wondering if I could come by your office today?"

"Of course you can. Want to come for lunch? It's pizza day."

"Wow! Pizza. That would be great," she said. "I just have a lot on my mind and I really feel like I need another perspective."

"Well, these days, perspective seems to be my specialty so why don't you come on over around noon? We'll grab a couple of slices and close my office door. We can powwow."

"That sounds great. I'll see you then! Thanks!"

I gave her the address and we hung up. I started to wonder. What was bothering Mary Beth that was important enough to reach out to me? When she was just a freshman in college, we used to have soul-searching discussions all the time. But that was a long time ago. I'd find out soon enough. Well, whatever the reason was, I was very happy for her to come to me.

We ordered pizza at work one day a week, just for the fun of it. It brought the office together and gave us a chance to talk to one another about work and things other than work. Tom had a place he liked that delivered, so he always did the ordering. Our full-time staff was made up of only nine people including Tom and me. There was Dee, the director of Program Services, Lee Ann, our shelter coordinator, Sam, who ran Client Services, and Meg, Kristi, Lisa,

Lee, and Barb, who did everything else. Our part-time staff provided counseling, advocacy, and all the other necessary help associated with Family Court and the Department of Social Services. Their backgrounds and experiences were as diverse as you could hope they would be. But here was the one lighthearted thing we all had in common: a passion for pepperoni and mushrooms on thin crust pizza. So Thursday was the appointed pizza day at My Sister's House and every week Tom bought us two extralarge pies and a huge mixed green salad. I was so happy I didn't have to eat boneless skinless chicken on a bag of salad that smelled like cellophane. And I didn't have to eat white meat turkey on rye with mustard. And for one more day I could forgo white meat tuna packed in water on a bed of raw spinach with lemon juice. It was Thursday and by golly, I was going to eat pizza like a teenaged boy.

The door opened at five after twelve and there stood Mary Beth. I saw her through my open doorway and called out to her.

"Hi! You're just in time! Lunch just got here and I'm starving. Come on."

"Great!"

We went to what we called the break room and helped ourselves, loading up paper plates. She followed me back to my office. I pushed aside files and my stapler and my pencil cup and she sat opposite me.

"Sorry, my desk is a mess, but I'm one of those people who works better with everything spread out in front of me."

"Oh, that's okay. I'm a slob too."

I thought, Oh brother, to be twenty-three again and to say those careless things without a second thought.

"Right!" I said and smiled at her. "So what's going on, Mary Beth?"

"Well, before I tell you why I called you, I thought I should tell you something. Remember that dinner where I helped you not long ago?"

"Sure. What a fabulous night that turned out to be! Thank you again."

"Oh, you're welcome. Gee, this pizza is really good. Where's it from?"

"Carmines on King Street. It's really perfect, isn't it? They have a full menu at night but they deliver pizza all day until midnight. It's the real thing."

"Yeah, it is. Um, so . . . remember that night I sort of hinted to you that I knew something about abuse?"

"Yes. I remember." Here it comes, I thought.

"Well, I do. Unfortunately. My father, who's a minister and supposed to be a man of the cloth and all that? Well, on Sunday he rocks the church with all these unbelievable sermons and his snake box."

"A snake box?"

"Yes, ma'am."

"Your father is a snake handler?"

"Yes. There are more than a few where I come from."

"You never told me this! Has he ever been bitten?"

"Oh, yes, ma'am. Half a dozen times. But he says if the Lord wants him to live he will live and he quotes that part of the Bible about *and you will take up serpents*? I'm pretty sure that's Mark sixteen. Anyway, so far he has lived. I think snake handling is dangerous and stupid and I wouldn't touch a snake if you paid me."

"Good heavens," I said, not knowing what else to say at that point.

"Well, that's the Sunday drill. Saturday night is the total opposite."

"What do you mean?"

"Do y'all have a microwave here?"

"Yes. We do. Why? Is your pizza cold?"

"No, it's just that it's hard to eat and tell you this story at the same time. Maybe I could just talk first and then eat?"

"Of course! Whatever makes you the most comfortable. We can zap your food later."

"Thanks," Mary Beth said and put her paper napkin down. "Well, on Saturday nights my dad goes out with his buddies and they get all liquored up and then he comes home and picks fights with everybody."

"Have you ever seen him hit anyone?"

"Oh, yeah. He beat the hell out of my momma, my two brothers, and me all the time. It's why I never went back home after college. We're all afraid he'll kill her, but we all just had to get out. He's really crazy. My momma won't listen to reason. I told her if she wants to live like that that it's her business. She's too scared to leave. She's afraid he'll kill her."

"Do you think he would?"

"I hope not but you know he mixes up the Bible and his rights as a man and liquor and bad things start to happen. He's always putting her down, saying she's stupid, that she has to obey him and all that kind of talk. He used to say the same things to me but I knew he was wrong so I just tried to stay out of his way."

"How did you know that at such a young age?"

"Because I had a teacher who was really nice. We talked all the time. She really saved me, I think. Miss Howe was her name. She was amazing. She's the one who arranged my scholarship to the College of Charleston. I even had a stipend for living expenses."

"You're very lucky, Mary Beth. I see girls all the time who don't have anyone to help them—at least until they find out about this place."

"I know. I wonder how many women would file complaints if they weren't so afraid."

"Well, intimidation is a big part of domestic violence. There are thirty-six thousand complaints of domestic violence filed every year in South Carolina alone."

"Did you say thirty-six thousand?"

"Yes. Thirty-six thousand. Nationwide? Three women are murdered by their husbands or boyfriends every single day."

"Every day? It's sort of like bullying gone crazy, isn't it?"

"If that's what they call homicide these days, then yes."

"Oh my goodness, I had no idea the number was that high. Terrible. Anyway, I wanted you to know that I've seen this stuff firsthand."

I looked at her face and I knew there was something she wasn't telling me then.

"Come on, Mary Beth. You're holding back on me. What else is bothering you? Do you want to try and get your mother away from your father? I can sure give you a ton of information on where she can go for help."

"That's a fabulous idea. It really is. But that's not the reason I asked to come over here today."

"Then let's figure out a way to get her out of there. Now tell me. What's the real reason you wanted to see me?"

"See? Here's the thing. I might be wrong. But I don't think so. And it would be very wrong if I knew something and I didn't say something and then something terrible happened."

What was she talking about? And then I realized what she meant and who.

"Ashley? What's going on, Mary Beth?"

"You have to swear this won't go back to her."

"You have my word."

"It's this guy she's seeing, the senator. Porter Galloway. Something about him is just too bizarre. He reminds me of my father because he plays head games with Ashley all the time. He's telling her all this weird stuff."

The resemblance to her father's behavior wasn't good, but it wasn't exactly grounds for an order of protection either.

"Like what's he telling her?"

"Well, he told her he fell in love with her the minute he saw her the first time and that he's been waiting for a girl like her all his life?"

"I think that's kind of sweet, personally," I said.

"Yes, but he thinks he owns her."

"How so?"

"Well, he doesn't want to know her friends, which is a bad sign if you ask me. And he always decides where they're going and what they're doing."

"But Ashley's friends are a good bit younger, aren't they?"

"True. Look, I don't know but he's always telling her not to say yeah but say yes and not to say awesome, like he's using mind control or something."

"Well, he is a public figure and how she conducts herself would, silly as it seems, reflect on him. At some point. If their relationship really went somewhere that is. The public is fascinated by all that stuff. Remember when Kate Middleton and Prince William were dating? My goodness! They couldn't go to the movies without someone having something to say about it."

"Yes, well, here's the story that really upset me. One night I was coming into the house and Galloway was running down the steps like I don't know what. When I got inside, there was Ashley on the floor and her head was bleeding. Now, granted, she had obviously been drinking some wine—too much, to be perfectly blunt. But how could he leave her like that?"

"Maybe she fell after he left?" I said. I didn't like that one bit.

"Then why was he in such a hurry to get out of there?"

"Maybe they'd had an argument? I don't know but it's a reasonable assumption, isn't it?" Or not, I thought.

"Maybe. Look, maybe I'm wrong about this but I just don't like him."

"I've only seen him on television and he seems a little full of himself but then most politicians are overly confident. Clayton says they're seldom right but they're never in doubt. That always makes me laugh. Ah, that Clayton is such a card sometimes."

"So then he's doing okay, I guess?"

Had my mother sent an engraved announcement to every resident of Charleston County that I'd gone to the Big Apple to kick my husband's behind for fooling around on me?

"Of course he's fine. Why wouldn't he be?" I narrowed my eyes at her.

"Right," she said. "Anyway, Ashley thinks she's going to be the next Jackie Kennedy or something. It's just annoying. And I was just really worried."

Mary Beth was plainly jealous and that's what this visit was all about.

"Who knows?" I said. "She *might* be the next Jackie, or she might be the next Mary Cassatt! Or both! You girls are so young. You don't have to be the reincarnation of anyone yet. So tell me, Mary Beth, do you have a boyfriend?"

Now that Mary Beth's suspicions had been met with reason and dispelled, she was a little uncomfortable. And like many people would when they're in the hot seat, she began to babble, but something told me she was still holding back.

"Yeah. Sort of. I mean, my taste in men is probably worse than Ashley's."

"How so?"

"Well, this guy I'm seeing isn't exactly the type I'd take home to Tennessee. And he comes from another culture where they treat women like cattle or something, you know, the women wear burkas and aren't allowed to drive or go to school?"

"He sounds interesting to me! My son has a partner who's Asian."

"That's different, believe me. This guy, Samir is his name, is peculiar in the intimate department."

"How peculiar is he?"

"Well," Mary Beth said and then she told me in excruciating detail exactly what it was that made Samir peculiar. "Sick, right?"

Her story nearly knocked the wind out of me.

"It's a strange one, okay. Let's go heat up your pizza," I said. "Then you and I are going to have us a little girl-to-girl chat."

I put her slice in the microwave, set it for thirty seconds on high, and pressed the start button. I had thirty seconds to figure out what to say to her. The television was on, as it usually was, and tuned to the Weather Channel. We stood there staring at it like most people did. Basically, during August and September the Lowcountry lived on storm watch. This had been a particularly busy hurricane season so far but luckily, except for late-afternoon thunderstorms, Charleston had been spared. Still, we watched and tried to figure out the path of one after another as they skirted our coastline and blew out to sea.

"What do you think about Melissa? She's a Category One," Mary Beth said.

"That's not so scary," I said. "I think we watch it and see. Right now it's stalled. It might fizzle out. But if it comes directly for us, I want you and Ashley downtown with me. And Maisie and Skipper."

"House party! I'll make togas from top sheets!"

The microwave timer went off.

"Darlin'? No one but my husband ever sees me in sheets," I said as I rolled my eyes at her and reached in the microwave for her plate. "I think I'll take another slice for myself."

She giggled and said, "Good one."

I heated my second slice, and when the timer pinged, we went back to my office. I sat down and took a big bite of my pizza and thought for a moment while she practically devoured hers. In fact, we didn't speak at all until we were finished eating.

Mary Beth? Mary Beth? Who was this lost child before me? She was trained as an elementary school teacher. She only subbed occasionally and worked intermittently for a caterer. She had to be broke. But she had a darling personality.

"You still working for that caterer?" I asked.

"Yeah, when they need me, which is about three times a week, on a good week."

"I know you majored in elementary education. What was your minor?"

"Psychology."

Perfect! She'd be a natural in fund-raising for an organization like ours. I had an idea.

"Mary Beth? It's time you got your life on a better track. You need a master's degree in psychology. You have to go back to school."

"Can't afford it," she said.

"Yes, you can. I'll pay the tuition if you come here and do volunteer work for me in return. I need help in development for the campaign we just launched. Then when you graduate, you'll already have business experience and no student loans to pay."

"But I think I might like to open my own catering company."

"I know. We've talked about that. Here's what's wrong with that. If you're successful, you'll never have a free night, weekend, or holiday."

"But! I'll also go to a fabulous party every night on somebody else's money."

She wasn't wrong. She was just young.

"So you can take some business courses too. No reason why you can't. And if you think a degree in psychology won't help you in business, you're dead wrong!"

"Are you really serious? I mean, you'd pay my tuition and all I have to do is help you here? Why would you do this for me?"

"For a lot of reasons. I've known you since your first day at the college. You're family to us. Someone needs to help you off the hamster wheel and I can do that. And maybe this should be the primary reason: you *understand* domestic violence so I think you'd be really great at this kind of work. It would give you a chance to reassess your own self-worth. We'll take graduate school one semester at a time. And don't worry. This isn't really a gift. You know me—you'll *earn* your tuition money."

Clayton said to start spending, so here I go!

"Would I actually be working with abused women and children, because I'm not sure I could take it. I mean, let me rephrase that, I couldn't take it. I'd cry all day long."

"No worries, darlin' child, you'll be answering phones, making phone calls, running errands, and setting up appointments. When you get your *doctorate* in psychology, you can decide if you want to get more involved with the cause. And I expect you will. How are your Internet skills?"

"About the same as anybody my age," she said.

"Which puts you light-years ahead of me and Tom. Good. We have a website and a presence on all the social media sites too. You can help manage them. Here. Take this folder. It has all the information you need to come to work here. And Mary Beth?"

"Yes?"

"Tell Samir your aunt Liz said he should go to hell and stay there. Clayton and I will find you a nice young man."

"That would be awesome. Can I really call you Aunt Liz? And can I give you a hug?"

"Oh, what the heck. But call me Mizz Liz, okay?"

I stood up and she hugged me with all her might. The poor child.

"Oh! And please don't tell Ashley about what I said. I was just so worried. And here's the thing. Right now they're broken up? But by tomorrow they might not be. I just don't want her to be mad with me."

"You secret is safe with me."

Wasn't it sort of wonderful that I was able to look at Mary Beth's situation and inside of an hour we'd hatched a plan to get her life moving in a stronger, more positive direction? Now I needed to do the same thing for Ashley. I wondered if there was any reason to worry for Ashley's safety and decided there probably was not. All the same, something in the back of my head told me to be vigilant, not unreasonably intrusive, just vigilant.

When Mary Beth left, I called Ashley.

"Hi, Mom! What's going on?"

"Nothing too much. Just watching the new hurricane, Melissa. So far it's not so scary. But it's Noreen that looks to be a stinker. Maybe."

"Whatever. How's Dad?"

"Dad's great. He's here for a while. I thought maybe this weekend you might like to come home. Bring Mary Beth. We can have a hurricane party."

"Well, since my social life blew up again . . . how's Saturday night? We can help you cook and clean up. And Mary Beth makes awesome eggs Benedict. Maybe we could do that for Sunday brunch?"

"That sounds great. See you!"

She had not said a word about Clayton and I wondered then if she even knew I went to New York at all. Was it possible that Ivy and Maisie didn't blab it to the world? Well, stranger things have happened.

CHAPTER 19

Ashley—Tied Up

When I wasn't wallowing in despair and painting like mad, I was still furious with Porter. Just who did he think he was anyway? God's gift to women? Well, he wasn't. And he wasn't going to tell me how to live my life anymore either. But the truth? He was really an idiot because I had loved him and I would've been so good for him. I had the perfect résumé to be the flawless politician's wife. Maybe I was young and a little naive but the world loved a new fresh face, especially one with deep roots and a solid family to back . . . okay, maybe my family was from another planet sometimes. But basically, we loved one another, in spite of the things we did. Loving one another was the most important thing. And we weren't that different from the rest of the population, really. Were we? Didn't every family have at least one relative they wished they could stick in the attic? I liked to think of us as sweet eccentrics, evolving past our own quirks together, finding new quirks. Okay, I'll admit it; if we were held up to public scrutiny, we might not show so well. But who does? Dad says only butt-kissing lightweights run for public office and that the real power in the United States is in the boardrooms and on Wall Street. He's probably right. Anyway, it didn't matter because I wasn't seeing Porter anymore. Besides, I'm only twenty-three and I still just want to paint. Someday my prince will come. I was just really disappointed because I thought he already had.

It was early Monday afternoon and the gallery was closed. Mary Beth and I were home, doing laundry and cleaning up the house. I had been in my studio all morning and went back to the house to do chores. Mary Beth was acting odd, like she wasn't telling me something. It could've been anything. Maybe her hormones were giving her a fit. We had decided that, in spite of the hurricane that was hovering over the Virgin Islands, we were going to throw one more party that Friday night and then go out of the party business. Forever. I had over a thousand dollars in my shoebox and it seemed like that ought to be enough for a while. I'd just sit on it until we came up with a new scheme.

"It's too risky," I said.

"Well, it was fun while it lasted," she said.

"My mom, who suddenly has ESP," I said, "thinks this stupid hurricane Melissa is going to give us a wallop on Saturday. She called me and she wants us to come over to her house to spend the night. She says we can have a hurricane party. I told her you'd make eggs Benedict Sunday morning."

I was folding towels and Mary Beth was scrubbing the countertops with a disinfectant cleaning spray and a vengeance. The whole room smelled like lemons. I loved the scent.

"Sure. That sounds like fun, actually."

"Did you call Tommy about Friday?"

"All taken care of. He's superexcited about some expensive new tie he just bought from Ben Silver. Apparently it's got itty-bitty martini glasses all over it. So he's going to wear it Friday."

"That's pretty sweet," I said. "He's a nice guy."

"Yeah, and he's got Ed lined up to bartend, and I've got Ursula coming to help with the kitchen."

"Ursula? Is that her name? Really?"

"No. I call her Ursula like the octopus from *The Little Mermaid*? Remember her? She has so many arms she can load the dishwasher in like ten minutes?"

"That's funny." I laughed.

"Yeah, well, anyway, I'll go to Costco tomorrow and get everything." She stood back from the counter and scrutinized it, looking for streaks. "This looks clean enough, doesn't it?"

"Gosh! The counters look brand-new! For real!"

"Thanks! I did a booze inventory and all we really need for Friday are two liters of vodka. No biggie. And of course, we need white wine."

"I can come with you and help carry everything. I'm only working until six."

"I wish you could, but I've got a gig tomorrow night. Hey, have you heard from Porter?"

"No. And this time I'm sure I won't."

"Oh, yes, you will. He'll turn up. They all come back, sniffing around until something else makes them stop, like another alley cat."

"Maybe, but I really don't want to see him, Mary Beth. Not after what happened."

"Yeah, there's nothing like date rape to leave a bad taste in your mouth about a guy. What a complete and total piece of shit he is. If you'd *say* something, you could put a stop to him, you know. You could do the world a huge public service and take him off the stage."

"Sorry, let somebody else do that. And listen, at some point I would've gone to bed with him anyway. The worst part was that we were *so* incompatible."

"Ashley, listen to me and listen good, okay? Don't kid yourself. The worst part is that he forced himself on you. Beyond a doubt *that* is the worst part. And you know what? I'm glad you were so incompatible. You deserve so much better than him. I hope he's out of your life. If he comes back begging, please don't let him in."

"I know. I won't. I just can't bring myself to face what he really did to me. And here's the extremely crazy part—some part of me sort of still misses him, Mary Beth. What's the matter with me? I can't help it."

"You don't miss him. You miss what could've been. You were dreaming up a fairy tale for yourself but who knows? You might wind up as first lady of the United States anyway, if that's what's meant to be."

"It's just such a disappointment," I said.

"I know. I told Samir to shove it too. I'm just too normal for him. He needs a freak, and I mean that in the nicest possible way."

"Bless his weird little heart," I said. We sort of laughed then and some tension seemed to have disappeared. "What happened?"

Mary Beth paused for a long moment and then she spoke.

"Well, you're going to find out anyway so I may as well tell you now."

"What? Tell me what?"

"It was your mom who made me see how stupid it was to be

wasting my time with him. I went to have lunch with her because of you, only because I was so worried . . ."

"*You did what?*"

"Hang on! Let me explain!"

Here came the whole story tumbling out of her about how she went to see my mom and told her about Porter and all, except she didn't tell my mom what happened the last time I saw him. I will never be able to call it what it was, maybe because it would paint me as a victim and I couldn't stand the thought of that. At first I was really angry that Mary Beth told my mother the things she did, but then I heard new details about her family, things that I'd never known. And my mom, formerly known as the Impossible (one half of a very impossible duo), was getting Mary Beth off her derriere to apply to graduate school? And she was going to work at My Sister's House? By then I was so proud of Big Liz I could've cried. So I did. I cried my heart out because Mary Beth was crying too. All the anxiety and bitter disappointment we felt had turned into a flood of tears. We just let it all go.

"How come you didn't tell her about what he did to me?"

"Because she had an excuse for everything I *did* tell her."

"What? She did?"

"Ash, even *you* don't want to admit you were raped!"

"I know. And I probably never will. To tell you the truth, I still don't understand how you found the guts to tell her anything."

"Because I was scared, Ashley. Look, if you were really my sister, I would've told our mom what was going on. And you're practically my sister, aren't you?"

"Of course I am! We've been sisters since the first day of college."

"And your mom is more a mother to me than my real one. She's just up there in Tennessee letting my dad whale on her whenever he feels like it."

"That's just so wrong. How come you never told me about your dad?"

"Because I was ashamed, Ashley. And I guess when your family is so violent and dangerous you're afraid to talk about it because it might make it worse. It was so terrible living in that house. The secrets! The manipulation! You can't imagine how glad I am to be away from them. I still have nightmares all the time. And I probably will for the rest of my life."

"Oh, gosh. I'm just so sorry, Mary Beth. But you're safe here."

"I know. But *you* weren't safe. I just couldn't stand by and watch it go on. You couldn't see it but Porter is exactly like my father. Everyone thinks he's so nice and all, but he's Dr. Jekyll and Mr. Hyde. I never knew which one was in the house when I came home. It was so scary. And it's the same thing with Porter. Everyone thinks he's this saint but he's not. I mean, Ash, Porter shows every single classic sign of being an abuser."

She went to her purse and pulled out some papers.

"Read this," she said, flipping through them until she found the one she wanted. "Your mom gave this to me."

The headline read, "Profile of an Abuser." Porter fit every single characteristic. He claimed that he loved me at first sight, he wanted a commitment, he wanted to stereotype me into some female archetype from the 1950s, he was jealous and possessive, and he didn't like my friends. On and on it went and I could find him in every line, especially the part about nonconsensual sex. And when I got to the part about the *learned responses of the victim,* there *I* was on every single line, especially the section about defending him.

Now we really started to cry. I got a box of tissues and put it in between us on the kitchen counter. I pulled two and handed them to her and took two for myself. I had been headed into an abusive relationship and my dear friend who had suffered so badly at the hands of her own father had tried to save me from a similar fate.

"This makes me wish I had the courage to stand up to him and tell him what I really think of him, you know?"

"Well, maybe someday you'll get the chance. At least you're out of that screwed-up situation."

"Yeah. We've *got* to get your mom out of there, Mary Beth."

"I know, I know. Once I admitted to your mom how bad it was at home, it took on a whole different meaning. I couldn't believe what was coming out of my mouth. I realized I was in denial about it all these years. Sort of like, if I didn't ever verbalize it, then maybe it wasn't true? And now with my brothers out of the house, my mother takes the brunt of all his anger. What's the matter with me?"

"I'm no better." Somehow through all my sniffling and blowing my nose I said, "My mom will help her. She will. It's what she does."

"She said she would."

"Then she will. Oh my God. My poor mother. Between my father's stupid fling, and your stuff and now mine? I have to do something nice for her. I haven't been thinking about her at all. I really haven't."

"Maybe this weekend we could take her like a ton of flowers or something?" Mary Beth said.

"Awesome idea. She loves flowers. If we spend fifty dollars at the Bi-Lo we can fill up the house."

"Awesome. Let's do it."

We dried our eyes and hugged and went back to the business

of planning Friday's soiree and saying yeah and awesome. Life was already so much better.

I worked Tuesday and Wednesday without much to report except that Dad had gone back to New York. He was retiring. He was also packing up the apartment and putting it on the market. I knew it was a good idea, but I was sort of sad about it for my own reasons. I liked the idea of having an apartment there that belonged to us. I was still hoping against hope that I'd be able to scrape up enough money to go and stay there for a few weeks. I seriously needed to see all the museums and all the galleries or else I may as well give up on being a painter altogether. Yes, I could paint commissioned portraits without the inspiration of other artists, but I didn't want to be that kind of an artist. The very idea of it was depressing and made me feel like I'd always be a local amateur. The alternative was to open my own gallery and represent younger artists who made edgier stuff. That was my fallback. And I could show my own stuff from time to time.

By late Thursday afternoon, the ocean was looking pretty crazy. Mary Beth and I were standing on the portico. The salt spray was stinging our faces, causing us to squint. The ocean was churning and roiling. And the color of the water was deeper, closer to black than blue. The charcoal sky was filled with fast-moving clouds and the wind was picking up, whipping all the palmettos and oleanders around like they were destined to take off and fly away. There was no question that a really nasty storm was coming to town.

"Do you think we should cancel tomorrow?" Mary Beth said, trying in vain to hold her hair in a ponytail.

"I don't know. I mean, it might be exciting for people to see the harbor like this. It's getting wilder, but I don't think it's dangerous, do you?"

"Nah, but we should keep watching the weather."

"Call Tommy. See what he thinks."

"Okay," she said, tapped his number into her phone, and walked back inside. "Hey! You got a minute?"

My cell phone was ringing too, so I ran inside to answer it. By the time I got there it went to voice mail. It was Porter. I wasn't calling him back.

Mary Beth walked back toward me. I was standing just inside the room off the portico, watching the weather.

"What did Tommy say?" I asked.

"He said we should turn on Eyewitness News and keep it on. We both agreed that since we already have a dump truck's worth of food, we should try to have it. But if they start talking about closing bridges, we should cancel."

"I think we should have everyone come in trench coats and dark glasses and call it a spy party," I said. "Tommy doesn't stand to lose anything except his tip jar. We've got a boatload of shrimp salad and it wasn't cheap."

"You and your theme parties!" she said. "Why are you holding your phone? Who called?"

"Who do you think?"

"Did you talk to him?"

I shook my head. "No message either."

"What an ass."

"Yeah," I said. "He sure is."

The rain started on Friday morning, right after I got up to go to work. I stared out the bathroom window while I was brushing my teeth. The yard was already starting to puddle. It seemed like the wind wasn't nearly as bad as it had been yesterday. Still, in this kind of weather there wouldn't be a single soul in the gallery that day so it was kind of stupid for me to even go in. It would be like stealing money from the Turners. I'd wait until nine and then I'd call and see what they thought. I pulled on a cotton sweater and a skirt. I'd need my rain boots if I went out. I wondered where they were.

Mary Beth was in the kitchen making coffee.

"Good day for the ducks, like Maisie says," I said. "What do you think?"

"I think it's a mess out there. Let's flip on the news." She picked up the remote and clicked through a few stations until she found a local weather report.

A very serious meteorologist with his shirtsleeves rolled up as if he'd been up all night spoke to the camera while the map behind him came to life. Various ribbons of colors moved across the coast, blinking and undulating like neon-colored snakes.

A hurricane warning is in effect tonight through Sunday as Hurricane Melissa makes her way toward the Lowcountry of South Carolina. Winds are out of the east/southeast and expected to exceed seventy-five miles per hour as the storm approaches with gusts maybe as high as ninety miles per hour. This is still a Category One storm but what happens in the next twenty-four hours can change all that. And just to remind our listeners, this might be a good time to bring in your porch furniture, secure those garbage cans, and make your property storm-ready. Make sure you have plenty of working batteries and drinkable water in case you lose power. For more comprehensive information on how to hurricane proof your home and to protect your loved ones go to Live5news.com.

"I'm not too impressed," I said. "Looks like more of a wind maker than a rainmaker."

"You're not impressed?" she said.

"Heck no. I grew up with hurricanes always threatening to blow us to kingdom come. This is going to be messy but it's not really dangerous. Unless it gets here on a high tide and a full moon. The moon's not full, is it?"

We googled the phases of the moon on our phones.

"On the wane," I said.

"Yeah, but it's still pretty full."

"Yeah, that's not so great," I admitted. "When is it supposed to make landfall here?"

"I don't think they're too sure it's going to make landfall in South Carolina at all. At least not yet."

"So let's just leave the television on then. You feel like breakfast?"

"French toast made from diet bread, egg whites, and low sugar syrup?"

"Why not? I'll nuke us some center cut bacon," I said. "Three strips for only seventy calories."

"Well, now that we are both officially back on the market, we have to watch it, don't you think?"

"I think I'm not thinking about it yet," I said as I poured a lot of real half-and-half into my mug of coffee. "Dieting is too stupid, and so is thinking of us as merchandise."

"You're right, of course. But my clothes are too tight."

"That's different. Let's give up meat and dairy."

"Except for bacon and yogurt."

"Deal. Starting Monday."

It made me laugh to think about how we'd devise these ridiculous plans to save calories when it seemed like we never lost a pound unless we flat-out starved and worked out like Olympians.

I never went to work. Bill and Judy Turner said they weren't really expecting to see anyone that day. Rain was bad for business. I was just as happy to stay home and help Mary Beth make sandwiches.

Tommy rolled in around three with Ed and Ursula and they began bringing in all the boxes of glasses and the party tables from the cottage.

"Check out my very cool bow tie!" he said, unwrapping the tissue paper and holding it up to his neck.

"Awesome," I said and giggled.

"I'll just put it on the piano until later," he said and left the room.

"Like an art object," Mary Beth said and laughed.

"Exactly!" Tommy said, stepping back into the kitchen and smiling. "But I have to tell y'all, I think it's getting worse out there. Seriously. I said to Ed that maybe we should try to set the bar up indoors but he said, and he's right, that the whole point of this party is to be out on the portico and watch the sun going down. The sun, my friends, is nowhere to be seen."

"How about the Ravenel Bridge is swinging in the breeze a little?" Ed said. "I didn't say anything about it when I first came in because it seemed like the rain and wind were letting up. Bottom line? It's not."

"And the harbor out front is crazy water, choppy, swirling around like it shouldn't be doing," Tommy said. "I don't know, y'all."

"This is *not* good," Mary Beth said.

We flipped on the television, and, sure enough, over the past few hours the storm had been upgraded to a Category Two and was predicted to go to a Three by nine that night. The airport was a ghost town, speed limits were reduced to twenty-five miles per hour on the bridges, and Charleston was all but officially closed.

"That's it," I said. We looked at one another already knowing our party was not going to happen. No way in hell! "Y'all? We need to cancel this thing. It's insane. What if there are wrecks or whatever? What if somebody gets hurt? We might get sued, which means my parents will get sued and then Mary Beth and I would be homeless."

"Shoot," Mary Beth said. "You're right."

"What about all the food?" Tommy said.

"The only thing we'd really lose is the shrimp salad, which y'all should take some home, or we could just come back here Sunday when the storm is gone and have our own party, couldn't we?" I said.

"My mother would just save it and serve it on Sunday. She'd give the shrimp more lemon juice and tell us to eat it anyway," Mary Beth said.

"Classic," Tommy said and smiled his goofy lopsided smile, loading big scoops of the salad into a plastic bag for himself and then another one for Ed. "Ursula? You want some?"

"Sí!" she said.

"I'm betting very few people would show up anyway," Ed said. "I mean, who goes out in this weather?"

He was probably right, but we started texting and tweeting as fast as we could, putting the kibosh on what was supposed to have been our final soiree. We agreed that maybe we'd just reschedule for a couple of weeks later. The shelf life on vodka, frozen pigs in blankets, cheese and crackers and tortilla chips was pretty much good until Thanksgiving or longer.

In the middle of our flurry of messaging and racing around, transferring things back to the cottage, my phone rang. It was Porter. I walked out to the hall and answered it.

"Hello?" I was very unexcited to hear his voice.

"Ashley? It's Porter."

"I know that." I hoped it sounded like I was saying, *so what?*

"What's the matter?"

I could detect a trace of panic in his voice.

"What do you mean, *what's the matter?*"

He was silent then. Did he think all he had to do was pick up the phone and everything would be okay between us again?

"Are you staying out at the beach during the storm?"

"I haven't decided," I said as evenly as I could, hoping it sounded like, *why should I tell you?*

"Ashley? You haven't told anyone, have you?"

So was this what he thought somebody with a conscience acted like?

"You mean, did I tell anyone what *you did* to me?"

"You wouldn't dare. And besides, you know you wanted it. Anyway, it would be your word against mine and who would believe . . ."

"Don't you dare threaten me, you, you . . . bastard!" I said and pressed the end button.

Was he serious? No one would take my word over his? If I'd gone to the ER that night they could've had enough DNA to hang him by his toes! I went back into the kitchen where everyone was still frantically repacking glasses into boxes and putting food back into shopping bags. I was so angry I was practically hyperventilating. I had to hold on to the side of the counter while I tried to calm myself down.

"What's wrong?" Mary Beth said. "He called again? What now?"

"I can't talk about it," I said. My face and neck were so hot and my heart was pounding in my ears. *He threatened me. And he said I had no credibility.*

Tommy was standing there with the last load of boxes in his arms, listening but not saying a word.

"I think I'm going downtown," I said. "Mary Beth, let's close up the house and go to my mom's. I'll call her on the way and let her know."

"I agree," she said. "Let's get out of here."

"Good idea," Tommy said. "Let's get off the island. I'll take Ed."

"I can drop off Ursula," Mary Beth said. "You want to ride with me, Ash?"

"No, I'm going to take my car and I want to just go over all the windows and everything once more before I leave."

Within the next fifteen minutes or so, everyone was gone. It didn't seem like it was raining so badly then. I thought about just staying the night by myself. I didn't really feel like being with my mom and a houseful of people. But I knew the storm would get worse. It would. And the wind would grow even stronger. Of course, there were other dangers to be considered. The house might flood, a tree might come through it, or we might lose power. You just never knew. The whole house might blow away. But I knew enough to know when to head for the hills and that was the plan. I was going to my mother's and somehow I would suppress my anger at Porter and no one would know.

I threw pajamas and a bunch of underwear in a tote bag and my cosmetics that I thought I'd want. I took my laptop and my chargers and threw them in too. Then I took what jewelry I had that was worth anything and put it in a sock, burying it in the bottom of my tote.

I checked and double-checked to see that all the windows were locked and then I locked the front door and raced to my car. I didn't set the alarm because who robs houses in a hurricane? I called my mom.

"Mom? Are you home?"

"Yes! We closed early. I'm here with Maisie and Skipper. Are you coming home? I'll tell you these fool weathermen had me thinking tomorrow was the worst day of the storm, but no! They're wrong again."

"I'm on my way and Mary Beth too."

"Well, thank God. Just take your time, all right? The wind is fierce. Go slowly on the bridge."

"I will. Don't worry. I'm already in the car. I'll see you soon."

I drove on and it was true, the weather was just dreadful. The water was almost to the top of the causeway. And just as I came to the traffic light at Rifle Range Road I realized I'd left my shoebox of cash behind. I swung my car around through the gas station and headed back to the island. I was only ten minutes away from the house. With my luck it would be the first hurricane in the history of Sullivans Island besieged by looters.

I pulled into the yard and there were pools of water everywhere. I looked at the cottage once more, thinking about my paintings and wondering if it would be better to move them to the second floor of the big house. I should have thought of that a couple of hours ago, I decided. I hopped out of the car with just my keys and made a run for the front steps. It took a minute to get the door open but I finally did, the ferocious wind grabbing the door away from me and slamming it against the wall of the foyer. The doorknob left an indentation in the plaster. My mother was going to give me the devil about that.

"Oh, fine!" I shouted to the house and left the door open, making a beeline for my bedroom closet.

As quickly as I could, I emptied the contents of the box onto my bed and stuffed all the money into another purse that had a zipper running across the top. I hurried out toward the front door and there stood Porter.

"What are you doing here?"

"I thought we needed to have a little talk, Ashley." His tone was threatening.

"About what?" I said. I was suddenly frightened.

"About what you said to me. Do you understand what would happen if anyone thought I had raped a woman? Do you understand that it would ruin my whole career? Do you?"

All I could think at that moment was that I wasn't going to lie for him, not then or ever. I don't know what possessed me to give me such courage.

"Well, Porter, you didn't seem to care about that when you held me down on my bed, did you?"

I never even saw his fist coming, but he hit me on my cheek, and then with the back of his hand he slapped my face, splitting my lip. I fell back against the wall and he started choking me. I couldn't breathe.

"You insignificant little whore," he said, "you'd better learn to keep your mouth shut or next time . . ."

Right before I thought I was going to black out, I saw Tommy's face. He grabbed Porter by the back of his jacket and spun him around. Then in a series of moves that had to be the chops and kicks of some kind of martial arts, he whipped Porter's ass. When Porter was knocked completely unconscious, Tommy looked at me.

"You okay?"

"Yeah," I said, but my voice was raspy and I was shaking from head to toe.

He pulled out his cell phone and dialed 911.

"I never liked this guy. Told you he was an asshole." Tommy came over, put his arm around me, and gave me a squeeze. "Let's get you a cold cloth."

We stumbled to the kitchen, threw a clean dish towel in the sink, covered it with cold water, and wrung it out. Tommy gave the details of what had happened to the authorities and where we were. In minutes I heard sirens.

There was a police car, a fire engine, and an ambulance in the yard.

"Why'd you come back, Tommy?"

"To get my tie. That thing cost almost a hundred dollars!"

"Really?"

"And I had a bad feeling." He smiled at me.

I could feel my lip starting to swell. And there was blood all over me.

The police were suddenly inside the house and when they saw Porter on the floor, they recognized him and called for a stretcher.

"What happened here?" said the police officer. "Isn't that guy a senator? What did he do?"

"He was trying to choke her when I got here," Tommy said.

"No, he wasn't," I said and then I stopped.

My mother, Mary Beth, and Maisie were also there.

My mother said, "We've been calling your cell phone for almost an hour! I was frightened out of my mind! Are you all right? Oh my God! What did he do to you?"

"What the hell, Ash?" Mary Beth said.

"Oh, my poor sweet girl! Come here and let me see your lip," Maisie said.

Before I could move, the officer said, "It looks like the senator has some explaining to do. Do you want to press charges, young lady? I'm gonna need everyone's names and some ID."

"No," I said.

"Yes," my mother said. "She wants to press charges. Ashley. You have to. It's the right thing to do."

"I don't know," I said.

"Liz!" Maisie said. "Why in heaven's name do you want to subject your daughter to a public free-for-all? It won't do any good. It won't change anything."

"Oh, yes it will. Do you understand that if this sweet young man—what's your name, son?"

"Tommy. Tommy Milano."

"Mother, if it hadn't been for Tommy here, we'd be planning a funeral for my daughter for the same reasons we buried Juliet."

"What are you talking about? Juliet died from an aneurysm," Maisie said.

"An aneurysm caused by a head injury caused by *abuse*. Her stupid abusive boyfriend banged her head on the *floor*!"

"He did no such thing."

By now, there was a small audience of people with dropped jaws, just listening. Except for Galloway who was handcuffed to the gurney and bellowing about his rights.

"Ashley!" he screamed. "Tell them the truth! Tell them Tommy did this to you and I was trying to save you! It was not me! Tell them!"

I walked over and looked him right in the eyes.

"I'm not lying for you, Porter," I said.

"We really could have had something," he said and closed his eyes.

"Juliet's boyfriend did no such thing," Maisie said again. "He was a lovely man."

"No, he wasn't and, yes, he did," my mother insisted. "You knew it and I knew it and we denied it for years! Why do you think I do the work I do?"

"I'm sorry, Liz," Maisie said and she started to weep. "Oh, God."

"What's done is done, Maisie."

"I should've been more honest with myself and you. All these years, we've carried Juliet's tragic death in our hearts and silently, I blame myself."

"Don't do that, Mom."

My mother called Maisie *Mom*.

"But you don't understand! Ashley is just so much like my Juliet. I just wanted to do the things for her that I would've done for your sister if she had lived. That's all."

"We can't change the past. If I couldn't help my only sister, at least I can help others. But, most of all, I'll be damned straight to hell if I'm going to stand by and watch my daughter be strangled and pummeled by this scum."

"You're right," Maisie said.

"So, yes, we're going to court and, yes, it's going to be messy but this is the last time Porter Galloway is going to hurt anyone and most of all, my daughter. Ashley? Are you with me?"

"One hundred percent," I said and I began to cry. This was all too much for me. I was completely overwhelmed.

I watched and listened as the police officer read Porter his Miranda rights and the EMS attendants rolled him out of the house.

"You're going to regret this!" Porter screamed.

Mom leaned over Porter's face and said quietly, "No. We won't, but you will."

A chill ran through my body.

"You okay now?" Tommy said.

"I think so. Tommy—thank you."

"Sure," he said. "Officer? Do I need to come with you?"

"Yes, you do. I just want to get a few more details from Ashley. You all right, sweetheart?"

"I'm fine," I said.

But I wasn't fine. Mary Beth put some ice in a baggie and covered it with a thin towel and handed it to me.

"Hold this on your cheek for a few minutes and then switch it to your lip," she said.

"Thanks," I said, and we exchanged looks of horror and disbelief.

I answered the officer's questions while my mother, who was also weeping, held my free hand. I had never loved her as much as I did then. She only left me for a brief moment when she walked the police officer and Tommy to the door and then it was just us— Maisie, my mother, Mary Beth, and me.

"Y'all hungry?" Mary Beth said, breaking the loudest silence ever.

Maisie blew her nose with a tissue from somewhere up in her sleeve. "Is there any gin in this house?"

"No, I don't think so. But there's vodka," I said.

"Good," said my mom.

"Vodka's fine," Maisie said. We all stared at her. None of us had ever seen her drink a drop of anything except gin. "Hell, there's a hurricane raging out there. We have to make do, don't we?"

And, to my complete surprise, we actually laughed.

"And we've got food for a hundred," Mary Beth said, spilling the beans.

"What are you talking about?" Mom said.

"Oh shoot, I guess there's a little more to tell," I said.

"I'll fix up a quick buffet," Mary Beth said. "Ash? You want a glass of white wine?"

"Well, maybe a little one will get my pulse back to normal. What do you think?"

"There's medicinal value in it," Maisie said. "I need to call Skipper."

"Therapeutic too," Mom said, dialing her home phone and handing it to Maisie.

"I got this," Mary Beth said and hurried to the kitchen.

"Tell me, Ashley. What's going on, baby?"

"Let's wait for Mary Beth," I said.

Very soon after, Mary Beth and I confessed the story of our parties while we nibbled on plates of shrimp salad and cherry tomatoes stuffed with mozzarella and picked at a platter of cheese and fruit. My mother's eyes grew larger and larger until she finally burst out laughing. Maisie began to chuckle then too. My mother stood up and kissed me on the top of my head and she kissed Mary Beth on her cheek. She couldn't stop laughing.

"You think it's funny?" I said. "I thought you'd disown me!"

"Well, I'm torn between admiration for your cunning and ingenuity and by horror over who might have been here and come back in the night and murdered you in your bed!"

"I know, right?" Mary Beth said. "We were lucky."

"Speak for yourself," I said. "I was just almost murdered by a senator in broad daylight!"

"He was just a state senator. It wasn't like he was Fritz Hollings or somebody," Maisie said. "But here we are in a hurricane, three generations of survivors!"

"Here's to the sister I never had!" Mary Beth said, holding up her glass to me.

"And here's to the sister I lost!" my mother said, raising her glass to Maisie.

Maisie looked at us and said, "All right now. No more sadness. From here on in, we're going to live life to the fullest! Life is for the living. Here's to us, we're the Hurricane Sisters!"

"Yes," I said. The Hurricane Sisters. I liked that. I liked it a lot.

We all toasted one another and quietly acknowledged that something very special had happened that night. I guess it would be similar to how men say it is when they've fought a war together. In the trenches, or wherever it is that men go when they have to fight a war, there's a bond they form. A bond that lasts forever and supersedes the stupid mistakes we all make. Because they lived and survived combat together, just as we had survived a literal hurricane and some long overdue but painful truth telling.

Eventually, we walked out to the portico to check out the storm.

"Looks like Melissa must've changed her mind and gone on up to Cape Hatteras," my mother said. She sounded wistful but most of all, she was relieved.

We were all relieved.

The wind had died down, but the water was still crashing against the shore.

"Skipper thinks we should probably all stay here tonight," Maisie said.

"What if Porter gets out of jail and no one believes me?" I said.

"Won't happen," Mom said.

"You've got witnesses," Mary Beth said.

"Don't worry, sweetheart. I've got a plan up my sleeve that will keep him away from you forever," Maisie said.

"What are you thinking?" I said.

"Don't you worry," Maisie said. "But I'll give you a hint. It involves a lady of a certain age, a llama, and a short trip on Highway 17 South."

No one wanted details. We didn't want to ruin our own surprise. And we didn't doubt the cleverness of Maisie's idea one bit. After all, it was she who dubbed us the Hurricane Sisters, a team of clever girls who could get through everything as long as we stuck together and told the truth. And as to my mother? I had to admit, Liz knew what life was all about. Deeply and completely. The rest of us still had much to learn.

Liz

It was the Saturday night before Thanksgiving. Bill Turner was taking Judy to Paris the next day to celebrate her fiftieth birthday. We joked with them that they'd have a hard time finding a turkey in Paris, but I don't think they cared about that too much. They'd tough it out and dine on truffles, foie gras, and caviar instead in some gorgeous French restaurant like Le Taillevent or Lasserre.

In any case, when the news broke about the Porter Galloway attack on Ashley, the Turners were the first people to come to Ashley's defense. She took a leave of absence from work because of all the attention Galloway's trial drew, a decision fully sanctioned by her father and me. We had wanted her to come stay with us downtown until it was all over, but she insisted on staying at the beach. She needed her space, she said. Reluctantly, we agreed but checked on her well-being and state of mind every day.

The Turners were so upset they drove over to Sullivans Island where they found her in the cottage, painting like mad.

"Binge painting is excellent therapy," Bill said.

Ashley, as you might imagine, was traumatized by the attack and a bit depressed. As predicted, she didn't enjoy the negative attention the trial brought. The most debilitating remnant was that she was so disappointed in her own judgment. She had really believed in Porter's integrity at one point and she had placed herself in a risky situation at another. She blamed herself for both and wondered when she could trust herself again. Still, she handled herself with a grace I didn't know she had.

"I didn't do anything wrong," she said.

"You certainly did not," I replied every time she said it.

The irony was not lost on me that even with a career of learning about domestic violence—I was supposed to be an expert on the subject—I still had failed to spot the signs in my own daughter's life. Even when they were staring me in the face and even when I was warned.

Maisie and I had been in a similar situation that resulted in the death of my poor sister. Maisie knew Juliet was being abused because *I told her,* but she wouldn't believe it because she had not seen it herself. And we paid a horrible, horrible price by not acting on the facts and our intuitions. This was the wound between us that festered for all these years. There was nothing to be done about that now except to try and forgive ourselves and each other.

But back to my other point, the Turners were among Ashley's first and strongest supporters. What the Turners didn't expect when they visited her studio was to be astounded by Ashley's work. To Ashley's complete surprise, they offered her a show. She was happy for the first time in a long time. And we, Clayton and I, were so touched that I told them so.

"Thank you for doing this for her," I said. "Maybe this is just the thing that will bring her back to her normal self."

"That's not why we're doing this. Ashley deserves a show on the merit of her work. I wouldn't even entertain the idea unless she did. None of us realized that your daughter has such an extraordinary talent," Judy said. "Fresh and new . . . I just love her point of view."

Of course, Maisie, on hearing the news, piped up and said, "Well, I always thought so. I said so from the time she was this big."

She held her thumb and forefinger just slightly apart in front of my face, to show us just how long ago she knew. I just wanted to pinch her, you know?

When Clayton and I saw Ashley's paintings all lined up against a wall, we were shocked. There was a series of palmettos and birds painted in bold and vivid colors, but her figurative paintings had a powerful emotional punch and were very moving. Even a little strange. Especially the one of Ivy, at least I thought it was Ivy, sitting all alone on the front steps of a big building. It made me want to sob because all I could think about was all the unnecessary pain we inflicted on one another. But that was buried in the attic of the past where it belonged.

There was a very strange acrylic of a wolf dressed in a uniform with a wolf's tail, hands, and feet. He was playing cards with a bunch of other wolves, and oddly, he looked familiar through the eyes. I didn't know what the symbolism meant, but I was sure Ashley would tell me. And there was a portrait of a young woman on a balcony. Juliet. My sister. Except she was Ashley. Or was she? Then there was some kind of homage to *The Birth of Venus* that looked a bit like me and another of Mona Lisa except that the face was clearly Maisie's. What did they mean? Well, Maisie surely kept secrets when she wanted to and she certainly considered herself to be all-knowing. Me? There was no question that I had been reborn.

So had my marriage and in fact, the whole darn bunch of us had taken a huge turn for the better. I took it upon myself to be sure we stayed on the right track.

So after weeks of planning, my entire family, including a fully recovered Skipper and of course Ivy's James, were all gathered at the Turner Gallery for the opening of Ashley's first exhibition. The Turners used their extensive mailing list and sent beautiful invitations to everyone they knew. I had invited Tom and Vicki and of course the Malcolms and the Karols.

In less than an hour, guests would start to arrive. Clayton had offered to underwrite all the catering, which Mary Beth was hired to provide, but the Turners wouldn't hear of it. They wanted to give Ashley a grand debut because they loved her. And they said she would always remember that they hosted the first professional show of her career. So contracts were drawn up; canvases were insured and transported, installed, and lit; and a catalog was produced with a price list. How the Turners determined the prices was beyond me, but it was amazing to Clayton and to me that they thought her smallest canvas could bring fifteen hundred dollars.

"I've got my doubts about that," he said.

"What do we know?" I said.

He shook his head in agreement.

Despite our misgivings, we were, all of us, bursting with pride over the confidence the Turners had in Ashley's talent and about the dignified way she continued to handle herself. She was fully emotionally prepared to enter the ranks of professional artists. By the way, Tommy Milano was at her side and had been a fixture in her life for quite a while.

"We're just friends," she said. Nevertheless, she bought him a new bow tie with tiny pianos all over it. And any fool could see they were very fond of each other.

I can't tell you that the past few months were easy. Buckets of tears were shed, especially between Maisie and me as we struggled to bury our hatchets. But a new peace was forged at last, and things between us would be remarkably kinder for the rest of our days. I hoped.

Just last week, we were on the portico of our house on Sullivans Island talking about Ashley's show and the subject of Juliet came up.

"For once and for all, you have to stop blaming yourself," I said. "You talk to me about forgiveness? It has to start with you, Maisie. I'm sure Juliet doesn't blame you or me."

"She was my firstborn child," she said. "I lost my beautiful daughter."

The anguish in her voice had diminished over the years but the profound sorrow was still there. Her eyes, the color faded from her years, were rimmed in red and brimming with tears.

"She was my only sister," I said. "I lost my only sister."

Suddenly, she threw her arms around me and said for the first time, "I'm so sorry, Liz. I'm so sorry."

"Me too," I said.

"I should have tried to comfort you."

That was all I had *ever* wanted to hear her say.

Needless to say, Clayton was a changed and better man. Retirement agreed with him. He decided he wanted to spend more time on the island and said that in the fall he was going to renovate the whole house.

"It's a sin not to take care of this old place," he said. "Hey! Maybe next month Maisie can show me how to plant tomatoes. It would be nice to have tomatoes all summer. What do you think?"

"I think she'd love to plant a whole vegetable garden with you," I said.

It would be a good project for him. He was as sweet as a little lamb and I'm so happy to report that he played golf with Skipper three times a week and with David and Steve on the weekends. Now I wouldn't have to chase a stupid little ball all over the place for hours in the blazing sun. Thank you, Skipper. Really.

But the best news of all was that Porter Galloway resigned from office and was rumored to be moving to East Africa on a mission sponsored by his mother's church. His plan was to try and redeem himself and his reputation by becoming a member of the clergy. Please, I know. But he could only leave the country after he served a little time as a guest of the state. He made as many public apologies as he could until none of the press would take his phone calls. Apparently his hubris and violent nature were no longer news. All I cared about was that soon he was headed to the other side of the world, away from my daughter. I hoped he'd stay there forever. And just to be sure he stayed away, Maisie walked a llama down Highway 17. He could never reconcile with Ashley or, heaven forbid, try to marry her when her grandmother had such a loose screw. Especially if he had delusions about running for public office ever again.

And, I have to say, my Ashley looked so beautiful at her opening. She was wearing a new dress her father and I bought her. It was a simple design, a deep blue lightweight wool dress. Maisie's triple strand of pearls hung around her neck.

"Jackie O would've loved this dress," I said.

"So would Audrey Hepburn," she said.

"Audrey Hepburn?"

"Yes," she said, quite seriously. "I'm closing my chapter on politics and politicians' wives. I'm moving on to Hollywood and old film stars."

Now, who would blame her for that?

We opened the doors at six and people drifted in, showing their invitations and giving their names to a pretty young girl with a guest list. By six thirty, the gallery was quite full. Among them was a young lawyer named Cindy Lue Elder. Ashley brought her over to introduce her to me.

"I thought y'all should meet," Ashley said.

"Oh? Well, hello, Cindy, and welcome!" I said. "How do y'all know each other?"

"I used to be the princess of denial," she said, and when she saw my puzzled expression, she added, "I used to be involved with Porter Galloway."

"Oh, dear. Denial. Classic victim response," I said.

"Now I do legal work for a battered women's shelter in Cleveland," she said. "I'm just so glad Ashley is okay."

"So are we," I said.

Soon Ashley had been photographed by all the local papers and interviewed as well. Clayton was holding court in one room and Maisie in another, both of them going on about how Ashley inherited her talent from them. It really made me laugh. And Ivy? He was making sure that Ashley worked the room and didn't miss meeting anyone who might be a potential buyer. His retail experience was invaluable that night because by the time we left the gallery for dinner at Charleston Place, every canvas but one was sold.

"Which one didn't sell?" I asked after we had toasted Ashley so many times it was just ridiculous.

"The wolf," she said.

"Give it to me," Maisie said. "I'll give it to Porter's mother. I never liked her anyway."

"What?" I said. "That wolf was Porter?"

I whispered Porter's name for the sake of our family's privacy. I was still afraid that if we mentioned him in public it would wind up in all the media.

"Who else could it have been?" Tommy said.

"That is so perfect," Ivy said.

"I love your family," James said. "I mean *love!*"

"So do I," said Tommy. "Hey! Where's Mary Beth?"

"She's cleaning up. She'll be along soon," Clayton said.

"She's a treasure," I said and thought about how hard she worked at My Sister's House.

"Well, Ashley?" Skipper said. "It's time to go bohemian, don't you think?"

"Paris?" she said, and her pretty eyes were filled with dreams once again. "Montmartre?"

"You can't afford . . . ," Clayton said and stopped. "Wait. Yes, you *can* afford it. You made a small fortune tonight and you know what? If you run out of money, let me know. I'll help you."

"I will too," Maisie said. "Artists have had patrons throughout history."

I gave my mother a look.

"What?" she said.

"Nothing," I said. Soon, Ashley wouldn't need a dime from anyone.

"I was thinking maybe next April?" Ashley said.

"Should I sing it?" Ivy said. "Hmmm?"

"Juliet would have loved Paris. I'll have to paint for two."

April in Paris. Maybe I'd go with her, help her find a safe apartment in a suitable neighborhood. We could use a mother-daughter trip. And she was right. Juliet would have loved Paris.

I looked around the table and marveled at how our lives had changed so much in such a short period of time. We were an imperfect family. I knew that. But at last we were on each other's side, dug in with a new and more profound commitment. Our happiness was hard won, it was ours and I was determined to keep us whole. The world had not heard the last of this Hurricane Sister or of the others as well. We all still have a lot of noise left to make. You can count on it.

AUTHOR'S NOTE

Dear Friends,

While doing research for *The Hurricane Sisters* I came across the startling facts about South Carolina's high ranking in cases of domestic homicide in the United States. I began to dig and ask questions only to discover that the problem is dramatically worse than I ever would have imagined. The statistics at the national level are even more staggering.

In the United States every year, an estimated 1,300,000 women are victims of physical assault. The crimes are usually committed by an intimate partner. The 1,300,000 are only the cases that are reported. One point three million. Many, many more women remain silent because of denial or fear. And ultimately, an estimated 1,800 women in America die each year as a result of domestic violence.

On September 12, 2012, on just that one day, across the country over ten thousand cries for help from victims were unmet because of limited resources and funding.

I didn't know any of this before I started writing this book. I mention it here because I want to start a conversation with you and for you to have conversations with each other. What can we do? Battered women's shelters all over the country are in constant need of support—goods, services, and, of course, money. If you live in South Carolina, please consider a donation of any kind to support

My Sister's House. If you don't, please support the battered women's shelters near you. They save women and children, help to make them whole again, and, most of all, give victims hope.

Many thanks.

Dear Readers,

For the third time in a decade, South Carolina ranks FIRST in the nation for the number of women murdered by men, per annum.

Although this novel is a work of fiction, the statistics are a hard fact. My Sister's House, Inc. is a real nonprofit organization, located in Charleston, SC, and was founded in 1980. Women and children in immediate danger from verbal, emotional, physical, or sexual abuse are eligible for services at no charge. The organization provides 24-hour temporary emergency shelter and a crisis line to victims of domestic violence in addition to group and individual counseling, children's programs, outreach programs, and a host of other services. My Sister's House, Inc. strives to improve community awareness of and an appropriate response to the devastating effects of domestic violence.

In 2013, My Sister's House touched the lives of 4,286 clients, answered 2,043 crisis calls, supported 462 advocacy cases, hosted 1,584 participants in our outreach programs, made 2,526 referrals, sheltered 197 women and children, and spent 84 cents of every dollar raised on programs and services for our clients. In order to provide a safe, more spacious environment where victims can not only make decisions but also take action to make those decisions a reality, a new facility is the next large endeavor. At 9,500 square feet, the current shelter accommodates up to 36 residents and the new facility would accommodate 46. No waiting lists! It is clear that a new facility is not just a "want" but rather a "necessity" in our continued efforts to help victims, to educate the public, and to eradicate abuse. Currently, we are in the process of launching a 3.5 million dollar capital campaign to raise funds for the project.

We invite you to visit our website at www.mysistershouse .org and to learn more about our organization's mission, programs, and services. Then please consider making a donation to our capital campaign at www.mysistershouse .org/donate. Your contribution will make a significant difference in the lives of so many women and children who have chosen to flee an abusive, potentially life-threatening situation. Please help us in our mission to provide a "home away from home" for victims who long to feel safe and secure.

Thank you in advance for your generosity!

Warmest regards,

Mackie Moore
Director of Development
My Sister's House

ACKNOWLEDGMENTS

Using a real person's name for a character in a book has been a great way to raise money for worthy causes. And in *The Hurricane Sisters* four generous souls come to life in these pages as my characters. I have never met two of these folks so I can assure you that the behavior, language, and personalities of the characters bear no resemblance to the actual people. My thanks go to Cindy Lue Elder for her generous support of the Lamb Institute, and to Porter (and Lorraine) Galloway for their support of the auction my dear friend Catherine Hay organized for the Regional Medical Center of Orangeburg, South Carolina.

However, I do know Bill and Judy Turner well, as they are my neighbors and friends in Montclair and strong supporters of the Van Vleck Gardens Gala. Thank you for letting me rewrite your lives and I hope y'all get a kick out of this.

Now, truth—Joyce Cerato does not operate a llama farm. We've been great friends for an obscene amount of years and if she starts talking, so will I! Love ya, girl! If you need an interior designer, she's your girl.

More truth—Annie and David Malcolm live in San Diego, California. And Michelle and Steve Karol? They live in Boston and I'm always trying to lure all of them to Charleston so we can see each other more often! I hope y'all will be pleasantly surprised to find yourselves in this drama. It was fun being reminded of you each time I wrote your names!

And make sure you do stop in for dinner at SALT at Station 22 on Sullivans Island. Say hello to the owners, my old friend Marshall Stith and my new friend Richard Stoney. Tell Marshall to buy you a beer and to give the bill to Richard! Love y'all! And to the iconic Magwoods—thanks for the wonderful memories!

Thanks to Art Seiber of Seattle for the restaurant tip on Pam's Kitchen. And heartfelt thanks to Colleen Bozard and Rebecca Williams-Agee of the South Carolina Coalition Against Domestic Violence and Sexual Assault for their helpful information. But the biggest thanks of all go to Mackie Moore of My Sister's House in Charleston, South Carolina, for her endless patience and knowledge.

Special thanks to Mikie Hayes of the Medical University in Charleston for helping me visualize the hospital and to George Zur, who is not a politico in real life but a computer webmaster, for keeping the website alive. If you are ever in Charleston and need a lift, call Walter Whaley at Chauffeurs Unlimited. He's a living doll and we love him! (I suspect his wife, Joyce, is a saint!) And JoAnna Marie Tedesco for cluing me in on the real meaning of YOLO! Lastly, Maisie Pringle's deceased husband, Neal, is alive and well and living in Atlanta. I suspect he has never owned a llama.

I'd like to thank my wonderful editor at William Morrow, Carrie Feron, for her marvelous friendship, her endless wisdom, and her fabulous sense of humor. Your ideas and excellent editorial input always make my work better. I couldn't do this without you. I am blowing you bazillions of smooches from my office window in Montclair. And to Suzanne Gluck, Alicia Gordon, Eve Attermann, Samantha Frank, Claudia Webb, Cathryn Summerhayes, Tracy Fisher, and the whole amazing team of Jedis at WME, I am loving y'all to pieces and looking forward to a brilliant future together!

To the entire William Morrow and Avon team: Brian Murray, Michael Morrison, Liate Stehlik, Nicole Fischer, Lynn Grady, Tavia Kowalchuk, Ben Bruton, Kathy Gordon, Frank Albanese, Virginia Stanley, Rachael Brenner Levenberg, Andrea Rosen, Caitlin Mc-Caskey, Josh Marwell, Doug Jones, Carla Parker, Donna Waikus, Rhonda Rose, Michael Morris, Gabe Barillas, Deb Murphy, Mumtaz Mustafa, and last but most certainly not ever least, Brian Grogan: thank you one and all for the miracles you perform and for your amazing, generous support. You still make me want to dance.

To Buzzy Porter, huge thanks for getting me so organized and for your loyal friendship of many years. Don't know what I'd do without you!

To Debbie Zammit, it seems incredible but here we are again! Another year! Another miracle! Another year of keeping me on track, catching my goobers, and making me look reasonably intelligent by giving me tons of excellent ideas about everything. I know, I owe you so big-time it's ridiculous but isn't this publishing business better than Seventh Avenue? Love ya, girl!

To Ann Del Mastro and my cousin, Charles Comar Blanchard, all the Franks love you for too many reasons to enumerate!

To booksellers across the land, and I mean every single one of you, I thank you from the bottom of my heart, especially Patty Morrison of Barnes and Noble, Tom Warner and Vicky Crafton of Litchfield Books (not of My Sister's House), Sally Brewster of Park Road Books, and once again, can we just hold the phone for Jacquie Lee of Books a Million? Jacquie, Jacquie! You are too much, hon! Love ya and love y'all!

To my family, Peter, William, and Victoria, I love y'all with all I've got. Victoria, you are the most beautiful, wonderful daughter and I am so proud of you. You and William are so smart and so funny, but then a good sense of humor might have been essential to your survival in this house. And you both give me great advice, a quality that makes me particularly proud. And William, my sweet William, my heart swells with gratitude and pride when I think of you and you are never far away from the forefront of my mind. Every woman should have my good fortune with their children. You fill my life with joy. Well, usually. Just kidding. Peter Frank? You are still the man of my dreams, honey. Thirty-one years and they never had a fight. It's a little incredible to realize it's only thirty-one years, especially when it feels like I've been loving you forever.

Finally, to my readers, to whom I owe the greatest debt of all, I am sending you the most sincere and profound thanks for reading my stories, for sending along so many nice e-mails, for yakking it up with me on Facebook, and for coming out to book signings. You are why I try to write a book each year. I hope *The Hurricane Sisters* will entertain you and give you something new to think about. There's a lot of magic down here in the Lowcountry. Please, come see us and get some for yourself!

I love you all and thank you once again.